Highland Intrigue

Duncurra Book 3

By
Ceci Giltenan

Duncurra LLC
www.duncurra.com
Copyright 2014 by Ceci Giltenan
ISBN-10: 0-9904876-7-9
ISBN-13: 978-0-9904876-7-8
October 2014
Cover Art by Earthly Charms
Cover Models: Justin Thomas and Patricia Dubyoski
Cover Photograph by Bradley Nguyen Photography
Produced in the USA

Praise for Ceci Giltenan

"Few authors touch hearts so deeply."
-    *Sue-Ellen Welfonder, USA Today Bestselling Author*

"Fine historical romance writing at its best."
-    *Suzan Tisdale, Bestselling Author of Scottish Romance*

"Ceci Giltenan continues to leave me spellbound weaving her trail of exceptional books that are absolutely magnificent the ones that stay with you long after you have read it. Yes, Highland Intrigue is definitely one of those kind of books."
-    *Barbara, Tartan Book Reviews*

"Ceci Giltenan tells beautiful stories with strong characters and an intriguing storylines"
-    *Lily Baldwin, Bestselling Author of Scottish Romance*

"Ceci's books get better and better"
-    *Tarah Scott, Bestselling Author of Scottish Romance*

Other Books by Ceci Giltenan

Highland Solution, Duncurra Book 1

Highland Solution Audio Book

Highland Courage, Duncurra Book 2

Highland Courage Audio Book

Highland Intrigue Audio Book

The Scrolls of Cridhe, Volume 1 –
Highland Winds, a collection of seven
novellas including:
Highland Revenge, by Ceci Giltenan

Dedications

For my dearest Eamon, you are
My rock and my soft place to land;
My greatest strength and my deepest need;
My steady course and my wild ride;
My one and only and my whole world;
I love you with all my heart.

For Natalie, without your love and support I would never
have written the first book. There isn't a word that can sum
up what you mean to me. Best friend falls woefully short so I
will go with beloved sister. Someday, I will give you fairies.

For Rhonda, another beloved sister, who has blessed my life
in countless ways, thank you.

For my beta readers, Ann, Annie, Annie (hmm, there's a
pattern here) Barb and Maria—a heart-felt thank you for the
gift of your time and feedback. Highland Intrigue is better
because of you.

For my editor John Robin, thank you for everything. You are
the best!

Pronunciation Guide

Ailsa	ALE suh
Bhaltair	VAHLtare
Eadoin	AY dunn
Eithne	EN ya
Fingal	FINN guhl
Gillian	GILL ee ahn
Kieran	KEER an
Maeve	MAYve
Niall	NIGH uhl
Nuala	NOO lah
Olghar	O luh ghur
Rhiannon	RHEE ann un

Glossary

Bairn	(BAREn) a baby
Brathanead	(BRA huh need) the MacLennan stronghold
Carraigile	(Kah rah GHEEL) the MacKenzie stronghold
Cluitie	(CLOO tee) a euphemism for the devil
Duncurra	(Doon KOO rah) the MacIan stronghold
Kertch	(KERTCH) Also called a *brèid* (BREEDt); a square of pure white linen folded in half and worn by married women to cover their hair. It is a symbol of the Holy Trinity, under whose guidance the married woman walks.
Léine	(LAY in ah) A full tunic-like garment. A woman's *léine* is a full-length dress with full sleeves that is worn belted at the waist. A man's *léine* would only come to his knees, similar to a long shirt. Both men and women generally wore a plaid over this garment.
Naomh-dùn	(NEEVE doon) The MacKay stronghold.
ramsons	(RAMsuns) Pungent wild garlic.
Wheesht	(WHEEsht) hush or shhh

Prologue

Brathanead Castle, The Highlands, October, 1354

"Gillie, what are ye doing up there lass?"

Gillian MacLennan sat perched between two branches of a tree with her face buried in her knees. She didn't answer her da's question because she didn't want him to know she was crying. When she told her mother the problem, her mother had just gotten angry and told Gillian she was being silly. She didn't want her father's disappointment too.

"Come down out of the tree lass and tell me what's wrong."

Gillian wiped the tears away with the heels of her hands before reluctantly climbing down.

Her father gently took her face in his hands. "Gillie, ye've been crying. What happened?"

"Oh Da, everyone teases me about being so tall. They call me 'Gillie the Giant.'"

"But, pet, ye know they are joking. I've heard ye laughing with them."

"That's just because I don't want them to know it bothers me. I don't like being a giant."

"Ye aren't a giant, sweetling. God just stretched ye out a wee bit more than other lassies."

Gillian thought that was an understatement. She towered over all of the girls her age and she was even taller than some of the lads.

"Gillie, just ignore them. Words won't hurt ye."

She loved her father, but he was wrong. Maybe words didn't hurt when ye're a strong warrior, but words did hurt her. Still, she knew he wouldn't understand that, so she ignored the statement. It wasn't the things other children said that most upset her. What hurt the most were her mother's words. "Mama says I'm hopeless and that no man wants a tall awkward woman."

"Yer mama isn't an expert on what men like. When ye're

all grown up, ye will make a fine wife for a braw young warrior."

"Ye think?"

"Oh aye, ye will be a beautiful, tall, strong lass. I can assure ye, men like that. I will have to fight them off."

"But I'm awkward. I trip and bump into things. People laugh. Look what happened at dinner yesterday." She had tripped on her own feet hurrying to the table and went sprawling. Her father's lips twitched now at the memory but he had the good grace not to laugh.

"Gillie, ye are a growing lass. Ye are all feet and elbows at the moment, but it happens to every youngling when they start to grow. Lads are much worse. Ye are but ten and three. It will change, I promise ye."

"Fallon isn't clumsy."

"Yer sister is two years younger. Her clumsy years are still in front of her and by then ye will be poised and practically grown. Mark my words." Her father pulled her into the kind of hug that always made her feel better. Gillian was closer to her da than to any other person. Her mother was critical and always too busy for her but she could count on her da to fix things.

Chapter 1

Brathanead Castle, February, 1361

A relentless pounding noise penetrated her dream. It was a good dream. She was with her father again. "Go away," Gillian moaned, turning over to bury her head in the pillow. The pounding persisted, followed by the sound of a guardsman's voice. It couldn't be morning yet. The fire was still burning brightly in her hearth. She must have just barely fallen asleep.

"Lady Gillian, the watch reports that an army, at least a hundred strong, approaches."

The lingering warm, happy feeling brought on by her dream fled as surely as if the guardsman had doused her with cold water. "Please give me just a minute," she called through the door. Jumping out of bed, she pulled on her clothes. She wrapped a plaid around her shoulders before opening the door to Gavin. "What's happening? Whose army is approaching? Can we defend against them?"

"My lady, they bear the king's banners, but MacIan's banner was also spotted."

"MacIan? In the middle of the night? This can't be good. Are the gates still barred?"

"Aye, they are," Gavin assured her, "but we can't refuse to allow a representative from the king to enter Brathanead."

"Nay, but we can sure as well find out what they are here for before we open the gates."

Brathanead was a simple tower keep with four floors above the great hall. Two sets of stairs gave access to the upper levels. Gillian hurried down the front stairs with Gavin, through the great hall, and out the main doors of the keep. Stepping into the cold night air, she pulled her plaid over her head, wrapping it tightly against the biting wind.

She glanced up. More men than usual had taken up positions on the curtain walls. The foreboding sight chilled her more than the winter wind. She hurried across the courtyard, entered the barbican, and climbed the stairs to the top of the tower. Other guardsmen, including the captain of her guard, awaited her. "Eadoin, how long until they reach us?"

"They will be close enough to parlay within a quarter of an hour."

"Do ye have any idea what they've come for?"

"Nay, my lady."

Eadoin's frown worried her. She wasn't sure he was telling her everything. "Do ye think MacIan seeks revenge?"

Eadoin shook his head. "I would have trouble believing that, my lady. If he had been planning to lay siege to Brathanead, he would have done it last spring while we were severely weakened and the weather was not so foul. Nay, they bear the king's standard and we have done nothing to anger the king. Be patient. We will know his purpose soon enough."

"Aye, I suppose we will."

If Eadoin had other suspicions, he clearly wasn't going to share them with her at the moment. She turned away from him. The moonlight illumined the approaching army. A quarter of an hour seemed like an eternity as Gillian waited on the cold wall. Dear God, how had she ended up here? She wished nothing more than to be able to change the events of the last year.

It was hard to believe it had been just over a year since the MacLennan army had ridden forth from Brathanead on the eve of Candlemas, expecting an easy victory. Unbeknownst to many of his clan, Laird Malcolm MacLennan had systematically worked to weaken the MacIan clan for years, while pretending to be a staunch ally. His ultimate goal had been to attack Duncurra, claiming it and all the MacIan lands for his own.

To everyone's surprise the MacLennans were not victorious and a mere remnant of Malcolm's men returned to Brathanead following the attack. Not only had they not taken Duncurra, but many of their men had been killed or were held for ransom. For a while the clan held onto hope that their laird had escaped. According to some of the men who had made it back immediately after the battle, he had captured Laird Niall MacIan's wife and escaped with her. Gillian had been particularly hopeful that her father, Duncan, the laird's second-cousin and captain of his guard, was still alive.

Gillian remembered waiting in the frozen courtyard weeks

later with her mother, sisters, and Aunt Meara, searching for her father among the returning ransomed men. Eadoin had been with them. When they hadn't spotted her father immediately, her mother had grabbed Eadoin's arm as he passed. "Eadoin, where is Duncan?"

"Lana, I'm sorry. Duncan is dead."

Her mother screamed. "Nay, ye're lying, ye're lying!" She continued to scream as Aunt Meara tried to calm her.

At the time, Gillian too believed there must have been some mistake. "He can't be dead, Eadoin. We heard he escaped with Lady MacIan." Her sisters had looked on in horror. Fallon sobbed while silent tears slipped down little Ailsa's cheeks.

"Gillie, I'm sorry but it's true. Yer da did flee with Lady MacIan and met up with the laird, who also managed to escape from the battle at Duncurra. But Niall MacIan caught up to them. Lady Eithne was riding with yer da."

"Lady Eithne? Why was she riding with Da?" The MacLennans had known for some time that their laird and Laird MacIan's step-mother were close friends. Frankly, they expected them to marry. Surely if Eithne didn't have a mount of her own she would have ridden with Laird Malcolm.

"I'm not sure why, but she must have been afraid of what MacIan would do when he learned about her part in what was to have been the MacIans' downfall. She stabbed yer da in the gut and tried to shove him off the horse. I suppose she was trying to escape Laird MacIan and figured she would never be able to riding double. But as yer da fell, he pulled her off with him. They were both trampled. I'm sorry lass."

Gillian had been so sure her da had survived and would return to them. She remembered standing in silent shock, trying to make sense of what she had heard. Dead. Her da was dead.

Her Aunt Meara stopped Eadoin before he walked away. "What about the laird?"

"He's dead too. He escaped briefly into the snowstorm, but evidently his horse lost its footing. They were found at the bottom of a ravine several days later."

Remembering that day now brought back the same searing pain she had felt then. How could her father be dead? She loved him. She needed him. She wanted to retreat, to run and hide as she had when she was upset as a child. Da had always found her; he could make everything better. But she couldn't hide on that horrible day any more than she could now, and outside of her dreams her da would never seek her out to comfort her again.

Watching, waiting for the approaching army—one year later—the memories from that day flooded her relentlessly, as though they were happening today. Her sister Fallon, who was only two years younger than Gillian, clinging to their mother, both of them sobbing uncontrollably. Her youngest sister, Ailsa, eleven at the time, weeping silently, her whole body trembling. Aunt Meara, bereft. Over the years Meara had lost practically everyone she loved, her parents, husband, her own children, and now her brother. All around Gillian people were either elated to be reunited with a loved one or devastated by loss. There was nothing between the extremes.

She remembered asking Eadoin that fateful question, "If the laird is dead, who becomes the chief? He has no family. Who is the laird now?"

Eadoin answered, "As ye well know, Malcolm had no brothers or sisters and neither did Laird Kelvin before him. As a second cousin, yer da would have become laird. With him gone, it would be yer Aunt Meara, but things aren't exactly clear. There are some that say it should be Eithne's son, Fingal."

"Fingal MacIan? Why in the name of all that's holy would anyone suggest that? He isn't a MacLennan."

"Apparently that's debatable. It seems that Malcolm was his natural father. One reason Malcolm wanted Duncurra was to claim Fingal as his heir to ensure he inherited both Brathanead and Duncurra."

Shocked, Gillian said, "Nay, that isn't possible. The clan won't stand for it."

"Lass, some of the men are already clamoring for it. We are in a bad state now. If Niall MacIan wanted to—and I can see how he might—he could crush us. If Fingal were made laird the MacIans would once again be powerful allies."

"Surely there is someone else who can lead the clan and keep it strong," she said.

"Well, there is yer Aunt Meara or ye. The two of ye are now the laird's closest relatives, but ye are women. Ye can't lead this clan without a man. The elders will have to discuss it."

Over the next weeks the elders had indeed discussed it. Incessantly. At least half of the clan was united in their desire to petition Fingal MacIan to be their chief for the very reasons Eadoin had told her. The other half of the clan was only united in who they didn't want to be their leader: Fingal MacIan. She remembered the perpetual arguments.

"If the MacIans are the cause of all our woe, why would we hand the clan over to one?" asked Owen, the oldest of the clan elders.

"The MacIans are not the cause. Malcolm's greed brought this on. The MacIans were our allies. Niall would have given his own life for Malcolm and see how he was repaid," said Daniel, another one of the elders who in his younger years had been captain of the guard and a close friend of Malcolm's father. "Nay, it is better to have a strong leader with powerful allies and Fingal is that. God's teeth, man, Laird Chisholm and Laird Matheson both stood with MacIan against us and that was more likely due to their relationship with Fingal than anything else."

"Aye, and we have all known for years that Fingal was really Malcolm's bastard," said Archie, another elder.

"Nay, I tell ye, if Fingal had wanted to lead this clan, Malcolm gave him that chance when he attacked Duncurra. Damnation, Fingal stood to gain the leadership of both clans but he turned his back and let Niall MacIan chase Malcolm to his death, father or no. I will not go crawling to him now. Nay, we need to choose a leader from within." With barely three score years behind him, Nolan was the youngest of the elders and arguably Malcolm's closest friend among them.

"Aye, Fingal turned his back on his father—a father who betrayed his allies. At least we can all agree that Malcolm was Fingal's natural father. Therefore, Fingal is the rightful heir," Daniel said, and the whole argument started over again.

Gillian smiled, remembering the moment when her Aunt Meara had reached her limit. She'd stood, banged an empty tankard on the table and called for silence. "This arguing must stop. The fact is, Fingal is not here and by all accounts has no love for the MacLennans. Malcolm may have brought this on, but I agree with Owen and Nolan we shouldn't humble ourselves further by begging Fingal MacIan for help." At the shocked expressions Meara said, "That's right, I said Fingal MacIan. He may have been Malcolm's bastard, but he was raised by Eithne and Alistair MacIan and that is where his loyalties lie. For the love of God, his mother gutted my brother, the man who should have become our laird. Ye should not be arguing about whether or not to ask Fingal

MacIan for help but rather who among us can lead the clan." Her statements had been met with some murmured agreements.

Archie looked stunned. "Meara, other than Fingal ye are Malcolm's closest relative but ye have no husband and no heirs. Are ye suggesting that we should make ye our leader?"

Meara laughed. "Nay, not me, Archie. Gillian."

Gillian remembered the looks of surprise on the elder's faces. "Gillian?"

Shocked by her aunt's comments herself, she squeaked, "Me?"

Archie tried to reason with her aunt. "Now Meara, I'll give ye that Gillian is a fine strong lass. Smart as any, but she is inexperienced and unmarried."

Gillian's mother had never been overly affectionate, but even so Gillian was surprised when Lana said, "Gillian can't lead this clan." Frankly, Gillian had never thought about it and while she too wasn't sure she was up to the task, her mother's absolute assurance that she couldn't be a leader hurt.

Aunt Meara scowled at Lana before saying, "With my help and the help of the elders, Gillian can lead this clan until an appropriate husband is chosen for her."

"That is not a bad idea," Owen said.

"It is a bad idea," Lana said. "Gillian is completely unprepared. Fallon would be a better choice."

Meara looked flabbergasted. "Fallon? Have ye lost yer mind Lana? Fallon is but ten and six, and is certainly no better prepared to be a leader than Gillian. At least Gillian has a head on her shoulders."

That finally shook Gillian from her silence. "Aye, Aunt Meara, I do. I have enough sense to know that, at the moment, I am not capable of leading this clan and neither is Fallon." She silenced her mother with a glare. "Ye, on the other hand, at least have their respect."

Meara did have their respect. Ultimately, they recognized her as the clan's leader and Meara agreed to this for the short term. However, against Lana's wishes, Meara insisted that Gillian begin to learn about the management of the clan and keep. She intended only to lead the clan until the elders decided who should marry Gillian and become laird.

Still, things hadn't gone well. The clan remained divided in spite of all Meara's efforts. Then a little over two months ago, in early December, Meara had died. She simply didn't awaken one morning. Some thought her heart gave out while others suspected she was poisoned. Gillian thought this was the product of over-active imaginations. There were always people who were willing to see conspiracy in anything. Aunt Meara hadn't felt well for days. She was not a young woman and the leadership of the fractious clan had taken a toll on her health. It was as simple as that.

Upon Meara's death, the elders had named Gillian their leader and continued to argue over whom she should marry. Now at only nineteen, Gillian stood on the barbican tower, the leader of her clan, at least in name, and the approaching army was within hailing distance.

Even though Eadoin had doubted it, she still couldn't help but wonder if Niall MacIan sought revenge. Were the MacIans attacking? Did Niall plan to seize Brathanead to give it to Malcolm's bastard?

She remembered the revulsion she felt a year ago at the thought of making Fingal MacIan the head of their clan. She hadn't cared who fathered him, his mother killed her da. Gillian would never accept him as her laird.

Chapter 2

Fingal MacIan rode silently towards Brathanead, accompanied by his brother, Laird Niall MacIan, a substantial contingent of MacIan men-at-arms, and an even larger number of the king's men. They had battled terrible weather for nearly two weeks, much longer than the journey would normally take, and were not far now. Rather than stopping for one more night, they pressed on, riding into the night to reach their goal.

Fingal was not remotely happy about the current state of affairs. It was difficult to believe that only a little more than a year had passed since the MacLennan army rode against Duncurra and his life had changed forever. Malcolm MacLennan and Fingal's own vile mother had informed him that Malcolm had sired him before she married Alastair MacIan, destroying Fingal's very identity.

The unholy pair told him that they were attempting to conquer Duncurra for him, regardless of the fact that he had wanted no part of their scheme. Malcolm, in his greed, attacked anyway and the decimation of his own clan was the end result. Niall ransomed the men who lived through the battle but the MacLennan losses were profound nonetheless. Fingal wanted nothing more to do with the MacLennans, ever.

Then King David II had summoned both Niall and Fingal to court. They'd travelled to Edinburgh shortly after Epiphany. Although the king indicated that the issue was urgent, he still made them wait for several weeks after they had arrived before he summoned them for an audience.

When they finally stood before him, the king didn't mince words. "Gentlemen we have a problem. Clan MacLennan is without a clear leader."

Niall responded, "My liege, I understood that a relative of Malcolm's, Duncan's sister Meara, was given the leadership."

"She was, and while we had our doubts about the

suitability of a woman leading a broken clan, we were inclined to wait and see. However, the infighting continues and Lady Meara is dead."

"I am sorry to hear that, my liege. What happened?"

"The information we have is vague. She died suddenly. When that happens one can never be sure it isn't murder. The fact remains, the MacLennans have no leader."

"Aye, my liege. I understand," Niall said. "What do ye wish from the MacIans?"

"A weak clan without a laird can change quickly from a simple annoyance to a dangerous liability. Now that the power struggle may have turned deadly, we cannot ignore it. Your brother, Fingal, is both a strong warrior and as we understand it has a valid claim to the leadership of Clan MacLennan."

Fingal stepped forward. "My liege, under the law I am a MacIan, not a MacLennan. My mother was married to Laird Alistair MacIan when I was born."

"You forget yourself, sir. We are the law. If we say you are a MacLennan, then you are, but there is more than one way to make you Laird MacLennan. When Meara died, her niece, Gillian, was nominally given the leadership of the clan until a suitable husband could be selected. We are happy to help them in this. It is our wish that you marry her. Thus you will assume leadership of the clan both as Malcolm's natural son and as Gillian's husband."

"With all due respect my liege, if Laird MacLennan sired me, would that not make the lady in question a relative? A cousin of some sort?"

"A very distant relative Fingal. We believe that she is your third-cousin. This is certainly not a close enough relationship to prohibit your marriage to her. Many royal marriages occur between cousins."

"Sire, ye are asking me to marry the daughter of one of the men responsible for the plot against my brother."

"No, Fingal, you are mistaken. We are not asking you to marry her. We are commanding you to marry her and be a stable leader for Clan MacLennan."

Fingal bowed his head. "I understand, my liege. What if the lady refuses to give her consent?"

"She will greatly displease her king and will be sent to a cloister. She has two younger sisters. I would prefer that you marry one of Duncan MacLennan's daughters, Malcolm's only legitimate heirs. To do otherwise could create more dissention. Still, while a marriage to one of the chits would be ideal it isn't necessary. I am naming you Laird MacLennan in any event. If they presume to refuse their king's command and do not accept this decision, you will instruct Clan MacLennan that my full wrath will fall upon them.

"You look less than pleased by this prospect, Fingal. Be warned, if you are unable to accomplish the task we have set for you, we will not be pleased with Clan MacIan either." The king shot an accusatory look at Niall. "Laird MacIan, have you already forgotten the solution which we provided to your financial woes several years ago?"

Two years earlier, when Clan MacIan was facing financial ruin, King David had arranged a marriage between Niall MacIan and Lady Katherine Ruthven, a wealthy lowland heiress. Fingal almost laughed at the memory. Initially Niall was as displeased with that arrangement as he himself was with this one. However, Niall soon fell very much in love with his wife. Their marriage has become quite a happy one and in addition to their foster son, Tomas, they recently had a lovely baby girl who was just beginning to toddle. Fingal knew King David would always have Niall's unswerving loyalty and as he expected, Niall offered his full support, much to his chagrin.

As a result, now Fingal rode ever closer to a fate he would rather avoid. They were almost within hailing distance of Brathanead when Fingal noticed a lone woman standing on the barbican tower among the MacLennan guardsmen. If he was not much mistaken, this was the woman who would be his wife.

The voice of a guardsman rang out through the frigid air, "Halt and state yer business, MacIan."

His brother, Niall, rode to the forefront calling, "Eadoin, I am here under the command of our king with a message for Clan MacLennan. Open the gates, we mean ye no harm."

Gillian MacLennan called, "The king's messenger needn't enter Brathanead to deliver his message. It's the middle of the night. Tell me the message now, or come back at a reasonable hour."

"I am the king's messenger, Lady Gillian, and I will not have a shouting match with ye. I have assured ye that we are here on peaceful matters. Open the gates now."

"Pardon me Laird MacIan but the last time MacIans and

MacLennans met it was definitely not peaceful."

"And that was no fault of mine. Yer laird betrayed me. I am not here for revenge."

"Nevertheless, ye can deliver yer message and be gone."

"I'm sorry Gillian," Niall persisted, "ye must let us in. Ye have known me since ye were a wee lass. I promise ye as long as the MacLennans do nothing to provoke violence, there will be none."

"Aye, I know ye. My laird and my da are dead because of ye. Deliver yer message!"

Over the last few days, Fingal had learned the captain of the king's guard was not the most patient of men. He clearly had reached his limit. Urging his mount forward the captain yelled, "Enough of this. Lady Gillian MacLennan, in the name of King David II you will open Brathanead and receive the king's messenger now or suffer the consequences!"

As Fingal watched the lass on the wall verbally spar with his brother he couldn't help but admire her. It took a very bold woman to try and force her will on a representative from the king. Now she fairly bristled with anger. The plaid had slipped down off her head, the wind whipped long strands of her dark, thick hair, and her jaw was clenched rigidly. Was she going to let the king's guard make good on the threat? Surely the lass had more sense than that.

When she failed to answer immediately, the captain demanded, "I want an answer now! What will it be Lady Gillian?"

"Fine, I will open the gates, but there is no reason why Fingal MacIan needs to enter."

Fingal chuckled quietly. "This should be interesting."

Niall rewarded his sarcasm with a quelling stare. Niall hated defiance and clearly Lady Gillian was pushing his temper.

In a tone, only slightly more tolerant than the king's captain had used, Niall demanded, "Lady Gillian, in the name of King David II, ye will open the gates now. I have promised ye a peaceful meeting, but I will remind ye, ye are in no position to set any conditions. I will decide who enters Brathanead. Is that understood?"

~ * ~

Gillian turned to Eadoin and the other guardsmen on the wall. "We have no choice if we don't want to bring the king's wrath down upon us."

Eadoin nodded grimly. "We could defend against them for a while, but ye are right. It would ultimately be the ruin of Clan MacLennan."

Gillian sighed heavily. "I suspect the faster we comply, the faster the message can be delivered and they can be sent on their way." Eadoin arched an eyebrow at her. "Never mind, I know that is wishful thinking. This is about me, isn't it? That's what ye didn't want to say earlier."

Eadoin's expression was full of sympathy. "Aye, Gillian. When the king's guard accompanied the MacIans, I suspected it might be about ye."

She had no choice. She called, "Aye, Laird MacIan, I understand. Tarmon, raise the portcullis!"

Eadoin asked, "Where do ye wish to receive them?"

"Honestly? In the courtyard, but I suspect Niall will object and I'm already tired of bending to his will. Bring them to the great hall."

Gillian hurried down the steps, across the courtyard and into the great hall. Servants had been roused from their beds and were preparing to receive their unwelcome guests. Unwelcome? There was a time when the MacIans were always warmly welcomed. Niall had completed his training at Brathanead when Gillian was just a girl. She remembered him being strong and handsome. All the older lasses mooned over him. While Fingal didn't train here, he had been a guest quite a few times too. Very tall and broad shouldered, with dark hair, he too was handsome and also had his share of mooning maids. She remembered Fingal as being warm, friendly, and affable, whereas Niall was quiet and brooding. She shook her head. None of that mattered anymore. Even if they were once considered friends, they weren't now.

Eadoin entered the hall moments later. "Lady Gillian, they are riding into the courtyard. They will only be a few minutes. Ye should sit in the laird's chair at the refectory table. I want ye surrounded by guardsmen and a table between ye and our visitors. I have sent for the elders—they will need to be here. They should flank ye."

"Thank ye, Eadoin." He was a good leader and a great warrior. He would have made an excellent clan chief, but he was already married to a lovely woman named Alana. They had a wee daughter named Kiora and Alana was expecting their second child in May. Eadoin and Alana were perhaps her dearest friends.

"Gillie, don't react to anything they say," Eadoin warned her.

"I don't see how I can do that."

"Just listen to them. If ye don't understand something, ask for clarification, but for the love of God, don't commit to anything. When MacIan has delivered his message, tell him ye would like to confer with yer advisors. We'll go with the elders to yer solar and discuss whatever it is. Gillie, for the next little while, icy water has to flow through ye."

"Aye, Eadoin, I understand." Gillian moved behind the table and had just taken her seat when the main doors to the hall opened. Guardsmen preceded the visitors into the hall and as Eadoin had promised they assumed positions near her. Nolan and Archie hurried into the hall, joining her at the table, just as Owen and Daniel, both of whom resided within the keep, emerged from the tower stairs. Gillian's mother and her sister Fallon also slipped into the room from the tower stairs. *Well good news certainly does travel quickly.*

Niall MacIan entered, flanked by his brother Fingal and the captain of the king's guard. A substantial number of his men followed them, but more remained outside.

Niall bowed. "Lady Gillian, thank ye for receiving us at so late an hour."

"There is no need to thank me Laird MacIan. I wouldn't have welcomed ye if I had been given any choice in the matter."

Daniel, who had taken the seat to her right, leaned in and whispered, "Gillian, lass, don't antagonize the man."

Niall scowled at her. "Lady Gillian, I understand ye are upset, but I bear a message from yer king. Regardless of how much ye dislike me, ye will hear his message. Is that understood?"

"Aye, Laird MacIan. Get on with it then."

"King David sends his condolences on the death of yer aunt, Lady Meara. As ye are a very young woman, he is concerned about yer ability to lead this clan, especially considering the events of the last year."

"She doesn't lead this clan on her own. As the elders of the clan, we guide her," Owen said.

"Aye, that we do. And we will ensure she marries a man who will be a solid leader," added Nolan.

Niall nodded in acknowledgement. "I'm sure the king will

be glad to hear ye have been so ably guided until now. However, he has selected the man he wishes ye to marry, who will be the laird of this clan."

Gillian clenched her jaw. She suspected she was not going to like what she was about to hear but she could not stop herself from asking, "And who is the lucky man the king so dislikes he would saddle him with me and a clan in disarray in the bargain?"

Niall actually laughed. "I don't think the king views it as a punishment, but he wishes ye to marry my brother, Fingal."

Marry Fingal MacIan? That simply could not happen. "And if I decline his generous offer?"

"Ye will be sent to a convent, and yer sister Fallon will marry Fingal." Her mother gasped at Niall's announcement.

Gillian saw exactly where this was going. "And if Fallon doesn't consent, he will marry Ailsa. Shall we save some time here? What if we all refuse?"

"His grace hopes ye will not be so difficult," said the captain of the king's guard. His clipped tone suggested he was becoming angry. "However, a marriage to ye or one of yer sisters is little more than a formality. He has already acknowledged Fingal MacIan's legitimacy as Malcolm MacLennan's son and heir. Regardless of what ye and yer sister's choose, his grace has named Fingal laird of Clan MacLennan."

The MacLennans in the room erupted with shocked exclamations varying from approval to disgust. Gillian, however, did not react, although it was a struggle to remain calm. Just as Eadoin had instructed, she tried to appear as if icy water ran through her veins. Surely this couldn't be happening. She could have accepted almost anything from the king, but how could she accept this? How could she marry Fingal MacIan? She had an option. Nay, it wasn't really an option. She truly didn't wish to enter a convent either. Even if she did, she felt sure her mother would be all too happy for Fallon to marry Fingal. The end result would be the same—he would be laird of Clan MacLennan. She needed time to think and she couldn't do that in the middle of this uproar.

Banging her fists on the table she yelled, "Silence!" Perhaps her forcefulness shocked those present, but the room fell instantly quiet. In a calmer tone she added, "I would like to discuss this with my advisors."

Niall shook his head. "My lady, there is nothing to discuss.

Ye need only decide whether ye will marry Fingal or enter a convent. This is yer decision—not one for the MacLennan elders."

"Nevertheless, Laird MacIan, I will not give ye an answer until I have considered the matter. My servants will see to yer comfort while I do so." She rose to leave.

Fingal had remained quiet until then, but now he stepped forward. "Nay, Lady Gillian. Perhaps ye didn't fully understand the king's message. Ye are no longer the leader of this clan. I am. Ye have a decision to make that is solely yers and it must be made today. The king has ordered that the wedding take place immediately."

"Immediately? That isn't possible. The banns must be posted, and even so Lent has started. Weddings can't be performed during Lent."

"My lady, at the king's request the bishop has waived the posting of the banns and given us a special dispensation to marry during Lent. The wedding, if there is to be one, will take place today. But, my lady, before anything more is said, I wish to speak with ye alone. Please join me in the solar." Fingal held his hand out to her.

Gillian's mother rushed to the center of the room. "Nay, Gillian, ye mustn't be alone with him." She wrinkled her nose in disdain. "I will go with ye."

Gillian clenched her jaw. She wanted to speak with her advisors, but her mother tended to be overbearing and Gillian didn't want to deal with her now.

Frankly, she was relieved when Fingal replied, "I said I would speak with her alone and I meant it." At that moment, Fingal, the man whom Gillian had once thought of as genial and good natured, looked every inch an angry Highland warrior.

"It isn't proper, *Laird*." The sneer in Lana's voice clearly told the room what she thought of the king's directive.

"Lana, like it or not, I am yer laird. Ye will not instruct me in what is or isn't proper. Gillian will decide whether she will marry me today or enter a convent. This decision dictates the course of the rest of both our lives. I will not have anyone forcing their will on her. Furthermore, her reputation will not suffer, nor will either outcome be affected by a private conversation with her laird."

That pronouncement successfully silenced Lana and Gillian was certain no one else would challenge him or attempt to prevent this private meeting. In fairness, she couldn't deny he was right. By royal command, Fingal was Laird MacLennan regardless of whether she chose to marry him or not. She believed that Fallon was not capable yet of fulfilling the role of Lady MacLennan but in time she could learn. Therefore the two people most affected by Gillian's decision today were Fingal and herself. She walked around the table, toward the tower stairs with her head held high, feeling every eye in the room follow her.

Falling in step beside her, Fingal and Gillian climbed the stairs together in silence. When they reached the dark, cold solar, Fingal walked to the hearth, stoked the fire to life, and lit several candles as if it were his solar. *It is his solar now, Gillian, ye eejit.*

"Come sit with me by the fire, Gillian, we have things to discuss."

"I don't want to sit with ye by the fire."

He chuckled. "I expect ye don't, but ye are about to make a much bigger decision regarding me, and ye have to start somewhere."

She sighed resignedly and took the chair opposite him.

He smiled. "That's better."

Chapter 3

Fingal considered her for a moment. He had visited Brathanead last nearly two years ago. He had been accompanying Niall and his new wife, Katherine, home to Duncurra when Katherine fell desperately ill. Fingal had been charged with taking care of Tomas while Katherine recovered. Outgoing and talkative, Tomas chatted with anyone who would listen and Gillian not only listened but was as charmed by the lad as Fingal was himself. She managed to find a small wooden sword for Tomas to play with.

He remembered her as being tall and gangly but time had a way of smoothing out awkwardness. Now Gillian was...the word "lovely" didn't quite do her justice. She was stately and poised. Thick brown hair reached her waist. Although slim, she was well curved in the right places. No longer gangly, she moved with a fluid grace that suggested supple strength. *This lass does not belong in a convent.* She didn't fidget or blush under his perusal but met his gaze with gold flecked brown eyes which, at the moment, glittered with anger. He wasn't particularly pleased himself, yet they had no choice but to reach an agreement. He smiled as he remembered how she had ordered silence in the hall and everyone complied. At the tender age of nine and ten, she was already a woman to be reckoned with.

She arched an eyebrow at him. "Do ye find this amusing?"

"Nay, lass. Nothing about this situation is amusing. I was just remembering my last visit here. Ye gave me a wooden sword for young Tomas. That was very kind of ye. It is still his favorite toy. He has slain many imaginary wild beasties with it."

At the mention of Tomas' name, she too smiled for a moment. The smile transformed her countenance, her brown eyes sparkling warmly. *Stunning.* Yes, now that word does her justice.

"He was a sweet lad. We heard that Laird MacIan accepted him as a foster-son. Laird MacLennan didn't approve, but I was very pleased. Is he well?"

Fingal grinned. "Aye. He's happy and loved at Duncurra."

"That is good to hear." Her face grew serious again. "Still, I doubt ye brought me up here to chat about Tomas."

"Nay, my lady, I didn't." He thought a moment before choosing his next words. "It is obvious that neither one of us wants this marriage."

Her spine stiffened. She clenched her jaw for a moment, an icy chill returning to her eyes. "Ye are right. I don't want to marry ye. I shouldn't have to marry ye. Yer brother was responsible for Laird MacLennan's death and yer mother killed my father. Ye do not belong here and the king had no right to make ye our laird."

"Ah, lass, he had every right. He is the king and words such as those, if uttered in the presence of the wrong people, namely the king's guardsmen below stairs, will get ye arrested."

"Why do ye care whether I am sent to Edinburgh or a convent? They are both prisons of one sort or another. Ye've arranged this rather nicely. I have two sisters, marriage to either of whom would legitimize yer spurious claim."

"Gillian, that will be the last time ye accuse me of having any hand in this. I had nothing to do with the king's decision. Laird MacLennan may have sired me, but he was never my father and I had absolutely no desire to lead his clan. He conspired with my mother and together they betrayed the man who I will always consider my brother. Had Malcolm not done that, he might still be sleeping in his own warm bed this frosty night and so would many MacLennan men, not to mention a few MacIan men who were slain that day. As to yer father's death, I am deeply sorry for yer loss. My mother was more cruel and self-centered than ye can possibly imagine. The only person she ever loved was herself. I was not there, but if I could have stayed her hand, I would have. Yer father was a good man."

She thrust her chin out in a defiant gesture, but her eyes held only grief. "Aye he was."

"Gillian, we can't change the past, nor can we defy the king. Ye must never suggest publically that ye disagree with his direct order. Doing so will not simply land ye in prison, it would likely result in yer head parting company with yer shoulders. Do ye understand me?"

"Aye. But if ye didn't want this, why is the king forcing it on ye?"

"A clan without strong leadership can become a dangerous liability. Internal strife often creates an enticing target to outsiders. For the time being, there is a fragile peace in the Highlands and the king doesn't wish to upset that."

"The only threat we have is from the MacIans," Gillian insisted.

"Nay, lass. Niall has no desire to lay claim to any of the MacLennan lands. However, he does not want anyone else to either. Stabilizing the MacLennans is in his best interests."

"Why must we marry to do that? Ye said the king has already named ye laird. I won't oppose it. Why must I go to a convent if I don't wish to marry ye?"

"Were ye in the hall when the king's order was announced? Did ye not hear the opposition?"

"Aye, but if I renounce the clan leadership what can they do?"

"Sadly, Gillian, if I do not marry ye or one of yer sisters, any of ye can become a standard around which those who oppose my leadership will gather. Essentially, as long as ye have a valid claim that isn't exercised ye enable division within the clan. The king cannot allow that. As laird, I cannot allow that."

"I don't want to marry ye."

Fingal sighed. He didn't want to send this strong, beautiful woman to a convent, but he had no choice. "Then ye have made yer decision? Ye choose the religious life?"

She looked away. "Nay, I don't want that either."

"Lass, it is one or the other."

"Ye don't understand. I don't love ye. In fact, I hate the very sight of ye. I cannot begin to imagine what kind of hell being married to ye would be."

Would marriage to him truly be a hell for her? As much as he understood her resentment, hearing her say that stung and he couldn't stop himself from snapping back. "Although ye have a lovely way with words, lass, at the moment I am not particularly fond of ye either. Perhaps it would be best if ye took the holy vows. Maybe one of yer sisters has a sweeter disposition."

She glared at him. "This is my home. I don't want to leave my family, my people."

Fingal's frustration was rising. "Honestly, I didn't want to leave my family either but I had no choice in it. Ye at least have an option, regardless of how unappealing ye find the alternatives."

"Can it be a marriage in name only?"

"A marriage in name only?"

Gillian clearly missed the underlying anger in his question. "Aye. We could be married to satisfy the king, but not live as a married couple. I mean, ye could have the laird's chamber of course. I would stay elsewhere."

Fingal's voice was deadly calm. "I see. Ye wouldn't share my bed."

"Aye. That would work. Ye could seek yer comfort elsewhere."

"Let me make sure I understand. We would marry, but ye would live yer life and I would live mine, *seeking my comfort elsewhere*. And what about ye, Gillian? Would ye *seek yer comfort elsewhere?*"

Perhaps Gillian finally heard the menace in his voice. "I-I-I only meant to say, I w-w-wouldn't stand in yer way. I-I-I wouldn't be unfaithful. It would be no different than a convent, only I could stay at home."

"Nay, Gillian, it would be very different from a convent. Do ye believe that I could live under the same roof with ye, as yer husband and laird of this clan, while parading a stream of lovers in front of ye? Even if ye believe that I am completely without honor, do ye think yer clan would stand for it?"

She paled. "L-L-Laird MacLennan took lovers. It was commonly known."

"Aye and while he had been a widower for many years, sadly I am sitting here and we are in this position because he wasn't faithful to his wife. Nay, Gillian, I won't do that and neither will I live as a monk within the bond of marriage. If ye wish to live chastely, then ye will need to accept the religious life."

Gillian's eyes flashed with anger. "Ye would force yerself on a woman who hates ye?"

"I would hope if the woman in question holds only hate for me, and sees no possibility for affection, she would not choose to marry me."

"This is my clan. I don't want to leave them!"

Fingal sighed, his irritation fading. As bold and strong as she appeared, Gillian was still a very young woman facing an incredibly difficult and, frankly, unfair decision. "Gillian, I know ye are in a terrible position. I know ye love yer clan and ye believe ye have good reasons to hate me. Please set yer anger aside for a moment and listen." Her mouth was set in a grim line, but she nodded. "I have known ye for years and while I wasn't here as much as Niall was, I wasn't a stranger either. Is that fair?"

"Aye."

"Have I ever done anything that scared or hurt ye?"

"Nay."

"Have ye ever heard stories whispered about me?" Gillian raised her eyebrows, causing him to grin. "I mean stories about my evil nature?"

Her lips fluttered briefly, giving him an all too fleeting hint of her smile. "Nay. There were surely enough whispers about ye, but no one ever accused ye of being unkind."

"Did yer laird or yer da ever say a word against me?"

"Nay."

"Based on the reaction in the hall, clearly some of the clan's elders support the king's decision to name me laird."

"Aye, there are several who have mentioned it before."

"And the ones who didn't? Have any of them ever accused me of being cruel or unreasonable?"

"Nay."

"Then there are only two reasons that ye have to hate me. One is because my brother defended himself against an attack by yer late laird. Although I know it is hard to accept, Gillian, it is the way of things. Malcolm chose that course, not Niall." Gillian said nothing, but didn't argue so Fingal continued. "I understand the other reason is much harder to resolve. My mother did a terrible thing and I am truly sorry for yer loss. But the fact remains, as much as we might wish to, we cannot change the past. We can only come to terms with it. It doesn't have to dictate our future."

Gillian looked down. Her chin quivered ever so slightly. For the first time since he had arrived, Fingal caught a glimpse of the scared lass that hid behind the resilient, poised front she presented. Dear God he hated this. He hated compelling her to do something she found so repugnant and he silently cursed the king for forcing both of them into it. "Perhaps there is a middle ground, lass."

"I don't see one. Ye have made yerself clear, Laird. Either I marry ye and live as yer wife or I enter the convent."

"What if we give ourselves a bit of time? Perhaps if ye get to know me better, ye will not find being married to me so distasteful."

"Ye said the king wanted us married immediately."

"Aye, that's true. However, I am willing to give ye a bit of time within the marriage. Mind ye, I don't think the king would approve, so ye can't reveal this to anyone. We must share a bed and we must appear to be living as a married couple. However, I promise not to force myself on ye. I will wait until ye are ready— until ye ask me to."

"Share yer bed without...without..."

"Aye, until ye are ready."

She arched an eyebrow at him. "What if I'm never ready? Ye said ye wouldn't live like a monk within marriage."

"And I won't, at least not forever. But I am willing to give ye—"

"A year?"

A year? Is she daft? "Nay, Gillian, I don't think so."

"Why not?" Her brown eyes stared in challenge.

Why not, indeed. What would he do if the year passed and she still refused him? Would he force her then? He knew he wouldn't, but once they were married, there was no going back. Perhaps he could seek an annulment, but not if they appeared to live as husband and wife. Surely he could win her consent within the year. For the love of all that's holy they would be sharing a bed. "Gillian, I don't think it is reasonable to set a limit. I am willing to give ye whatever time ye need. Truthfully, I could never force an unwilling lass. But by the same token, ye can't enter this marriage expecting that ye will never truly be my wife. If ye think ye will always hate me, do us both a kindness and enter the religious life."

~ * ~

Did she really hate him? Would she ever be able to get past everything that had happened? He asked her not to agree to the marriage if she thought she would always hate him. *What does it matter?* What better revenge could there be than to marry a man who agreed never to force himself on her and then always refuse him? *Once we're married, what can he do?* He would never hurt her, Gillian thought confidently. Damnation, it was true. Aside from everything else, she firmly believed he would never hurt her. She couldn't deny that he had always seemed to be a good man.

How then could she marry him? She firmly believed she would never get past who he was and what his family had done. *If ye think ye will always hate me, do us both a kindness and enter the religious life.* She could not ignore the truth of his words. Living the rest of her life married to someone she hated would be torturous for both of them. *Do us both a kindness.* Painfully, her choice became clear.

Just as she opened her mouth to tell him, a knock sounded at the door. Before either of them could answer, the door opened and her little sister Ailsa poked her head in. Like Gillian, Ailsa had lovely brown eyes and chestnut colored hair, but where Gillian's hair was sleek and straight, Ailsa's was a sleep-tousled riot of curls.

"I heard ye talking, Gillie. It woke me up. Ye sounded upset. What are ye...oh." Ailsa's eyes landed on Fingal. Putting her hands on her hips she demanded, "what are ye doing here?"

"Ailsa, pet, this isn't a good time." Gillian gave her a quick kiss on the forehead and attempted to usher Ailsa from the room. "Go back to bed, sweetling, and I will tell ye everything in the morning."

Ailsa pulled away from her. "I will not go back to bed." She turned on Fingal. She didn't appear remotely intimidated by the huge warrior sitting by the hearth. "Ye don't belong here and clearly Gillie doesn't want ye here. Ye can leave now." She pointed at the door.

Gillian cast a worried glance at Fingal but was surprised to see a grin spreading across his face. "Ailsa, I'm very sorry we woke ye, lass. The king has asked us to consider something very important. We were discussing it."

Ailsa stared at him for a moment. "Well I think ye should discuss it in the morning. Gillie has a lot of responsibilities and needs her rest."

Fingal's grin only broadened and it was hard for Gillian not to laugh at her imperious little protector. "It is all right, pet. Go back to bed."

"Not until ye tell me what is going on. I am not leaving ye alone with him."

Gillian glanced at Fingal, who gave her an almost imperceptible nod. "Ailsa, do ye know who this is?"

"Aye. Fingal MacIan. The one people say is really Laird Malcolm's son."

"That's right and because of that, the king has asked him to be our laird."

"But the person ye marry is supposed to be our laird."

"Aye, that is also true, so the king wants me to marry Laird—uh—Fingal."

"And what if ye don't want to marry him?" Ailsa glared at Fingal.

Gillian sighed. "That doesn't really matter."

"Of course it matters."

"Nay, pet, when the king tells us to do something we must obey. However, he has given me a choice this time." Ailsa looked at Gillian expectantly. "If I don't wish to marry him, I can join the holy sisters and he will marry Fallon instead."

"What if Fallon doesn't want to marry him?"

Gillian hadn't given this a moment's thought. Fallon would surely marry him. Gillian was certain their mother would insist on it. Hadn't she wanted Fallon named chief? Before she could tell Ailsa this, Fingal said, "Then *ye* have the great good fortune of marrying me."

Ailsa looked askance. "I don't want to marry ye."

Fingal chuckled. "There seems to be a lot of that going around."

When his words sank in, Ailsa turned back to Gillian, grabbing her hands. "Nay, nay, nay. Gillie, tell me that isn't true. Ye can't go to a convent. Ye can't leave me. What would I do without ye? Mother only cares about Fallon. I need ye."

"Ye don't understand, pet."

"I do understand. If ye don't marry him, ye will leave me and Fallon will be Lady MacLennan or I will be. I don't think I want to be Lady MacLennan and I'm sure I don't want Fallon to be, but mostly I don't want ye to go away." Ailsa threw her arms around Gillian and held on as if she could keep her close with sheer force. "Please, Gillie." She started to sob.

Gillian wrapped her arms around Ailsa. More than any other member of the clan Ailsa needed her. *Mother only cares about Fallon.* As hard as it was to admit, Ailsa was right. Gillian had never understood it. Mothers were supposed to love and protect their children—all of their children. However, their mother doted on their sister Fallon. She had rarely shown Gillian and Ailsa the same affection. With their father gone who would be there for her youngest sister? How could she leave her sweet sister with no one to love and care for her? If she could put aside her hatred of the MacIans for anyone, she surely could for Ailsa. She held her sister quietly for a moment before kissing the top of her head. She looked across the room to Fingal. "Ye'll give me time?"

"Aye, lass, I will. Ye'll try to get past yer hatred?"

"I don't think I can love ye, but aye, I suppose I can try not to hate ye."

Chapter 4

Gillian entered the great hall on Fingal's arm. She was not happy about it, but if she were going to go through with this, she may as well start acting the part. The hall grew silent as all eyes turned toward them. She cleared her throat slightly. "After discussing the matter with the laird, I have decided to obey the king's request. I will marry Fingal MacIan, who is laird of Clan MacLennan." The room erupted as it had earlier with a mixture of elation and disapproval. She didn't have the energy left to bring the hall to order, but Fingal stepped in.

He raised his voice over the din, "Enough." The room fell still. "I know not all of ye agree with the king's decision in this regard. However, the dissent must stop now. A clan divided will fall. I will not allow that to happen and neither should any of ye. It is late and everyone is tired. Gillian and I will be married later this afternoon. Ye will have until then to decide where yer loyalties lie. After the wedding, the members of the clan must give us their fealty or leave MacLennan land."

A voice called out from the back of the room, "But laird, 'tis still winter. Ye would turn us out of our homes?"

The room was silent but for the crackling of the fire in the hearth. Gillian glanced around at her people. She didn't want Fingal to turn any of them out. Before she could argue with him, he answered, "I certainly would not wish to. I would prefer to have ye stay and help me rebuild this clan. However, that can only happen if ye accept me as yer laird. For the sake of the clan, I cannot agree to anything less."

As much as Gillian despised the idea, she couldn't argue. He was right. To tolerate less than complete allegiance would surely ruin them. Although it killed her to agree with him, she had to. "It must be this way. Whether or not ye accept that it is his birthright, Fingal MacIan is Laird MacLennan by the king's order. After we are wed, he is laird as my husband too. No one can deny that. If ye choose not to accept it, then it is to yer own folly." She looked into Fingal's warm green eyes and was shocked to see admiration. Suddenly, it was all too much for her. "Please excuse me now. I suggest ye all find yer beds and get a bit of rest. I suspect it will be a busy day."

Gillian edged her way through the dumbstruck crowd. Perhaps she should have seen to the comfort of her guests, but she needed to escape. Then again, if Fingal was laird now, she would not be Lady MacLennan until after they were wed. Let him handle it. She rushed up the stairs and into her bedchamber. Her rumpled bed linens reminded her that less than two hours ago she'd awakened from a sweet dream about her father to the nightmare in which she found herself now. She slid to the floor, with her back against her chamber door. "Oh Da, how can this be happening? What am I going to do?" How she wished it was only a nightmare, or even better that the events of the last year were just a nightmare and her father would wake her from it.

Before she settled her jumbled thoughts, someone pounded on her door. "Gillian, let me in." It was mother. Gillian should have known better than to expect the woman would give her a few moments of privacy. She stood with a sigh and opened the door to her mother and her sister Fallon.

Her mother charged into the room, anger washing off her in waves. "That man is horrible. This cannot be allowed."

"Mother, please, it is done."

"It isn't done until it's done. We have to think."

"Nay, Mother, we don't. I will marry Fingal MacIan in a few hours. Ye must accept that."

"Don't tell me what I must accept, Gillian."

"Please, I don't wish to argue. I know ye probably would prefer that I step aside for Fallon—"

"Good heavens, no! That man cannot marry Fallon under any circumstances."

"Then I don't see what the problem is. She doesn't have to marry him." Fallon stood silently to one side.

"The problem, *Gillian*"—her mother hissed her name as if it were an invective—"is he should not be the leader of this clan. I know this is not the way things were meant to be."

"I'm not sure why ye are so certain of the way things were meant to be. Things are as they are and frankly the more I consider it, the more I believe we only have Laird Malcolm to blame. He wanted Fingal to lead this clan enough to betray a staunch ally and waste too many lives to see it done. Perhaps this isn't the way he intended it to happen, but happen it has."

"Ye know nothing, Gillian MacLennan!"

"Mother, I know that this is beyond our control and I'm tired of arguing with ye. I can only follow the king's dictate and do what I must to help preserve our clan. It is as Fingal said. Ye must decide where yer loyalties lie. Mine lie with the clan."

"As do mine. How dare ye suggest otherwise?"

"Good, then there is nothing more to discuss. Good night, mother." Gillian opened the door as a not so subtle hint for them to leave.

Her mother narrowed her eyes and she snarled, "Yer father would be so ashamed!" before leaving in a huff.

Fallon remained behind for a moment, looking a bit stunned. She gave Gillian a quick hug and whispered, "Nay he wouldn't, Gillian," before following their mother.

Would he? Dear God, in a few hours she would marry his murderer's son. Would her father understand that it was her only option? It made her head hurt. The course was set; she had to try to make it work for the sake of her family and her clan.

~ * ~

Fingal had watched with admiration as Gillian left the hall, her head high and her back straight. He found her simply remarkable. After arguing tooth and nail against marrying him, she could have remained stubbornly silent, or worse yet, openly disagreed with the demand he had placed on her clan. Clearly she recognized the need for clan unity and in spite of her personal feelings she fully supported him in that. Perhaps there was hope for this marriage.

The remainder of the MacLennans appeared to follow her suggestion to "find their beds" as many of them left the hall while others bedded down on the floor as was their custom.

As the hall cleared and they were afforded a bit of privacy, Niall interrupted his musing. "She seems to have accepted this better than I expected."

Fingal shook his head. "Nay, she hasn't."

"She was agreeable just now."

"Aye, because she is smart and she cares about her clan. She is not happy. She blames me for my mother's actions."

"She will get past that, Fingal."

Fingal hoped so, but he wished he could be as confident about it as Niall. Before he could say so, Eadoin approached. "Lairds, can I be of any service?"

"Eadoin, ye were made the MacLennan commander?" Niall asked.

"Aye, Laird MacIan."

Eadoin and Niall had trained together and Niall still considered him a friend in spite of all that had happened. During his captivity, after the battle at Duncurra, Eadoin told them that Malcolm's decision to attack Duncurra did not have the whole-hearted support of many of his men, but nevertheless they were sworn to follow their laird.

Niall asked, "What can we expect from the MacLennans?"

"I wish I knew for sure. There are some, many in fact, who are thrilled. There is no denying we are vulnerable. Having the might of the MacIans and their allies behind us again is a relief. Niall, after the battle at Duncurra ye dealt fairly with us. We were well treated and our wounded cared for. Ye allowed us our dignity. The ransom ye requested was laughably small. Many of us won't forget that." He turned to Fingal. "Most of the MacLennans accept that ye are Malcolm's rightful heir. The king has effectively silenced any opposition to that by insisting ye marry Gillie. I will swear my fealty to ye."

Fingal nodded. "I appreciate that. However, I fear there is something ye aren't telling us."

Eadoin seemed to consider his words for a moment. "Malcolm kept secrets and I suspect he wasn't alone. Two of the elders, Nolan and Owen, have been dead set against the idea of ye being made laird. Nolan particularly was close to Malcolm and perhaps knew more about what Malcolm kept hidden than anyone. I believe ye will have the support of most of the clan even if some of it is grudgingly given. Just don't let yer guard down until we know for sure."

"Aye, Eadoin, I won't. I appreciate yer candor."

Eadoin's demeanor became solemn. "Laird, I will serve ye faithfully. Malcolm wanted ye to be his heir. I do not respect the method he chose to accomplish it, but the fact remains this is what he intended to happen eventually. However, before I declare my fealty tomorrow I would like to make something clear."

Fingal nodded and Eadoin continued. "I have known Gillie

since she was a bairn. She is like a sister to me. Duncan was my commander, and I considered him a friend. He had both my respect and admiration. I do not hold ye responsible for what yer mother did but ye must know that Gillie adored her father. When she became our chief, we learned how strong and dedicated to this clan she truly was. She was destined to marry someone who could serve as laird and she was unlikely to have any say as to whom it would be—I don't dispute that. As far as it goes, I know ye are an honorable man, and a better choice of husband than many. However, in spite of her willingness to follow the king's demands, ye must know she has a broken heart and mourns the loss of her father deeply. I will not swear my fealty to ye until ye have sworn to honor and protect her in yer marriage vows. Never give me cause to regret my oath to ye."

Fingal returned Eadoin's solemn gaze before carefully choosing his next words. There was a time when Niall, the man whom he respected more than any other, but who had been blinded by old hurts, behaved like a complete arse towards his lovely wife Katherine. Fingal understood what it felt like to be trapped between fealty to his laird and concern for his lady. "Eadoin, there are men who would consider that statement a threat. However, I appreciate the respect ye hold for Lady Gillian. Tomorrow, I will vow before God to love, honor, keep, and guard her. If ye ever think I am in danger of failing those vows, I give ye leave to address it with me privately."

"Thank ye, laird."

Eadoin's relief was palpable and Fingal's respect for the man grew. "Oh, and Eadoin, if I ever seem less than willing to hear ye out, ye need to say but one word—Katherine."

Niall arched an eyebrow at him and Fingal laughed. "Niall, ye can't deny it, ye were an arse and if ye had listened to me from the start, it could've saved ye loads of misery."

Niall laughed too. "Aye, brother, ye needn't rub it in."

Eadoin chuckled. "Well, Lairds, it is late and if ye wish to get some rest before morning I will show ye to rooms upstairs. Yer men can bed down here in the hall."

"Thank ye, Eadoin," Fingal said. "Since it is so late, we won't keep ye any longer. We will stay with the men in the hall tonight and sort out other arrangements tomorrow."

"So be it. Good night then, Lairds." Eadoin gave a small nod and left the keep.

As the men settled in for the night, Niall and Fingal sat alone at the table. "Niall, what think ye of Eadoin? Would I be wrong to leave him as commander?"

"Eadoin is a good man and I believe he will be loyal. However, I think ye should also have someone here whose loyalty ye would never question. Ye know I am leaving men-at-arms to bolster yer ranks, but ye need someone else."

"Aye, that would ease my mind a great deal. Who do ye suggest?"

"In the short term, Diarmad can stay here."

"Nay, he is yer commander, Duncurra is his home. I don't want ye to do that."

Niall insisted, "There is no one I trust more. He would be a solid advisor and a strong right arm just until things are more settled. But ye also might want to bring in a few guardsmen of yer choosing—maybe Peadar and Quinn MacKenzie. Ye trained with them at Chisholm and ye know they would be worthy guardsmen."

Fingal laughed. "Ye just made Rowan MacKenzie one of yer guardsmen. Cathal will declare war if we lure more of his sons away. Besides, Peadar is married and settled at Carraigile."

"Then just ask Quinn. Another man ye should consider is Bran MacBain. He trained here when I did but left well before Laird Kelvin died, while Malcolm was at court. He won't have had strong ties to Malcolm but the MacLennans will respect him. And, of course, Hogan MacBain is a solid ally."

"Aye," Fingal agreed, "so is Laird Ross, and Bran is married to his youngest daughter, Tira. I may also eventually contact Laird MacKay. His nephew, Dougal, is old enough to begin training as a squire."

"That would also give ye ties with MacLeod as Dougal is his nephew too. I think it's a good plan, Fingal."

"Still, I need to learn what resources I have available before I act."

"Don't wait too long," Niall cautioned. "When Malcolm turned on me, he severed more ties than he knew. Ye will need to take steps to rebuild allies as quickly as ye can."

"Aye, Niall, I know ye are right. But I may not have the funds required to do this."

"Fingal," Niall said in exasperation, "ye are more stubborn that I ever knew. Yer mother left a small fortune to ye."

Fingal frowned and clenched his jaw. "I will not take that

money. She stole it from Da. It should go back to the MacIans."

"And I am tired of arguing with ye about this. We do not need it. Ye do."

"Nay. Eithne and Malcolm are to blame for all of this. I want nothing from her."

"Aye, brother, they are to blame for all this and that is *precisely* why ye should accept the money. It may be the only way to repair a small portion of the damage they did."

"I will not discuss this anymore tonight."

Niall shook his head in frustration. "And ye say I'm hard-headed."

Fingal attempted to change the subject. "So, Diarmad will stay temporarily and I will try to bring on Bran MacBain and Quinn MacKenzie. The question remains, do I leave Eadoin as my commander?"

Niall appeared to consider this for a while before answering. "Give him shared leadership with Diarmad for now so as not to offend the MacLennan's, but know that Diarmad has yer back."

"Thank ye, Niall."

Niall lowered his voice, perhaps not wishing to be overheard by any of the MacLennans who might still be awake. "Spend the next few months assessing the situation here. I suspect the MacLennan warriors that are left need more training and discipline. Malcolm's father, Laird Kelvin, was a brilliant warrior and trained his men rigorously. From what we have seen in the last year, I suspect Malcolm was not as effective. If it becomes clear that ye need more help, ask for it."

Chapter 5

Gillian tried to get some rest in what remained of the night but it was to little avail. Before dawn pinked the frigid winter sky, she gave up. Although the front stairs were closer to the laird's chamber, which she had been given when the clan named her chief, she hurried through the quiet halls and down the backstairs. These exited into the back of the great hall, near the doors to the rear bailey and kitchens, her destination.

As she quietly entered the kitchen, she was not surprised to see Jeanne, the elderly woman who still managed the cooking, already at work. When she saw Gillian, Jeanne's face burst into a wreath of smiles and she opened her arms. Gillian rushed into her embrace. Enfolded in the warmth and love of a dear friend, something crumbled inside her and Gillian burst into tears.

"I-I'm sorry, Jeanne," she sobbed.

"Och, lass, ye have yerself a bit of a cry now. Ye'll feel better and we can tackle this together."

It felt good to cry. Gillian had held it in for so long. She hadn't even given in to tears when Aunt Meara died months earlier. The clan was in disarray, she was their leader, and she had to stay strong. Jeanne just crooned, "Wheesht, lass," and held her while she cried.

When her tears were spent, Jeanne motioned her to a chair near the hearth. "Sit here a minute while I fix us a nice warm tisane and we'll talk."

Gillian watched the stooped old woman busy herself making the warm brew. The peacefulness of the quiet, cozy kitchen surrounded her and she slowly regained control. After Jeanne poured the fragrant drink into two mugs, she pulled out a small jug and winked at Gillian. "Ye know I only use the water of life for medicinal purposes, but I think a wee drop is called for this morning." Gillian grinned as Jeanne poured more than a drop into each mug. Jeanne was a great one for discovering all of the medicinal uses of whisky. She handed Gillian a mug before drawing another chair near the fire and settling herself in it. Gillian took a sip and felt the warmth to her very soul.

"Now, lass, let's talk things through."

"Jeanne, have ye heard what's happening?"

"Aye, lass, news like that doesn't rest long. The king has seen fit to give us a laird and ye a husband."

"Aye. Fingal MacIan."

Jeanne chuckled. "Fingal MacIan, the demon."

"He isn't a demon, Jeanne."

"Nay? Well, by the way ye said that just now I thought ye were namin' one of the devil's own."

Gillian gave her a wan smile. "He isn't a bad man. It's just—it's just..."

"Ye feel cornered. It feels as if everything is spinning out of control. Ye miss yer da with every breath ye take and Fingal MacIan's mother is the one who took him from ye. Not to mention that yer own mother only makes things worse."

Gillian blinked in astonishment at the accuracy of Jeanne's summary. "Aye."

"Well, my sweet lass, this is what ye will do. Ye will rise to this. Ye will marry that young MacIan. Ye will honor the vows ye take before God and ye'll work to be yer husband's partner."

Gillain looked aghast. "His partner? I want as little as possible to do with him."

"Tell me, what is to be gained by that?"

"I-I-I'll be faithful to my father's memory."

"I see. And that is what yer father wants? For this clan to be divided and fall?"

"Nay, Jeanne. Ye twist my words, but the MacIans have—"

"Don't tell me what the MacIans have done. The MacLennans are not innocent in this but moreover that's in the past. Gillian, hear me well. Men live in the past. They hold grudges and fight wars over bygone things. Women must live for the future, for our children and their children. Sometimes we have to set aside old hurts, regardless of how painful they are, in order to ensure a better life for our children."

"But—"

"Nay, the best way to honor yer father's memory is to see this clan become great again. The best way to do that is to become yer husband's ally and see to the welfare of our people. Ye don't have to love the man, but ye must earn his respect and find a way to give him yers." Jeanne's face softened. "Oh, Gillie, I hate to see yer heart ache so. Years ago, I had my own dreams for ye. Ye were such a sweet thing and I wanted nothing more than for ye to marry my grandson." Tears clouded the old woman's eyes as she remembered her loss. "He was a good lad and would have made a fine warrior. Still, the good Lord had other plans for him and He does for ye as well. Ye will be the mother of our clan's leaders to come. Focus on that future now and ignore anyone or anything that drags ye into the past. Do ye understand me, lass?"

"Aye, Jeanne, I understand."

"Ye know yer own mother is likely to be one of them."

Gillian sighed. "Aye, sadly I do."

"Hold strong against that, lass. Maybe she will understand someday. Like it or not, yer future is with yer new husband, not yer mother."

Gillian nodded. Jeanne was right. Her future was indeed with Fingal MacIan and though she didn't like it she would do what she had to do.

Jeanne leaned forward and patted Gillian's hand. "Now, lass, break yer fast with me and then I will see that a bath is sent up to ye."

"I don't have time for a bath. I have a keep overflowing with unwelcome guests to see to. I'll just have a quick wash in the tub in the wash-house."

"Nonsense, 'tis yer wedding day. I'll make sure yer guests are fed."

~ * ~

As Gillian sank into the bath Jeanne had arranged, she was immensely grateful the old woman had insisted on it. It was a luxury she seldom indulged in, preferring to bathe, as most everyone else did, in the wash-house where the laundry was done or behind a screen in the kitchen; it was much less work for everyone. However, having a bath in the privacy of her own chamber was delightful. That was until a swarm of clanswomen, including her mother and sisters, descended on her.

The mixed feelings with which the clan greeted the news of their new laird and the king's edict were clearly expressed among the women. Some were joyous, others dolorous, but all were intent to see her wed with as much fanfare as possible, under the circumstances. Her friend Alana, plump with pregnancy, did her best to keep the mood light. Ailsa's continuous chatter also distracted Gillian.

These women who loved her were there to pamper her. They brought sweet herbs for her bath water and helped wash and dry her hair. They pulled out practically every garment she owned and argued over what she should wear. They created a controlled chaos that prevented Gillian from dwelling overmuch on what was to come.

By mid-morning, still only wearing a shift, Gillian sat with a blanket around her shoulders while her sister worked an intricate braid in her hair. The women had decided she should wear her dark blue *léine*. It was made of soft lamb's wool but had no adornment and apparently that *simply would not do*. Three women sat furiously embroidering scrollwork in yellow thread on the neck and sleeves. Peggy, who diligently worked on one sleeve moaned, "It is a shame we don't have any gold thread. I know Rhiannon has some but we just don't have time to go get it."

At the mention of Rhiannon's name, a look of horror crossed her mother's face. "Oh my, how could we have forgotten? Someone must go tell Rhiannon about the wedding."

Gillian shot her mother a quizzical look. "Why? She rarely leaves her cottage and she never comes to the keep anymore."

Lana wasn't the only one who frowned at Gillian. "Aye, she prefers to stay at home but she would be very hurt if we didn't let her know this was happening. She cares very deeply about this clan, Gillian."

Gillian didn't argue. Rhiannon was an old woman who lived in a cottage just beyond the village, at the edge of the forest. Many of the MacLennan women seemed to revere her. They gushed about how lovely and kind she was. Frankly, Rhiannon was rumored to have the gift of "sight" and Gillian suspected that was the reason people courted her favor. Everyone had heard stories about Rhiannon's wonderful predictions that had come true. Gillian wasn't sure she believed that Rhiannon was truly a seer but Lana had always considered her a good friend. "I suppose ye are right mother. Would ye mind going? Let her know about the wedding and tell her I would be honored if she would attend."

"I'm sure she won't approve, but aye, I will take the news to her."

"Thank ye, mother."

Lana turned to leave. "Come, Fallon."

Fallon continued to braid Gillian's hair. "Mama, I can't. Gillie needs me." Gillian noticed Ailsa had become quiet and sidled out of her mother's line of vision. Gillian smiled. Obviously her littlest sister didn't want to go either.

"Nonsense," said her mother. "Alana or one of the other women can do that."

Alana stepped in, taking the strands of Gillian's hair from Fallon, whispering, "Go, Fallon. Let's not push things today."

Fallon sighed, but followed her mother. Once they had left and it was clear she wouldn't be dragged along too, Ailsa flopped happily on the bed and resumed her chatter.

~ * ~

It was well after noon and time for the wedding before her mother and Fallon returned. Gillian was already dressed in the newly adorned *léine*. It was cinched at the waist with a braided leather belt and she had to admit that the yellow embroidery at the neck and sleeves added a beautiful touch. Around her shoulders she wore a red plaid with green and gold stripes. Alana had woven a wreath of ivy for her which held a fine woolen veil on her head.

The clan's healer, Agnes, brought her a small bouquet of herbs. "Gillian, lass, I only have dried herbs at this time of year, but this contains burnet for a merry heart. My lady, I know this is hard, but try to keep yer heart light. The clan loves ye and will always support ye. I have also put in lavender for devotion and luck, sage for long life, marjoram for joy, and yarrow for everlasting love." Gillian tried not to roll her eyes at this. She didn't believe any amount of yarrow would help bring everlasting love to this union. "I have also added a bit of mint for warm thoughts because it is a bitter cold day."

"Thank ye, Agnes. Ye have all been great friends to me. I understand that some of ye are not happy about this wedding. I can't say he would have been my first choice either. However, I swore to ye, when ye made me yer chief, that I would always consider the good of the clan first. This is what our king has asked of us and I can only believe it will help stabilize us and once again give us strong allies."

Her mother clenched her jaw, her lips pressed into a tight line, but everyone else offered their good wishes.

A knock sounded at the door. Alana opened it to Daniel, who stepped into the room before exclaiming, "My lady Gillian, ye are beautiful lass. Yer da would be so very proud of ye."

"Thank ye, Daniel. I hope so. Are they ready for me?"

"Aye, my lady, they await ye on the steps of the chapel. I would be honored if ye would allow me to escort ye."

She hadn't had enough time to think of who would give her away. It should have been her father with her today. The pain caused by the memory of his loss nearly took her breath away. She took a deep breath, forcing back the tears that threatened. This was political. This was to protect the clan. She would not give in to sentimentality. "Of course, Daniel. Thank ye."

Ailsa frowned. "Ye said that Fallon and I would stand with ye?"

"And ye will, pet. Daniel is just going to do what Da would—would have done were he here." Gillian paused a moment in order to maintain her control. When she saw tears well in Ailsa's eyes she pulled her into a hug. "I need ye and Fallon to stand with me when I take my vows. Run now and get yer mantle, it is bitter cold out. Then ye'll walk ahead of me to the chapel doors." With Ailsa still on the edge of tears Gillian leaned down and whispered. "I need for ye to be strong with me, pet. Da would want it and I can't do it without ye."

Ailsa nodded. Releasing her and swiping at the moisture on her cheeks, she hurried from the room. The rest of the women followed, each giving Gillian a hug and wishing her well as they went. Fallon and her mother were the last to leave. Fallon, who also looked close to tears, hugged her silently for a long moment.

"That's enough, Fallon. Let's get this over with and by the saints stop crying. At least it isn't ye." Lana pulled her away and out of the room.

Daniel arched an eyebrow at Lana as she left, but said nothing until the sound of their footsteps faded. He stepped close to Gillian, taking both of her hands in his. "Gillian, I know the leadership of this clan has weighed heavily on ye these last few months. Ye have done very well. Ye do not belong in a convent, ye belong here with us and ye made the right decision in marrying Fingal MacIan."

"I'm glad ye think so, Daniel, but I wish there was another way."

"I know ye do, but ye'll be fine, lass." She nodded. He

gave her a kiss on the cheek. "Are ye ready?"

She smiled. "Not really, but time won't change that."

He chuckled. "Nay, it won't." He took Gillian's elbow and walked with her down the stairs and through the deserted hall. Fallon and Ailsa waited just inside the doors. When they reached her sisters Daniel stopped for a moment and grinned. "Are we ready, lassies?" Both Fallon and Ailsa nodded. "Then I suppose we shouldn't keep them waiting. Go on now and part the crowd. We will be right behind ye."

Just moments after Fallon and Ailsa left the keep, Gillian followed, on Daniel's arm. As they stepped out the main doors a cheer went up from the members of her clan, their show of support bolstering her flagging confidence. Daniel was right. She had made the right choice and her reasons for agreeing to the wedding stood all around her. She belonged here with her clan. Snow had started to fall and a bitter wind blew. She turned her face to the blowing snow and laughed. "Lovely day for a wedding, wouldn't ye say, Daniel?"

He laughed too. "Ah, lass, don't ye know? If snow falls on yer wedding day, 'tis a good omen for a long, happy marriage."

"Well if the severity of the storm has any impact, 'twill be positively blissful. Like my mother said, let's hurry and get this over with, otherwise I'll be frozen to death before it ever starts."

Chapter 6

Although Fingal had stretched out on a pallet near the hearth in the great hall, he hadn't slept much that night. He had worried about the huge responsibility he was about to undertake. Just before dawn, a soft noise from the rear of the hall woke him. He had watched as his betrothed slip out the back of the keep. For a moment he had wondered if she was running away. As soon as that thought had crossed his mind, he set it aside. She might not like this, but she was strong and bold; she would not sneak away like a thief in the night. Wherever she was going, he was certain that she would marry him as she promised.

He had spent most of the morning taking stock of the clan's assets, most importantly their manpower and defense measures. The steward, Ailbert, was both accommodating and enthusiastic. He had clearly been one of the MacLennans who welcomed Fingal's leadership. After saying his piece the previous night, Eadoin too had been helpful, providing much needed information about their military strengths and weaknesses. When Niall approached at one point to suggest that he prepare for the wedding he had been shocked at how late it was. There had only been time for a quick wash and a change of clothes before the ceremony. Now he stood solemnly on the steps of the chapel with Niall and the MacLennans' priest, Father Stephen.

Gillian's mother and several other women had just exited the keep and were winding their way through the people who had gathered for the wedding. A hush fell over the crowd as they waited expectantly. Fingal wished he were almost anywhere but here. He had never aspired to leadership and yet it had been thrust upon him, along with an unwilling bride. These people were *his* people now. Their success or failure, their safety—their very lives—were his responsibility. God's teeth, could he do this?

His concern must have shown on his face. Niall leaned close. "Fingal, never doubt that ye are up to this challenge. Ye are a skilled warrior. Ye are both intelligent and compassionate. I respect ye more than any man alive and I am confident ye will be a great leader."

"Thank ye, Niall." Before he could say more, the doors opened again. Fallon and Ailsa stepped out of the hall followed moments later by Gillian, on Daniel's arm. A great cheer went up from the crowd. The wind picked up and the snow swirled around them. Gillian turned her face into the wind and laughed. Dear God, she was spectacular. Perhaps she would never love him, hell she might never even like him, but by all that was holy, he could think of worse things than waking up next to her every day for the rest of his life.

Daniel led her through the crowd to his side. Before Father Stephen could utter a word, Daniel said, "Father, I know it is traditional for the couple to exchange vows in front of the church, but since the bishop is allowing us to break with several other traditions, do ye think God would mind terribly if we took this inside on such a blustery day?"

Father Stephen looked flustered at Daniel's request. "Well, ah...well—nay, I don't suppose so." He turned, opened the door, and led those assembled inside out of the wind.

"That's much better, Father." Giving the priest a roguish wink, Daniel added, "frankly, I don't think our Lord himself could've heard their vows in that wind." Gillian chuckled and Fingal found the sound entrancing.

Father Stephen administered the wedding vows without preamble. Practically before he knew it, their promises had been spoken and Fingal held the blessed, gold ring, symbolizing their eternal bond in his hand. He took Gillian's cold hand in his, capturing her gaze for a moment. Looking into the amber depths of her eyes he saw neither hate nor fear, only uncertainty mixed with determination. *Well at least that's something.* He slipped the gold band on her ring finger saying, "With this ring, I thee wed, in the name of the Father and the Son and the Holy Spirit."

Father Stephen finished the ceremony with the final blessings before saying, "Laird MacLennan, ye may kiss yer bride."

Fingal caressed her cheek tenderly. She arched an eyebrow at him, but he cupped her jaw in his hand before leaning in to give her a gentle kiss. Cheers of approval filled the little church. Gillian's lips were soft and warm. He had the sudden urge to pull her closer and deepen the kiss, but he refrained. When he stepped back, she looked bemused and a small gasp escaped her lips. Fingal smiled, pleased to see she was not unaffected. "My lady, shall we lead our clan back to the keep? I understand something of a last minute feast has been prepared to celebrate our nuptials."

Still looking perplexed she answered, "Aye, Laird."

Fingal suppressed a grin. This formidable young woman, who argued with the king's messenger from the top of her curtain wall and laughed in the face of wind and snow, was knocked off balance by his kiss. Aye, there was hope for this marriage.

~ * ~

Jeanne had indeed managed to pull together a modest feast. They were served a creamy fish stew, roasted salmon and root vegetables, fresh bread, preserved fruit, and one of Gillian's favorites, a rich dense cake made with dried apples. It was a good thing Ailsa, who sat on her left, kept up her usual running chatter because Gillian had trouble focusing on anything. She couldn't possibly have made intelligent conversation with anyone.

Fingal's kiss had surprised her. It was sweet and gentle, almost loving. She knew their vows would be sealed with a kiss, but she hadn't expected to *like* it. Well at least it was over, she thought.

But it wasn't. All through the meal he did little things that unsettled her. He touched her hand seemingly randomly or brushed her arm with his. He served her food and filled her goblet with wine. He leaned in to whisper a comment or ask a question. Each time it caused her stomach to flutter.

At the end of the meal, their new laird called for quiet. "This has been a wonderful feast. My thanks to ye Jeanne for pulling it together so quickly. The welcome is most appreciated." He waited while a cheer went up praising Jeanne's efforts. "Although the king's dictate named me Laird MacLennan, today Lady MacLennan and I have made the holy vows of marriage to each other. Now, by both proclamation and marriage to yer lady, I am yer laird. Therefore, Lady MacLennan and I will accept yer pledges of fealty." He reached for her hand and pulled her up to stand beside him.

This wasn't what Gillian expected. Of course she knew he was going to ask for their fealty, but she didn't expect him to include her. She didn't know what to say, so she stood beside him dumbly as each member of the clan present gave their promises of loyalty to both of them.

It took quite a while but when everyone had spoken the words, Fingal made one last announcement. "Thank ye all for yer show of support and commitment to this clan. Now I give ye my vow that I will serve faithfully as yer laird and that I will consider the good of this clan foremost in all actions. Although I was named Fingal MacIan at birth and I will always consider Alistair MacIan my father, and Niall MacIan my brother, today I stand before ye as Fingal MacLennan, Laird of Clan MacLennan."

That was the last thing Gillian expected to hear and to her surprise, a deafening cheer went up. She wasn't quite sure how he had done it, but Fingal seemed to be winning the hearts of her clan. Oh, it wasn't unreserved on everyone's part, but still it was a better response than she had expected when Laird MacIan announced the king's order earlier that morning. The memory of it reminded her of how very little sleep she had had the previous night and how utterly exhausted she felt now. She couldn't suppress a yawn.

Fingal smiled at her, addressing the clan again as the cheering subsided. "Thank ye. Now, I must apologize. I realize that it's early, but all things considered, it has been a rather long day. Lady MacLennan and I will retire now."

More cheers went up. Some members of the clan yelled bawdy suggestions while others called for the bedding ritual. Gillian blushed hotly. Dear God, how had she forgotten that? She didn't think she could face it. Perhaps sensing her panic, Fingal took her hand in his and silenced the crowd again. He grinned cheekily. "While I appreciate all of yer kind words of advice, and offers of assistance, I'm sure ye will agree that Lady Gillian might prefer some privacy. After all, this whole wedding came as a bit of a shock." Many of those present greeted this with disappointment although there were also murmurs of approval around the room. "Still, I wouldn't want this union to start with a bad omen, so Father Stephen, would ye be so kind as to come with us and bless the wedding bed?" The members of the clan seemed satisfied by this and Gillian was profoundly relieved.

The priest nodded. "Of course, Laird, I would be happy to."

"Thank ye, Father." Fingal led Gillian through the crowd as people called well wishes to them.

When they reached the entrance to the stairs, someone

yelled, "Now, Laird, are ye sure ye know what's what? I'm the father of three, I'd be glad to talk ye through it."

To the delight of the clan Fingal called, "Aye, I think I have the basics down, Tarmon. With any luck, I'll be catching up to ye soon enough." The result was another thunderous cheer.

Gillian said a silent word of thanks to God that she was already through the door because if possible her blush grew deeper. Father Stephen was well ahead of them on the stairs. When they reached her chamber—their chamber now—Father quickly blessed the bed. If anything he looked more embarrassed than she did. He wished them a good evening and hurried from the room. Fingal closed the door behind him before turning to face her.

Unsure of what to do, she clutched her hands in front of her and looked down. Fingal crossed the room and nudged her chin until she had to meet his eyes. "Gillian, I know today was very difficult for ye. The steps ye've taken—we've taken—will ensure the safety and unity of this clan for the future. No chief in yer situation could have done more. I am honored that ye are my wife."

Gillian was at a loss. "Laird, I—"

"Lass, we are married. Please, call me Fingal."

She sighed. "Fingal, I don't know what to say."

~ * ~

Her reluctance to marry him and her assurance that she could never love him weighed heavily on Fingal from the moment she had agreed to the wedding. He didn't want to spend the rest of his life with someone who could barely tolerate his presence. Then he kissed her after they exchanged vows and he had a moment of clarity. A woman who could hate a man forever didn't become flustered by a chaste kiss. Perhaps she had been simply caught up in the moment. Still, he put this new insight to the test. He intentionally touched her casually throughout dinner. He spoke low in her ear, forcing her to lean close to hear. He served her food and wine. Fingal was fully aware that he had a reputation for being charming. In truth, he had never consciously tried to win anyone's affections. So during the wedding feast he simply did what came naturally and to his delight, he kept her off-balance well into the evening.

He had vowed, perhaps foolishly, that he would not push her; he would give her all the time she needed. He had agreed to wait until she was ready, in fact until she asked him. He never promised not to do everything in his power to get her to ask him. He smiled to himself. *I can win this battle.*

Now he stood with his very flustered bride in their chamber. "Gillian, ye needn't say anything. I simply wanted ye to know." The desire to kiss her almost overwhelmed him but instead he turned away and began to remove his boots.

"What are ye doing?" There was a slightly shrill edge to her voice, perhaps brought about by her nervousness.

She couldn't see his grin. "I'm taking off my boots. I didn't lie to the clan. It has been a long day, and frankly, I am ready for bed."

"Bed?" The pitch of her voice went even higher.

"Aye, Gillian. I'm exhausted, I need to sleep." However, he was fairly certain he would not sleep well with this beautiful woman sharing his bed chastely.

"Oh. Aye. Sleep."

His grin broadened. He schooled his features before turning to face her. "Aye, lass. I made ye a promise and I intend to keep it. I won't truly make ye my wife until ye ask me to." He continued to undress until he stood in front of her wearing only his *léine*. He had to force himself not to laugh at the shocked expression on her face. "Is something the matter?"

"Nay, I just—well I didn't think—I mean—ye're undressing."

"Aye lass, I told ye, I'm tired. I'm going to bed."

"But, there is only the one bed. Ye look as if—do ye mean to sleep without clothes?"

He stood and gave her as surprised a look as he could muster. "Are ye in the habit of sleeping in *yer* clothes?"

"Nay, but—"

"Well, neither am I."

"But surely ye don't mean to—"

"Gillian, we are married. We talked about the need to appear married to everyone. Although I don't expect visitors, it would look terribly odd if for some reason we were found sleeping in our clothes, especially on our wedding night. I have given ye my word that I will give ye all the time ye need, but now I need to get some rest or I will collapse."

He walked past her to the bed, placed his sword and dagger within easy reach and pulled off his *léine*, giving her an unhindered view of his bare arse before climbing under the covers. Her shocked gasp nearly made him laugh aloud, but he forced down his amusement, turned his back to her, and pulled the covers over his shoulders.

"Ye don't expect me to—to..."

Fingal gave what he hoped sounded like an exhausted sigh. "Gillian, lass, ye too are practically dead on yer feet. The only thing that I expect is that ye will get in this bed and get some rest. Please, lass."

She must have stood still for several moments. He tried to make his breathing smooth and regular as if he were relaxing into sleep. Eventually she moved around the room. She took an inordinately long time to undo the braids from her hair and brush the thick dark tresses. He would dearly love to run his fingers through that silk instead of lying here imagining it.

Eventually, he heard the rustle of her clothes as she removed them before padding softly to the other side of the bed. Through squinted eyes, he saw that she still wore her shift, but it left very little to the imagination. The outline of her full breasts made him want to caress them. The merest glimpse of her long beautiful legs as she climbed into the far side of the bed sent his imagination reeling. Oh, what heaven to have them wrapped around him. God's bones he had to put such thoughts out of his mind. She curled into a ball, as close to the edge of the bed as she could without falling off. *Control yerself man, it will be sometime before ye win that prize.*

Fingal watched her surreptitiously until she finally fell asleep. Awake she seemed so serious and capable, so very in control he had forgotten she was just nineteen. In sleep however, her features softened and the worry lines relaxed. He could see a bit of the carefree lass she had been up until a year ago. Damn Malcolm; he had ruined so many lives.

Fingal wasn't sure how long he watched her sleep, but eventually he must have fallen asleep himself. He woke at some point in the middle of the night. The covers had been kicked off and the fire in the hearth had burned too low to fend off the chill, but a warm body lay curled tight against him. Gillian's shift rode high on her thighs and her bare legs were entwined with his. It was exquisite torture having her so close and not being able to move or caress her. However, to do so might wake her and send her scurrying to the edge of the bed again. Her nearness was worth the torment. As gently as he could, he eased the covers back over both of them.

~ * ~

Gillian came slowly awake. She was so very cozy and warm she nearly ignored the pink light of dawn and nodded back to sleep. *Cozy and warm*? Her eyes flew open; something was amiss. Oh dear God, Fingal lay sound asleep on his back, snoring softly and perhaps, drawn to his warmth, she had wrapped herself around him. Her head lay on his chest and one leg was thrown over his, resting between his thighs on his naked groin. The only thing that could possibly be more embarrassing would be for him to wake and find her there. She would simply ease herself off and out of the bed. He would never know.

Ever so gently, she tried to raise herself off his chest only to have him throw his arm around her in his sleep, pushing her firmly back down. She wasn't at all sure how she had slept so well pillowed on that chest in the first place. Although toasty warm, it was rock hard. After a few moments she felt his grip relax a bit so she tried again. This time his other arm encircled her, effectively trapping her where she lay sprawled on top of him.

She decided to give it one more attempt. She wiggled a bit to try to slip from under his arms. Evidently her movements woke him. To her dismay he groaned and opened his eyes. They twinkled oddly bright for someone just rousing from sleep. "Good morning, Gillian."

She blushed furiously. "Uh...good morning, Laird."

"Really, lass, do ye suppose ye could call me Fingal? After all, we are married and yer knee is perilously close to unmanning me."

"I'm sorry, Fingal, I-I-I must have gotten cold."

"Aye, I can tell." He released his hold on her and she scrambled away, taking the covers with her. When she realized that she left his body gloriously uncovered she gave a squeal and tried to cover him. He chuckled heartily and stayed her hands. "Tis alright, Gillian, I was getting up anyway." He rose from the bed in all of his spectacular nakedness. By the saints, he was a well-formed man—tall, lean, and well-muscled. She realized she was staring at him boldly when he turned and caught her gaze. She looked quickly away, more embarrassed than she thought possible. He chuckled and pulled on his clothes.

Not wanting to sit in the bed staring at him, she too jumped up. Thankful for the meager covering provided by her shift, she began to dress with her back to him. When she turned around she found him watching her. He seemed captivated. She found that odd but before she could parse out what it might mean he picked up his dagger, pulled up his left sleeve and made a small shallow cut on his forearm. "Fingal, don't, what are ye doing?"

He smeared the blood on the sheets, wiping his arm clean. "I am giving no one reason to think our marriage isn't real or that ye didn't come to me as a pure bride. That is the evidence of yer virginity."

"Fingal, I'm sorry. I didn't think about that. Thank ye. Ye didn't have to do that, I could have..." What could she have done?

He cocked his head and gave her an odd look. "Gillian, yesterday I vowed to honor and protect ye. I would be a cad worthy of yer scorn if I did anything less."

Chapter 7

Gillian's first morning as a married woman was starting in as bewildering a manner as the previous day had ended. The man who she married, who she firmly believed she could not even learn to like, had left her confused and off-balance. It wasn't only the respect and gentleness he demonstrated that surprised her. The reaction she had to him as a man was completely unexpected. When he looked at her or touched her, she felt an oddly pleasant fluttering in her belly. However, when she woke draped over his naked body then was treated to an unimpeded view of his spectacular masculine form, that fluttering went to an entirely new level.

Her mother only added to her confusion when she greeted Gillian in the great hall with a kertch she had made. All married Highland women wore this square of pure white linen covering their hair. It was folded into a triangle to represent the Holy Trinity, under whose guidance the bride would walk. A married woman wore it tied around her head, or held on by strings tied under her chin. Generally a bride's mother placed it on her the morning after her wedding. The fact that her mother did this didn't shock her. She might not have wanted the wedding, but she would have been mortified if Gillian didn't wear a kertch. Gillian still remembered how scandalized her mother had been when Lady Katherine MacIan had dined in the great hall with her hair uncovered.

What surprised her was the warmth her mother displayed. Gillian and Fingal were already seated at the table breaking their fast when her mother entered the hall and rushed to the table. "Oh, Gillian, ye are up already. Good morning. I had hoped to be waiting for ye. Are ye well, lass?"

Her mother's enthusiastic greeting alone was a bit of a surprise. "Good morning, Mother. Aye, I'm very well."

"I have brought ye yer kertch, lass." Her mother moved

behind her, placing it on her head, wrapping the ends under her hair and tying them on the top of her head. "Gillian, as ye begin yer marriage in the sight of God, may ye continue to be guided by the Holy Trinity throughout yer days. May a hundred thousand blessings go with ye under this kertch." Then her mother put her arms around her from behind, embracing her warmly.

This was terribly out of character and Gillian didn't quite know what to say. She settled on basic politeness. "Thank ye, Mother, please sit and break yer fast with us."

Her mother agreed, took the seat next to her, and chatted happily while they ate. It wasn't that she never did this; she just usually reserved this behavior for Fallon. Gillian loved her mother but their relationship had always been a bit strained. Over the last year things had been tenser than ever. Perhaps Lana had finally realized no one could alter the course of events put in place by the king. Still, on top of the internal upheaval she experienced over her reaction to her new husband, this chattiness left Gillian dumbfounded.

Her mother managed to occupy her full attention while they were eating. At one point, Fingal laid a hand gently on her arm, drawing her attention. "Gillian, there is much to be done here to ensure our defenses are adequate. The king's guard left this morning to return to Edinburgh. Niall will be staying with his men for few more days. We have some plans to discuss. Is there anything ye need before I go?"

Fingal's gentle concern surprised Gillian. All she could manage to say was, "Nay, thank ye for asking."

He leaned in to give her a quick kiss before leaving the table. The unwelcomed fluttering returned to her belly at this sweet gesture.

When Fingal was out of earshot Lana wrinkled her nose. "Thank goodness he is gone."

This was the mother Gillian knew. "Mother, please don't say things like that. This is his hall, he is our laird."

"I pledged my loyalty. That doesn't mean I have to like the man. Tell me ye aren't falling for him. He is a charmer, always has been, but don't be fooled, Gillian. Never forget who his mother was."

"I couldn't possibly forget that, Mother," she snapped. The warm fluttery feeling from Fingal's kiss was replaced by the cold, hard reality of her mother's words. However, she remembered what Jeanne had said to her yesterday. *The best way to honor yer father's memory is to see this clan become great again. The best way to do that is to become yer husband's ally and see to the welfare of our people.* Jeanne was right. She was also right when she predicted that Lana would be one of those who would try to interfere. Gillian needed to put some distance between herself and her mother so she could try to process all of her strange feelings. "Please excuse me now, Mother, there is work to be done."

"Aye, there is, but first ye must go with me to see Rhiannon today."

"Mother, the snow must be nearly knee deep and I have hundreds of things to attend to here. Surely it can wait."

"She was heartbroken that she couldn't see ye wed. Bless her, she has grown a bit frail this winter. A visit would mean so much to her."

"She has never been overly concerned about a visit from me before."

"Ye are Lady MacLennan now."

Gillian leveled a stare at her mother. "I have been Lady MacLennan since Aunt Meara died."

"I know, but now, with the king's order and the wedding and all, it's somehow more official. Please, it won't take long, Gillian. She wants to hear about it all from ye."

"Not today, Mother. Perhaps I can go in a few days when things have settled down a bit."

"She may not be up for a visit in a few days. I promised her ye would come today. She will be very upset if ye don't stop in."

Gillian couldn't believe her ears. This was beyond foolish and so very typical for Rhiannon. She liked receiving attention, but only on her terms. Although the MacLennan women seemed to dote on her, she kept them at arm's length until she wanted them for something. It had always been that way with her mother and yet Lana adored her just like the rest of the clan's women. Gillian knew there was no use arguing. Her mother would harangue her all day until she gave in. Better to have done with it early.

"Fine. We will go for a short visit, but only a very short one. I have too much to do here."

Her mother beamed. "She will be so thrilled." Leaning closer, she whispered, "she might have some words of wisdom for ye. Perhaps she has *seen* something ye should know."

Gillian sincerely doubted it. "Let me just fetch some warmer boots and a mantle. I will meet ye back here in a few minutes."

Before long she and her mother crossed the courtyard to the curtain wall and out into Brathanead's village. Everyone they met offered her warm wishes for a happy marriage. A little part of her wanted to scream, but she accepted their kindness with grace. Before long they reached the edge of the village. They still had a little way to go before reaching Rhiannon's hut at the edge of the forest.

"Mother, why does Rhiannon choose to live so far away?"

"I think this is where Olghar wanted to live."

"But he has been dead for years. Surely it would be better and safer for her to live in the village."

"Perhaps, but she cherishes his memory. I suspect she doesn't want to leave the home they shared. Besides, it isn't as if she lives there alone, Gillian. She has Coby living with her."

"Aye, she has Coby, but he is a guardsman and spends much of his time at the keep anyway. Ye left our cottage in the village after Da died."

"That isn't the same at all. Meara had become the chieftain and was training ye to take over. We needed to be in the keep. Besides, Rhiannon enjoys the quiet and solitude. She also has her little Blaze to keep her company when Coby isn't there, although I will never understand why anyone wants a dog in the house."

Gillian smiled. Blaze was a lovely little dog and in her opinion he had been the highlight of any visit with Rhiannon for several years. "Aye, Blaze is a sweet little beast."

"Don't get any ideas, Gillian. Dogs don't belong inside."

It occurred to her that she was Lady MacLennan now and if she wanted a pet, she could have one. She very nearly said so but decided not to risk goading her mother at the moment.

By the time they reached Rhiannon's cottage, Gillian was chilled to the bone. They knocked on the door and heard Blaze's wild barking. After a few moments Rhiannon appeared. "Lana, Gillian, what a surprise. Oh, I suppose I should call ye Lady MacLennan now, but ye have always just been sweet Gillian to me. Ye don't mind, do ye?"

"Of course not, Rhiannon."

"What brings ye all the way out here on such a cold day?"

Gillian was at a loss for words. Hadn't they been invited,

or more accurately, compelled? Lana spoke up. "Rhiannon, ye asked me to bring Gillian by today so ye could hear about the wedding."

"Ah right, I remember now. It slipped my mind. I'm a little busy this morning, but I suppose ye could come in for a bit."

"Oh we'd love to, wouldn't we, Gillian?"

Gillian sighed. "Yes, thank ye for inviting us in." In Gillian's experience this was typical for Rhiannon, but she was getting on in years, maybe her memory was suffering.

Once inside Gillian and Lana took chairs by the fire and Blaze immediately put his head in Gillian's lap for some attention. Rhiannon busied herself making them a warm tisane to drink as they chatted. The aroma was very strong, smelling of mint, thyme, and some herbs Gillian couldn't identify. The flavor was equally strong, but liberally laced with honey it was not unpleasant. "I don't think I have ever tasted an infusion quite like this one, what is in it?" Gillian asked.

Rhiannon smiled. "It is my secret recipe. It is an ideal tonic. It contains thyme, comfrey, camomile, and several kinds of mint. It is wonderful for the digestion. It can help relieve a headache, toothache, or joint pain. It is good for gout. Why, it works miracles for a colicky baby. In fact, speaking of babies, it can help a woman conceive fine strong sons." The old woman winked cheekily at Gillian. "I'll give ye some to take with ye."

Gillian blushed and sputtered into her mug, causing Rhiannon and Lana to laugh.

Rhiannon grinned. "Gillian, lass, ye are a married woman now, and to Fingal MacIan no less, as braw a warrior as ever drew breath. Ye have no cause to blush like a maid."

She had no intention of telling Rhiannon she was, in fact, still a maid and thus had no use for such a beverage. "Aye, I suppose ye are right but he isn't Fingal MacIan anymore. He has taken the name MacLennan."

"Has he? Now that does surprise me."

The conversation moved on to other things including the wedding. However, their mugs were barely empty when Rhiannon said, "Well it was lovely of ye to stop by. I really do have some work that I must take care of. I am not the lady of the castle after all." She tittered merrily.

Gillian wanted to tell Rhiannon the "lady of the castle" had tons of work to do herself, which she should have done instead of trudging through snow all the way out here, when they clearly weren't wanted, but for her mother's sake she refrained. Instead she offered her thanks for the large packet of herbs that Rhiannon insisted she take.

"Don't forget," instructed Rhiannon, "brew a cup and drink it every morning and ye will be with child before spring."

Gillian smiled. That was one of Rhiannon's predictions that she felt sure wouldn't come true. "Thank ye, Rhiannon."

"Ah, 'tis no trouble at all. Perhaps next time ye can stay longer and we can have a nice long chat." With that she ushered them out the door, shutting it firmly behind them.

Chapter 8

As they started the long slog back to the keep, Gillian could not keep from commenting on Rhiannon's reluctance to see them. "Mother, ye made it sound so urgent that I see Rhiannon today, but she clearly had no time for a visit."

"Gillian, don't be petulant. Rhiannon is very busy and she did want to see ye. She was very clear about that. She made time for ye dear. She wouldn't have done that if she didn't want to see ye."

There was no point in arguing. Gillian had already wasted too much time walking out to see the old woman in the first place. She should be thankful that the visit itself hadn't taken long. Perhaps if she didn't make further conversation her mother would take the hint and remain quiet too, but that hope was in vain.

"Gillian, now that ye are married, we have a new laird, and things are settled we should think about Fallon."

"Things are settled? Mother, I'm barely married a full day, Fingal has been laird ever so slightly longer, and absolutely nothing has been settled."

"Why must ye always be so contrary? Ye are married, yer husband is laird and that is the main thing that needed settled. It is all the elders have argued about for months."

Sometimes her mother's short-sighted view of things was astounding. But again, she didn't wish to argue. "Fine, if that is how ye define settled then aye, I'm settled. Still, I don't think we need to worry about Fallon just yet."

"She is almost eighteen. It is well past time she was married."

"She won't be eighteen for several months and I don't see the rush."

"Ye wouldn't. Ye are just like yer father—'Don't worry, Lana, everything will sort itself out.' Now look where we are because of that. Ye must address this with the laird. It is a matter of great importance to the clan."

Gillian laughed. "Fallon's betrothal is a matter of great importance to the clan? I'm sorry mother, I don't think the clan cares about whether Fallon is married or not."

Her mother frowned, shaking her head. "Ye are far too short-sighted then, Gillian. Have ye already forgotten? Ye are Lady MacLennan. Until ye have a child, Fallon is yer heir. What if something happened to ye? Imagine the state the clan would be in if we had to go through this again."

"Something would have to happen to both Fingal and I for the leadership to fall to Fallon and that is highly unlikely."

"Still, I would feel much better and the clan would be more secure if Fallon had a strong husband. We can never risk that uncertainty again."

"Mother, I really don't think finding a husband for Fallon is the most important order of business for the laird at the moment."

"I'm sure it isn't, but I already know *who* Fallon should marry. I just need ye to get the laird's blessing."

Gillian couldn't quite believe she was having this conversation but she simply had to ask, "Who do ye think she should marry?"

"Rhiannon's son, Coby."

Gillian stopped in her tracks, flabbergasted. "Is that what all this was about? Is that why ye wanted me to chat with Rhiannon today? Are ye planning on opening betrothal negotiations?"

"Nay, Gillian, that had nothing to do with our visit. It is as I said to ye, Rhiannon was heart-broken that she couldn't see ye wed. She just wanted to hear about the wedding from ye. Nay, I have been thinking about Fallon's betrothal for a long time. Coby would be perfect. He is a respected guardsman. His mother—well, everyone loves her."

"Mother, now really isn't the best time for this." Gillian started walking again, picking up the pace. She did not want to have this conversation and thankfully they were nearing the gate tower in the curtain wall. She would extricate herself from her mother soon.

"There is no better time than the present," her mother insisted. "I think it would be a wonderful match."

"What does Fallon think?"

"It doesn't matter what she thinks. She will do her duty just as ye have."

They entered the courtyard, but before Gillian could tell her mother exactly what she thought of that notion, Fingal came striding towards her.

"Gillian, where have ye been?"

"My mother and I went to visit an elderly clanswoman. Is something wrong?"

"Ye were seen leaving the village alone."

"I wasn't alone, I just told ye I was with my mother."

"Nay, I meant without protection."

Gillian laughed. "I don't need protection just to walk to Rhiannon's cabin. She lives just a wee bit beyond the village near the edge of the forest."

"Gillian, I learned from the guards that ye are accustomed to coming and going freely without an escort, but it probably isn't the best idea."

Lana put her hands on her hips. "What utter nonsense. Gillian knows this land and our people better than anyone, certainly better than ye. She is perfectly safe and always has been."

"I'm sorry Lana but I have to disagree. I have learned today that there have been persistent small raiding parties attacking MacLennan land for the last year."

"Aye, that's true," Gillian said. "We suspect the Grants are behind it. Aunt Meara sent raiders to recoup our losses and I increased patrols as much as I could."

"I know ye did, and that was prudent. But ye are Lady MacLennan now. Ye would be an extremely enticing target if the Grants wished to take ye and hold ye for ransom."

Lana huffed. "They wouldn't stroll into Brathanead village during broad daylight."

"Nay they probably wouldn't," Fingal agreed, "but ye left the village and ye were near the edge of the forest. That is a little too far away to be completely safe. Can ye not see the risk it might pose?"

Her mother pursed her lips and didn't answer but Gillian had to admit she had never considered it. "I didn't really think about it. As Mother said, it has never been a worry before."

"It certainly wasn't," Lana added hotly.

Fingal did not seem remotely bothered by her mother's agitation. "I suppose it wasn't, but Gillian, do ye understand why it is now?"

She hated to admit it but he was right. Their defenses were spread rather thin. Although it might not be likely, it could be possible for raiders to avoid detection and get as close to Brathanead as the forest. She had never thought of herself as a valuable target, but if captured, aside from the horror of it, the Grants could demand a huge ransom. "Aye, I suppose I do. I really never looked at it that way. But by the same token, I can't stay locked up here in the keep."

He grinned. "I don't expect ye to. I would just like for a guardsman to accompany ye if ye leave the walls."

Her mother bristled. "Even just to go to the village? That is simply ridiculous."

Gillian absolutely agreed. However, taking the opposing view to her mother on this very trying morning was too much of a temptation. "Nay mother, he is right. It isn't likely that anything could happen so close to the keep, but if it did, if we had to forfeit a ransom because of something that could have been so easily prevented—well, that just can't be allowed to happen."

"Bah, I never thought I would see the day when my daughter wouldn't be free to roam anywhere she wished to on her own lands."

"I'm sorry Lana, but the rule also applies to ye, Fallon, and Ailsa. As Lady MacLennan's mother and sisters, ye could be targets too."

"Ye do not have the right to tell me where I can and can't go."

Gillian cringed. Malcolm would not have tolerated such disrespect but to her surprise Fingal remained calm. "I'm sorry, Lana, perhaps I have made a mistake."

Triumph shone in her mother's eyes. "Clearly ye have."

Fingal went on as if he hadn't heard her. "I could have sworn ye swore fealty to both of us yesterday."

"I did, but-but that has nothing to do with this."

Fingal's voice became deadly calm. "I disagree. I am yer laird and ye will never again presume to tell me what rights I do or do not have. I absolutely have the right to dictate yer movements in so far as they impact the well-being of this clan. Is that clear?"

"Gillian, are ye going to let him—"

Fingal didn't let her finish. "Lana, I asked ye a question. Have I made myself clear?"

She gritted her teeth. "Aye, Laird."

"Good." His serious tone left immediately. "Then do ye also understand that I don't want ye or yer daughters to leave the castle walls without an escort?"

"Aye, Laird."

"Excellent. I'm glad we understand each other."

Her mother looked as if she had swallowed something foul tasting. "Excuse me, Laird, I have work I must do." Lana gave a curt nod and walked off.

When her mother was out of earshot, Fingal smiled. "I'm sorry, Gillian. I didn't wish to upset her, but this really is in the best interest of yer family as well as the clan."

"I understand. I really never gave it much thought. So much has changed since..."

He took her hands in his. "It will get easier, Gillian. I will do whatever I can to help, it will just take time." She nodded and he squeezed her hands. To her surprise, he continued to hold one hand as he turned to walk with her towards the keep. "So ye were visiting an elderly clanswoman?"

"Aye, she wasn't able to come to the wedding." In a whisper she added, "why are ye holding my hand?"

"We are meant to appear married," he whispered back. "Is she ill? Does she need anything?"

Gillian was once again flustered by his nearness and the simple intimacy of him holding her hand. "What? Does who need anything?"

He laughed and raised her hand to plant a kiss on the back of it. "The clanswoman ye visited. I believe ye called her Rhiannon."

"Nay, she isn't ill. She just keeps to herself." *By all the saints get a hold of yerself.*

"Perhaps she shouldn't live so far from the village on her own."

"She has a grown son who lives with her. Perhaps ye've met him? His name is Coby. He is one of the guardsman. Are ye going to hold my hand all day?"

"I'm going to hold it until I get ye inside the keep where it is warmer. Yer hand feels like ice. And aye, I know Coby. But as a guardsman he isn't exactly with her all of the time. I'm sure we can find a home for them in the village."

Gillian sighed. There was no way around it; she had to

consciously stop letting him befuddle her. "Fingal, I don't think she wants to live in the village. Mother thinks it is because she misses her husband so she doesn't want to leave their home. I think she just likes to keep a bit of distance. Perhaps it adds to her mysterious air." Fingal arched an eyebrow at her and she laughed. "People have always whispered that she has the Sight. I suppose if the local seer is seen to be just like everyone else, emptying her slop bucket or hanging out her wash, it makes her seem, well...ordinary."

Fingal laughed. "Surely she is ordinary. Has she always been a seer? Even as a child?"

"I don't know and I suppose no one else does. She isn't a MacLennan, or at least she wasn't born one."

"Then how did she come to be here?"

"As I understand it, she was a MacRae and was widowed as a very young woman."

"Ah, then she came here when Nuala MacRae was married to Malcolm?"

"Exactly. Rhiannon was Lady MacLennan's friend and confidant. Eventually Rhiannon married a MacLennan guardsman named Olghar and had Coby. Olghar passed away years ago."

"Well, whatever the reason is, I will try to find an opportunity to discuss it with Coby. I can't imagine he wants his elderly mother to live so far away from the security of the village. Perhaps we can talk her into moving closer. Then ye can visit as often as ye wish and everyone will be safer."

They had reached the keep and Gillian decided not to tell him that visiting Rhiannon wasn't one of her favorite things. As they entered the great hall Ailsa ran headlong to her. "Where have ye been? Jeanne was looking for ye to discuss meals." Ailsa turned her attention to Fingal. "Laird, have ye met Jeanne yet? She runs the kitchens. She makes the very best honey cakes in the Highlands. Well, I guess I can't say that for sure because I haven't tasted every honey cake in the Highlands, but I'd like to. I love honey cakes. Do ye like honey cakes? I'm sure she would make them for ye if ye do—maybe even today."

Gillian laughed. "Ailsa, ye little weasel. Ye just want an excuse to ask her to make honey cakes for ye."

Ailsa looked contrite. Fingal grinned at her which oddly restarted the fluttering in Gillian's belly. "Aye, lass, I do like honey cakes. But if ye like them so well, maybe ye should ask

Jeanne to teach ye how to make them."

"Oh, maybe she would. Gillian, do ye think she might?"

"Aye, sweetling, I'm sure she would but she may be too busy today. We'll go talk to her just as soon as I put on a dry *léine*." She held up her skirt to show Ailsa the snow encrusted hem.

"That is a good plan," Fingal said. "Ye will catch yer death if ye stay in those wet clothes." He let go of her hand and as much as she told herself she shouldn't care, she missed the warmth of his touch.

~ * ~

Fingal watched as Gillian hurried out of the hall and up the stairs. When he learned that she and Lana had left the curtain walls without an escort he had wanted to pound some sense into the men-at-arms guarding the gate. Instead, he remained calm and asked why. It had apparently never been the practice at Brathanead, so he couldn't very well hold them accountable this time. The relief he felt when he saw them entering the gates surprised him.

"Ye look angry." For a moment, lost in his thought, Fingal had forgotten Ailsa still stood there.

"Nay, Ailsa, I'm not angry. I was just a bit worried earlier."

"Why?"

"Because I found out that Gillian and yer mum left Brathanead with no one to guard them."

Ailsa made a snorting sound. "They don't need guards."

He smiled at her. "Aye, they do. And ye do too, Ailsa. I don't want ye to leave the walls of Brathanead without a guardsman."

"Me?" she asked incredulously. "Why do I need a guard? That's silly."

"Nay, sweetling, it isn't. Someone who might want to hurt our clan could do that by capturing ye and holding ye for ransom."

"Me?" Ailsa laughed. "Ye worry too much. No one would want me. I'm not important."

"Nay Ailsa, ye are very important. Ye are Ailsa MacLennan. Besides that ye are also Gillian's sister, which make ye my sister now."

Ailsa's brow furrowed. "Do ye really think it could be

dangerous to go to the village alone?"

Fingal ruffled her curls. "I doubt it sweetling, but I don't want to take even the slightest risk with ye. Do ye understand?"

She grinned broadly. "Aye, I suppose I do. I'm important and ye want to protect me."

Fingal laughed. "Exactly."

Ailsa threw her arms around him tightly for a moment before letting go. "Thank ye." She lowered her voice. "Don't tell anyone I said this, but I like that ye are worried about us. It is a little like having Da back."

The thought was sobering. "I will do my best to keep ye safe, Ailsa. I promise."

Ailsa looked at him for a moment, as if sizing him up. "Gillian didn't want to marry ye."

"Nay, she didn't."

"I like ye."

He grinned. "I'm glad to hear it." He wished her sister were this easy to win over.

"I think Gillian would like ye if she gave ye a chance."

"Ye needn't worry about it, Ailsa. It will all work out. We just need to give it time."

"Time's all right, but a puppy is better."

Fingal laughed. "What?"

"Ye want to make Gillian happy so she will like ye, right?"

"Sweetling, I—"

"Give her a puppy. She loves dogs. I do too. We have always wanted a pet and Mama wouldn't let us have one."

"Is this a ploy like the honey cakes? So ye can have a puppy?"

Much to his surprise, Ailsa grinned. "Of course it is, but that doesn't mean it won't make Gillian happy too." Gillian entered the hall again, wearing dry clothes. "Shh. Don't tell her I told ye. We'll let her think ye thought of it on yer own."

"Ailsa, I don't think—"

"Shh." Ailsa turned away, walking to meet her sister. "Let's go see if Jeanne will make the laird some honey cakes."

Gillian shook her head. "Ailsa, ye are incorrigible."

Fingal just laughed.

Chapter 9

Fingal spent yet another restless night sleeping chastely next to the beautiful young woman who he had married but who professed to hate him. They had been married over a week now and no matter how gently he wooed her, she showed no signs of relenting. Aye, she had fulfilled her end of the bargain. She appeared united with him in front of the clan. She accepted his leadership of the clan and publically supported his decisions. However, every night she fell asleep curled up as far away from him in the bed as possible. And every morning he awoke with her lush warm body snuggled next to him. This was a torture that he wasn't sure he could stand for long. Still, she continued to be inordinately flustered by his slightest touch, so he held out hope that her attitude would soften.

Sighing, Fingal rose from the bed as quietly as he could in the predawn gloom, leaving Gillian to sleep. There was an endless amount of work that needed to be done to bring Brathanead's defenses up to an acceptable standard. Furthermore, his brother would be leaving early this morning. Fingal needed to see him off.

Gillian stirred as he dressed. "Fingal?"

"I'm here, Gillian. Go back to sleep for a bit." She too had been working tirelessly and could use a little extra rest."

She woke more fully. "Nay, I have too much to do to sleep the day away. Besides, Niall is leaving this morning is he not?"

"Aye, but he would understand."

"He would think me lazy, rude, and unfit to be Lady MacLennan if I stayed abed instead of seeing visitors off."

"Nay, he wouldn't Gillian, but suit yerself. I will go down to the great hall and give ye a few minutes of privacy."

She joined him moments later. After attending morning Mass, they bid Niall farewell together before heading their separate ways to start their daily work as had become their pattern. One of the most pressing needs was the training of Brathanead's warriors. Clearly Malcolm had not put as much effort into this as he should have but that would change. However, another serious problem was the condition of Brathanead's curtain wall. It wasn't terribly large—most of the village lay outside the walls. Even so, it had fallen into disrepair and was critically weak in spots.

Unfortunately, it took men to rebuild the wall and if they were rebuilding a wall they were not training to improve their skills. Fingal had divided them into two divisions, one led by Diarmad and the other by Eadoin. They alternated between training and working on repairs.

He ensured that Diarmad had training well underway today before joining Eadoin where his men worked on the southwestern side of the wall. "How are the repairs coming?"

Eadoin shook his head. "Things are worse in this section than we imagined. Rory here has some experience with masonry. He has something to show us."

"Aye, Laird, have a look here at this." The older man reached forward and with just his finger was able to brush the mortar from between the stones. "The winds blow hard from the southwest much of the year. The rain and snow driven by the winds has broken down the lime mortar. Where that is the only problem, the loose mortar can be scraped out and patched to shore up the loose stones. However, in this part of the wall there are other problems. In most places the top of the wall is pitched to allow water to run off, but here the pitch was off and the top was a bit more level. In fact, between the effects of weather and years of sentries' footsteps, there is no pitch left at all. It has allowed water to pool and penetrate into the heart of the wall. The effect of the water freezing and thawing within the wall has only made the problem worse. As we scrape out the old mortar, we just find more problems the deeper we go. I think it may be too far gone here to simply repair the damage on the surface."

Eadoin looked shocked. "I had no idea it was that bad."

"None of us did, Eadoin. Ye expect the surface mortar to break down over years, but none of us knew the heart of the wall was deteriorating too. Honestly, based on the damage we are finding, I think it would take very little force to break through this part of the wall. It's the reason so many stones have fallen along this side."

Fingal stepped forward to examine the wall. The mortar crumbled under his touch and he was able to feel slight movement in some of the stones. He turned back to Eadoin and Rory. "So, if ye can't repair the mortar, what do ye suggest?"

"I think the best thing to do at this point is tear down the sections where the worst damage is and rebuild them."

Eadoin frowned. "That will leave us very vulnerable, Rory."

"I know that, but I don't see a better way."

"How quickly could it be done?" Fingal asked.

"Well, it might take weeks, Laird, but we could work in sections so the whole southern wall isn't torn down at once."

"If it were only small sections of the wall down at a time, we could create a moveable wooden stockade that might offer some protection," reasoned Fingal.

"And post a heavier guard as an additional precaution," added Eadoin.

Just then, as if fate stepped in to illustrate the abysmal condition of the wall, a heavy stone came crashing down from the top. Eadoin yelled "Laird!" diving toward Fingal, pushing him out of the way. The stone barely missed them both. Eadoin shouted up at the men on the wall, "what in the hell are ye doing?"

"We were loosening the top stones to replace them, as Rory said to," called Coby from the top of the wall. "I'm sorry Eadoin, we didn't know ye were down there."

"For the love of God, watch what ye are doing," Eadoin admonished. "Ye can't just let rocks fall without a care for what is on the ground below. Ye could have killed us."

"Aye, sir, we'll be more careful."

Fingal sighed heavily. "I guess this is all the evidence I need that the wall is not only insufficient to protect us, but is dangerously unstable. Aye, Rory, tear down what ye need to in order to make it strong and safe. How long do ye think it will take?"

"At the rate we are going, months."

Fingal knew that wouldn't be sufficient. He had hoped by dividing the men's time between training and rebuilding, he could address both of the clan's most pressing needs. However, the winter weather itself provided some measure of protection for the clan. Anyone who might seek to lay siege or attempt to overrun Brathanead was not likely to do it in the dead of winter. "We need to have this wall repaired by Easter or shortly thereafter. Otherwise we present too tempting a target."

Eadoin frowned. "But Laird, Easter is but a month away. It will take all of our men working on the wall to finish it by then. Ye said yerself the skill of the MacLennan warriors is lacking. If ye think we are a target, don't we need well-trained warriors who can defend us?"

"Aye we do, but even the best trained warriors will have trouble defending Brathanead with the wall crumbling. I think we need to focus our efforts on the repairs while the weather keeps the Grants or any other potential aggressors close to their hearths. For now the men will train for a half day every other day, and the rest of their time will be spent rebuilding. Rory, will that give ye enough men to finish this by Easter?"

"Aye, Laird. I think we can have the worst of it rebuilt by then."

"Eadoin, do ye agree?" Fingal asked. "I can't see a better way forward, but if ye have any thoughts on it, I am happy to hear them."

"Ye are right. The wall must be the priority now. Have ye considered bringing in some men from other clans to bolster our ranks?"

"As ye are aware, Niall left a very large contingent of MacIan men with us, but he was only able to do this because Lairds Matheson and MacKenzie sent men to Duncurra in their place."

"Given that our threat comes primarily from the Grants and Laird Chisholm is also plagued by them, perhaps he would lend some aid?"

"Perhaps, Eadoin, but our resources are stretched as it is. I don't know if we could feed any more mouths, much less offer compensation for their service."

Eadoin squared his shoulders with resolve. "Then Laird, we will have to make this work."

~ * ~

At the evening meal Fingal discussed the changes in plans with Diarmad too.

"That is distressing news, Laird. I had hoped to use the next few months for training to bring the MacLennan warriors' skills up." Diarmad lowered his voice. "Too many of their most seasoned warriors were killed at Duncurra last year."

Fingal glanced at Gillian. Her furrowed brow told him she

had heard Diarmad's observation. He hated to remind her of her loss.

"Fingal, maybe so many would not have lost their lives if they had been better prepared," she observed. "Surely repairs to the wall can be accomplished over time. How can ye take men away from training?"

"I agree we need to ensure that the men are trained, Gillian, but the wall can't be ignored."

"Surely well-trained warriors are more important to our defense than patching mortar." There was an irritable edge to her voice.

"Sadly, it isn't just a case of patching mortar—"

She cut Fingal off before he could finish. "That wall has stood for decades. It will stand a few months longer. I think ye should focus on training the men."

Fingal did not want to argue with her publicly but before he could say anything, Daniel cut in. "Gillian, this is not yer concern and ye have no place questioning the laird in these matters."

She looked as if he had slapped her. Fingal covered her hand with his. "Nay Daniel, she loves this clan and I understand her concern. Gillian, I agree that we need a well-trained garrison but we also need a strong defensive curtain wall. I know it has stood for decades. However, there are places where the wall has been so damaged by the elements it is ready to tumble down."

At her look of disbelief Eadoin added, "Aye, 'tis true. Water has damaged parts of the southwestern side of the wall so severely that it could crumble without the aid of a battering ram. In fact it is crumbling now. A stone fell from the wall where the men were working today and barely missed the laird."

She turned her head sharply to look at Fingal. "Is that true? Were ye injured?"

"It is true but thanks to Eadoin's quick reflexes I wasn't injured. Unfortunately though, parts of the curtain wall are hazardous and can't be ignored. It is best to tear them down and rebuild now, during the remaining weeks of winter."

Gillian nodded, but still looked worried. Fingal tried to reassure her. "Gillian, the men will continue to train some while we are repairing the wall. I won't overlook that. I promised that I would help make Clan MacLennan strong again, and I will."

Chapter 10

The year since the death of Gillian's father had been difficult, but the weeks since Aunt Meara passed away were doubly so. If Gillian had been the daughter of a laird it might have been different. She would have been trained to run a keep and help lead a clan practically from infancy. However, she was the daughter of warrior and had expected someday to marry a guardsman, craftsman, or even a farmer. She could cook, clean, sew, and manage a family. That was all she had ever expected to do.

Aunt Meara had been doing her best to teach Gillian the basics, but running a keep efficiently took great skill. The truth be told, Aunt Meara hadn't been born to it either. She had only taken on the responsibilities of chatelaine at Laird Malcolm's request a few years earlier after the elderly woman who had managed the staff and the keep for years had passed away.

Even with all of the upheaval she had experienced recently, the first four weeks of Gillian's marriage was, without a doubt, the most confusing, frustrating, and oddly disquieting weeks of her life. Trying to keep the household running, a skill at which she was not quite adept, was hard enough. Now she had to pretend to be married to Fingal in every way. Many of her clanswomen teased her good-naturedly about her braw new husband and speculated about everything from the cause of the dark circles under her eyes, to the month in which she would deliver her first bairn.

She couldn't tell them that the dark circles were because she was so tied up in knots about her feelings for Fingal she couldn't sleep. She avoided going to bed as long as she could in the evening only to lay awake for ages, disturbed by his nearness. Regardless of what Jeanne had told her the day of the wedding, Gillian couldn't put aside the fact that he was the son of her father's murderer. She had good reasons to hate him and she wasn't ready to let them go. However, any time he was near she felt off-balance. He was unfailingly kind and thoughtful; he seemed to charm everyone around him. Ailsa adored him.

Even those originally most opposed to his leadership were developing a growing respect for him, including Nolan. For the love of God, Fingal asked her for her opinion...*often*. And when she did have a concern, as she had over the decision to focus efforts on rebuilding the wall, he listened to her and explained his reasons.

Of course that only happened when she could manage to keep her wits about her. Sometimes she could barely think in his presence, much less offer anything worthwhile to the conversation. And if all of that wasn't bad enough, ever since the day after the wedding her mother nagged ceaselessly about a betrothal between Fallon and Coby.

There was only a little more than a week of Lent remaining. Not only was Gillian worried that they were running low on grains and salted fish, staples during the days of fasting and abstinence, there was an Easter feast to plan. Ailbert's records were usually good, but Gillian needed to double check the inventory. She thought she had found a few minutes of blessed solitude in the cellars and she relished the opportunity to just be alone with her thoughts for a while. However, she had barely started the task when her mother called to her from the corridor.

She thought about hiding, but knew it was pointless. "I'm in here, Mother."

Her mother's footsteps quickened until she reached the storeroom where Gillian worked. "Gillian, my dear, I have looked everywhere for ye. I couldn't imagine where ye had gotten to."

"I am checking supplies. Would ye like to help?"

"Oh nay, dear, I am hopeless with figures. I'll just keep ye company."

Gillian sighed. "Mother, I don't need someone to keep me company. In fact, I will be able to focus better *without* company.

"Well, that may be, but we don't often have time alone and I want to know what Fingal thinks of a betrothal between Fallon and Coby."

"I haven't asked him yet. There is so much to be done. Really, Mother, it can wait a little while."

"Ye are thoughtless and selfish, Gillian."

Gillian couldn't quite believe her ears. "Mother, I am

working myself to exhaustion for this clan. In what way am I selfish?"

"Ye have a new husband warming yer bed every night while yer sister grows into an old maid that no one will want."

Gillian snorted. "Ye can't believe that. Fallon is a lovely sweet lass and I sincerely doubt her thoughts at the moment are consumed with marriage plans or fears of becoming an old maid."

"It doesn't matter what ye believe or don't believe. It's yer responsibility to see her settled with a good husband."

"And I will, Mother. Please, just give things a few more weeks to settle down."

"Weeks?" her mother practically shrieked. "It has already been weeks. Nay, Gillian, this cannot wait that long. Mark my words, if ye don't address this soon, I will take matters into my own hands." Her mother spun on her heel and marched out of the cellar.

Gillian shook her head in frustration but went back to work. When she had finished her inventory, she made her way out of the cellars. She sought out Jeanne in the kitchens to tell her where their inventories stood. As always Jeanne welcomed her with a hot drink and a rest by the hearth. "Ah, my lady, ye look worn out."

"Jeanne, please don't call me 'my lady'. I've always just been Gillie to ye."

Jeanne chuckled but then sobered. "Gillie, ye are pushing yerself too hard."

"No harder than usual."

"Then why do ye look exhausted? Ah...are ye starting to appreciate yer new husband's charms?"

Gillian couldn't stop herself from rolling her eyes. "Nay, Jeanne."

"Nay? Is he not good to ye lass? There were always rumors about that one. I would have thought..."

"That isn't what I meant Jeanne. I...that is, he...I..."

Jeanne looked shocked. "Ye don't mean to say ye have refused him?"

"What? Nay, I...well not exactly." Gillian put her head in her hands.

"Did he agree to this? To a marriage in name only?"

"It isn't like that Jeanne. Everything was happening so fast. I didn't want to marry him but I knew it was the best thing for the clan."

"But lass, how could ye ask that of him?"

"I didn't—at least not forever. He just agreed to give me a little time to get used to the idea. Please, Jeanne, no one is supposed to know."

Jeanne looked at her sternly. "Gillian, ye have been married for weeks now. On the morning of yer wedding I told ye that ye didn't have to love the man, but ye had to earn his respect and give him yers. I said ye had to focus on the future and yer future was with yer new husband."

"Aye, I know ye did."

"Weeks, Gillian! Honestly, that young man has shown ye great respect in this. Much more than most men would have. Ye need to thaw yer heart lass or ye will remain firmly rooted in the past."

"I'm trying, Jeanne."

"Nay lass, by the looks of things ye are trying with all yer might not to."

"But—"

"Nay, don't argue with me. I see how ye are around him. Ye find him attractive, I know ye do. Any lass would. And when he is near ye, well I've never seen ye so flustered."

"But, Jeanne, he's—"

"Don't tell me he is Eithne's son! That is the past." Her tone became gentle. "Lower yer guard, lass, and let him in. Ye might find him more than just attractive. Ye might find someone ye can trust and learn to care for and who cares for ye as well."

"It is all so confusing."

"Honestly, I think ye need to stop worrying about what ye think ye *ought* to feel and give in to what ye *want* to feel. There is no going back now, Gillian. If ye keep doing what ye have been doing, ye will keep being miserable."

Gillian sighed. Maybe she had been causing her own turmoil. She knew Jeanne was right but she didn't know how to break the pattern she had started. "I don't know what to do."

"Don't think so much about it, lass. It is the simplest thing in the world."

"Where do I start?"

"Just let it happen. Let him woo ye. He seems to be doing a pretty good job of that. Let yerself enjoy his attention without feeling guilty about it."

"I guess I can try."

Jeanne laughed. "Lass, if I were forty years younger, I wouldn't have to try to enjoy that young man's attention."

Gillian left the kitchen feeling no less confused. She thought of their conversation all afternoon and knew her old friend was right. Although she had promised Fingal she would try not to hate him, she had actively been working to keep her hate alive. She had to try and let her guard down where Fingal was concerned. Maybe if she made an effort to get to know him better it would be easier.

In spite of her good intentions, as she sat beside him during the evening meal, she felt as awkward and unsettled as she always did. She decided not to try to resist the strange warm feelings that rose in her but it didn't help. If anything, she found the attention he paid to her, even his very presence, more disconcerting when she wasn't trying to resist his charm. She also felt the stark disapproval of her mother and a few other clan members. One thing was clear; she couldn't do this with an audience.

When the meal was over, she noticed the determined look on her mother's face. Fearing that she might bring up the topic of a betrothal for Fallon again, Gillian thought it best to escape. "Fingal, I am very tired tonight."

"Aye, ye look tired. Everyone has been working hard of late. Perhaps we should say our goodnights."

"Would ye mind terribly?"

"Nay, of course not." He rose from his chair and to those who remained at the table said, "please excuse us, Lady MacLennan and I will retire early."

"But Laird, there were some things I wished to discuss with ye," Owen said.

"I will address them with ye first thing in the morning, Owen. I think some rest could do us all good."

Hand in hand, they exited the hall. A quick glance back at her mother told Gillian that Owen was not the only person who was irritated by their early departure. Lana's jaw was clenched and her eyes narrowed. She was clearly not happy at missing the chance to speak directly with Fingal.

~ * ~

Gillian's sudden desire to retire early had surprised Fingal.

She usually waited until the latest possible hour to leave the crowded hall. Then, she would curl up on the edge of the bed, as far away from him as she could possibly get and *wouldn't* go to sleep. He knew this because, while he too tried, it was no easier for him to fall asleep with her lying beside him, knowing he couldn't touch her. He took a small amount of pleasure in the fact that he disturbed her as much as she did him.

He didn't have to wait long to learn the reason for the change in pattern tonight. After they were out of hearing distance of those left in the hall she said, "I thought maybe we could get to know each other a bit better. We have both been working so hard and haven't had much time together."

Get to know each other? She had done her level best to avoid time alone. While he wondered at her change in attitude, he wouldn't question it. They did need time alone if the barriers between them were ever going to come down. "Aye, I'd like that."

He thought it best to let her take the lead, so when they reached their chamber he unfastened his sword belt, sat in one of the chairs at the table by the hearth, and stretched out his legs, warming his feet near the fire. It was no surprise to him that she stood awkwardly in the center of the room. "Ye know, sometimes it is easier to get to know each other by doing something fun together."

The look of shock on her face caused him to laugh heartily. "Although there are many fun things we could do together. I was only suggesting that we play a game. Do ye have a board for fox and geese, or maybe chess? If ye don't know how to play, I could teach ye."

Her look of relief reminded him of just how far they had to go. "Aye, chess would be good. My grandfather taught me to play. He died when I was still very young. I tried to teach Fallon, but she didn't like to play. When I was a little older I played with Eadoin some or with my da."

Fingal worried that this might not go as planned. It could remind her too intensely of her loss, thus causing her to withdraw more, but she was already digging in a chest, evidently searching for a chess set. "Ye played with Eodoin?"

"Aye, when we were children. We have always been friends. His wife Alana is my closest friend. We taught her to play but she wasn't very good and always preferred to sit by Eodoin and watch." She grinned and confided, "Alana said it was so she could learn to play better but I knew what her real game was."

Fingal laughed and was relieved. Thankfully she had other wonderful memories of playing chess.

"Here it is," she announced when she found the board. She set it up on the table, fingering the pieces lovingly. "This was my grandfather's set." Before sitting across from him she asked, "would ye like me to call for someone to bring us some ale or wine?"

"Nay, I think I may need to keep my wits about me in this game." She laughed. Fingal hadn't heard much of that but he loved the rich sound of it and the way her face lit up.

She picked up a pawn of each color and put her hands behind her back for a moment before presenting him with her closed fists. "Pick a color." He tapped her right hand and she revealed the white pawn. "Ye go first."

Chapter 11

When Gillian had agreed to marry him, Fingal knew that winning her acceptance was going to be a challenge. He had been encouraged by her obvious physical reaction to him. During the first month of their marriage, he had done his best to woo her, but in spite of all his efforts she seemed rigidly determined to remain as distant as possible. That was until the evening they spent playing chess.

They hadn't talked about anything terribly important. She told him about her family and friends and various other members of the clan. He told her about the MacIans and what it was like training under Laird Chisholm. All in all, it had been a very congenial evening. When they finally retired she seemed less tense than she had earlier and sleep had come easier to both of them.

For the next several evenings it became their pattern to spend time alone, playing chess, before retiring. They chatted about a variety of things from the progress on the curtain wall to Ailsa's newest attempts to get their mother to let her have a pet. They assiduously avoided any mention of her father or his mother. He truly enjoyed this time spent with her, but he was acutely aware of the topics they avoided. He believed that for her to be able to set aside her hatred, they couldn't continue to ignore the source.

Fingal didn't want to spoil the easy comradery that had developed between them, but as he sat across from her tonight he knew he needed to broach the topic. As Gillian prepared the chess board he thought to raise the subject by asking about her mother. "I couldn't help but notice, yer mother seems a bit short-tempered with ye recently."

She laughed a mirthless laugh as she made the first move. "Recently? She is usually short-tempered with me."

Fingal moved a pawn. "Is she? Why?"

"I don't know. I suppose it has to do with all of the changes recently."

Fingal frowned as he remembered something Ailsa had said. "Gillian, the night I arrived, when we were discussing the king's dictate, Ailsa said something that puzzled me. She said she needed ye because yer mother only cares about Fallon. What did she mean?"

Gillian became flustered but tried to hide her disquiet by focusing on the chess board. "I-I don't know what ye're talking about."

"Aye, ye do. Ye wouldn't be so upset if ye didn't."

She sighed. "I don't want ye to think me disloyal, but, well—I suppose ye are bound to find out sooner or later anyway. My mother has always been much closer with Fallon than with me or Ailsa. I think it was less obvious when Da was alive but since his death everything is harder."

"I see."

"Don't get me wrong. I know she loves us all and wants the best for us. It's just, Fallon is so good-natured and sweet, everyone loves her. I'm...well...pricklier. I suppose it is normal to be closer to one parent than the other."

"I don't think ye are 'prickly' Gillian and I don't know if it is normal or not. I fostered with the Chisholms and they seemed to adore all four of their children as well as every lad who trained there, but I am fairly certain my mother didn't care a whit for me or Niall."

Gillian became very serious. "How can ye say that? She must have loved ye. She and Laird Malcolm laid siege to Duncurra all so ye could be laird of both clans."

"Gillian, I can assure ye, the only person Eithne ever loved was herself. She was downright cruel to us when we were lads. Niall had it worse than I did. She took a strap to him so often over the smallest things he always had bruises. She beat me too but I didn't have to suffer her harsh nature for as many years. I was still very young when she left for Edinburgh."

"How terrible. It's true mother isn't overly affectionate with me and Ailsa and she can be quick to find fault, but she has certainly never beat us. Why did yer da allow it?"

"He didn't know."

"How could he not know?"

"He was busy with the business of running our clan and she was very good at hiding her evil side from him."

"Fingal, I am so sorry. At least Ailsa and I had our da."

Until my mother killed him trying to save her own worthless skin. Fingal was sorry he had raised the topic, but he pressed on. "Eventually, I had the Chisholms. I couldn't love Lady Chisholm more if she had been my own mother. I would like for ye to meet her someday. Ye remind me of her in many ways." As soon as the words passed his lips, he knew they were profoundly true. Gillian was strong and self-reliant, but she had a tender heart just like Lady Chisholm."

Gillian smiled and her eyes lit. Clearly she understood how sincere a complement it was to be compared to the woman he loved as a mother.

They played in silence for a while before Gillian said, "My da always liked ye and Niall. All circumstances aside, I think our marriage would have pleased him."

"Tell me about him."

It was as if those four little words battered open the wall she had carefully erected between them. She told story after story about Duncan as they continued to play. Fingal's heart nearly broke for her loss as he came to know Duncan, the loving father, through Gillian's eyes.

The game ended when Gillian declared checkmate with glee. Fingal realized this beautiful, determined, resilient woman had captured his heart as surely as she had his king.

A bit later, as they lay in bed she said, "Thank ye, Fingal."

"For what?"

"For this evening...for asking about my da. I haven't been able to talk about him. Mother gets angry, and my sisters burst into tears. It was nice to just remember him and not worry about hurting someone else in the process."

"Maybe yer sisters need that too."

"Aye, I suspect they do. But now I know how."

"I don't understand."

"It was nice to just talk a little about happy things and not focus so firmly on how much I miss him. It made it easier. I can make it easy for Fallon and Ailsa now and I thank ye for that."

~ * ~

When they woke the next morning, Fingal sensed a subtle change in Gillian. The tension which had seemed ever-present with her had finally eased some. At last things seemed to be moving in the right direction. He started his day more hopeful than he had been in weeks. That was until they entered the great hall to break their fast. Diarmad met him with unwelcomed news.

"Laird, there has been a raid to the southeast, near Grant lands."

Fingal shook his head. Somehow it never failed. Ever since he became laird here, just when he started to see progress in one area, a new problem arose. "Was anyone hurt?"

"Nay Laird, but we lost a score of cattle."

Fingal swore, "God's holy bones!"

"That many?" Gillian asked. "We can't sustain losses like that and survive. Can we increase the patrols like Aunt Meara did in the fall?"

Fingal shook his head. "We don't have the men to both increase patrols and finish the work on the wall quickly."

Diarmad nodded. "And if we ignore this, it may tip the Grants off to our weakened condition."

Fingal pinched the bridge of his nose. The MacLennans' predicament—his predicament—was an utter lack of resources. The MacLennans didn't have enough skilled warriors to ride patrols and protect them from raiders so Fingal set about to train them. Then they discovered the curtain wall, their primary defense, was crumbling. So he stopped training men hoping the weather would deter raiders and set the men to repairing the wall. Now spring approached, the Grants had started raiding again, and he still didn't have enough trained men nor did he have a completed curtain wall.

"Aye, ye are right in that. If we let this pass, they will be attacking the keep next. With an unfinished wall and a depleted garrison, I don't want to risk that. The only thing to do is bluff."

Diarmad clearly agreed but Gillian's mouth gaped in disbelief. "Bluff?" she asked. "How can ye possibly do that?"

"As much as I hate to leave the keep less well guarded, I will take a large party of our best warriors on a raid. At the very least, we will recover our livestock and perhaps a few more. If we run into any Grants in the meantime, our numbers and skill will be impressive."

"Aye, they would never assume ye'd risk the cream of yer garrison on a wee raid. It will send the needed message. The MacLennans are strong and not to be trifled with."

Gillian's brow furrowed. "But what if ye run into a greater force of Grants? What if they kill or capture ye?"

The concern in her voice touched him. "Gillian, don't worry yerself over this. We will be fine. I suspect the Grants believe we are critically weakened. They will be expecting us to pull in and lick our wounds, not retaliate with any show of strength."

Diarmad tried to reassure her as well. "Aye, my lady, the men we will be taking can defeat a force three times as large. Furthermore, ye may not know this, but there are few men who can best the laird in a swordfight."

"Ye are certain?" she asked hesitantly.

"Aye, my lady, I'm certain," answered Diarmad.

"He speaks the truth, sweetling. There is no reason to worry. Finish yer breakfast. Diarmad and I will go now to make plans." Fingal kissed her cheek and took a bannock and some smoked fish from the table before leaving with Diarmad.

"It has been a while since I was on a raid, Laird. Who do ye propose to take with us?"

"Most of the men from Duncurra, Eadoin, and a few MacLennans of his choosing. But Diarmad, I want ye to stay here."

"Ye told yer wife ye'd be taking yer best warriors and I told yer brother I would guard yer back."

"I know ye did, but in spite of what we told Gillian, I am worried that drawing us out is exactly what the Grants meant to do. If we do meet an overwhelming force, we won't be able to hold them off forever. I will send a messenger back and I want ye to take Gillian, her family, and as many of the clan as will go with ye to Duncurra."

"She will never agree to go if she thinks her clan is in danger."

"Diarmad, if I send ye a message, it's over. There will be no way to defend Brathanead and attempting to do so will only result in more death and destruction."

"I understand that, but will she?"

"Ye will make her understand or ye will bind her and force her to go. Either way, I do not want to risk her or her sisters winding up in Grant hands."

"T'would be better to leave Eadoin behind. She trusts him."

"Aye, but if the worst happens, I'm not sure I can trust him to stand up to her and do what must be done to keep her safe."

Diarmad shook his head. "I don't like it, but ye have a point. Aye, I'll stay behind. But if ye have to fight, for the love of God give it all ye have."

Fingal grinned. "I intend to."

"Ye know, Niall will kill me if anything happens to ye."

"Well then, I promise to do my best to save my own skin as well as yers."

Fingal spent the rest of the morning preparing for the planned raid. Shortly after the midday meal, he rode away with twenty hand-picked men. It was many more than necessary for a raid, but not nearly enough to do battle with an invading force. Still, if he had taken any more, no one would believe that he simply planned a retaliatory attack.

~ * ~

Gillian couldn't help but worry as she watched Fingal, Eadoin, and a large contingent of their men ride out of Brathanead.

"Where is he going?" demanded her mother.

"Didn't ye hear? The Grants raided again last night. He is taking a few men to investigate."

"Aye, I heard but that is more than a few. Who is left to guard us or repair the wall and why does the laird need to go with them?"

"Don't worry mother, everything is under control. Fingal will be fine." Gillian had a bit of trouble believing this herself. It did seem foolhardy to take their very best warriors, leaving few skilled men to protect the castle and finish the work on the wall. At least Fingal had left Diarmad in charge while he was gone, although she would have preferred for Eadoin to stay behind.

"I'm not worried about his well-being. I'm worried about the leadership of this clan if something happens to him. He hasn't sorted out Fallon's betrothal yet."

Gillian couldn't keep the rein on her temper. "Mother, even if something happens to him, I am still very much here and alive. *I am Lady MacLennan*, not Fallon."

"Ye always take things the wrong way, Gillian."

"How am I supposed to take that? From the time ye raised the issue of Fallon's betrothal ye said it was because she is my heir."

"Well, she is."

Gillian didn't know what possessed her to say what she

said next. "How do ye know that? Maybe she isn't. Maybe I am carrying the next laird of the clan even now."

Her mother looked shocked but not unhappy. "Are ye, lass? Are ye expecting? Have ye been taking Rhiannon's special tonic? Oooh, a bairn, how exciting."

Gillian hedged, "It's too soon to know for sure, but I could be. My point is that ye are worried over nothing. Fingal will return with his men and our stolen livestock by tomorrow." Stalking towards the keep, Gillian fervently hoped that was true.

Her mother tried her patience to no end and their argument reminded Gillian of her conversation with Fingal from the previous evening. She heaved a sigh as she remembered how pleasant it had been to talk about her da. Yes, that is what had been missing, what had made things all the more tense with her mother. She had tried to handle the pain of losing him by blocking all thoughts of him, even the wonderful, happy memories.

When she was upset as a girl she would find a place to be alone and eventually her da would find her and help make everything better. That is what she needed now. She needed some peace. Lady MacLennan couldn't very well find a tree to scramble up, but there was a place where she could be alone with her thoughts and her memories.

It seemed her brain and her feet had come to the same conclusion because she found herself in front of the chapel. She entered its cold stillness and sat down, allowing her jumbled emotions to settle. When they had, she let the happy memories of her da wash over her. She couldn't stop the tears that spilled down her cheeks. She closed her eyes; she could nearly feel him with her—his warm, strong arm around her shoulder.

When her tears finally subsided, she felt calmer and stronger than she had in days. She dried her face, took a deep breath, and left the chapel.

~ * ~

The peace she found in the chapel stayed with her for the rest of the day. When she finally retired to her chamber that evening she fell asleep almost instantly. She slept soundly until just before dawn when she woke to the sounds of a commotion in the courtyard. She dressed quickly and ran down the stairs. The men who had been on the raid poured into the great hall and Diarmad had joined them as well. She thought things must have gone well because they were clearly jubilant but as soon as she spied Fingal she panicked. A bandage was wrapped around his left arm and blood soaked his sleeve.

She rushed to him. "What happened?"

"I'm fine. 'Tis just a scratch, Gillian."

"It isn't just a scratch. There is blood everywhere. How were ye hurt?"

Eadoin laughed. "He'll be grand, Gillian. Nothing important was injured."

"He's a lucky devil, I'll give ye that," called Tarmon.

Gillian was losing all patience. "I don't find any of this amusing and someone had better tell me what happened right now—"

Interrupting her tirade, Fingal pulled her toward him with his good arm and kissed her. She blushed crimson and all conscious thought fled her mind.

When he broke the kiss he said, "Gillian, my love, I'm fine. We didn't mean to upset ye so."

"Then tell me what happened," she said in a calmer voice.

"We found a trail we thought had been left by the Grant raiders. We followed it and, sure enough, caught a small group of them unawares with a few more head of our cattle. They engaged us but were outmanned and gave up soon enough."

"But how did ye get hurt?"

"Don't spoil the story, my lady," teased Diarmad.

Fingal continued his tale. "We had them unhorsed, disarmed, and face down on the ground. I considered holding them for ransom, but I worried if I brought them back here they would see the true state of things and once released tell their laird. So instead, we took our own cows, their weapons, horses, and anything else of value, trussed them up, and dumped them on Grant land. We left them with a warning that if we caught any more Grants on our land we wouldn't be so benevolent."

Tarmon laughed. "In fairness, they had some fine horses. I'm not sure ye could have gotten a better ransom from Laird Grant for them anyway."

"So ye were injured in the scuffle?" she asked.

"Nay, that is where the story gets a bit odd, my lady," Eadoin said. "We had long since turned back when an arrow flew out of nowhere. The laird had just turned to say something to me, otherwise it would have pierced his heart. Instead, it just barely nicked his arm."

"How could that happen? Who shot the arrow? Oh dear God, ye could have been killed, Fingal."

"But I wasn't killed. It is just a deep scrape. It doesn't even need a stitch. As to who shot the arrow, we can only assume we missed one of the Grants. Perhaps a squire stayed hidden until we passed again, thinking to have revenge."

"Perhaps? Ye don't know?"

"We searched in the area from which the arrow appeared to have been shot, but never found him. He must have laid in wait to take one shot. When he missed he either escaped us or more than likely simply hid himself well."

Eadoin added, "We decided one lone squire, without a horse, was no real threat. Furthermore, if we stayed in the area looking for him he might continue to take random shots and potentially kill someone before we found him. All things considered, the evening was a great success."

Gillian was relieved to hear this. "Well, I'm glad ye found our livestock and put the fear of God into some thieving Grants, but I want Agnes to look at that wound before I am willing to call the evening a success. Even the smallest wounds can be deadly if not properly tended. Please send for her."

"Aye, my lady," Eadoin said with a grin. She glanced quickly around the room, noticing that all of the men wore stupid grins. She harrumphed in frustration, took Fingal by his good arm, and practically dragged him from the hall.

"What are the eejits all grinning at?" she demanded when they were out of earshot.

"I think they are just pleased at the way things are working out."

"What on earth are ye talking about?"

He stopped, pulled her to him, and kissed her, again wiping her mind of all thoughts but his kiss. "I'm talking about that. I think the men are pleased that ye are flustered by my kisses."

"I-I'm not—I just—I just—ye are injured."

"Aye, that pleases them too."

"That ye are injured?" She was appalled at the notion.

"Nay, lass, not that I'm injured, that ye seem so concerned by it."

Before she had the chance to react he kissed her again.

Chapter 12

Like his men, Fingal was touched by how upset Gillian had been by his injury. It was obvious that she cared for him. Perhaps the going was slow, but he was winning her heart. When Agnes arrived she confirmed that the injury was indeed minor. She cleaned and dressed it before offering him a potion to help with the pain.

"Nay, thank ye, Agnes. It really doesn't hurt that much and if yer potion is anything like the foul swill Niall's wife dispenses, I can happily do without it. I think after a wee rest I will be fine."

He did sleep for a few hours and felt perfectly well when he awoke. The sun was fully up and Gillian had left their room. He knew they had had a close call with the Grants and he could not afford another one. He needed to get the wall finished and turn his attention to rebuilding the strength and skills of his warriors. He had to face facts; he needed to bring in additional manpower. Before the midday meal was served, Fingal sat down with Diarmad, Eadoin, and the four clan elders to discuss his plans for moving forward.

"Eadoin, I have mentioned it several times, but it bears repeating, ye have done remarkably well ensuring the clan's protection given yer limited manpower over the last year."

"Thank ye, Laird. I won't deny that having our ranks bolstered by yer brother's men has been a Godsend."

Daniel nodded enthusiastically. "Aye, I have been watching and they are highly skilled warriors to a man. Sure, didn't ye send the Grants packing right enough?"

Fingal nodded. "Aye, we did, but we took a huge gamble doing that. I don't ever want to leave the keep so poorly guarded again."

Daniel said, "Frankly, we could use the skill of some more of Niall's guardsmen. There are a lot of young men to train and we lost many of our best warriors."

Diarmad agreed. "Laird, given that the repairs haven taken so much time away from training, it might be prudent to ask Niall for the loan of another guardsman or two, to help with training once the repairs are done."

"Diarmad, I can't ask him for more."

"Aye, ye can. He worried that this might happen and he asked me to remind ye that ensuring the MacLennans stay strong is in the best interest of all yer neighbors. Besides, he owes ye."

"He doesn't owe me."

Diarmad became serious. "Aye, Fingal, he does. Ye saved Duncurra. Besides, when will ye learn not to argue with Niall? He is willing to send whomever ye need and I think it would be an excellent idea if Turcuil came for a while. He is particularly skilled as a trainer."

"Diarmad, I appreciate the help Niall is willing to offer. However, if he sends Turcuil he may as well come too because Edna will kill him."

Diarmad grinned. "Aye, she might."

"Are ye talking about the widow who helps runs the household staff at Duncurra?" Eadoin asked.

Fingal nodded. "Aye. Most of us think Turcuil will ask her to marry him—in a decade or two."

"Not anxious to be chained down?" Nolan asked with a chuckle.

Fingal grinned. "It isn't that exactly. It's more that she terrifies him."

"And this is the man ye want training our warriors?" Nolan asked incredulously.

Diarmad and Fingal both laughed before Fingal explained, "Aye, I do. Ye've seen him. Turcuil may be the fiercest warrior in the Highlands and he could pound ye into the ground as soon as look at ye. But it isn't just his size that makes him fearsome, his skills are renowned and he has always had both a knack and a fondness for teaching others. His only weakness is Edna and he is so smitten with her that he can barely think when she is near."

Eadoin arched an eyebrow. "Maybe this would be the push he needs to ask for her hand."

Nolan frowned. "Why is it that young married men are always so anxious to curse the rest of us with that affliction?"

Eadoin laughed. "Why is that old bachelors think marriage to a good woman is a curse? I assure ye, it is anything but."

Fingal smiled. A few days ago he might have wondered if marriage was a curse or not, but things were beginning to look up with his own bonny bride. "Turcuil really is the best man for the job."

Diarmad nodded. "Aye, and it wouldn't be forever. The wall will be completed very soon, probably by Easter. Perhaps he and a few other men could come then."

Fingal weighed his options. He hated to ask Niall for more help but he knew, with their limited resources, he had few choices. "I suppose that could work. However, we can't rely on MacIan men forever. I think it is also prudent to seek several highly skilled warriors to join the ranks as guardsmen permanently."

Archie asked, "Who do ye propose to ask?"

"Quinn MacKenzie, for one."

"Quinn MacKenzie is a friend of yers is he?" Owen asked, failing to hide a note of suspicion in his tone.

"Aye, he is. He is a fine warrior and the MacKenzies are the kind of powerful allies we need. Anyone would think twice before tangling with Cathal MacKenzie." Fingal answered.

"Ye have that right," agreed Archie. "That man has managed to bind himself to nearly every strong clan in the northern Highlands. Who else were ye considering?"

"Bran MacBain."

"Bran?" Daniel asked. "Aye, he trained here under Laird Kelvin. He is a fine warrior and well known to most of us. He is an excellent choice."

Nolan nodded. "They would both make fine guardsmen. There is only one little flaw in yer plan. Our funds are dangerously low. Ye have nothing to offer these men."

"He does, Nolan," Diarmad said. "Eithne left a large estate."

Fingal shook his head. "Nay Diarmad, I told Niall I wanted no part of that."

"Aye, but I think the elders of yer clan may see it differently."

"What are ye talking about?" demanded Nolan.

"Over the years, while she was bankrupting the MacIans, Eithne amassed a fairly large sum of money," explained Diarmad.

"Aye, she built her wealth by stealing it from them. It is MacIan money," Fingal insisted.

"Niall doesn't see it that way. They are once again

financially sound, ye are her heir, and there is more than enough money available to help resolve the MacLennan's most pressing issue, skilled manpower."

"Diarmad, I—"

"Be reasonable, Laird. Eithne played a major role in the tragic series of events that have landed us all here. Take the money and bring some good from it."

"He is right," agreed Nolan. "I understand why ye might not want it. Actually, I respect yer reasons. However, it's true, we urgently need the manpower and our resources are stretched thin."

Daniel nodded. "As much as I despised that woman, I have to agree. The clan needs those funds regardless of how she acquired them."

Fingal turned to the other elders. "Owen, Archie, are ye of a same mind?" Both men nodded their agreement.

"Then it is settled," Diarmad said.

"Aye, I suppose it is." But Fingal worried about Gillian's reaction to this. He believed the men were right. He would explain it to her but he knew, deep down, the idea of accepting Eithne's money would rankle her more than it did him. After the progress they had made over the last few days, he dreaded this discussion. He also knew that if she was adamantly opposed to it and he couldn't change her mind, he would have to find another way. He didn't want to cause her more pain.

~ * ~

Perhaps Gillian was over tired. Although she tried, she hadn't gone back to sleep after Fingal and his men had returned. She couldn't stop thinking of how close she had come to losing him. It was only by the Grace of God that he had turned in time to miss the arrow last night. She wasn't sure why it had upset her so badly. She had been distracted by these thoughts all day. That, coupled with her exhaustion, was the only explanation she had for why her guard was down at the evening meal and she had missed the determined glint in her mother's eyes.

The meal was nearly over when Lana cleared her throat and turned to Fingal. "Laird, I've been meaning to discuss something with ye."

Fingal gave her his attention. "What concerns ye, Lana?"

Dear God, Gillian knew instantly that Lana intended to raise the issue of the betrothal. If Gillian hadn't been so preoccupied, she might have seen this coming sooner and averted it more smoothly, but alas, she didn't. Her mother would be relentless and Gillian did not want this discussed in public, in front of Fallon. She jumped to her feet and offered the only excuse she could think of. "Mother, I'm sure whatever it is will wait until another time. I am exhausted and really must retire now."

"Go ahead, Gillian, 'tis the laird I wish to address anyway."

"I'm sorry, Lana, I too am anxious to retire." He stood and flashed a huge smile, generating some chuckles from around the table. "I assume it isn't urgent since ye have waited until now to raise the topic. Perhaps we can discuss this tomorrow?"

Her mother looked irritated for an instant but recovered quickly. "It is important, but aye, it can wait until tomorrow."

Fingal gave Lana a nod. "Very well, until tomorrow, we wish ye all good night." Then he took Gillian's hand and exited the hall with her as those assembled called their good nights. When they were halfway up the stairs and out of earshot of the hall he couldn't help but tease, "well done, Gillian. Ye give every indication of being a new bride anxious to be alone with her groom."

"That wasn't what I was doing."

Fingal laughed. "I know that, lass. I trust, when we reach our chamber, ye will tell me what topic of conversation ye wished to avoid with that rapid exit."

Gillian was aghast. "Was it that obvious to everyone?"

Fingal laughed again. "Probably not. I'm sure most of them think ye simply wished to be alone with me. I am the only one who knows ye want another chance to trounce me at chess."

Gillian blushed. Someone had thoughtfully placed a full decanter of wine and two goblets on the table. Apparently the servants had noticed their recent habit of spending evenings alone. She poured herself a goblet and although she usually drank watered mead or wine she thought perhaps a little extra fortification was in order. She dreaded talking about her mother's betrothal plans. After taking a drink she realized she should have offered some to Fingal as well. She turned to face him. "Would ye like some wine?"

He looked exceedingly amused. "Nay, thank ye Gillian."

Not knowing what else to do, she sat at the table and began to arrange the chess board even as she said, "We don't have to play chess tonight. Ye should rest."

"I'd like to play. I find it relaxes me." He took off his belt and weapons, placing them by the bed before joining her in the other chair. "Now, what unsuitable subject was yer mother about to raise?"

Gillian tried to appear affronted. "What makes ye think it would have been unsuitable?"

"Gillian, I'm not the one who rushed to avoid it but I would appreciate knowing what to expect tomorrow."

Gillian sighed. He was right. "My mother thinks, now that everything is 'settled', a betrothal for Fallon is in order."

Fingal arched a brow. "Settled?"

Gillian nodded her head. "Aye. I'm married so things are 'settled'."

The tone of her voice told him that she did not agree with her mother's assessment. "I see but I'm confused. The other evening ye said she was extremely close to Fallon."

"Aye. She is."

"If she is so close with Fallon, why is she anxious to see her married? I would have thought the opposite."

"I'm not sure. I remember her raising the issue of who they might seek as a husband for Fallon with Da on numerous occasions over the last few years. There was a time when she pushed for yer brother."

Fingal chuckled. "Anxious to make her Lady MacIan, was she?"

"Probably, but each time she started going on about it, Da would eventually silence her by saying he wouldn't consider a betrothal for Fallon until he had one arranged for me and he didn't want me to marry Niall MacIan. I always thought it was because he wanted me to stay here. Now I wonder."

"Gillian, don't. I doubt that anyone knew what Malcolm had planned much in advance."

Gillian found that oddly comforting. "Well, I suppose that is why she feels things are settled now and she can focus on her priority, Fallon."

"Fallon is seventeen?"

"She will be eighteen just after Easter."

"In truth, we need to begin reestablishing ties with other clans. Malcolm severed quite a few when he attacked Duncurra. One way to do that is with a betrothal."

Gillian gave a wry laugh. "That is not at all what mother has in mind."

"No? But ye just said—"

"Fingal, she already knows who she wants Fallon to marry. She'll just try to convince ye that it is a good idea."

"Who does she have in mind?"

"Rhiannon's son, Coby."

"Is Fallon fond of Coby? A strategic match would be better for the clan at the moment, but if they love each other, I would consider it. Ye and yer sisters have been through a lot."

"Fallon has never mentioned having any special feelings for Coby. Nay, I think this is something my mother has dreamt up."

"Any idea why?"

Gillian took another sip of wine. "Not really. Everyone has always held Rhiannon in very high regard. I'm not sure whether it was her status as Lady Nuala's companion, or because she is rumored to be a seer."

"Do ye think it is a good match?"

"My mother would be livid if she heard me say this, but no. I guess it isn't so much that I think it is a bad match, I just think it's the wrong time."

"How would ye handle it?"

"So much has changed for us over the last year, and even more so over the last few weeks. I don't think it's fair to Fallon to add to that stress. As ye said, if she wanted the match it would be different. If it were up to me, I would wait a while. When things are truly more settled, perhaps in a few months, I would discuss the idea of a betrothal with Fallon first. Then I'd figure out who the best candidates were."

"Then that is what I will tell yer mother when she broaches the subject tomorrow, as I'm sure she will."

"God's breath, Fingal, ye can't tell her I said that."

Fingal laughed. "Have ye no faith in me, lass? I won't tell her ye said it. I'll tell her that with all of the recent changes, I think it is better to wait a few months before discussing this."

Gillian was completely taken aback. He had asked her opinion and listened to her. "What would ye have done if I had said a betrothal for Fallon to Coby was a brilliant idea?"

Fingal grinned. "I might have slightly questioned yer judgment. I agree the timing seems wrong. However, ye know yer family and clan better than I do and if ye were wholeheartedly behind it, I would support ye." At her shocked expression he added, "Gillian, this marriage will work much better, for us and for the clan, if we view it as a partnership."

This was the last thing Gillian expected but it was exactly what Jeanne and told her days ago. She had no idea how to respond. Finally, she simply said, "Thank ye."

"Ye're welcome. Now there is something else we need to discuss. A few moments ago I mentioned that we need to rebuild our ties with other clans. One way to do that and reestablish our own internal strength is to add several highly skilled warriors to our ranks of guardsmen. As ye know as soon as we can finish the wall we need to focus on training our men. I intend to ask Niall for some additional men to help with that, but that's only a temporary solution. I want to ask Bran MacBain and Quinn MacKenzie to become guardsmen."

"I remember Bran MacBain, he trained here. My da always liked him."

"Aye, the elders think well of him too. I trained with Quinn MacKenzie and he is young but has solid skills."

"They seem like good choices then."

"I would also like to ask Laird MacKay if he would consider sending his nephew Dougal to foster with us. He is old enough to begin training as a squire and that would give us ties to both the MacKays and the MacLeods. As Lady MacLennan, ye would have a role in that as well. Are ye willing to take him on?"

"Aye. Of course I am. Ye are right, we need these alliances. I just don't understand how we can do it all. We have very limited resources."

"I understand, and that is what I need to talk with ye about. As it turns out, Eithne left a very large estate."

Gillian did not like the direction this was heading. She wanted nothing to do with Eithne's wealth, especially after learning even more about her evil nature from Fingal. Her reservation must have clearly shown on her face.

"I can see ye like that idea no better than I did. Until today, I had refused to accept it. Eithne built her wealth by stealing from the MacIans and I felt it should go back to them. Niall has always disagreed. However, I discussed this with Eadoin and the elders earlier today. They all believe, just as Niall did, that that money should come to our clan."

"I don't want anything that belonged to her."

"I understand. I don't either. However, we cannot do the things we must without funds."

"There has to be another way."

"I have been considering our options for weeks now and haven't been able to figure out another plan. None of the elders have any suggestions either."

"Ye've already discussed it with the elders and clearly they agree. Why did ye bother even asking me? If I flatly say no, it doesn't change anything. Ye will still use her money."

"Nay, Gillian. If ye flatly say no, and there is no changing yer mind, I will go back to them and we will have to change our plans. I won't lie to ye, it will leave us vulnerable and I'm not sure we can survive for long. But this is too important. Ye must understand where the money is coming from and agree, as repugnant as it may be, to use it for the good of the clan."

"Ye would do that? Ye would turn it down if I asked ye to?"

Fingal looked grim. "I think it would be the wrong decision but yes, I would."

Gillian stared into her goblet of wine and wondered what her father would think. She could almost hear him, *Gillian, don't cut yer nose off to spite yer face, lass.* "It is the only way?"

"It is the only way that any of us can see."

She swirled the wine in her goblet and thought about it a bit longer. As much as she hated to accept anything that belonged to that dreadful woman, he was right. They had no choice. She sighed in resignation. "Then I suppose we must use it."

Fingal was obviously relieved. He reached for the decanter and poured wine into the other goblet. "Here's to our partnership." They touched goblets and both drank, Gillian draining what remained in hers. Fingal wrinkled up his nose. "That isn't particularly good, is it?"

Gillian blushed. "Nay, I guess not. We brew heather ale, but we have to buy wine and we couldn't afford good wine. Sometimes Jeanne steeps herbs in it to improve the flavor but it doesn't help much. I just thought it was stronger than what I am accustomed to—I usually mix mine with water. It's gone to my head a bit."

"No matter, I would rather seal our partnership with something else entirely." He stood, put both hands on the arms of her chair, leaned down and captured her lips with his. There went every rational thought in her head and the butterflies that had seemed to take up residence in her belly all took flight at once.

He broke the kiss far too quickly. She wanted more. *Nay, Gillian, get a hold of yerself.* How was he able to do this to her? She was over-tired. That must be the explanation. She was, in fact, more tired than she realized. She had closed her eyes when he kissed her and waited far too long to open them again after he stopped. When she did open them, it was to see a bemused smile on Fingal's handsome face. She stammered, "I—uh—I—well—I'm awfully tired. Do ye mind if we don't play chess tonight? I think I'll turn in."

His smile became a wide grin. "Whatever ye wish, Gillian."

Chapter 13

To Fingal's delight, Gillian had become as befuddled as ever when he kissed her. After he broke the kiss and stepped away from her chair, she rose and wobbled a bit, tittering nervously. "The wine seems to have gone to my head. I really should have watered it down." She motioned toward the decanter, accidentally knocking his full goblet over, spilling the contents. "Fingal, I'm sorry. I can be so clumsy sometimes. I'll just clean this up and pour ye some more."

"Don't worry about it, lass. It isn't very good wine anyway."

She grabbed a towel from the washstand near the hearth, but in her hurry to wipe up the spill, she knocked over the whole decanter. "Oh for the love of all that's holy, what's wrong with me?"

Fingal righted the decanter and took the towel from her. "Ye are just tired, Gillian. Ye have been overworking yerself. Let me clean this up and ye can get ready for bed."

She looked distressed. "But ye are injured."

"It is just a scratch. I can manage this." He gave her a quick kiss. "Go on. I'll keep my back turned."

As he mopped up the spilled wine, she undressed quickly. In no time, the bed creaked softly as she crawled under the covers. When he turned around, she was curled in a tight ball on the edge of the bed just as always. He put the wine soaked towel in the wash bowl and wet another towel to wipe up any residual stickiness. When he was through, he hung it on a chair to dry. Then he banked the fire, blew out the candles, removed his clothes and climbed in bed beside her. Her slow, steady breathing told him she was already asleep.

He wanted to do so much more with his new bride than sleep. The changes in her over the last week were beginning to give him hope. Maybe she had finally stopped fighting with herself where he was concerned. Clearly logical, Gillian had had a list of reasons why she shouldn't love him but they were dwindling. Furthermore, logical Gillian was not always in control. There was part of her that was warm, affectionate and needed both to give love and be loved in return. When she had talked about her parents, this had been painfully clear. He could love her. He certainly admired and respected her. She was smart, strong, and beautiful. What man could ask for more? Aye, not only could he love her; he believed he already did. Now, she just needed to let him.

~ * ~

Fingal wasn't sure how long he had been asleep but he awoke with a start, alert that something was wrong. The room was filling with smoke and fire crackled loudly. He scanned the room quickly and saw that a log had rolled from the hearth and onto one of the woven rush mats. Thick smoke was filling the room.

He jumped out of bed and yelled to Gillian, "Wake up, there's a fire, ye have to get out!" The smoke filled his lungs and he was racked with coughing. He used the first tool at hand, his sword, to shove the log off the rug and onto the stone floor. He glanced back at Gillian. She hadn't wakened. "Gillian! Wake up!" He reached for the water pitcher to pour water on the smoking rush mat but it was empty so he grabbed the wet towel he had used earlier and beat at the mat. With the burning log removed, the mat appeared to be smoldering, but there were no remaining flames. Using the poker and fire tongs he returned the log to the hearth.

The immediate danger of fire had past but the thick smoke burned his throat and eyes. He turned, intending to throw open the window shutters and clear the air, only to realize that Gillian still hadn't stirred. Terror seized his heart. The smoke was so thick he feared she had already been overcome by it. He ran to her side and scooped her up blankets and all before rushing out of the room with her in his arms, closing the door behind them to keep smoke from filling the corridor. Between coughs he yelled for help. Diarmad was the first to arrive, followed by several men-at-arms and serving maids who had been sleeping in the hall.

Coughing, Fingal sank to the floor with Gillian still in his arms. "Diarmad, there was a fire. It's out, but the smoke—" He was overcome with a coughing spasm. However, Diarmad seemed to understand, cautiously entering the room while Fingal turned his attention to Gillian. He shook her. "Wake up, love. Please, wake up." Another coughing spasm gripped him.

Someone tried to remove her from his arms. "Nay, don't touch her. Send for Agnes. Please, love, wake up." Finally she seemed to rouse, coughing as she did. He rested his forehead on hers. "Thank God. My precious lass, ye're alive."

She coughed until tears ran down her cheeks. Finally she whispered, "What happened?"

"Gillian, my love, a log rolled from the hearth, catching a rush mat on fire. It is out but there was so much smoke. I couldn't wake ye. I was afraid I had lost ye."

"I must have been more tired than I thought. How could I have slept through that?" She rested her head against his chest, closing her eyes even now and making no attempt to move from his lap. He wouldn't have let her if she had tried.

Lana arrived moments later. "What in the name of all that's holy is going on? What is all this commotion about?"

When one of the men at arms explained, Lana rounded on Fingal. "Thank God Gillian is all right. Clearly ye must not have banked the fire properly Laird and ye nearly got my daughter killed. Why are ye just sitting there? Gillian, get up."

Fingal had to rein in his anger. "Lana, we were nearly overcome by smoke. Please, if ye wish to be helpful, see that a room is prepared where Gillian can rest."

"We could have all been burned alive. I have to check on Fallon." Lana turned in a huff and stomped away. Fingal was shocked by her lack of concern.

One of the maids, a lass named Peg, stepped forward saying, "I'll see to it Laird."

Diarmad came out of the room. "Lady MacLennan is all right?"

"Aye, thank God."

"I have opened the window shutters to air out the chamber. The smoke needs to clear and the room to be cleaned well but other than the rush mat, there doesn't appear to be any other damage. Ye must have woken right away—the mat was just blackened. If it had caught fully on fire, it could have been disastrous."

Fingal nodded, rising from the floor with Gillian in his arms. "Aye, I must have." However, something nagged at him—something was wrong. "Gavin, Tarmon, return to yer duties. The rest of ye should find yer beds. Things are under control now." He turned to Diarmad. "Thank ye. I want to see that Gillian is cared for now. I would speak with ye privately in the morning."

Fingal carried a still very drowsy Gillian to the bed chamber Peg had prepared, realizing for the first time that he was completely naked. He had barely tucked her into bed and wrapped a blanket around himself when Agnes, the healer, arrived. Agnes checked Gillian over, finally saying, "Lass, ye seem to be all right. I suppose this terrible ordeal has exhausted ye. Get some sleep and I will check on ye again in the morning."

"Aye, Agnes, I'll rest." Gillian curled up under the blankets and was instantly asleep.

Agnes turned to leave but Fingal stopped her. "Agnes, are ye sure she is well? I had trouble waking her. I worry that she breathed too much smoke."

"Well that could have made her hard to wake, sure enough." Agnes winked at him. "Did ye wear her out before sleeping lad?"

Fingal smiled at the old woman's teasing. "Nay, I don't think so. She did have a glass of wine before bed."

"That might have made her sleep a bit more soundly. She isn't accustomed to strong drink. I don't think there is any need to worry. She is breathing well now and although sleepy, she can be awakened. I think she will be fine in the morning."

Fingal showed her out. He washed the soot from his own face and hands before crawling in bed beside her. He pulled her close, and in her sleep she didn't resist. His mind was racing and he couldn't sleep. He thought back over the events of the night, trying to determine what left him feeling so uneasy.

Lana had accused him of not banking the fire properly, but he was certain that he had. He banked the fire immediately after cleaning up the spilled wine. He had awoken later as the room was filling with smoke from the smoldering rush mat. *Why wasn't it burning?* He had jumped out of bed, shoved the burning log off the mat and grabbed the water pitcher, which was empty. He beat it with the wet cloth, but there were no flames. None of it made sense. Dried rushes catch fire easily and the water pitcher was half-full when he went to bed. He had only used a little water to wet the towel he used to wipe the table.

He slipped quietly from bed, wrapped a blanket around his shoulders, lit a candle, and made his way back to their chamber.

He entered the room cautiously. The smoke had cleared and with the windows all open, the room was frigid. The wine soaked towel was still in the wash bowl where he had put it. The decanter and goblets stood on the table and the pitcher lay on the floor where he had dropped it when he discovered it was empty. He looked at the place where the burning log had rolled onto the rush mat. It was blackened, but barely burned. He ran his hand over it and found it wet. How had it gotten wet? The wine had spilled over the edge of the table, closer to the middle of the mat—he could see the stain. This whole corner of the mat was wet.

Well at least the wet rush mat explained the unusual amount of smoke. It would have smoldered and smoked for quite a long time before it caught fire. It was a blessing really. They could have been engulfed in flames otherwise. He just couldn't figure out how it had gotten wet. Perhaps Gillian had arisen at some point and spilled the water remaining in the pitcher. He would ask her in the morning.

Chapter 14

Gillian woke later than usual in the morning feeling cozy. Her back was against Fingal's chest and he held her close. Although she didn't want to admit it, even if only to herself, she felt safe and comfortable in his arms. She glanced around the room, confused for a moment because they weren't in their chamber. Then the events of the night came flooding back. There had been a fire. It was all a blur. Even with his injured arm he carried her from the room and she remembered being so tired. *Gillian, my love...I was afraid I had lost ye.* He saved her life. He had been worried about her.

Fingal's arms tightened around her for a moment and he kissed the top of her head, setting off the butterflies in her stomach. "Ye are awake, love?"

Love. "Aye. I didn't dream that fire, did I?"

"I wish I could say ye did."

"What happened?"

"I'm not sure. It appears that a log rolled from the hearth. It would have been much worse except that rush mat was wet and didn't catch fire quickly. Were ye up at all after we went to bed? Could ye have spilled water from the pitcher?"

"Nay, I barely remember waking when ye carried me into the hall. Oh, but I spilled the decanter of wine before we went to bed."

"Aye, that must have been it. We were very lucky." He gave her another squeeze.

She turned onto her back so that she could look him in the eye. "Ye saved my life."

"Gillian, I made a vow to ye before God. I would give my own life for ye." He brushed the hair from her face. It was a simple gesture and yet so very intimate it touched her. She felt...cherished.

"Fingal, I-I thank ye." That wasn't what she wanted to say and she frowned.

Fingal chuckled. "Ye are welcome, love, but it looks as if it pains ye to say that."

Love. "Nay, oh, I'm sorry. It's just I-I, well...I think I may have been wrong about ye."

He laughed outright. "I know ye were but it is nice to hear ye say that."

"I have pushed ye away without giving ye a chance and yet ye have been...kind—and thoughtful. I'm sorry, Fingal."

"Ye needn't apologize, Gillian. Yer life took quite a change in direction a few weeks ago and ye had very little control over the new course. I'm sorry for that."

"But it wasn't yer fault any more than it was mine."

"Nay, still I'm sorry it has been so difficult for ye."

Jeanne had been right. It was time she tried harder. "Fingal, I think—I think I'm ready to be yer wife."

He smiled and kissed her forehead. "Gillian, my love, I'm overjoyed to hear ye say that and I want to be yer husband in every way. However, we have just been through a terrible experience and I fear ye are just feeling vulnerable. I would be the worst kind of rogue if I took advantage of that. Sweetling, let's wait a few more days. When the events of last night are not so fresh, if ye are still sure of yer feelings, I will make ye my wife."

She couldn't quite believe her ears. While there was truth in his words, she didn't believe she had made this decision out of vulnerability. She was surprised that he hadn't jumped at her offer but what surprised her most was the disappointment she felt.

~ * ~

It was all Fingal could do to keep himself from capturing her lips, kissing all thoughts from her head and making love to her as he longed to do. This was what he wanted—Gillian willing and pliant in his arms. However, he worried. He believed she felt gratitude and perhaps a growing respect for him but somehow that wasn't enough. If not love, he wanted her to feel desire. Then, and only then, would she be his without reservation. He could wait a few more days.

"Gillian, I think ye should take things slow today. I am going to send someone up with breakfast and a bath."

"That isn't necessary, I am fine. The clan will worry if I don't attend to things as usual. I will have a bath this evening after the day's work is done."

Fingal sighed. "I would prefer ye rest, but I understand yer concern. Please promise ye won't overtax yerself."

"I promise."

"I'm going back to our room to get some clothes."

"I'll come too."

"Nay, the shutters were open all night and I'm sure it is freezing. Stay here where it is warm and I'll bring ye something to wear."

Fingal wrapped a blanket around his waist and made his way to their bedroom. It was cold and there were black smoke stains on the walls, but otherwise all was well. He dressed quickly and gathered clothes for Gillian as well. Their clothes had been in the wardrobe but they smelled of smoke. Everything would have to be scrubbed down and laundered.

Diarmad entered the room. "I saw the door open. Are ye and Gillian both well this morning?"

"Aye. There was very little damage really. Diarmad, some things aren't quite adding up." Fingal proceeded to tell him about the events of the evening leading up to the fire. "I know I banked the fire and I know there was a half jug of water left on the stand."

"Could Gillian have accidently knocked it over in the night?"

"Nay, she was sleeping so soundly I could hardly wake her during the fire."

"Does she always sleep that soundly?"

"We have both been working hard and are tired at the end of the day." Diarmad grinned, but Fingal ignored the innuendo inherent in it. "She blamed it on the wine she drank. She says she usually drinks it watered. Still, the night of our wedding I poured wine for her that wasn't watered. She didn't seem overly affected by it then."

"Laird, it was her wedding night, if a lass can't stay awake for that, I would worry."

Fingal chuckled at his jest. "I guess ye are right." He would tell no one that he had yet to consummate his marriage, not even Diarmad.

"Do ye think this fire was more than a simple accident?"

Although Fingal was concerned about circumstances surrounding the fire, he had no evidence to confirm that it was anything other than an accident. He didn't want to jump to conclusions that might ultimately worry Gillian. "Nay, I am probably overreacting. I will take a few extra precautions in the future, but I'm sure there is nothing to worry about."

"Well then, I'll go break my fast and then I'll arrange to send a messenger to Niall as we agreed."

"Very well, I'll join ye in a moment. I just need to gather a few more things for Gillian."

When Diarmad had left, Fingal went to the table where the empty decanter stood. There was a small amount of wine, a few drops, left in the bottom. He upended the decanter and let the drops spill on his tongue. They had the same slightly bitter aftertaste that he had noted the previous evening. It seemed familiar, but he couldn't place it. Maybe it was just from a bad cask, but it worried him. Had someone put something in the wine and then set the fire? Were there MacLennans who hated him sufficiently to risk killing Gillian too? If he had consumed drugged wine and slept as soundly as Gillian had, they both surely would have died. As it was, he had only swallowed a mouthful before Gillian spilled it. That couldn't have been enough to seriously affect him.

Perhaps he was overreacting as he had told Diarmad and he was seeing a conspiracy where none existed. He truly didn't believe he could he have slept through someone entering their room. Maybe the wine was just bitter and the log had simply rolled from the hearth. Nevertheless, he would take no chances. He didn't want to worry her, and she wasn't used to barring the door at night, but he would have to figure out a way to do so without raising her concern.

There might also be another way to help protect them both. He remembered what Ailsa had said the day after the wedding. *Give her a puppy. She loves dogs. I do too. We have always wanted a pet and Mama wouldn't let us have one.* He chuckled. A dog would serve several purposes. Not only would it please his wife and needle his mother-in-law, a dog could help alert them to unwanted nocturnal intruders.

~ * ~

Within the hour, Fingal had sent messengers to Niall as well as Lairds MacKenzie, MacBain, and MacKay with the requests for assistance. When they were gone, he left the keep in search of Hearn, the MacLennan stable master. Hearn also raised and handled Brathanead's hunting dogs. Fingal had known him for years and knew he treated the animals entrusted to him with care.

They responded to him without hesitation as only loyal gently-handled beasts do. Perhaps this was why Fingal liked and trusted him. However, before he reached the stables, Eadoin approached him, clearly angry.

"Laird, the night ye arrived ye told me that if I ever thought ye were in danger of failing to love, honor, keep, and guard Gillian, ye gave me leave to address it with ye. Does that still hold true?"

Fingal sighed. "Aye Eadoin, it does."

"Then how could ye have failed to do something as simple as bank the damn fire?"

"Eadoin, I believe I did bank the fire. I remember doing it."

Some of Eadoin's anger dissolved. "If ye banked the fire, how did a flaming log roll from it?"

"I don't know. I can't explain what happened. I assure ye, I don't take Gillian's safety so lightly." Fingal was not sure yet whether he trusted Eadoin completely. He wasn't comfortable saying more.

Eadoin frowned. "Laird, I swore fealty to ye and I will believe ye this time. Please don't make me regret that. Gillian is too important to this clan."

"I won't, Eadoin."

Eadoin nodded and having said his piece, walked away.

No, Fingal couldn't explain what had happened and that was why he needed to speak with Hearn. As expected, he found Hearn in the stables overseeing the work of the day. Although he had a stocky build, Hearn wasn't a very large man. Fingal stood a head taller but he knew Hearn was as strong as an ox. Even at well over two score and ten, he was stronger than many men half his age. "Hearn, do ye have a few minutes? I would like to discuss something with ye."

"Of course, Laird. The tack room is empty, we won't be interrupted there." Fingal nodded and followed him into the tack room, closing the door behind him. Not one to waste time, Hearn asked bluntly, "does this have something to do with the fire last night?"

"Aye, in a way it does."

Hearn crossed his arms over his chest. "As I hear it, a log rolled from the hearth. That rarely happens if a fire is banked properly."

"I agree." Fingal prepared to be castigated by yet another MacLennan for failing to keep Gillian safe.

"So Laird, either ye are careless, extremely unlucky, or ye think it wasn't an accident. Given how narrowly ye missed having an arrow pierce yer heart, I would say luck smiles on ye. I also wouldn't have thought ye were that careless even if distracted by a lovely bride."

Fingal smiled. Perhaps Hearn was not willing to blame him immediately. "Nay, I'm not a careless man. I banked the fire before retiring. Being born to Eithne MacIan is perhaps evidence enough to suggest I am unlucky in spite of what recent events indicate. This could have been the accident it appears to be. But, if it isn't, the only explanation is that someone slipped into our chamber."

"That's hard to believe, Laird."

"Aye, it is. For that reason, I am inclined to believe the fire was caused by pure misfortune. However, I am unwilling to risk a recurrence if it wasn't."

"And what do ye think I can do to prevent it?"

"Ailsa told me several weeks ago that Gillian has always wanted a pet, a dog, but their mother refused to allow it. While I understand our king's desire to ensure the welfare of Clan MacLennan, his edict has been extremely difficult on Lady Gillian. If a pet would add a small bright spot to the whole situation, I want her to have one. Furthermore, if we did truly sleep through someone entering our chamber, another set of sharp ears might prevent that happening in the future. I thought maybe ye could help me there."

Hearn grinned and chuckled. "Ailsa is a minx. She knows one of my sight hounds whelped an unusually large litter in early December. She comes to the kennels nearly every day. There are two pups that she has practically ruined."

"Two?"

"Aye, it's odd really. There was one huge male pup in the litter, and one scrawny one. Those two seemed to have an odd bond. Often larger pups in a litter will push a weak one around, so much so that a runt sometimes doesn't survive. But in this case, the big one seemed to look out for his wee brother. He didn't let the others edge him out at feeding time. Now, with four months growth, there is much less of a difference in size. They both look to be fine strong animals. Still, Ailsa calls the little one her 'wee

Duff'."

"Are ye willing to part with one of them?"

"Aye, but Laird, would ye consider taking them both?"

"Has Ailsa truly ruined them as hunters?"

Hearn laughed. "Nay, Laird, I don't believe affection can ruin an animal. I just have a soft spot for Ailsa. She is a sweet lass and losing her da broke her heart as ye can imagine. I believe a wee beastie of her own would help ease that pain. I thought maybe ye would give Duff to her and take the other one for Lady Gillian."

Fingal grinned. "Hearn, would ye be trying to get me in trouble with my new mother by marriage?"

"Laird, do ye honestly care what Lana thinks? Ye are the laird and if ye want dogs in the keep, ye can have them. A truly loving mother would have done something to help the lass bear up before now. I tried last year. One of the MacLennan crofters had a herder with a spring litter of pups. Knowing how much Ailsa was hurting, I thought she might like to have a pet, so I got a wee female pup off him and approached Lana. She flatly refused to let her have it. I ended up keeping her as a pet myself. I named her Lulu and I can't imagine life without her. My wife passed a few years ago. I can tell ye for certain, a dog helps ease that loss like nothing else."

"Ye are right, Hearn. Ailsa needs a pup as much as Gillian does. If ye are willing to give up both of them, ye have my gratitude."

"It is my pleasure. Come with me, I'll show them to ye." Hearn led him to the kennels which were just as clean and well cared for as the stables. Dogs surrounded Hearn, vying for his attention. "I keep the puppies in a separate pen until they are big enough to hold their own in the pack." Hearn let Fingal through the gate into a smaller pen where ten sleek coated puppies with small floppy ears wiggled excitedly. He scooped a large puppy up under each arm, handing the dark brindle colored one to Fingal. The other pup was only slightly smaller and was mostly black with a small patch of white on each paw. "This one is Ailsa's 'wee Duff' and the brindle is Duff's protector. I call him Bodie. It means 'shelter' in the old Norse language. Given his protective nature, it seemed appropriate."

Fingal smiled. "Aye, it seems so." While sometimes the men who trained hunting hounds didn't bother to give them names, naming them wasn't uncommon either. What surprised Fingal was the thought Hearn put into naming his animals.

"I'd give them to ye now laird, but if we want to tamp down a little of Lana's ire, bathing them first might be a good idea. I will have one of the lads take care of it and I'll bring them up to the keep after the noon meal."

"That would be perfect." Then Fingal frowned. The thought occurred to him that perhaps Fallon would feel left out. "Hearn, ye know Gillian's family better than I do. Will Fallon be hurt if I give a pet to Ailsa?"

"It's good of ye to think of her, Laird. Fallon is a sweet lass and she has always been fond of animals, mayhap not as much as Ailsa and Gillian but she has a soft spot for cats. However, she would be less likely to cross her mother than the other two. She would never ask for a pet, but if ye gave her one, I expect she would be thrilled. There is a mouser in the stable who had a litter of kittens at the end of the summer. Some of them are a bit on the wild side, but there is one tricolor female that is very affectionate. Honestly, I hate to let her go because, like her mother, she is an excellent mouser. But that could work to yer favor with Lana. She hates vermin."

"Does the cat have a name?" Fingal asked casually but he would have been willing to bet money on the answer.

Hearn looked a little embarrassed. "Well, aye, Laird, I've been calling her Maggie."

Fingal laughed and Bodie wiggled happily in his arms, straining to lick Fingal's face. "Ye're a good man Hearn. Bring her up after the noon meal with these two fierce beasts. If I'm going to irritate Lana anyway, I may as well do it with three pets as one."

Chapter 15

In spite of Gillian's desire to attend to things as she usually did, she had trouble focusing on her work. Her mother, Fallon, and two other women were helping to clean up the damage from the fire. The draperies, bed linens, and bed hangings had been carried to the wash house to be cleaned. Even the mattress would be replaced. The feathers were being salvaged. Several women were stuffing them into fresh ticking. The other women were washing down the smoke stained walls while Gillian emptied the clothing from the wardrobe. It all reeked of smoke and needed to be laundered. While she had slept soundly the night before, she still felt tired. Maybe it was caused by the overwhelming smell of smoke but she also had a slight headache. She stopped what she was doing and pressed two fingers into her forehead between her eyebrows, trying to relieve the pain.

"Gillian, are ye all right?" Fallon asked, concerned.

"Aye. I just have a touch of a headache."

Her mother glanced at her from where she stood on a stool. "Do ye have the packet of herbs Rhiannon gave ye? Rhiannon swears by it for a headache."

"Aye, mother, but—"

"Why do ye always argue with me, lass?"

Peg laughed. "Don't all lasses argue with their mothers? I know I do. But Gillie, if the herbs she gave ye are her 'special tonic' it really does work."

"Peg, ye will address Gillian as 'Lady MacLennan' or 'my lady' now," Lana said sharply. "It isn't appropriate for a servant to call her 'Gillie' any longer. She will not be respected if everyone treats her so casually."

"Oh mother, please," Gillian snapped, "Peg has been my friend since we were little. I don't want her to address me so formally."

Her mother looked ready to spout fire and Maeve, an older

woman who worked with them, intervened. "My lady, yer mother is right to remind us to remember yer station now but Lana, old habits die hard. Give us all a bit of time."

Gillian smiled at her. "Thank ye, Maeve. I still feel much more like 'Gillie' than 'Lady MacLennan'."

The older woman laughed. "Well all right then Gillie, listen to yer mum. After ye take those clothes down to be laundered, stop in the kitchen and make yerself a mug of Rhiannon's tisane. It will do ye a world of good."

Her mother glared at Maeve, but Gillian laughed, taking the packet of herbs from the chest where she had put it, then grabbing an armful of smoky clothes. "I think I will. Fallon, will ye help me?"

Looking as thrilled to leave the room as Gillian felt, Fallon grabbed up the remaining cloths and grinning said, "Oh, aye, *Lady MacLennan*, I will."

Their mother shouted, "I didn't mean ye Fallon!" as they left the room.

By the time they had taken everything to the wash house and made their way to the kitchen, the noon meal was nearly ready to be served. "Get out from under my feet now lassies and I'll bring ye a mug of my own tonic to have with yer meal in a few minutes," Jeanne said as she chivvied them out of the kitchen.

Being out of the smoky room and walking through the fresh cold air to the wash house and kitchens had done wonders for Gillian's headache anyway. When they reached the great hall people were gathering for the meal and Fingal was just coming through the front door of the keep. She smiled. He seemed light-hearted and happy. This was the charming, handsome young man she remembered from years ago and her heart leapt. Fallon nudged her. "Ye look happy sister. Is he winning yer heart?"

Just last week a comment like that would have made her angry. Today the butterflies in her stomach suggested that he might be winning her heart. She wasn't quite ready to admit it so she just rolled her eyes. "Fallon, that is a silly, romantic notion. I barely know him. Don't let mother hear ye even suggest it."

The knowing smile on Fallon's face indicated that her sister didn't believe her. To make matters worse, Fingal crossed the hall, wrapped her in his arms, spun her around, and kissed her soundly. There was simply no part of her that could muster anything but delight at his greeting. Perhaps he had been right that morning when he said she was feeling vulnerable. However, she knew she was feeling something else too. It was just as Jeanne had suggested. When she allowed herself to accept and enjoy his attention, she felt valued and cherished. She felt loved.

Fingal took her hand and walked with her to the head of the table, Fallon following behind them. "Are ye feeling quite well this afternoon, Gillian?"

"Aye, I am."

"No she isn't," announced Fallon, "she has a headache."

Fingal looked concerned. "Gillian, last night was terribly distressing. Please rest this afternoon."

Gillian glared at her sister. "Fallon exaggerates. I had a slight headache, but I think it was the smell of the smoke from cleaning our chamber. I was just outside in the fresh air and feel much better."

"Perhaps so, but ye were nearly overcome by the smoke last night. Leave the cleaning of our chamber to others."

His concern touched her and frankly, she had had enough of the smell of smoke. "I will. It is almost done anyway. All of the fabric has been removed for cleaning and the smoke stains washed from the walls. We should be able to move back into it soon enough."

Their conversation moved on to other things during the meal. Now that she had stopped trying to despise him, she didn't feel as flustered by his attention. Of course any time he touched her, it still set off the butterflies in her stomach, and as predicted she was beginning to like it. *Get a hold of yourself, Gillian, ye have only known this man for a little over a month.* Nay, that wasn't true. She had known him for many years and had liked him for most of them. It was only in the last year that she had felt differently and as he pointed out the night he arrived, he himself had done nothing to earn her hatred. It was time to move forward. He had rapidly earned her respect; maybe love wasn't out of the question.

Fingal interrupted her musings by laying a hand on her arm. "Gillian, I have something for ye. I know the last few weeks have been difficult. I wanted to give ye something that might bring ye some joy. I have it on very good authority that ye are fond of dogs."

At that statement, Ailsa, who had been chatting away with Fallon, stopped mid-sentence to stare at him in awe. "Laird, ye didn't. Did ye?"

Fingal grinned and motioned to Hearn who stood just inside the front door of the hall. One of the stable boys entered carrying a large, wiggling, brindle puppy. Gillian was too shocked to say anything. The boy brought the puppy to her and deposited it on her lap. She put her arms around him, rubbing his velvety fur. "Oh, Fingal. I love dogs. I have always wanted one of my own."

Ailsa was out of her seat and at Gillian's side instantly petting the puppy who started licking her face. "I told him, Gillian. Ye are so lucky. Hearn calls this one Bodie." There was an unmistakably wistful note in her voice.

To Gillian's surprise, Fingal motioned to Hearn again. "Ailsa did tell me ye have always wanted a pet, but it was clear she wanted one too. As it happens, Hearn tells me Bodie has a little brother that Ailsa is rather fond of."

Realizing what was happening, Ailsa looked up and squealed with glee, running to meet the stable boy who carried a large black puppy with white feet. She gathered her puppy in her arms and carried him to show Gillian. "It's my wee Duff. Is he for me, Laird? Really?"

"Aye, Ailsa. He is for ye. Take good care of him. Hearn will help ye if ye have any questions."

"I *will* take good care of him, Liard. Thank ye." With the puppy still in her arms she hugged him.

Her mother cleared her throat. "Ye should have asked me before giving my daughters animals, Laird. I don't approve of keeping animals inside."

Stricken, Ailsa looked at Fingal, silently pleading for his help. Fingal rested a hand on Ailsa's shoulder. "I understand that Lana, but I am the laird of this keep, and I do approve of keeping animals as pets. In fact, I think animals can be a great comfort to wee lassies who have suffered significant losses. Ye are certainly free to ban them from yer private chamber, but they are welcome everywhere else."

Gillian's mother didn't relent. "Ailsa is too young."

"I disagree, Lana. She needs him and she will care for him. Ye needn't worry. I will make sure of it."

Her mother looked angry but didn't argue further. Ailsa let out a huge sigh of relief and turned her attention back to her puppy. Gillian tore her gaze from the soft puppy who seemed to be all legs. She glanced quickly around the hall. She saw more looks of approval than she would have imagined.

Fallon reached to pet Bodie. "Gillian, he is lovely."

Ailsa looked momentarily concerned. "I'll share Duff with ye if ye wish, Fallon."

Fingal grinned, motioning to Hearn who crossed the hall to the table. "That is awfully nice of ye Ailsa, but Hearn mentioned that Fallon wasn't quite as fond of dogs and ye and Gillian are. He thought she might like this wee beastie for her own."

Fallon's mouth fell open and she gasped as Hearn pulled the young tri-color cat from under his plaid. She gathered the cat in her arms and nuzzled her face. "Maggie." After cuddling her for a few moments, she looked up. "Laird, thank ye. I love her."

"Hearn thought ye might."

Gillian looked at their mother. Her mouth was pressed to a thin line and she glared at the cat. Gillian was about to say something to try and cool her mother's anger when Fallon spoke up. "Mama, I know ye have never wanted pets but truly, I have wanted a cat for as long as I can remember. Please don't say I can't have her." Gillian was in awe. Fallon was brilliant. Even though Fingal had just said that allowing animals in the keep was his decision, Fallon had practically forced their mother to agree. There is no way mama would deny her this in front of the clan. And once she agreed to accept Fallon's cat, she would say no more about the dogs either.

Just as Gillian expected, her mother relented. "If ye want her so badly, I won't refuse ye, Fallon."

"Thank ye, Mama." Fallon walked to her and kissed her cheek. "Ye know...I hear she is quite a good mouser."

"Is she? Well at least there's that." Gillian was shocked to see her mother reach to scratch behind the cat's ears.

That seemed to be the cue the assembly had been waiting for. The animals were petted and admired by everyone in the hall. Ailsa told Gillian the story of how Bodie protected Duff when they were very little. And for the first time in longer than she could remember, Gillian didn't spend the afternoon working. She and her sisters...played.

~ * ~

As Gillian and her sisters became engrossed in getting to know their new pets, Fingal silently left the hall to join his men on the training fields.

"Laird, wait," Eadoin called from behind him, running to catch up.

"Is there something ye need Eadoin?"

"Nay, Laird. I just wanted to say, what ye did in there was—well ye couldn't have given those lasses anything they needed more."

"Eadoin, I meant what I said. This last year and especially the last few weeks have been exceedingly hard for them all. I cannot bring their father back. I can never make up for what my mother did. The love of a wee beast is a very small thing but perhaps it will give them some comfort."

~ * ~

Gillian and Bodie developed an instant bond. It was as if he knew she belonged to him. He stayed with her wherever she went as close as a shadow. That alone thrilled her.

Late that afternoon, she still had the remnants of a headache. At her sisters' urgings she went to the room she and Fingal had moved to after the fire, and laid down. Bodie settled on the bed next her. His warm, solid presence was oddly comforting.

Comforting. *I think animals can be a great comfort to wee lassies who have suffered significant losses,* Fingal had told her mother. He was right. She had to admit, the pure, unrestrained affection Bodie showed her was like a balm to her very soul. She didn't know how it was possible to need something so desperately and yet not realize it until it was in her arms but she had needed this warm, affectionate beast more than her next breath.

Fingal had done this. She remembered her ugly words when he had first arrived at Brathanead. *I hate the very sight of ye. I cannot begin to imagine what kind of hell being married to ye would be.* Hell? He started their marriage reinforcing her position as Lady MacLennan through heritage by insisting that the clan declare fealty to them both, not simply to him. He showed her nothing but respect and kindness. He had worked tirelessly for the last weeks, trying to find ways to fix problems that had been developing within her clan over years, not merely since Malcolm died. He would have forsworn his mother's estate if Gillian had asked. By all that's holy he had been injured chasing off her clan's enemies and had saved her life last night. Now he had given her the one thing on earth that she wanted, nay *needed,* more than anything else.

And yet, the only thing she had given him was a promise to try not to hate him.

Jeanne was right; she needed to thaw her heart. He had treated her so gently in the night. He had called her "love" and his "precious lass", and yet when she offered to be his wife in every way, he had believed it was only the vulnerability she felt that led her to it. What must he think of her to believe she wasn't sincere?

Bodie's ears perked a moment before she heard the sound of the chamber door opening. Fingal stepped in quietly. She sat up and pulled Bodie onto her lap. "Nay, lass, stay resting. I didn't mean to wake ye. I heard ye still weren't feeling well and I just wanted to check on ye."

"Ye didn't wake me. I'm fine."

Fingal crossed the room and sat on the bed beside her. "Does yer head still ache?"

"Ever so slightly, but it is much better."

"I'm glad to hear that. I was worried."

"I almost never get headaches. I'm sure it was just from the smoke last night."

"Aye, probably."

His expression held nothing but genuine concern for her and once again she was struck by how kind and considerate he was to her, even in the face of her obstinacy. She also allowed herself to enjoy how very handsome he was. She reached out to caress the strong line of his jaw, the shadow of his beard coarse against her fingers.

Before she knew what she was doing she leaned in and kissed him. It wasn't a long kiss, but she poured her heart into it. When she pulled away he looked befuddled by her boldness. Perhaps this is what she looked like to him when he kissed her, and all conscious thought fled. She felt a little surge of feminine power and grinned. Apparently two could play this game.

"Thank ye, Fingal."

He continued to look confused. "For what?"

She laughed. "Do I need to list everything? For being so very considerate of me, for working so hard to care for this clan, for saving my life, but most of all for this wee beast." She scratched behind Bodie's ears.

"I'm glad ye like him."

"I adore him." She leaned forward and kissed her husband again. Before he recovered from his surprise she climbed off the bed and smiled sweetly. "It is probably time for the evening meal. Shall we go down?"

Chapter 16

Gillian decided she would proceed cautiously. The Easter Triduum was upon them so she focused on the reverent holy days. Besides, she had been so rigid and unyielding that she wanted him to know it was not vulnerability she felt, but rather rising affection. After the feast of Easter, she put her whole heart into convincing Fingal of this. Although she wasn't quite sure how to do this, over the next few days she tried the same things on him which had left her feeling so unbalanced. She focused her attention on him, touched him casually, inclined her head and spoke softly to him during meals—forcing him to lean close and listen. Although initially her changed attitude seemed to confuse him, he recovered quickly and restarted his own efforts to charm her in return.

She was stunned to realize they were actively wooing each other. For several days the friendly banter and casual show of affection continued, culminating each evening in a chaste good-night kiss before they slept. Each morning they woke in each other's arms but started their day as they had for weeks now, with nothing more than a friendly "Good morning."

Initially Gillian found this more than pleasant. She began to welcome the fluttering in her stomach that these interactions stirred. However, after a few days, the fluttering became more of a gnawing need. She wanted more from him; she *needed* something more, but didn't quite know what it was. Their bedchamber had finally been completely put to rights and they were going to sleep in it again that night. In a way it was a new beginning, so she promised herself she would become his wife in every way.

She wasn't quite sure what she should do. The whole clan thought they were fully married well over a month ago. She had even suggested to her mother that she might already be carrying a child so she couldn't very well ask her. Well, Jeanne had guessed the truth but she had also already told Gillian: *It is the simplest thing in the world; just let it happen.*

When they retired to their chamber that evening, Fingal started to remove his belt and plaid as he usually did. Bodie had already curled up to sleep by the hearth as had become his habit.

Gillian unfastened her brooch and belt, removing her plaid. "Do ye mind if we don't play chess tonight?"

"Nay, of course not. I am a bit tired myself."

She pulled the kertch from her head, releasing the thick silky mass of hair over her shoulders. "Fingal, could ye help me a moment. I am having trouble untying the ribbons of my *léine*." She turned her back and lifted her hair out of the way.

"Certainly, my love." She felt his long warm fingers on the back of her neck as he worked to untie the fastenings. "There ye are."

Before he removed his hands from her, she turned and slipped her arms around his neck. "Thank ye," she whispered. Heat smoldered in his eyes. She gave him a quick kiss. With her hands still around his neck she grinned slyly. "I'll untie yers for ye."

He grinned back. "Will ye now?" He stroked her back gently as she released the laces of his *léine*. When she was finished he leaned down and kissed her. His kiss was slower and deeper than hers had been. She opened her mouth to him and he explored it greedily. She was breathless by the time he broke the kiss. "Thank ye," he whispered, just as she had.

She looked into his beautiful green eyes and was lost. "Fingal, I..."

"Gillian, I won't push ye. I made ye a promise. I said I would wait until ye were ready—until ye asked me to be yer husband."

Dear God, Gillian wanted this kind, beautiful man to love her. "I know ye did, and now I'm ready. I'm asking. Fingal, please, make me yer wife."

~ * ~

Fingal knew exactly when it had happened. He knew the moment the tide had turned. It was the evening she had kissed him, thanking him for giving Bodie to her. At that moment she shifted from prey to predator and after he recovered from the shock, it had delighted him. The interplay between them had become increasingly sensual as the days passed and yet every evening, she kissed him chastely and went to sleep beside him. It was becoming almost more than he could bear and he ached with need for her.

Still, he had made her a promise and he would not push her.

When she asked him to untie her *léine* he thought it might kill him. The idea of touching her, helping her undress and then turning his back and going to sleep was agonizing. Now she stood with her arms wrapped around him, asking him to make love to her. "Oh, Gillian, lass, I want nothing more."

He covered her lips with his own, kissing her deeply. She returned his kiss, hesitantly at first but responding more ardently at his coaxing. He pushed the *léine* off her shoulders, letting it fall to the floor. He inched her shift up as he kissed her, breaking the kiss to pull it over her head. He dropped the garment and captured her gaze. She stood before him, her tall willowy frame cloaked only in her silky brown hair, and he soaked in her beauty. She blushed under his gaze and looked away but he cupped her cheek, turning her face back to look at him. "Gillian, ye are magnificent and ye take my breath away." He kissed her again. She gave a little squeak of surprise and giggled when he lifted her in his arms and carried her to the bed. He pulled his own *léine* off, eliciting a shy smile from his beautiful bride, before joining her on the bed.

Gillian was tall for a woman and Fingal thought she had the longest, most beautiful legs he had ever seen. He leaned in to kiss her again, allowing his hands to travel down her body, feeling her slim taut waist and the firm muscles of her thighs. On the upward journey he caressed her soft round breasts, her nipples hardening under his touch. She arched against him and the soft moan that escaped her lips told him she enjoyed his caresses.

Emboldened, Gillian began her own exploration of his body. Her hands, as long and slender as the rest of her, roamed over his chest and shoulders. Although tentative and feather-light at first, her touch enflamed his passion. She slipped her hands down his sides and across his belly, brushing the crisp hair that led to his groin. He moaned and grabbed her hands. "Ah, Gillian, my love, I can't bear it."

She stilled. "I-I-I'm sorry, Fingal. I didn't mean to..." She looked embarrassed.

He pulled her hands to his lips and kissed them. "Nay, sweetling, ye have done nothing wrong. It is only—I have desired ye for so long and yer touch is heavenly, too wonderful. I need to go slowly for ye tonight, love." With her hands in his, he captured her lips again, before trailing kisses down the slender column of her throat. With aching slowness, he eventually reached his goal, her full creamy breasts. He enclosed one pert nipple in his mouth and suckled, gently teasing with his tongue. He released her hands, cupping the other breast, massaging it lightly before sliding his hand over her silky belly to the dark curls at the apex of her legs. She stiffened at his intimate touch.

He moved his mouth back to her lips and kissed her, hoping to calm her, but she remained still and tense. "Gillian, my beautiful lass, tell me what troubles ye?"

"N-n-nothing."

He raised up on an elbow and searched her face. "Yer beautiful, responsive body tells me otherwise. Please, lass."

"I—well I-I'm a little bit afraid." Her voice trailed to almost a whisper.

"What are ye afraid of?"

"I guess...well...that is, my mother said, well...that it hurts."

"Has anything I've done hurt ye so far?"

"Nay. But we haven't—we haven't..."

"Nay, we haven't. And sometimes, the first time for a lass can hurt a bit. But if we take our time, ye relax and trust me, ye will hardly notice it." He began kissing and nuzzling her neck.

She giggled and squirmed. "That tickles."

"Mmm. I know a few other things that tickle too." Once again he began his sensual assault, kissing and caressing her body. His hands drifting ever lower until he delicately brushed against her womanly curls. She didn't tense this time so he continued to lightly stroke her. When she arched against his hand, he began circling the sensitive spot just inside with his thumb, pleased when she writhed against his touch. As her pleasure built, he slipped a finger inside. She appeared lost in sensation. He slowed his movements for a moment, watching her.

She arched against his hand. "Fingal...what...ah, Fingal, please..."

"Sweet Gillian, ye are so very beautiful." He rained kisses over her neck and breasts and continued to stroke her most private spot as he positioned himself over her.

When she panted, arching her head back and beginning to tremble with her release, he slid into her with one firm thrust. He felt her muscles continue to contract, even as she gave a small cry. As much as he craved his own release, he held very still within her, watching as the tremors of her climax swept through her.

~ * ~

Gillian had never felt anything like that in her life. It was exquisite and overwhelming. As he started to caress her she enjoyed his touch. But at some point, those pleasant sensations became a burning need. Fire licked through her veins. Somehow she knew she had to move to quench it, but moving only seemed to fan the flames. Just when she thought she would surely be consumed it was as if something burst inside her and sent waves of pure pleasure through her body. At that moment, at the peak of her release, Fingal entered her. She cried out, but it wasn't from pain. Aye, there was some discomfort, but it became so melded with the waves of bliss coursing through her she didn't care.

She became aware of him kissing her and she had a burning need to kiss him back. She took his face in her hands and pulled him to her lips. She kissed him with abandon, threading her fingers through his dark hair and holding him to her. She felt the need to move again and did.

Fingal groaned, "Lass, I don't want to hurt ye."

"Ye aren't hurting me. I need—I need—oh Fingal, I don't know what I need but lying still isn't it."

He groaned again but began to move very slowly. As he moved, she felt the heat growing in her belly once more. She moved with him, rising to meet him, pushing him to move faster. As the fire coursing through her reached fever pitch she trembled as her body was awash with ecstasy yet again.

She was vaguely aware that Fingal too cried out and she felt the warm rush of his seed within her. "Dear God, Gillian..." His voice trailed off. He panted and lowered his forehead to hers. "I'm sorry. I tried to hold back. Ye are just so...please tell me I didn't hurt ye too badly."

Gillian too panted. "Hurt me? Nay Fingal, but that wasn't at all what I expected."

Fingal laughed and moved to lie beside her, pulling her close to him. "What did ye expect then?"

"Well...I guess..." She looked up at him with a contented smile. "Honestly, I don't know—but not that. That was...wonderful."

He fixed his warm green eyes on her and brushed the hair from her face. "Ah well, my bonny bride, I aim to please."

Under the heat of his gaze, she became self-conscious until she blushed and looked away. "And what about me, did I—did I—

please ye?"

He put a finger under her chin, lifting it until he was looking into her eyes. "Aye, Gillian, my love. Ye please me more than ye can know. Never doubt that." He kissed her. "Now the thing that would please me is for ye to sleep here in my arms, instead of curling up on the opposite side of the bed."

"Aye, I think I'd like that too." She snuggled close to him, filled with a more profound sense of warmth and belonging than she ever thought possible.

Chapter 17

Fingal woke the next morning blanketed by Gillian. Her head rested on his chest, her silky hair spread over them both. Her long slender legs were entwined with his, one thigh nestled snuggly against his groin. He chuckled, remembering the first morning they had awoken together, when thinking he was asleep she tried unsuccessfully to extricate herself. She opened her eyes at the sound. Still half asleep, she looked so young and untroubled this morning. He needed to see her like this more often. "Good morning, my love."

She smiled a drowsy smile. "Good morning."

He brushed the hair from her face, cupped her cheek, and gave her a deep, languorous kiss. She stretched her long lithe body like a cat, wrapped her arms around his neck, and kissed him back. When he broke the kiss, she sighed heavily and nuzzled her face against his chest, closing her eyes again. Aye she was even more beautiful when worry lines didn't mar her face. Fingal only had a moment to admire her however, because as she woke more fully she stiffened suddenly, bumping her head into his chin. "Dear God, the day is already bright and we are still abed. What will people think?"

Fingal laughed. "Don't worry so, love. It isn't that late and ye have been working yerself ragged. Everyone will think ye needed a bit of extra rest." He gently rubbed her back. When she relaxed into his embrace he winked at her. "Either that or ye decided to stay locked away for the day to do wicked things with yer husband." He rolled her onto her back and knelt over her.

She blushed hotly and slapped playfully at his chest. "We can't do that."

He wiggled his eyebrows. "Aye, lass, we could if we wanted to. After all, I am the laird. Who is there to say me nay?"

She chuckled. "Fingal! Stop teasing." He buried his face in her neck, nibbling and kissing until her laughter turned to purrs of pleasure. She smiled at him when he pulled away. "We can't stay abed any longer. There is too much to do."

Even as she said the words, he heard the longing in her voice. But as much as he would like to stay closeted away with her today, he knew she might be sorry later. "Aye, my precious lass, ye are right, there is work to be done. However, I promise ye, someday we will stay locked away and spend a day, maybe a week, in each other's arms. Someday soon." He kissed her again.

"Someday soon," she echoed when he broke the kiss. Then she popped out of bed. "But not today." She dressed quickly and as much as he would have liked to simply watch her, he too rose and dressed. Once dressed, she dug through the contents of a chest, clearly having trouble finding something.

"What are ye looking for?"

"I had a small packet of herbs that Rhiannon gave me the day after the wedding."

"What do ye need them for?"

She sat back on her heel to look up at him. "She says it is a marvelous tonic to help with all manner of things." She gave him a saucy grin. "It is apparently especially good at helping one conceive fine strong sons."

Fingal laughed and pulled her to her feet, kissing her again. "I'd like that very much."

~ * ~

As Fingal began another day of exhausting physical labor it was with renewed purpose. In spite of his misgivings about the marriage forced on him over a month ago he was happier than he ever imagined possible. He also was beginning to see the fruits of all the clan's hard work. There had been no more raids on their land. The weakest portions of the wall had been torn down and rebuilt. Only minor repairs were left. He had already received word from Niall. Rowan MacKenzie's wedding was to be held several days after Roodmas. If everything continued to go well, he and Gillian would attend the wedding and return afterward with Turcuil and several other men. Then the real work of training his men could begin. He had also received word from Laird MacBain, telling him Bran and his family would also come to Brathanead in a few weeks.

That afternoon during the midday meal a messenger arrived from Laird MacKay. Fingal's brow furrowed as he read it.

"What is the matter? Is he opposed to sending his nephew to us?" Gillian asked.

"Not exactly. He is just cautious. He is concerned about the stability of clan MacLennan and therefore the safety of his nephew. He doesn't wish to send Dougal to me to train as a squire just yet."

Eadoin too looked troubled by that news.

Gillian looked confused. "I don't understand why ye both seem so upset. Can ye not seek a squire from another clan? Doesn't Laird Sutherland have several young sons?"

Fingal clarified, "It isn't just that I need a squire. I do, and one of Laird Sutherland's sons would also be a good choice. What worries me is exactly what worried King David in the first place. Other clans see us as weak and vulnerable."

"But we aren't. Not really. We are rebuilding and much stronger than we were before ye arrived."

"Aye, we are, sweetling, but while things are getting better, we have quite a way to go yet. The fact that other clans see us as potentially weak is a problem."

Eadoin nodded and spoke softly, "It means that anyone who might want to attack is likely to try. Even if we were as strong as ever the fact that others think we aren't makes us a target. That is probably what emboldened the Grants."

"We need other clans to see not only are we strong, but that we have strong allies so they will think twice about attacking," Diarmad added.

"What can we do?"

Fingal hated the concern he saw reflected now in Gillian's expression. "We are doing much of what we need to do. Bran MacBain will be here in a few weeks and several of Niall's men will come after Roodmas. I have never prayed for bitter weather, but as long as April stays blustery and cold it may afford us some protection. After that we will have the clear support of Clan MacIan, MacBain, and perhaps even Clan MacKenzie."

"And ye don't think that is enough?"

"It is a start. But honestly, if Laird MacKay will send his nephew here, other clan leaders will see that as a good sign."

"How can we convince him?"

"Dougal's father is Laird MacKay's brother. Perhaps if we invite Tasgall and his wife for a visit at midsummer, they can see for themselves that we have both rebuilt our clan and reestablished strong allies."

"Aye, Laird," agreed Diarmad, "The MacKay's are well connected in the northern Highlands. If they believe it is safe for Dougal to train here, that will go a long way to convincing other clans that the MacLennans are strong and stable."

"But what if they won't come?"

Although generally seated at the laird's table, the normally quiet Father Stephen rarely joined in the table conversation. However this afternoon he cleared his throat, before saying, "My Lady, I may be able to help there. Lady MacKay is my cousin, more like a sister really. We grew up together. I will send her a letter and assure her that things are well here."

Fingal was dumbfounded. "Father Stephen, if ye are a cousin to Lady Mackay, that makes ye either a MacDonnell or a MacNicol."

"A MacNicol, aye. Bhaltair MacNicol was my father, God rest his soul. I am Laird MacNicol's cousin too."

"That surprises me," Fingal said.

"That I'm a MacNicol?" Father Stephen asked.

"Nay, that ye are Bhaltair MacNicol's son and yet ye became a priest. He had a fearsome reputation."

Father Stephen gave a rare laugh. "I'm sure my father wanted me to be a warrior, but I was hopeless. Still he mellowed a bit in his later years. As he grew older, it became clear that he loved my mother and would deny her nothing. She knew I was never meant to be a warrior. Eventually he saw the wisdom in letting me study and pursue the priesthood. Still, I am not uneducated in what is required to keep a clan safe and whole. Ye are accomplishing that here. I wouldn't ask for Laird MacKay's support if I felt otherwise."

"Thank ye, Father. I appreciate hearing that."

Fingal knew Father Stephen's letter might go a long way toward helping convince Tasgall MacKay and his wife to come for a visit but he still worried.

As if the news from Laird MacKay wasn't enough, Lana finally cornered him immediately after the meal to raise the issue of a betrothal for Fallon. "Laird, I have wanted to talk to ye about something for days and haven't had the opportunity."

"Lana, this isn't a good time."

"It never seems to be a good time for ye," she snapped, "but this is important and it cannot wait any longer."

Fingal had trouble not showing his frustration. "What is more important than seeing to our clan's defenses?" Fingal hoped his question would shame her into silence for a bit longer, but that hope was in vain.

"A betrothal for Fallon."

"Ye can't be serious."

"Of course I'm serious. She will be eighteen in a few weeks. This can wait no longer."

Just as he had promised Gillian he would, Fingal replied, "Lana, with all of the recent changes, I think it's better to wait a few months before discussing this."

"That isn't acceptable, and there is really nothing to discuss anyway. I know who Fallon should marry and simply need yer blessing. I think yer guardsman Coby would be perfect for her. We can post the banns and have the wedding in a few weeks."

"Coby? Is this a marriage that Fallon wants?"

"What Fallon *wants* is not the issue. She will do as she is told. It is a good match and good for the clan."

Fingal had intended to be more sympathetic for Gillian's sake, but his patience was sorely tested. "Good for the clan? I'm sorry, Lana, I disagree. Even if it were Fallon's fondest wish to marry Coby, I would not agree to it. Not now. We need to do everything we can to rebuild strong ties with other clans. Forging an alliance through marriage is one of the best ways to do that."

"Ye can't mean to use Fallon as a pawn."

"Not immediately, nay. However, when things have truly settled down and Fallon has had time to adjust to all of the recent changes, I will consider a political marriage for her. That is truly in the best interest of the clan."

"But Laird—"

"Lana, ye have my decision. I will hear no more discussion of Fallon marrying Coby or anyone else." Lana was dumbstruck, which pleased Fingal more than it should have. Although he had no intention of forcing Fallon into a marriage that she didn't want, perhaps if Lana believed he would, she would stop pushing the issue.

~ * ~

If the news that arrived at the midday meal was distressing, the discussion with his mother-in-law that followed was more so. However, to Fingal's pleasure and relief, Quinn

MacKenzie arrived with six other MacKenzie warriors and ten Matheson men just before dark.

Fingal met them in the courtyard after the watch announced their approach. "Ye are a welcome sight indeed, Quinn, and so are the men ye brought. Join me in the great hall. The evening meal will be served soon. Afterwards, I will have my steward see to quarters for ye and yer men. Frankly, I'm a little surprised to see ye before yer brother's wedding."

"I'm glad ye asked me to join yer guard, Fingal, but I can't say the same for Da. He's still angry about Niall luring Rowan away, but he realizes that peace is best maintained with a show of strength. I thought it better to leave while he was open to the idea. However, I will need to go to Duncurra for the wedding in a few weeks."

Fingal laughed. "I understand. If possible, Gillian and I will go too."

"I'll warn ye, Da will make certain ye know once the MacLennans are strong and stable. There will be no reason for me to stay any longer."

Fingal's brows drew together as they walked toward the head table. "I had hoped ye'd stay on for good. I need a strong guard."

Quinn laughed. "Ye know that, and I know that, but I haven't quite broken that to Da yet."

Fingal shook his head. "Yer Da may declare war on me himself when he finds out."

"Nay, he won't. He'll bluster over it every time he sees ye for the next decade or so, but he'll come around."

"Has he found ye a bride yet?"

"Thankfully, nay. Right now he is focused on Rowan's wedding to Eara Fraser. It is good that ye're planning to go. Ye may have the opportunity to solidify ties with some of the clans in attendance."

"Aye, that is an opportunity I wouldn't like to miss." As they entered the hall, Fingal spotted Gillian, with Bodie at her heels. "Ah, here is my bride now. Gillian, I would like for ye to meet our newest guardsman, Quinn MacKenzie. Quinn, my wife, Lady Gillian MacLennan."

Gillian smiled. "It is a pleasure to meet ye, sir. We are most grateful that ye have come."

Quinn took her hand, bowing low. "My lady, the pleasure

is mine. Please, call me Quinn." Quinn offered his hand to Bodie to sniff before scratching him behind the ears. "And who is this beastie?"

Gillian grinned and crouched beside the dog to rub him and give him a cuddle. "This is Bodie, although 'Shadow' might have been a better name as he is never farther away from me than that." Standing again she said, "The evening meal is ready. Please join us at the head table.

If Fingal had been worried about Quinn, an outsider, being accepted by the clan, his worries were laid to rest during the meal. Quinn was outgoing and friendly, but had an unassuming manner that naturally drew people to him. Fingal wasn't surprised by the attention paid to Quinn by Brathanead's serving maids. Tall, blond, and muscular, with crystal blue eyes and a charming smile, he was extremely attractive and had always turned the head of any lass in his vicinity. Gillian's sisters practically fell over themselves when they met him. Not even Ailsa, at two and ten, was immune to his charms. She drew his attention and peppered him with questions at every opportunity.

When Fingal and Gillian retired for the night he couldn't help commenting, "Ailsa seems quite taken with Quinn MacKenzie."

Gillian snorted. "Why should she be different than any other skirt-clad person in the room? I've never seen Fallon blush so much. Even Jeanne was smitten. By all that's holy, I think a maid was at his elbow to refill his cup after every swallow."

Fingal laughed until tears ran down his cheeks. "And ye, my lovely bride, were ye not equally captivated?"

"Well, I won't lie, he is a fine looking man. But I am rather partial to dark hair, green eyes, and roguish smile."

He pulled her close. "Are ye now?"

She gave him a saucy grin. "Oh, aye, I am. Do ye suppose he has any brothers like that?"

"Cheeky lass. Nay, he has five brothers and not a single one with green eyes."

"Then I suppose it is a good thing I have ye." She wrapped her arms around his neck and kissed him.

"Aye, a very good thing," he said when she broke the kiss. "Gillian, love, now that ye mention Quinn's brothers, I need to ask ye something. His brother Rowan is one of Niall's guardsmen. He is to be married at Duncurra a few days after Roodmas. We are invited to attend the wedding." She looked pensive. He was worried that a visit to Duncurra would be painful for her. Although it wasn't where her father was killed, it was certainly Malcolm's ill-fated siege of Duncurra that ultimately resulted in her father's death. "It is an opportunity for us to reestablish ties with other clans."

She sighed heavily. "Aye, we should go to the wedding. I'm sure it will be nice for ye to go home for a bit."

"It will be nice to see my family, but Gillian, love, I am home."

~ * ~

Gillian lay in his arms, drowsy and replete after their love-making. She remembered the lie she had told her mother about possibly being with child. Perhaps it wouldn't be too long before it would be true. She would like to have children with Fingal. After the persistent kindness and tolerance he had shown her, she knew he would be a good father. She had been taking Rhiannon's herb tonic. It was supposed to help her conceive fine strong sons and she prayed it would soon.

Bodie padded quietly across the floor and climbed up on the bed, settling himself at her feet. She reached down and scratched his ears. "Are ye cold, lad? Is the fire dying too low for yer tastes?"

His only response was a sigh as he drifted off to sleep.

Perhaps she shouldn't let him stay on the bed. He was large already but perhaps when he was fully grown he would be too big to be on the bed. Still, she didn't care. Held in her husband's warm embrace with her devoted pet warming her feet, she had never been happier.

Chapter 18

In just a few days Quinn MacKenzie had already proven himself an excellent addition to the MacLennan guard as the training of the MacLennan men began in earnest. Once a few more skilled warriors joined them, with any luck by the end of summer the MacLennan warriors would be significantly better prepared to defend the clan.

Now that Lent was over, they needed to replenish their stores of meat. During the evening meal, Fingal discussed plans to send out a hunting party the next day.

Coby said, "Laird, we have had reports of boar sightings by some of the crofters to our east. They are worried about the damage the beasts can cause to newly planted fields. Perhaps that is the prey we should aim for."

"Aye, that is a good plan. One boar can be a farmer's nightmare. Do we have any idea where to start hunting?"

Coby nodded. "We have found fresh signs of a wild boar foraging not far from here, just inside the forest, not too far from my mother's cottage."

Eadoin grinned in anticipation. "If it is feeding that close, it is likely we could bring the beast down within a day, perhaps two. Laird, ye haven't been on a hunt since arriving. Ye should join us on this one."

The idea was tempting. With everything that needed to be taken care of at Brathanead, Fingal had been working himself to exhaustion alongside his new clansmen. The opportunity to escape for a while and go on a hunt was hard to pass up. Still, having just recently won Gillian's trust and affection he wasn't anxious to leave her. "Nay, I should stay and attend to things here."

Gillian cocked her head to one side. "Fingal, there is nothing here that can't wait a few days. Go on the boar hunt. I can tell ye want to."

"Aye, Laird, it'll do ye good. I'd go if I were a few years

younger," Nolan said.

"As would I," added Daniel.

"It has been too long since I went hunting. And ye're right, Gillian, a day or two should not be a problem."

"Then it is decided ye will ride with us in the morning," Eadoin said.

"Ah, but I don't want to risk leaving Brathanead undermanned."

"I don't think ye have anything to fear, Laird. I will stay behind with a sufficient number of men to see to our defenses," Diarmad assured him.

"I will stay behind too," offered Quinn.

Fingal grinned. "Well then, with Brathanead in good hands, I will go."

~ * ~

Rising well before dawn the next morning, Fingal was surprised when Gillian too arose. "Sweetling, go back to sleep, it is still early."

She ignored him and began to dress. "Nay, Fingal, I will join the clan in seeing ye off."

"Seeing me off?"

"Aye, it has always been a tradition here to gather the men and beasts for a blessing just before a boar hunt. Boar hunting is dangerous."

"Well, I suppose it can be a bit more dangerous than hunting other prey but if adequate precautions are taken, there should be no problems."

"Aye, and one of the precautions we take is a blessing."

Fingal chuckled. "When did this tradition start?"

"Years ago, back before my great-grandsire's time. I think one of the laird's sons was killed on a boar hunt. As the story has it, he boasted that he would kill the boar with only his dirk."

"Aye some men think it is more sporting to kill a beast at close range but it is very dangerous to try and kill a boar that way."

"I expect so," Gillian said dryly. "It's probably even more dangerous if ye drink yerself stupid first."

"He was drunk?"

"So the story goes. Still, since then we always gather to bless the hunters."

"I certainly won't stand in the way of tradition then." He

smiled and offered her his hand. "Shall we go?"

When they reached the courtyard a large number of MacLennans had indeed gathered there. Even Donald and Owen, who were not known to be early risers, were in attendance. Added to the many men going on the hunt, there was quite a crowd. When the horses were saddled and the men ready to leave, Father Stephen invoked God and his holy angels to watch over them. The normally soft-spoken priest had to practically shout to be heard over the baying of the hounds.

When they were all properly blessed, Fingal turned to Gillian and kissed her. She wrapped her arms around him and kissed him back, to the delight of the crowd. "Be careful," she whispered.

"I will." He assured her. "I have no intention of either drinking myself stupid or trying to kill the beast with my hands."

She grinned. "Good plan."

He gave her another quick kiss before mounting his chestnut stallion. The horse tossed his head and danced. "Con, lad, are ye excited? Ye want a bit more than just exercise too, don't ye?"

As dawn broke they rode out of Brathanead village, across the small heath, and entered the forest near Rhiannon's cottage before turning south. The hounds ran ahead of the men as the light morning mist swirled around their feet.

They hadn't ridden far before they saw gouged tree trunks and other signs of the boar they sought. The hounds picked up a scent several times but then seemed to lose it. The path eventually took them in a northward arc. They stopped to rest the horses and eat near midday. Hearn took one of his best scent dogs scouting to see if she could pick up a trail. Before long he was back. "Laird, I think Bea has found a strong trail just to our west heading back towards Brathanead. She's mad to follow it. There is a cliff just a little north of where we entered the forest this morning. If we drive the boar that direction, it will be trapped."

"Well then, mount up men and we'll follow her."

Sure enough, once Bea led them to it, the baying hounds found a solid scent trail and they were off. Fingal found charging through the forest on a hunt invigorating. Soon they heard the boar crashing through the forest ahead of them and the men whooped with delight. Now they simply needed to run the boar until the dogs could corner it at the cliff. The terrain was rugged, but Con was strong and sure-footed. Horse and rider were one as they raced through the trees following their prey. The boar was tiring and the dogs would soon have him surrounded.

In hot pursuit, Fingal soared with Con, over a fallen tree, but as Con's front feet hit the forest floor, the saddle gave an almighty lurch. Fingal was thrown to one side, head first. Heavy undergrowth broke his fall, but he still managed to hit his head. Everything went black.

~ * ~

"Laird, Laird, can ye hear me?" Eadoin's voice penetrated Fingal's pounding head. He opened his eyes to see Eadoin kneeling over him. "Laird, oh praise be, ye are awake."

"Eadoin, what happened? God's teeth, the boar!" Fingal struggled to sit.

"Nay Laird, ye took a bad blow to yer head. Ye need to rest a bit. The others have gone ahead to bring down the boar."

"Where is Con? What the hell happened?"

"Laird, it looks like the cinch on yer saddle gave way."

"Is Con all right?"

"Aye, he stumbled a bit and seems to be favoring one leg, but Hearn thinks he will be fine. He is seeing to the beast now."

Fingal struggled to rise again, pushing past Eadoin's objections. "I have to check on him." The man he considered his father, Laird Alastair MacIan, had given him Con when he went off to train with Laird Chisholm. Fingal had learned to be a warrior as Con learned to be a warrior's horse. It was almost as if Con could anticipate his next moves. Fingal made his way to where the big stallion stood. "Hearn, is he hurt?"

"Not seriously, Laird. He will need a few days' rest but he should be fine."

Relieved, Fingal stroked the big steed's neck. "Ye hear that, lad? It takes more than a wee stumble to stop ye, eh?"

"Laird, he's not badly hurt, but I can't rightly say the same for ye. Ye've busted yer head open."

Fingal touched his head and winced. He had a painful knot and bloody gash just above his hairline. His arms and face had been thoroughly scratched by the underbrush. "I'm sure I'm a fine sight, but I'll be all right. I don't know how this happened. The cinch on my saddle was a bit worn, but not thin enough to break."

Hearn walked over to the damaged saddle and frowned as

he examined the cinch.

Eadoin asked, "Is something wrong Hearn?"

Hearn seemed startled. "What? Oh, nay, nothing is wrong. Just a broken cinch, as I said. Ye were lucky, Laird."

Hearn looked directly at Fingal before glancing at Eadoin briefly. "Very lucky." Clearly something was amiss and Hearn didn't want to speak in front of Eadoin.

"Aye. I'm just thankful Con is not badly injured." Fingal needed to be alone with Hearn. He turned to Eadoin. "Perhaps I should take yer horse and catch up with the rest of the men. I'll tell them what has happened."

"Certainly, Laird." Eadoin led his mount from where he had been tied.

Fingal started to mount the horse, feigned dizziness, and stepped back down.

"Are ye all right, Laird?" Eadoin asked, taking the horse's reins.

"Nay, I'm a bit light headed. On second thought, perhaps ye should go. I'll stay here with Hearn and see if I can shake this dizziness."

"Are ye sure, Laird? Ye may need me. They will come back soon enough."

"Aye, I'm sure I'll be fine. It is as ye said, I need to rest a bit." Fingal lowered himself to the ground, leaning back against a tree, closing his eyes.

"If ye're sure. I won't be long." Eadoin mounted his horse and rode away.

After a few minutes he opened his eyes. "Now, Hearn, what's wrong."

"Come look at this, Laird." He picked up the cinch. "Ye see here? The strap broke where the leather is worn."

"Aye, but that is what ye said, isn't it? The strap gave way under wear?"

"Aye, but look at the split leather. The front edge of the strap, where the wear is greatest, is darkened with age. If it gave way purely because of wear, I would expect the last bit of it to look torn. But see here, along the back side of the strap? It isn't torn. It looks as if it has been cut."

Fingal couldn't believe what he was hearing. "What are ye saying? Ye think someone damaged my saddle on purpose?"

"Aye Laird, I think so. They cut into the cinch just behind

the spot where it was most worn. The thing is, Laird, I saddled Con for ye myself. I checked his tack and it was fine. It hadn't been damaged then. Someone did this after he was saddled. Being on the back side of the strap, ye wouldn't have noticed the cut. Whoever did this weakened it enough to ensure it would break during the hunt while ye were riding hard or jumping."

Fingal looked closely at the broken strap and the evidence seemed conclusive. "Hearn, why didn't ye want to mention this in front of Eadoin? Do ye have some reason to suspect that he was involved?"

"Nay, Laird. I believe Eadoin is a good man. But this was a foul deed. If I'm right, someone was aiming to kill or injure ye. I wouldn't have imagined any MacLennan capable of it. Still, I thought it better to let ye and ye alone know my suspicions first."

"It must be one of the men with us."

"I don't know. It could have as easily been done before we left Brathanead. There were a lot of people gathered for the blessing. Someone could have gotten to Con then."

"Aye, I suppose they could have." This was hard for Fingal to believe. He knew a few of the MacLennans still resented his becoming laird. However, things were going well, they were becoming a stronger and more secure clan. "Hearn, don't mention this to anyone. If someone means me harm, I don't want to tip them off just yet."

"I won't, Laird, but have ye considered that it might not just be ye they mean to harm?"

"What makes ye say that?"

"The fire in yer chamber a few weeks ago. Ye said ye were sure ye banked it properly."

"Aye, I did."

"If ye hadn't wakened in time, both ye and Lady Gillian would have perished."

Fingal hadn't wanted to believe the fire was anything other than misfortune. In light of the damage to his saddle that caused this accident, he knew Hearn was right. Gillian would have been killed too. But even if some still hated him, how could someone wish to hurt her? It didn't make sense. "Hearn, the king's edict was not unanimously welcomed by the MacLennans. In spite of their pledges of fealty, there might still be some who would wish me dead. But Gillian is loved. I can't imagine that anyone wishes to kill her."

"I can't either, but the facts are the facts and ye need to face them in order to protect her."

Dear God, could she be in danger? "I can't understand why anyone would wish to harm her, but ye're right. I can't risk her life. I promise, I will find out who is at the bottom of this and I will protect her, Hearn."

Chapter 19

The hunt was successful. The hunting party returned to Brathanead with a huge boar. Gillian went to greet the returning huntsman with Bodie at her side. She was as elated as the rest of the clan until she saw her husband. If the huge knot and gash on his forehead were not enough, his face was streaked with dried blood and his left eye was blackening. She rushed to him and put her arms around him. "By the saints, Fingal, what happened to ye? I thought ye said ye wouldn't tackle the beast bare handed."

Fingal returned the hug and gave her a quick kiss. "Are ye referring to this wee thump? Aye, well, I can't rightly blame the beast for this. 'Twas but an accident. The cinch on my saddle gave way. Luckily I landed on my hard head or I might have been seriously injured."

The men around them chuckled at his jest but Gillian was worried. "Fingal, don't tease. This *is* a serious injury. Eadoin, please send for Agnes."

Fingal caressed her cheek. "Really, Gillian, it will be fine. But I wouldn't say nay to a bath."

"I'll arrange for a bath for ye *after* Agnes has seen to yer injury."

Fingal did not protest when she led him to their chamber, Bodie on their heels. When they entered, Bodie settled into his spot by the hearth while she gathered what she needed to clean the gash. "Fingal, tell me what happened."

"It is just as I said, Con and I had jumped a fallen tree and the cinch on my saddle broke. I guess it was more worn than I thought."

Something in his tone of voice concerned Gillian but before she could ask him anything else, Agnes arrived.

"Och, Laird." She gave a wheezing cough. "The gash isn't too bad. I'll put a few stitches in it for good measure." She coughed again.

Gillian had been so worried about Fingal she hadn't noticed that Agnes herself appeared pale and drawn. "Agnes, ye don't look well yerself."

"Ah, Gillian lass, I feel a bit of a catarrh coming on. 'Tis nothing to worry about." She coughed again before prodding the wound on Fingal's head. "Laird, the size of that knot makes it look like ye rattled yer skull but good. Are ye dizzy at all? Can ye see clearly? Did ye lose consciousness when it happened?"

"I'm fine, Agnes. Ye need to look after yerself. I think this bump looks much worse than it is."

"I'll be the judge of that. Answer my questions."

Fingal chuckled at her authoritarian manner. "I am not dizzy and I can see fine. I did black out for a moment when it happened but I've been fine since then."

She coughed again before accusing, "Eadoin said ye were dizzy for a while afterward."

Fingal looked slightly sheepish. "Ah...well, aye. I suppose I was for a few minutes but I'm fine now."

Agnes frowned. "Laird, ye mustn't make light of this. A blow to the head is a fickle thing. Sometimes a man can take a blow so hard he lapses into a sleep so deep ye'd believe he'd never come out of it. Then in a few days, he wakes up right as nails with no permanent damage. Yet another man takes a hit that doesn't even knock him out. He seems fine but days—maybe even weeks—later, he starts complaining of dizziness, confusion or a headache. Then he falls into a sleep from which he never wakes."

"I'm sorry Agnes. I know head wounds can be unpredictable. But the damage is done."

"Aye, but if ye take things slow for the next few days and don't overwork yerself, it likely won't cause ye any trouble. It's folks that ignore an injury like this and don't give themselves time to heal that have more problems." She was caught by a spasm of coughing.

"Says the woman who should be tucked up in her own bed taking care of herself."

"Don't try to turn the tables on me, lad. Do as I tell ye."

"Agnes, I can't stay in my bed for the next few days just because of a wee bump."

Gillian put her hands on her hips and scowled. "Ye can if she says ye must."

Agnes chuckled. "Laird, ye needn't stay in bed any more'n

I do. Just take things a bit easy. Don't do any heavy lifting or over strenuous work."

"I will on one condition—ye do the same."

She scowled, but after another coughing spasm agreed before stitching his wound. The servants arrived with the tub and water as she worked. "Normally I would have given ye something for the pain, but with a head injury, it is better if I don't."

"Don't worry. If the potion ye brew for pain is anything like Katherine's, I'd rather take the pain."

Agnes grinned. "Aye, Katherine MacIan is a smart lass and we use a similar recipe. Find it a tad bitter, do ye?"

"More than just a tad." As he said that an odd expression crossed his face.

"Is something wrong, Fingal?"

He smiled at Gillian. "Nay, love. It just smarts a bit."

Agnes finished the last stich and left with another stern warning for him to rest.

When they were alone, he started to undress. "Here, let me help ye."

He laughed. "Sweetling, undressing is hardly heavy labor."

She pouted coyly. "But I like helping ye undress."

"Well then, I certainly wouldn't want ye to feel deprived."

She giggled and helped him remove the rest of his clothes. He climbed into the tub, groaning as he sank into the warm water. She took a cloth and gently washed the dried blood from his hair and face before moving onto the rest of his body. "Ye are covered with scratches. Did ye land in a thorn bush?"

"Not a thorn bush, but aye, some fairly heavy underbrush. That was lucky really as it broke my fall. I might have broken something useful—like my neck."

She knew he was trying to underplay what had happened, but she realized that he could have been killed and she sent up a quick prayer of thanksgiving that he hadn't been more seriously injured.

She soaped her hands, massaging his arms and shoulders as she bathed him. He closed his eyes, relaxing.

"Do ye like this?"

"Aye, love, I do."

She slipped her hands lower, washing his belly. Her fingers brushed the long red scar on his side. "How did ye come by this scar?"

His brow furrowed and then he winced and touched the lump on his head. "I must remember not to frown for a few days."

She kissed his forehead lightly. "Ailsa says kisses make hurts better."

He cupped her head in his hand and pulled her lips to his, giving her a soft kiss. Letting her go he said, "I think Ailsa is right."

"They also seem to make a man forgetful," she teased. "I asked about yer battle scar."

"It was nothing, really. It looks much worse than it was and I can't even claim it as a battle scar. It happened on the training field well over a year ago now. It was simply an accident."

"I'm not sure whether ye are very lucky or simply accident prone."

"Why do ye say that?"

"Well, just in the short time ye've been here, a stone from the wall nearly fell on ye. We've had a fire. Ye barely missed getting an arrow shot through yer heart and yer cinch broke while ye were hunting today."

He said, "I would prefer to think of it as lucky," but again his tone concerned her.

She sat back on her heels. "Something is amiss."

"Nay, love. Why would ye say that?"

"Please don't lie to me, Fingal. I can tell. When ye told me the cinch must have been more worn than ye thought, it was as if ye didn't believe that. And just now, ye said ye would prefer to think of it as luck, yet it seems ye think something else."

Fingal sighed. "I'll finish bathing and then tell ye what concerns me."

~ * ~

Gillian was too perceptive by far. He had hoped not to worry her with his concerns but he now realized he couldn't keep it from her and maybe it wasn't even in her best interest to do so. He had more reason than ever to believe that the fire was not an accident. As soon as Agnes had mentioned not giving him anything for pain, he remembered the God awful tasting brew that Katherine had given him when he had been injured the previous year.

The morning after the fire, he had tasted the drops of wine that remained in the decanter. There was a bitter aftertaste that he couldn't place at the time. Now he knew what it was. The wine had been laced with the ingredient in that pain draft. Dear God, if they had both consumed enough of it, he would not have awakened in time to put out the fire. They would have been killed. Hearn was right.

Gillian didn't push him for details until he was out of the bath and dressed. When the servants arrived to remove the tub he said, "I haven't had a chance to get report from Diarmad today. Would ye send up the evening meal and ask him and Quinn Mackenzie to dine with us here?"

The servants agreed and left. Gillian looked irritated. "I thought ye were going to tell me what has ye worried, not discuss the events at Brathanead today."

"Gillian, I am concerned about several things and I would like them to hear as well."

"If it is that serious, perhaps we should include Eadoin and maybe the elders?"

He took her hand and kissed the back of it. "Nay, lass. I would like to just talk with ye, Diarmad, and Quinn for the moment."

"But why not Eadoin at least?"

"I know this is hard to believe, but I don't think my cinch breaking was an accident. In fact, I know it wasn't."

"And ye think Eadoin is involved?" She looked outraged.

"Nay, love, I don't. However, I just want to be cautious for now."

"So, no MacLennans. Perhaps I should leave?"

"Gillian, please. Let me just explain things to the three of ye and we will decide what to do then."

"Eadoin is one of my oldest friends. I would trust him with my life. Until very recently I would have trusted him more than I would *Eithne MacIan's son.*"

Her words hurt more than he wanted to admit. He thought she had let go of her anger. He sighed. "I know ye would, Gillian."

She must have read the hurt in his expression because she immediately became contrite. "Fingal, I'm sorry. I don't know why I said that. I love ye and I trust ye. I just—I just..."

"It's all right, sweetling, I understand." He kissed her hand again. "Really, I do." How could he explain it to her? "Gillian, ye aren't going to want to hear what I have to tell ye and neither will Eadoin. The fact is someone partially cut the cinch on my saddle.

They did it after Hearn saddled Con this morning."

"Nay, Fingal. Surely ye don't believe that. Cinches wear down. Have Hearn look at it. He'll tell ye it was just misfortune."

"Gillian, love, 'twas Hearn who found the damage. It wasn't misfortune. The person who did it sliced into the leather behind a worn spot. The damage weakened the cinch enough to cause it to give way under stress. I suspect they intended it to look like an accident."

"But ye could have been killed. Surely ye don't think...nay, Fingal, ye can't think that. Everyone swore their fealty to ye. This is a mistake."

"I pray God it is. But can ye understand why I want to talk with the people I trust the most first?"

"And ye don't trust the MacLennans." The resignation in her voice pulled at his heart.

"I trust ye, and ye are a MacLennan."

They were interrupted by a knock at the door. Quinn and Diarmad arrived along with several servants carrying trays of food and two extra chairs.

"Laird, are ye sure ye're up to this tonight? I can give ye report tomorrow," offered Diarmad.

"I'm fine Diarmad, and I am anxious to hear about progress on the wall."

Diarmad frowned but said, "As ye wish."

They engaged in casual conversation until the meal had been served and the servants were dismissed. Then Diarmad said, "I am fairly certain ye don't wish to talk about the wall. What has happened?"

As quickly as he could he told them about what Hearn had discovered.

"Cut?" Diarmad asked. "Ye are certain?"

"Aye, there is no question."

Quinn glanced cautiously at Gillian before asking, "Do ye trust this man, Hearn?"

Gillian's eyes had been downcast until this and she looked up sharply, waiting for his response. "Aye, I do," Fingal answered firmly.

Diarmad nodded. "I agree. He seems to be a very good man, Laird. Father Colm often says that children and dogs are the best judges of character. Clearly the hounds trust and obey him, but ye can't be too careful. Does something else bolster yer confidence?"

Fingal took Gillian's hand in his and gave it a squeeze. "Hearn is singularly concerned about Gillian and her sisters' welfare. Both Hearn and I believe whoever is behind this may be willing to take Gillian's life too."

Gillian recoiled, yanking her had from his. "Fingal, I can't believe someone is trying to kill ye and now ye are suggesting that they might try to kill me too? That is preposterous. Why would ye or Hearn, for that matter, think that?"

Quinn too seemed shocked. "That does seem a bit of a leap. After all, cutting the cinch to yer saddle would be unlikely to cause Lady Gillian any harm."

However, a look of stunning realization crossed Diarmad's face. "The fire," was all he said.

"Aye, the fire," agreed Fingal.

"What fire?" Quinn asked.

Fingal filled him in on the story.

Gillian shook her head in confusion. "But Fingal, ye said yerself it was an accident—a log rolled from the hearth."

"At the time I couldn't imagine that it was anything other than an accident. But I know I banked the fire before coming to bed. I also know the pitcher was nearly full, but when I grabbed it to throw water on the burning log, it was empty."

"Ye didn't tell me that."

"Nay, I didn't want to worry ye."

"Maybe ye were mistaken about the water."

"I'm sure I wasn't and the rush mat was wet. I still don't understand why someone would do that. The room might have been ablaze before I woke otherwise. The smoke from the rushes was bad enough. Still, even if I am mistaken, what concerns me the most is the wine ye drank. Do ye remember? I had only taken one sip before ye knocked my goblet over."

She blushed. "Aye, I remember."

"I said it didn't taste very good and didn't drink any more but ye had had a full goblet. Do ye remember thinking it had gone to yer head a bit? Ye fell asleep as soon as ye hit the bed."

"Aye, but I usually water my wine."

"Ye said that at the time, but ye don't always water yer wine and it hasn't happened since. However, there is something else which I only realized tonight. The next morning when I went to check the damage, I tasted the tiny bit of wine that remained in the decanter. I noticed the bitterness again."

"But I told ye we couldn't afford good quality wine."

"I know ye did. Ye also said sometimes herbs were added to improve the flavor. I thought perhaps that is what I tasted. The flavor seemed familiar to me, but I couldn't place it, at least not until Agnes mentioned pain potions earlier and I remembered the one Katherine had given me when I was injured last year."

Diarmad chuckled. "Ye complained like young Tomas over the way that tasted."

Fingal smiled. "It's bitter swill. But, Gillian, it is what I tasted in the wine."

Gillian was aghast. "Ye think someone drugged it?"

"I'm sure of it."

"But why?"

"I suspect it was to make certain we slept soundly while they slipped into our room and pulled a log from the fire."

"But ye said ye didn't drink the wine," observed Quinn.

"I didn't, not more than a mouthful anyway."

"That hardly seems like enough to knock ye out. Ye were never a heavy sleeper and the hinges on yer chamber door are far from silent. I remember as a lad the noise of a mouse in the rushes could wake ye and have ye reaching for a weapon."

Fingal chuckled. "I am not quite as light a sleeper as I once was, but ye're right, I can't explain that. I suppose a mouthful of drugged wine might have made me sleep a bit more soundly. But if it was that potent, an entire goblet could possibly have killed Gillian. Still, I am no longer willing to believe it was an accident."

He had to be wrong. She asked again, "But why, Fingal? Why would someone want to kill ye, or me? Who would stand to gain from it? Ye have only helped make us stronger since ye have been here. The king made ye laird and by requiring that we wed. No one else has any claim to the title. There is simply no reason for anyone to do this."

Fingal had been wrestling with the same question but he had no intention of telling her who he suspected. She was right that the clan's circumstances had improved since he arrived, but there *was* someone who stood to gain if both he and Gillian were killed—Fallon.

Fingal did not suspect that Fallon herself was behind any of this. As much as it sickened him to admit it, their mother Lana was a different story. She was one of the few members of the clan who still treated him with open disdain. The way she favored Fallon over Gillian and Ailsa was obvious to everyone. Even more damning, she had been pushing for a betrothal for Fallon since Gillian and Fingal were married. If she wanted Fallon to be Lady MacLennan it would certainly be better for the clan, and avoid the king's interference again if she were already married. Lana would have had the opportunity to drug the wine and cut the cinch. Hell, if he had awoken to Lana entering the room the night of the fire, she could have blustered in her usual fashion and come up with some excuse for being there.

Nay. Fingal could not tell Gillian this—not without proof and perhaps not even then. Even though his own mother had been cruel to him as a child, the pain he felt at learning how completely she betrayed the MacIans devastated him. He did not want Gillian to suffer this, especially if there was any chance he was wrong. But if he was right, Gillian was every bit as much a target as he.

"I don't know what the reason might be, Gillian, but I am not willing to risk yer life simply because I don't understand why it is in danger."

"But Fingal—"

"Nay, Gillian. Quinn asked me if I trusted Hearn, and I do. Do ye?"

"Of course I do."

"Then even if ye doubt me, put yer trust in him. He fears for yer life."

As the realization sank in, Gillian's shoulders sagged and she blinked rapidly, as if holding back tears. Fingal took both of her hands in his. "I'm sorry, love. I know this is painful. I will find out who is at the bottom of this but until I do, I will take no chances. Do ye understand?"

She bit her lip and nodded, avoiding eye contact, still obviously fighting to maintain her composure. Her distress caused him more pain than he thought possible. Even Bodie must have sensed it because he crossed the room and laid his head in her lap. *Dear God, what would it do to her if her mother was actually behind this?* Fingal had to make sure that if Lana was manipulating things, she didn't have a reason to continue. And if it wasn't Lana, Gillian still had to be protected.

He cupped her cheek in his hand and lifted her chin to look into her eyes. "I love ye, Gillian. I will not see ye harmed in any way. Until I am sure ye are not at risk, I want ye guarded at all times. If ye are not with me or in this room with the door barred and Bodie at yer side, a guardsman will be assigned to watch over ye. Promise me ye will abide by this."

"I still don't believe I am in danger from someone in my own clan."

"I know ye don't, but please, love, give me yer promise."

She heaved a sigh and stroked Bodie's head. "I don't like it and I hope ye are wrong, but ye have my promise."

Chapter 20

Fingal woke early the next morning. His head still ached some but other than that he felt fine. He slipped out of bed, leaving Gillian asleep. There were things that he needed to do immediately to ensure her safety. First, he needed to speak with Eadoin. After his discussions the previous evening he had weighed the value of telling Eadoin his suspicions against the risk that Eadoin was involved in some way. Aside from having no motive, Gillian trusted Eadoin implicitly. She viewed him as she would a brother. Fingal had to take a leap of faith and trust him too.

As it was early, he sought Eadoin out at his cottage in the village. Alana came to the door with Kiora on her hip. "Laird, this is a surprise, please come in."

Eodoin appeared behind her instantly, laying a protective hand on her shoulder. "Laird, is something wrong?"

Fingal smiled and tickled Kiora. "Nay, Eadoin. I just wanted the opportunity to speak with ye alone."

"Certainly, Laird. We can talk outside if ye wish. Or I can come to the keep with ye."

"We can talk out here."

"Very well." Eadoin stepped around Alana, giving her a quick kiss before shutting the door.

Fingal furrowed his brow. He anticipated as difficult a conversation as he had had with Gillian the previous evening.

"Something is wrong, Laird. What has happened?"

Fingal sighed. There was no easy way to do this. "Eadoin, my fall yesterday was not an accident. Hearn found evidence that someone cut the leather behind a worn spot on the cinch."

"He is certain?"

"Aye, he is. He believes someone was trying to kill me."

Eadoin frowned. "By all the saints, Laird, I can't believe it. But if Hearn is certain, that is the only explanation. When did ye learn this? Who else knows?"

Fingal proceeded to tell him about his discussion the previous evening. "Eadoin, I'm sorry. It isn't that I don't trust ye. I just needed to—"

"Laird, say no more. I understand. I'm sure Gillian was irritated, but if someone is trying to kill ye, ye can't be too careful."

"Eadoin, there is more. I worry that I am not the only target." He told Eadoin about the suspicious circumstances surrounding the fire and his realization last evening that the wine Gillian drank was drugged.

Eadoin was stunned but did not argue against the facts. "I agree. Gillian is in danger, but I am relieved to know the fire wasn't yer fault. I will admit, Laird, it worried me to think ye had been so careless."

It was Fingal's turn to be stunned. "It's easier for ye to believe it was an attempt on our lives instead of my carelessness?"

"I don't want to believe someone in the clan wishes to see ye dead, Laird, and I can't fathom why they would. But aye, ye swore before God to love, honor, keep, and guard her. I'm glad to know ye haven't failed in that."

"This new danger makes keeping those vows harder than ever."

"Do ye have any clues as to who it might be?"

Fingal shook his head. "As far as I can tell the only one who stands to gain by both of our deaths is Fallon and nay, I don't think she is remotely involved in any of this."

Eadoin looked away, clearly waging some internal battle.

"Don't tell me ye think her capable of plotting this evil."

"Nay, Laird. Ye are right, she wouldn't...but Lana might."

Fingal nodded. "I hope ye're wrong, but I feared as much."

"I don't want to believe she would do this. It's true Lana isn't as warm toward Gillian and Ailsa as she is toward Fallon, but it's more than that. She has always believed great things lay in store for Fallon. Even last year, when Malcolm and Duncan were both dead, she pushed the elders to make Fallon chieftain."

Fingal stared, aghast. "Ye aren't serious. Over Gillian?"

"Aye, and Meara. Gillian put her foot down and insisted on Meara leading the clan. Lana wasn't happy."

"What would have made her think Fallon was a better choice than Gillian?"

"It's like I said, she has always said Fallon was destined

for greatness."

"Why does she believe that?"

"Ye've met Rhiannon?"

"Aye."

"Well, folks believe she is a seer."

"Is she?"

"I don't know. She does seem to have a gift. Lots of people can point to accurate predictions she's made. Sometimes though, I think people see what they want to see."

"What do ye mean?"

"Well, for example, she predicted profound changes for the clan before Malcolm attacked Duncurra last year."

"It would seem she got that right."

"Aye, but people find a way to fit reality into a prediction. Had Malcolm been victorious, doubled the size of our holding, and brought ye back as his heir the same thing would have been true."

"I suppose it would have been but what does this have to do with Fallon?"

"Apparently, before Fallon was born, Rhiannon told Lana that the bairn would rise above all others. She didn't say how. If she had said it about Gillian, everyone would have said it came true years ago because she is the tallest lass in the clan."

Fingal chuckled. "I see what ye mean."

"Some say Rhiannon was simply predicting Fallon's great beauty. But Lana has always believed it meant something else."

"Gillian told me that she had pushed Duncan for a betrothal to Niall."

"Aye, exactly. Sometimes I think predictions such as these compel people to make them true. If Duncan had done that, Fallon would be Lady MacIan, but not because of any inherent greatness in her. It would have been simply because her mother pushed for an advantageous marriage."

"Do ye think Lana would harm Gillian just to see a prophecy realized?"

"I hope not. I just thought ye should know. Superstition is sometimes hard to battle."

"Aye. Thank ye, Eadoin. Like ye, I hope Lana does not intend to harm Gillian but it helps to understand what her motive might be if she does. I will consider all of this. At any rate, the attempts on our lives have failed so far but I can't rely on luck to keep us safe. Until I can figure out who is behind this, I want her guarded at all times. If she is not with me, or barred in our chamber, I want either ye, Quinn, or Diarmad seeing to her safety."

"No one else? There are other Duncurra men here."

"Eadoin, I have no idea who might be behind this. I can't say for sure that one of the Duncurra men doesn't hold some sort of grudge. I am not willing to trust anyone unless I am absolutely sure of their loyalty."

"And ye are sure of mine?" Eadoin looked surprised.

Fingal chuckled. "Aye. Gillian trusts ye above all others and for that reason, I trust ye too."

~ * ~

Immediately after leaving Eadoin's home, Fingal sought out Diarmad and Quinn. Although he would not share his fears about Lana with Gillian, after having Eadoin confirm them, he needed to discuss them with Diarmad and Quinn.

Quinn was stunned. "By God's bones, Fingal, do ye really think Lana would kill one daughter simply to see the other one rise in status?"

Diarmad was less shocked but still skeptical. "Lana clearly favors Fallon over her other daughters. That is painfully obvious. But still, I have trouble believing she would wish any ill on the other two, even to see a prophecy realized."

"Is it easier to believe that Fallon herself is behind this? She is the only one who stands to gain by killing both Gillian and me."

Quinn clenched his fists, clearly angry. "Ye can't possibly believe that. She is sweet and guileless."

Fingal was both surprised and pleased by Quinn's immediate defense of Fallon. "Nay, Quinn, I don't believe Fallon has anything to do with this. My point is, if she is the only person who stands to gain by our deaths, and her mother believes she is destined for greatness, I don't think we can rule Lana out as the culprit."

Quinn shook his head. "If that is true, it will crush Fallon."

Diarmad agreed. "Aye, and I'll warrant it'll do the same to Lady Gillian."

"I don't doubt that and I don't want either of them to know my suspicions. However, I do want both of ye to be watchful. Furthermore, if Lana is behind this, I may be able to solve the problem simply."

Diarmad cocked his head. "Exactly how can ye do that?"

"Arrange a betrothal for Fallon to a close ally of mine."

Diarmad grinned, but Quinn became angry. "Ye can't mean that. She is young still, and has been through so much. Ye can't force her to marry someone simply because of her mother."

Fingal laughed. "Ye have become quite a champion for the lass, Quinn. Ye know as well as I do that a strategic marriage for my wife's sister is in the best interests of the clan. Besides, her mother has already raised the issue multiple times."

"Fingal, don't do this to her. She doesn't deserve it. She isn't ready to leave home."

"If the man I have in mind agrees, she may not have to leave home."

"What man do ye have in mind?" Quinn ground out through clenched teeth.

Fingal slapped him on the shoulder. "Ye would seem an obvious choice. Especially since the idea of a betrothal for her to someone else seems so repugnant to ye."

"Me? Marry Fallon?"

"Aye, do ye object? Do ye think Fallon would object?"

He smiled. "I can't speak for her, but nay, I don't object."

Fingal turned serious. "I trust ye, Quinn. Ye are a good man. From everything I can see Fallon is quite taken with ye too. Not only might this marriage stop whatever plans Lana is hatching for Fallon, it would solidify an alliance with yer father."

"Ah, my father. I can't guarantee that he will agree to this."

"I understand but as long as ye don't oppose it, I will broach the subject with him at Rowan's wedding."

"I won't lie to ye. She is lovely and I can't think of anyone I would rather marry. Still, I would like to know for certain that Fallon wishes to marry me. I don't want her to feel pushed."

Fingal chuckled. "Well then, ye have three weeks to woo her. I will discuss this with Gillian but no one else until ye tell me otherwise."

Chapter 21

Gillian woke much later than she usually did. Fingal was already up and gone in spite of the fact that Agnes told him to rest. "What am I going to do with him, Bodie?" Bodie wagged his tail and nudged her hand. She rose and started to dress. In spite of sleeping longer than usual, she felt tired and a little queasy. She smiled and patted her stomach. She had been taking Rhiannon's herbal tisane ever since the first night Fingal had made love to her. Maybe it was working. Alana said the first sign she had with both pregnancies was an upset stomach. She also said that Rhiannon's tisane helped sooth her stomach like nothing else did. Gillian put the packet of herbs in her pocket and went downstairs, Bodie at her heel.

Although the tisane did seem to quiet her stomach for a while, she had a hard time focusing on her work and she still didn't feel well even after the midday meal.

"Ye look a bit pale, Gillian," observed her mother.

"I'm fine. My stomach is just a tad upset."

Her mother's eyes brightened and she whispered conspiratorially, "Are ye carrying, then?"

Gillian smiled. "Maybe. I don't know for sure."

"How long has it been since ye've had yer courses?"

"I don't know exactly. It was sometime before the fire."

"How long before the fire? That was only three weeks ago."

"I don't remember. Maybe a week, or more."

"Well, it's early, but ye could be. I knew I was carrying before I even missed my courses when the smell of ramsons blooming made me ill."

"But ye like ramsons, mother."

"Aye, I do, but not when I was pregnant."

Gillian laughed. It felt good to share this with her mother. "I've been taking Rhiannon's tisane. Alana swears it helps with the queasiness."

"Aye, it would. I'm not sure what all she puts in it, but there is plenty of mint and chamomile. That alone will soothe yer stomach. That wasn't a very large packet she gave ye. Ye must be nearly out by now."

Gillian didn't want to tell her mother she had had no need for a tonic to help her conceive "fine strong sons" until a little over a week ago. "Aye, I suppose I could use some more, especially to help with this sick feeling."

"I was planning to visit her later today—if *the laird* can spare an escort."

"Mother, after the Grants raided I would have thought ye'd see the wisdom of having protection."

"I suppose I do. I just hate having to ask *him* for anything."

Gillian sighed. She guessed her mother would never change. "Ye needn't ask Fingal if ye don't want to. Just ask the guardsman on duty at the gate and he will see to an escort for ye."

"I know. I just ask *the laird* so he knows how much it irritates me."

"Mother, ye are hopeless. On the one hand, ye say ye *hate* asking Fingal for anything and on the other ye only ask Fingal to arrange a guard for ye to let him know it irritates ye."

Lana harrumphed. "Never mind that. Ye should come with me. Rhiannon would love a visit from ye."

"Nay, mother, not today. I really don't feel like it. Besides, I wanted to check on Agnes this afternoon."

"Is something wrong? Wasn't she just here last eve sewing up *the laird's* fool head?"

Gillian rolled her eyes. "Mother, please."

"Well, wasn't she here?"

"Aye, she was, but she seemed to be taking ill. She is rather old and lives alone. I just want to check on her."

"Then I will go on my own. Perhaps ye will feel up to a visit with Rhiannon next week."

Gillian smiled as her mother left the hall. Even with the ever-present barbs, she hadn't had such a pleasant conversation with her mother in months. Maybe Lana was truly becoming used to all the changes. She clearly was happy about the prospect of being a grandmother.

Gillian walked to the back door of the hall which led to the kitchens, with Bodie loping beside her.

Eadoin called to her, "My lady, where are ye heading?"

"Eadoin, How many times do I have to tell ye not to call me that."

He caught up to her, grinning. "Several more, I fear. Are ye going to the kitchen?"

"Aye. Ye may as well come with me. I am going to visit Agnes and will need a guardsman with me. She seemed to be taking ill yesterday. I thought I would get a parcel of victuals from Jeanne to take to her."

When Gillian and Eadoin arrived at Agnes' cottage, she was no better. In fact, she lay huddled in her bed and her catarrh was worse.

"Agnes, it's freezing in here. Yer fire has gone out."

"Aye, lass, I was just too tired to tend it."

Eadoin went straight to the hearth. "I'll take care of it, Agnes. We'll have it toasty in here soon."

Gillian was worried. "At least ye took yer own advice and rested today. I brought ye a crock of soup from Jeanne. Let's see if ye can eat a bit of it."

Getting Agnes to eat was harder than Gillian expected. Although she tried, she was only able to take a few sips before becoming exhausted. Even Bodie sensed something was wrong. Instead of making himself comfortable by the hearth, he stood near the bed, watching vigilantly.

"Eadoin, I fear she is desperately ill. We can't leave her here alone."

"Aye, we could send for Rhiannon or maybe Eleanor."

Gillian frowned. Agnes had never liked Eleanor, but it would take much too long for Rhiannon to get here. "Eleanor is closer. Go get her. I'll stay here until ye return. We should probably move her to the keep then where there are more hands to care for her."

Eadoin became very serious. "I can't leave ye alone Gillian, but I'll send for her." He stepped out the door and called to someone. Moments later he was back. "Tarmon's son was playing in the lane. He is running to fetch Eleanor, then he will find the laird."

Fingal arrived first, having met the lad before he reached Eleanor's house. "Gillian, what's wrong?" he asked softly so as not to wake Agnes.

"She is much sicker than she let on yesterday. I sent for Eleanor. She is a midwife but she knows some healing skills."

"Does the clan not have another healer?"

"Rhiannon, but she lives so far out of the village I feared it would take too long. I'm very worried."

Eleanor arrived before long. Clearly Tarmon's son had conveyed the urgency because Eleanor, short and plump as she was, looked as if she had run the whole way. Gillian told her what she knew about Agnes' illness before Eleanor approached the bed, taking Agnes' thin bony hand in her own plump one. With her other hand she brushed the silver hair off Agnes' forehead and crooned, "Agnes, love, Lady Gillian tells me ye are feeling a wee bit poorly."

Agnes opened her eyes, coughed, and said weakly, "Eleanor, I'd say that's an understatement."

Eadoin chuckled at the acerbic old woman's dry wit but Eleanor became serious. "I know, Agnes. Lady Gillian and I want to get ye up to the keep and see if we can make ye feel a bit better."

"I know ye spend more time bringing souls into the world," she wheezed, struggling for breath, "but surely even ye can tell when a soul is ready to leave, Eleanor. I'd just as soon be in my own bed for that."

Gillian gasped. "Nay, Agnes. Yesterday ye said it was just a bit of a catarrh."

"I was wrong." Agnes lapsed into another paroxysm that left her gasping for air. When she could breathe again, she motioned for Gillian to come closer. Eleanor stepped aside. Gillian left Fingal's side to kneel by Agnes' bed, taking the old woman's hands in her own. Agnes nodded towards Fingal, whispering, "He is a good laird. I know this was hard, but I'm proud of ye. Now, I want ye to go. I don't want ye here when I die."

"But Agnes—"

"Don't argue with a dying woman." She succumbed to yet another spasm.

Tears slid freely down Gillian's cheeks. She leaned forward and kissed Agnes' leathery cheek. "I love ye."

Agnes whispered, "Ye're a good lass. Laird, take her home now."

"I will, Agnes. Rest easy now." Fingal lifted Gillian from the floor.

"Nay, Fingal, I can't leave her."

"Wheesht, love. 'Tis what she wants and I understand why. Come now." He ushered her, weeping, from the little cottage. Bodie whined and followed.

Once outside in the lane she turned on him. "Fingal, why? I can't stand the thought of just going back to the keep as if nothing is wrong. Why can't I stay with her?"

"Because she doesn't want yer last memory of her to be as she gasps and struggles for breath. It is a hard way to die, and even harder to watch. She knows this and she wants to spare ye. It is her last gift. Let her give it to ye."

"But she shouldn't be alone."

"Gillian, she isn't alone. Eleanor is with her and so is Eadoin."

"She has never liked Eleanor much."

Fingal smiled. "That was obvious. Still, this is the way she wants it." He gathered her in his arms and kissed the top of her head. "I'm sorry, love."

She began to sob. Hot tears fell in rivers and she could barely catch her breath. He lifted her in his arms and she buried her face in his chest, unable to stop weeping. She was vaguely aware of Bodie whining as Fingal carried her to the keep. When he reached their chamber, he sat in a chair, continuing to cradle her in his lap. His work roughened hands felt cool against her cheeks as he brushed her tears away.

When she could finally speak again she said, "I-I'm sorry. I don't know wh-what came over me. I didn't cry like that f-for Aunt Meara. I-I didn't even l-let myself c-cry like that for D-da."

"Gillian, sometimes sorrow just builds up until it all bubbles over. These were all of those tears ye have kept locked away. Ye needed to let them go."

~ * ~

Gillian was clearly exhausted, but Fingal could not get her to go to bed. Even though Agnes wouldn't allow Gillian to stay at her bedside, she kept a vigil all the same. It the wee hours of the morning when Eadoin brought them word that Agnes had passed. The news brought on a fresh wave of tears but when her tears were spent, she slept.

Fingal didn't leave her when he woke the next morning. He continued to hold her in his arms until she finally stirred.

She blinked sleepily against the bright morning light. He expected her to jump up instantly, complaining that she had overslept as she usually did if she woke past dawn. However, she moaned and pulled a pillow over her head.

Concerned, Fingal gently rubbed her back. "Are ye feeling ill, love?"

"Aye. My head aches something fierce and I feel sick to my stomach."

"Yesterday was a hard day and ye had very little sleep last night. Perhaps ye should stay in bed for a while."

She rolled on her back and pulled the pillow away from her face. "Nay, it isn't that. Well, all of my tears and lack of sleep may be adding to the headache, but I have been queasy for a few days now. Rhiannon's tisane helps a lot."

"Ye've been sick for days? Gillian, ye should have told me."

"I don't think it is anything to worry about, Fingal. My mother thinks I might be expecting."

Fingal grinned. "Really? That's wonderful. But, sweetling, it hasn't been very long, are ye sure?"

"Not completely. My monthly courses are due. Perhaps overdue a day or so but mother says she knew she was pregnant almost before she had missed her monthly because things made her sick immediately."

"Gillian, I couldn't be happier." He rested his hand on her flat stomach, filled with awe. "A bairn."

She smiled, but then groaned and rolled to the edge of the bed. Fingal was beside her instantly, supporting her as she heaved several times but brought nothing up.

He helped her wash her face and rinse her mouth before saying, "Stay in bed and rest until ye feel better, love."

"Nay, really it isn't necessary. As soon as I drink the tisane and eat something, I will feel better. Besides, there is much to do to prepare for Agnes' funeral. She served this clan well and we must bid her an appropriate farewell."

~ * ~

Gillian and the other women of the clan did work to prepare a fitting farewell for the beloved healer. She worked no harder than usual, but was utterly exhausted at the end of the day. As soon as the evening meal was over, Fingal ushered her from the hall.

"We should have stayed a bit longer," she scolded half-heartedly as they reached their chamber.

"My darling, ye look ready to drop. Ye need to rest. Besides, there is something I have been meaning to speak to ye about but with Agnes' passing I haven't had the opportunity."

"Is something wrong? Has something else happened?"

"Nay, love. Nothing is wrong. I have just been thinking about yer mother's desire to arrange a betrothal for Fallon."

Gillian sighed. "I thought ye agreed it was too soon."

"I did, but I have considered it a bit more."

"Fingal, I don't think Fallon particularly likes Coby. Don't let mother talk ye into this."

He grinned at her. "I am not considering a betrothal for Fallon to Coby. I was thinking perhaps Quinn MacKenzie would be a good husband for her."

"Quinn? Really? Aye, he is very nice." Gillian hadn't given any thought to a husband for Fallon. The fact that Fingal had, frankly, surprised her.

"So ye think it would please her?" Fingal asked.

Gillian laughed. "Please her? Honestly, she practically swoons when he glances in her direction. If she can stop blushing long enough, aye, I think she would like the idea. What does he think?"

"Ye are so sure I have already spoken to him?" She leveled a glare at him that ended in a grin. He laughed. "He likes the idea too. But he wants to give her a chance to get to know him a bit."

"Is he free to choose his own wife then?"

"Not exactly, but as long as they are both amenable, I will speak to Laird MacKenzie about it when we go to Duncurra for Rowan's wedding."

Gillian grinned. "I think Mother will be pleased to have Fallon marry a laird's son. Not to mention the fact that Mother seems as charmed by him as every other woman here. Aye, I think it is a good match and I hope Laird MacKenzie agrees to the betrothal."

"I do too, but it may take some convincing. He thinks Quinn is just here to lend some temporary aid."

"I thought he was meant to be a permanent addition to yer guard."

"Aye, he is, but Cathal won't like that. He prefers his children to stay close to home."

"That hardly bodes well for him accepting the betrothal."

Fingal grinned. "We may avoid that wee fact until the betrothal is signed." He put his finger too her lips. "Can ye keep a secret?"

She smiled coyly. "Perhaps if ye keep my lips busy doing something else, I can."

"I am happy to oblige, my lady." Fingal captured her lips with his own and she returned his kiss with ardor. Eventually he broke the kiss, whispering against her lips, "ye are tired and need yer rest."

"I'm not too tired for this," she whispered back, looping her arms around his neck.

Chapter 22

Even after retiring earlier than they usually did, Gillian woke the next morning feeling weak and sick. Fingal hadn't been around many pregnant women, but he had heard of the sickness that comes with pregnancy. Still he was inclined to worry. He urged her to rest more but she insisted that it would all pass soon.

Then, a little over a week after Agnes died, Fingal woke before dawn to the sound of Gillian sobbing and Bodie whining.

She was curled in a ball on the edge of the bed. "Sweetling, what's wrong?" He reached for her, but he immediately saw the source of her tears. The sheets were bloody. "Oh, Gillian, Gillian, my love." He gathered her in his arms and held her while she cried.

"I think I lost the baby," she sobbed.

"I am so sorry."

"I-I was s-so happy and mother was t-too."

"I was happy too, sweetling. I know yer heart aches because my own does."

"I-I'm s-s-sorry."

"Wheest, Gillian, this isn't yer fault, love. It isn't anyone's fault. It just happened. We will get through this together."

When her tears had slowed, he kissed her before laying her gently on the bed. Bodie stood beside her as if he understood the pain she felt. "I will be right back, love. I am going to send for Eleanor."

She nodded, but said nothing, putting her arm around Bodie.

Fearing what he did about Lana, he was loath to ask the next question, but he had to. "Shall I send for yer mother too?"

She nodded again. Although she tried to hold them back, fresh tears spilled down her cheeks. She buried her face in Bodie's soft fur.

After he sent a servant for Eleanor and Lana, he returned

to her side. "Sweetling, let me help ye wash."

"Nay, a woman's blood is harmful to a man."

"I know there are people who believe that, but I think it is nonsense. Every man is born from a woman, how can her blood be harmful? There is nothing else I can do. Please let me help ye."

She looked up at him, her eyes filled with sorrow, and nodded. "I am so tired. Aye, thank ye."

He brought the wash basin to the bedside and helped wash the blood from her legs. She placed linen toweling between her legs to staunch the flow. By the time he had her dressed in a clean shift and sitting by the hearth, wrapped in a soft plaid, Lana arrived.

"What on earth do ye need me for at this ungodly hour?" she demanded before entering the chamber. On seeing the bloodstained sheets her demeanor changed instantly. "Oh, Gillian, I am so sorry. Please leave us, Laird. I will help her from here. This is no place for a man."

Fingal stiffened, preparing to argue. He would not leave her alone with Lana. But before he could protest, Gillian spoke up. "Nay, mother. I want Fingal to stay. I love him. I need him here."

Her words gripped his heart. He went to her, took her hand and kissed her head. "I love ye too, my precious lass."

Lana glared at him for a moment, but her expression softened. "Aye, Gillian, he can stay if that is what ye wish. What can I do?"

"I feel dreadful, queasy, and my stomach hurts."

"Rhiannon's tisane will help. I will go brew ye some. She gave me a new packet of herbs yesterday. I'll bring fresh sheets for yer bed when I come too."

Lana had no sooner left than Eleanor arrived. "Laird, I came as quickly as I could. Although I don't know what need ye would have for a midwife." As she entered the room, she clucked when she saw the bloody sheets. "My lady, are ye having trouble with yer courses?"

"Nay Eleanor, I think I have lost a babe."

"Ye poor dear. I didn't know ye were carrying. Ye should have told me."

"I only just began to suspect it."

She walked to the bed to examine the sheets more closely. "Did ye now? How long has it been since yer last courses came?" She turned away from the bed to face Gillian. "Och, Laird, forgive me. I forgot ye were here. Leave us now and we'll see what's what."

Gillian grasped his hand as if holding on for dear life. Fingal had no intention of leaving Gillian regardless of what the midwife said. "Nay, I'll stay. Gillian needs me."

Eleanor clucked again. "Nay she doesn't. She has me here now and this is no business for a man. 'Twill ruin yer sword arm, so it will. Tell him, my lady. Tell him to run along now and we will put everything to rights."

Not only did her overly cheerful tone irritate Fingal, the look of horror on Gillian's face told him she believed Eleanor's dire predictions. Fingal was known through the Highlands for his skill with a sword. The notion that anything other than serious bodily injury could damage his swordsmanship was laughable. He had to quiet her fears. "It will do no such thing unless ye plan to cleave it off with a sword yerself. I will stay."

Gillian relaxed, resting her head against him.

Eleanor looked affronted. "Well, this is highly irregular, but ye are the laird so I guess I have no say in it." She huffed. "So my lady, how long has it been since ye bled last?"

"I'm not sure exactly. A little over a month."

"Is that all? What makes ye think ye were carrying? Maybe ye were just a bit late. It happens."

"I have been over-tired and sick for about a week now. And this...this feels different. It is more painful and...well, there is more blood and clots than usual."

"Come lay on the bed and let me examine ye."

Fingal helped Gillian walk to the bed and when he would have stepped away she held his hand, so he stayed by her side.

Once again Eleanor clucked her disapproval, but she examined Gillian with Fingal at her side.

When she finished her examination, she went to the basin to wash her hands. "My lady, I'm not sure whether ye were pregnant or not. The sickness ye describe suggests that ye might have been. Also, the pain and heavy bleeding ye are having is what happens with a miscarriage. However, sometimes when courses are very late, even with a maiden, the same thing can happen. Either way, ye are not pregnant now. Just be thankful it was so early ye didn't have time to think about being a mother."

Fingal was shocked by her words. The fresh tears in Gillian's eyes told him she felt the same way. If he had only believed for a moment that they were expecting a baby, the loss would be as devastating. Before he could form a response, Lana returned with several servants in tow.

"Ah, Eleanor, how is my poor lass?"

"She'll be fine in no time. She lost it very early, if she was pregnant at all."

Lana was clearly affronted. "It? No matter how early the loss came, that was my grandchild Eleanor, not an 'it' and I'll thank ye to remember that. Ye can go. I'll take care of my daughter from here." She turned her back on Eleanor. "Gillian, I've brought Rhiannon's tisane and I added a bit of willow bark, to help with the pain."

Eleanor grabbed her arm. "Ye mustn't give her that if it contains willow bark."

"Why on earth not?"

"If she wasn't pregnant—if she is just having unusual pain and bleeding because she is late—it goes against God's will to stop her pain. Women are meant to suffer for Eve's sin."

Fingal couldn't believe what he was hearing. Perhaps this was the reason men should stay clear of these sorts of things. At that moment he wanted to use his sword arm on Eleanor. He opened his mouth to tell her what he thought but Lana beat him to it.

"I will give my daughter whatever I think she needs and will sort it out with God when I meet Him."

"*If* ye ever meet Him, ye mean," Eleanor snapped before she left the room.

Lana turned back to Gillian. "Pay no attention to her, Gillian. She has a knack for bringing even the most reluctant bairns safely into this world, but if God put a more annoying woman on this earth, I pray I never meet her."

Fingal glanced at Gillian. While tears still stood in her beautiful brown eyes, a small smile played at her lips. For the first time since marrying Gillian, he felt a bit of respect for her mother.

~ * ~

It took Gillian longer than she expected to recover from the miscarriage. A little over week later the bleeding had all but stopped but she remained tired and queasy most of the time. She tried not to worry Fingal with it. Eleanor had said to let her know if the bleeding lasted more than ten days or so and not to overwork herself during that time. She hadn't mentioned that the nausea would persist that whole time. Gillian had no energy, feeling exhausted after the slightest activity. Both Fallon and Lana stepped in to help see to things.

As expected, Bran MacBain arrived near the end of April with his wife Tira, their three children, and an escort of MacBain soldiers.

Gillian, Fingal, the elders, and many other MacLennans gathered in the courtyard to welcome them. As Bran had trained there, he was well known and respected by many of them. Quinn was there with Fallon at his side. Gillian had felt so ill she had barely noticed the burgeoning affection between them. Although Fallon still blushed shyly when she talked to him, at least she was able to speak.

Ailsa too was there with Duff whose head came to her waist now and who, like Bodie, was never more than a few yards from his mistress. She had been excited about the MacBains' arrival ever since she heard that they had a daughter who was only a few years younger than her.

Fingal gripped Bran's forearm in welcome then introduced him. "Gillian, do ye remember Bran MacBain?"

Bran took her hand, bowing low over it. "My lady, ye were no older than my daughter Maeve here when I saw ye last."

"Aye, it has been a long time."

"This is my wife Tira and our children, Maeve, Kieran, and the wee lassie hiding behind her mother's skirts is Aileen.

"I'm very pleased to meet ye all."

Introductions were mostly not required. Even Quinn knew them well as his oldest sister Annag was married to Bran's brother, Laird MacBain.

Gillian motioned to the doors of the keep. "Please join us in the hall. We have prepared a feast to welcome ye."

Ailsa looped her arm through Maeve's, pulling her towards the door. "I'm so glad ye are here. We are going to be friends. Do ye like honey cakes? Jeanne makes the best honey cakes and I helped make them for the feast. This is my dog, Duff. Do ye like dogs? I like dogs."

Gillian smiled and called, "Let her get a word in, Ailsa."

Tira laughed. "Don't worry. As soon as she takes a breath, Maeve will take up where she left off."

"I am glad ye've come too," said Gillian. "I know it must

have been hard, leaving yer home. Bran is very well respected here and we truly do need skilled guardsmen."

"Don't worry. I'm sure this will feel like home soon enough."

"I have prepared rooms for ye in the keep. If ye would prefer a cottage in the village there are several ye can choose from. But the keep will be more comfortable until ye get settled."

"The keep will be fine," Tira assured her, "and it will give us a chance to get to know one another better."

She offered Tira the seat next to her so they could chat during the meal, but as the evening progressed Gillian felt dull and unable to focus. Ailsa and Maeve sat across the table and kept a steady stream of chatter flowing.

Gillian actually nodded off at one point, jerking awake, startled. Tira rested her hand on Gillian's and asked, "My lady, are ye well? Ye look a bit pale and ye've eaten almost nothing."

"I'm so very sorry. I-I-I'm just over-tired. I'll be fine. I haven't shown ye to yer chambers yet."

"I can do that, Gillian," Fallon said gently. "Perhaps ye should retire now."

Fingal eyed her with concern. "I'll go up with ye, love. Please excuse us."

"Nay, Fingal, it isn't necessary. Please don't desert our guests." She stood to leave, swayed, and collapsed.

Fingal caught her before she hit the floor. "Gillian, are ye all right?"

"I guess, I'm a bit dizzy." That was perhaps an understatement. The room spun wildly, forcing Gillian to close her eyes.

He lifted her in his arms and carried her from the hall, her mother and Bodie close on his heels. Fingal called over his shoulder, "Send for Eleanor."

She opened her eyes when he laid her on the bed. "I'm sorry. I'm sure I'll be better soon."

"Gillian, wheest. There is nothing to be sorry for. Ye are ill."

Her mother wrung her hands. "Gillian, lass, ye must be working too hard. Laird, ye should insist she rest more."

Fingal arched an eyebrow at her. "Believe me, Lana. I have tried."

"Then ye need to listen to yer husband, Gillian."

If she had had the energy, Gillian would have snorted. "Fine, I'll rest more. Just, both of ye go back to our guests now."

"Ye've gone daft if ye think I will leave ye until Eleanor has seen to ye," said her mother. "Although I think it would be better if we sent for Rhiannon. Eleanor isn't much good unless someone is in labor."

There was a knock at the door. Lana turned to open it saying, "Well, it's about time—oh I'm sorry, Tira, I thought ye were someone else."

"I know. Apparently Eleanor has gone to an outlying croft to deliver a bairn. I am a midwife too. I thought maybe I could help."

"Please come in, Tira. Thank ye," Fingal said.

She walked to the bed, took one of Gillian's hands in hers, and felt her forehead with the other. "Fallon said ye lost a bairn last week. I am so very sorry for ye. She says ye have been very tired. Are ye still bleeding, my lady?"

"Nay, that stopped a day or so ago."

"And was it very heavy for long?"

"Not really. Not after the first day or two."

Tira palpated Gillian's belly. "Do ye have any pain here?"

"Nay."

"And ye have been overly tired since the bleeding started?"

"I have been tired since a week or so before that."

"'Twas that and the nausea that made us think she was carrying," offered Lana.

"I think that is the worst part. I thought the sick feeling would go away after I...lost the baby."

Tira frowned. "Did it not?"

"Nay. It is almost worse. Rhiannon, she is a healer, she's given me a packet of herbs to make a tisane that helps a little."

"What herbs does she use?"

Lana smiled. "She says it is her secret blend but it doesn't take much skill to know it contains mint, thyme, comfrey, and chamomile. I added some willow bark when the pains were bad in the beginning."

"All of those should help settle yer stomach. Would ye like me to brew ye some now?"

"Nay, I had some just before ye came. I just want to sleep now." Gillian patted the bed. Bodie hopped up, settling himself beside her. "Fingal, please return to our guests."

"Just long enough to assure everyone ye are well. I will be back in a few moments."

"I'll stay with her 'till ye return," Lana said.

"Perhaps it would be best if we all left and let her sleep, Lana," her husband said, holding the door open for Lana and Tira to pass.

With Bodie's solid warmth beside her, Gillian fell instantly asleep.

~ * ~

Once they were in the corridor Fingal asked, "Tira, what's wrong?"

She shook her head. "I don't know."

"It isn't just the miscarriage?" Lana asked.

"I don't think so. The fatigue and mild dizziness might be normal for a few days, especially if she had lost a lot of blood, but it doesn't sound as if she did. Sometimes, a fever will set in after a miscarriage, but she doesn't seem to have one. Besides, her belly would hurt with it and she has no pain. The thing that is most puzzling is the nausea. Morning sickness should have stopped immediately. Occasionally a lass will have bleeding like when she hasn't actually miscarried, but she isn't pregnant."

Fingal frowned. "If this isn't still a result of the miscarriage, what could it be?"

"I don't know. This Rhiannon is a healer ye say? Has she examined Lady Gillian?"

"Nay. We thought this was all because of the miscarriage."

"I'll go for her first thing in the morning," Lana said.

Chapter 23

After Tira had examined her the previous evening, Fingal had been close to panic. He lay beside her throughout the night, but could not sleep. He couldn't imagine what was causing her to be so ill and it terrified him. It had been a little more than two weeks since she started having the first signs of pregnancy and just ten days since her miscarriage and yet she seemed to be fading away. She was pale and much too thin. He had heard of wasting illnesses like this and prayed fervently through the night that she did not have one—that she would wake in the morning refreshed.

But when Gillian woke the next morning little had changed. Unlike the previous days, she was so weary she didn't even attempt to get out of bed, not that he would have let her. Lana was true to her word and fetched Rhiannon shortly after daybreak. Just as Tira had the night before, Rhiannon examined her, asking many of the same questions.

She too spoke with Fingal and Lana in the corridor.

"Laird, I believe she suffers from melancholia, perhaps brought on by the miscarriage."

"Aye, she is sad. The miscarriage came as a blow to both of us. But it is the nausea and the fatigue that has me concerned. Surely sadness isn't causing that."

Lana's brow furrowed. "Rhiannon, how could it be melancholia? She was heartbroken after Duncan was killed. We all were, but she pushed through and did what had to be done. Then Meara died and she was forced to marry. None of these things brought on melancholia. Surely something else is wrong now.

"Lana, perhaps all of those things led to this and it has only been made worse by the miscarriage. Her humors are out of balance because of the excess bleeding. An abundance of black bile causes melancholia."

"What can be done to help her?"

"Old Laird MacRae had a physician in his employ for

many years. I learned much of my skills from him. He would have treated an excess of black bile with a purgative."

Fingal groaned. Gillian had been through so much he hated the idea of putting her through more with a purgative.

Rhiannon went on. "However, I am not sure that is what she needs. Since the humoral imbalance was caused by losing too much blood, we need to build up her blood."

Fingal sighed in relief. "So we just need to make sure she rests until she is stronger?"

"Oh, nay, that is the last thing she needs. If ye leave her to rest in bed, she will become a target for the devil himself. Old *Cluitie* likes nothing more than to swim in a bath of black bile. He will take her soul for certain if ye leave her idle. Work is what she needs to build up her blood and keep the devil away. Ye must get her up and have her do as much of her daily routine as ye can."

"But that is what she has been doing and she only grows worse," Lana said.

"Still, 'tis the best thing for her, Lana."

"We had been planning to travel to Duncurra today for the Roodmas celebration and Rowan MacKenzie's wedding to Eara Fraser," Fingal said. "After she collapsed last eve I had decided against it but if normal activity is what she needs, perhaps we should go. Niall's wife, Katherine, is an excellent healer. Perhaps she will know something that will help as well."

Rhiannon looked momentarily horrified. "Nay, work is one thing, travel is something else. Going to a strange place where there will be throngs of people celebrating a wedding is the worst thing she could do. It will just remind her painfully of her losses. The black bile will simply increase. Ye will be practically inviting *Cluitie* to the wedding. Nay, she mustn't travel to Duncurra now. Keep her here, in her own home, doing her normal routine and she will snap out of this. Lana, do ye have the packet of herbs I gave ye? Have ye been giving her the tisane?"

"Aye, she says it helps some with the nausea. At least for a bit."

"Good. Keep giving her that for now. I will mix a new blend when I get home and add a bit of St. John's wort. It's said to repel the devil. Send someone for it later this afternoon. If she is not better in a few days, it will be a sign that Satan has taken hold of her. We will have to be more aggressive at driving him out. I sense a darkness around her and I fear the worst if we don't act quickly."

When Fingal went back into the room, he was relieved to see Gillian had gotten out of bed and was dressing. He didn't want to scare her with Rhiannon's dire predictions and if she kept to her normal routine, he saw no reason to.

"Don't tell me to stay in bed, Fingal. I don't think I can stand it. Besides, we are travelling to Duncurra today. I need to get ready."

Fingal smiled, wrapping her in his arms. Perhaps Rhiannon was right. "I won't tell ye to stay in bed, love. Maybe continuing to do what ye always have is best. Still, I don't think we should travel."

"But ye were going to speak with Laird MacKenzie about a betrothal for Fallon and Quinn." Even as she protested, he felt her body relax in relief.

"Now that Bran MacBain is here, Diarmad will return to Duncurra. I will send a letter to Laird MacKenzie and ask Diarmad to represent me in discussions. Quinn himself is more than capable of helping his father see the benefits of this marriage.

After Gillian was downstairs and attempting her normal routine, Fingal sought out both men. Diarmad was discussing the ongoing training of Brathanead's warriors with Bran and the other guardsmen.

As Fingal approached them, Diarmad stopped addressing the men. "Laird, how is Lady Gillian this morning?"

"She is no worse. Rhiannon has been to see her and thinks she will be fine with time." Fingal heard the doubt in his own voice.

Diarmad frowned. "Is she up for the journey? We can set a slow pace. Perhaps it will be good for Lady Katherine to see her."

Fingal sighed. He fully agreed. Most healers, like Rhiannon, believed that the power of evil was the root of a great many illnesses. Evil certainly was present in the world. Like most people, he prayed for protection from Satan and his malevolence. Therefore Rhiannon's belief about the source of Gillian's illness seemed reasonable and was consistent with much of his experience with healers. That was until he met Katherine.

She treated illnesses among the MacIans with an array of herbs, potions, and poultices just like many other healers, and she often prayed for God's aid in healing, but she never mentioned driving out the devil. "I would love to have Katherine's opinion but Gillian isn't well enough for the journey. I thought we could take a wagon, so she wouldn't have to sit a horse for so many hours. However, Rhiannon says she shouldn't make the journey."

"Not even in a wagon? We can make a comfortable place for her to rest and go very slow. It is only a half-day's ride at a regular pace."

"Rhiannon believes that the best thing for her is stay here doing what she normally does. If the journey made her worse, I could never forgive myself.

Eadoin said, "Rhiannon is an experienced healer. Most of the clan sought aid from Agnes because she lived in the village and was more accessible. Still there are those who always turned to Rhiannon, my wife included."

Fingal nodded. "That is why I am unwilling to risk Gillian's health with the journey."

"Then there is only one answer," Diarmad said. "I will ask Niall to bring Katherine here when Quinn and the other men return after the wedding. It should only be a week. If Gillian is improving by then, she will enjoy the visit. If not, Katherine may be able to help."

Chapter 24

Well over a week passed and Quinn had not returned with Niall and Katherine. Neither was Gillian any better. Rhiannon visited daily. She added more herbs to the tisane and instructed Lana to see that Gillian drank it three times a day. Strong and committed to overcoming her illness, Gillian continued to push herself but it became harder every day. She was getting worse and Fingal was beside himself.

He discussed it with Tira MacBain, who like Fallon and Lana stepped in to help with the running of the keep.

"I have heard of melancholia occurring after a miscarriage, sometimes even after a live healthy birth. Some say it is the devil's work. I don't know."

"Do ye think encouraging her to keep doing what she usually does is the right thing? She seems so very tired."

"When I have seen it, staying abed hasn't made it better. Usually, it passes after a time. I just don't understand why she is so sick. I'm sorry, Laird, I don't know what to do."

Then on the Friday before Pentecost, he began to lose hope. For the first time in over three weeks since the miscarriage, Gillian refused to get out of bed.

"Fingal, I can't. I am too tired. My head aches and the light hurts my eyes. Everything seems too bright and oddly green."

"Please, love, I know ye feel terrible but Rhiannon says ye will not get better if ye don't get up."

"I don't care what Rhiannon says," she snapped. "Getting up every day and trying to ignore whatever is making me ill hasn't worked so far."

"Just sit in the chair for a bit. Perhaps ye will feel stronger then."

"Why are ye pushing me like this?" Tears filled her eyes. "I'm sorry. I can't force myself anymore. I just need to rest."

Tears stung the back of his eyes. He hated seeing her so ill.

He knelt next to the bed, taking her hands in his. "Sweetling, Rhiannon says it will only get worse if ye stay in bed."

"Sleep has always been the cure for tiredness. When did that change?"

There was nothing to do but tell her Rhiannon's fears. "She thinks it is more than just tiredness. She believes ye are suffering melancholia and to stay abed will allow it to fully take hold. Please let me help ye up."

He started to lift her from the bed. "Nay, Fingal!" she yelled. Bodie growled at him. "Leave me be!" She started to sob.

"Wheesht, love," he crooned, stroking her cheek. Forcing her to get up—upsetting her so—couldn't be good for her. "I will let ye rest. Please, stop crying." When she had quieted, he washed her face with a cool cloth.

Then she said the words that chilled his soul. "I'm sorry, Fingal. I don't think I can get better."

"Nay, I won't hear ye say those words. Ye will get better. I am sending for Katherine immediately. She will know what to do."

He sent a servant for someone to sit with Gillian. After he sent for Katherine, he would visit Rhiannon to see if there was anything else to do.

Fallon arrived in a few minutes and once he was sure Gillian was as comfortable as possible, he sought out Eadoin. He would trust no one else to carry the message to Duncurra. Eadoin left immediately. Fingal too saddled Con and rode out of Brathanead. Coby and Tarmon stood watch at the gate. "Laird, where are ye going?" called Tarmon, but Fingal didn't answer. He had but one thought, to help Gillian in any way he could.

He arrived at Rhiannon's cottage in a few minutes. Her little dog, Blaze, announced his presence before he reached the door. He raised his hand to knock, but she opened it before he had the chance.

She smiled. "Laird, this is a surprise. Come in. Sit down."

He entered the cottage. "She is worse, Rhiannon. I can't get her out of bed today. When Quinn and Diarmad left for Duncurra, even though I had hoped it wouldn't be necessary, I asked them to bring Lady Katherine MacIan back after the wedding. She is a very gifted healer. I don't know why it has taken so long. The wedding was to have been last week. I have sent an urgent message for her to come now but I'm worried. Rhiannon, she has given up." He couldn't keep the dread he felt out of his voice. "There must be something else to do. I'm begging ye."

"Laird, I feared this. The devil is taking hold of her."

"Don't say that. There must be something to do."

Rhiannon thought for a moment. "Well, I know a few of the old ways—charms and the like. Mind ye, we must make sure to use our faith in God as well or old *Cluitie* will make his own use of them."

It was a measure of his desperation that he said, "I will do anything. Please, I need to keep her alive until Katherine gets here."

Rhiannon nodded. "Very well. I will tell ye what ye need to do. Ye know that the rowan tree was sacred in the old ways. Even now, people place great store in its ability to ward off evil. If we need to turn the devil back, I reckon a rowan charm is the best way."

"What do ye need to make it? I will get it for ye."

"Ye have to be the one to make it, Laird. Ye will need to cut two small twigs, each about the same length, from a rowan. Cut no more than that. Never take more off a rowan tree than ye need. Ye will bind the twigs together, with red thread, into the shape of St. Andrew's cross. Then we will have Father Stephen bless it and we will bind it over her heart with a red ribbon."

"Is that all? That is simple enough."

"There is a bit more to it. Ye need to pray to the Blessed Mother and all the angels as ye are cutting the twigs."

"I have been praying constantly anyway. That will pose no problem."

"Also, ye need to cut the twigs from a rowan tree that ye have never laid eyes on before and the stronger the tree, the stronger its protection."

"How can I tell a strong tree from a weak one?"

"Strong trees grow in inhospitable places, in rocky soil or better yet out of a crag or cliff wall. Lucky for us, I know of just such a tree and I will warrant ye have never seen it. It isn't far from here. Perhaps an hour's walk or less."

"Can ye ride with me? There is no time to waste."

Although he meant no insult, her tone told him that he had affronted her in some way. "Aye, Laird, I am perfectly capable of sitting a horse. Let me just get my walking stick. The terrain near the cliff is rough and I wouldn't want to lose my footing."

After she had fetched her stick, he lifted her onto Con's

back and mounted behind her. He took a trail that led northward and soon the trees thinned and he could see the edge of the cliff rising ahead of them.

"Now just turn eastward a bit. The tree I'm thinking of isn't far from here."

This was the general area where they had killed the boar weeks ago. She was right. Because of his accident, he had not seen the cliff that day.

"Here, now. We will need to walk the rest of the way."

He dismounted and lifted Rhiannon from the saddle. Using her walking stick, she began to pick her way carefully toward the cliff's edge. He looped Con's reins around the branches of a small shrub and followed.

When they neared the edge she said, "Aye, this is the spot. I fear I am not steady enough on my feet to draw closer to the edge, but if ye just lean out a bit, near that boulder, ye will see it growing from a fissure there."

Fingal did as she said. Holding onto the boulder for balance, he leaned out. Sure enough, a young rowan grew out of a fissure but it was far enough away he wasn't sure he could reach it. He turned to tell her so and was struck full force in the chest by her walking stick. Losing his balance he fell backwards over the edge of the cliff.

Chapter 25

"I am rid of ye at last." Rhiannon stepped closer to the cliff and looked over the edge. She expected to see Fingal's mangled corpse at the foot of the cliff but she didn't. His bloodied body was caught upside down in another rowan tree about a third of the way down. He must have bounced against the rocks several times before being caught in the tree. His left arm hung at an odd angle, clearly broken. The back of his head was a bloody mess. From this distance she couldn't tell if he was still breathing, but even if he was, he wouldn't be for long. If he did manage to regain consciousness, he wouldn't be able to climb out with that broken arm.

Just to be sure, she would send Coby back tonight to make sure he was dead. She just had one more thing to attend to. She walked past the spot where Con was tethered. It would be so much easier to simply ride him back and set him loose but she feared he would be found and a search would start for Eithne's git before he had a chance to die—if he wasn't already dead.

Nay, it would be better to leave him tethered here. She would try to eliminate any signs of their passing as she walked back to her cottage. Furthermore, it would look more like an accident if his horse was still tethered where he left the beast.

It was nearly midday when she reached her cottage. She gathered the supplies she needed then made her way to the keep as she had every day since Gillian had taken so ill. That lass had proven much stronger than she had hoped. Foxglove had an unusual spicy flavor. Putting enough of it in a tisane to kill someone instantly was hard to do as they would be unlikely to drink enough of it after tasting it. Small amounts of foxglove given regularly could kill a weak person fairly quickly. It had taken no time for Meara to succumb. In fact, it had happened a little too fast. That was the reason she had put very little in the herbs she first gave Gillian.

She had hoped Gillian would sicken and die soon after her wedding. But she didn't. The lass seemed totally unaffected. Rhiannon had to add more to the second batch. She added still more as the days went on and Gillian failed to die. It was taking so long at one point Rhiannon had feared Agnes might figure it out. But for once, fortune had smiled on her. Agnes succumbed to a lung infection at the perfect time. Even so, Rhiannon could wait no longer. The laird had sent for another healer. If she was as skilled as he believed, she would know the signs of foxglove poisoning and be able to taste it in the tisane Lana dutifully prepared.

Now, Rhiannon simply had to give Gillian something that would assuredly kill her, remove the tainted herbs from her chamber before anyone was the wiser, and mourn with the rest of the clan. Imagine Gillian succumbing to melancholia on the same day the laird tragically fell to his death. She smiled to herself. It was all working out now.

She walked through the village and past the gate to Brathanead.

"Hello Mother," Coby said warmly. "Please tell Lady MacLennan she is in my prayers and I hope she is feeling better today."

"How thoughtful of ye. I will tell her."

"Rhiannon, have ye seen the laird?" Tarmon asked. "He rode out of here a couple of hours ago with the devil on his heels and he hasn't come back yet. It looked like he was heading towards yer cottage. I feared something had happened to Lady Gillian."

"Nay, Tarmon. I haven't seen him. He has been under a fair strain these last weeks. Maybe he just needed some time alone to clear his head."

Rhiannon continued on her way. She met Lana as she entered the hall.

"Rhiannon, I'm glad ye've come early today. Gillian is in a bad way. She is too weak to get out of bed. Fallon has been with her all morning and I am on my way up to sit with her now. I have her tisane here but she refused to drink it this morning."

"Give it to me. I will see she drinks it. She won't get better otherwise."

"I'll come with ye. I want to give Fallon a break. Worrying herself sick over Gillian will do no good."

"I have nothing pressing this afternoon. I will sit with

Gillian for a while."

"Ye needn't. I am so worried about her. I want to tend her for a while."

Rhiannon looked at her sternly. "Lana, I didn't want to say this to ye, but I fear ye have been too soft on her. Ye and the laird both let her have her way. She would be up and fighting this if ye didn't. Ye are letting her give up."

"That's not true. She is much worse today than she has been. She simply can't get out of bed."

Rhiannon patted her arm. "I know ye think ye are doing what is best, but perhaps if I try I will have better results. See to things down here and unless the devil has her completely in his grasp, I will get her up."

"If ye really think ye can, I suppose that is best."

Rhiannon took the tisane from Lana. "It is best. I will send Fallon down. See that she gets some fresh air. We wouldn't want the black bile building in her either."

"Oh dear, I didn't realize that could happen. Nay, we can't have that. Send her down."

"Of course, Lana." She sniffed the cup. "I think this needs to be a bit stronger. Is the packet of herbs in her room?"

"Nay, I have it here." Lana reached into her pocket, producing the packet.

Rhiannon took the packet from her and continued up the stairs. She knocked softly at the door and entered.

Fallon smiled wanly when she entered. "Rhiannon, I was expecting Mother, but I'm glad ye're here. Gillian is feeling very poorly today."

"Aye, so yer mother said. I'll set her to rights though. I have her tisane here."

"She wouldn't drink it this morning."

"I'm not deaf and I don't want it," snapped Gillian from the bed. "It isn't helping anymore. Just leave me alone."

Rhiannon frowned. "Fallon dear, perhaps ye should go help yer mother. With yer sister abed, there is much to do. I will sort things out here."

Fallon went to Gillian's side and caressed her cheek. "Gillian, I will go help mother but if ye need me for anything, send for me."

"I'm sorry I was cross with ye, Fallon. Thank ye."

"It's all right. I understand. I'll be back later." Fallon

kissed Gillian's cheek and left the room.

Rhiannon crossed the room, put the mug containing the tisane on the table and pulled a small flask from her pocket, pouring its contents in the mug. "I understand ye are being very contrary today, Gillian. Yer family loves ye and only wants the best for ye. Lying abed and failing to take yer medicine isn't very considerate. I thought better of ye than this." Her words had their intended effect. Tears welled in Gillian's eyes. "Now, I have prepared a new medicine for ye. I think it will pick ye right up. Be a good lass and drink it down."

Bodie growled from his spot on the bed beside Gillian as Rhiannon approached.

Gillian put her hand on him. "Bodie, stop. It's all right."

Gillian reached to take the mug from her. Bodie growled and snapped. Rhiannon pulled her hand away and took a step back. "Ye see, Gillian, even Bodie is upset by ye staying abed. He needs fresh air. I will just let him out, shall I?" She walked to the chamber door, opened it, and clicked her tongue. "Come on, lad. Ye want a nice run now don't ye?"

~ * ~

Gillian wasn't sure why Bodie had snapped at Rhiannon. That wasn't like him. She wouldn't have stopped him if he did want to go out, but she was glad when he stayed put. "I don't want him to go. He'll be fine," Gillian assured her.

"If ye say so." Rhiannon sat in a chair across the room.

Gillian lifted the mug to her lips and took a sip. It was bitter as gall. She frowned.

"Is something wrong, Gillian?"

"It's too hot, and it tastes different."

"Let it cool a bit if ye must, but the new medicine I added is a tad bitter."

For days Gillian had felt as if she were in a fog but for some reason she remembered something Fingal had said the evening after the hunt. He was talking about pain medicine. *It's bitter swill. But Gillian, it is what I tasted in the wine.* She took another sip. Bitter swill was right. This tasted horrible. "What do ye think this new medicine will do?"

"It will put everything to rights, dear. I should have thought of it days ago. Drink up."

What was Rhiannon doing? The wine she drank that night

had a faint bitter aftertaste and yet it had put her into a deep sleep. This was almost impossible to choke down. If this was the same thing, there was enough in this mug to kill her. *Rhiannon wouldn't try to kill me. What possible reason could she have?*

The night of the hunt she had asked Fingal why anyone would want to kill her. He'd said, *I don't know what the reason might be, Gillian, but I am not willing to risk yer life simply because I don't understand why it is in danger.*

She raised the mug to her lips again, taking another sip, shuddering at the taste. Bodie whined. The night of the hunt she had promised Fingal that she would accept a guard at all times, unless she was in this room with the door barred and Bodie at her side. *What am I doing? Something is wrong. For whatever reason, Rhiannon is trying to kill me and Bodie knows it.*

She wanted to get out of bed, to escape, but she was so weak she didn't believe she had the energy to reach the door. She had to make Rhiannon believe she was drinking the tisane. She put the mug to her lips again, but turned her head slightly away, letting the liquid dribble out of the cup and onto her pillows. The few sips she had taken were already making her a little drowsy but Gillian suspected Rhiannon would need to see that she drank much more if she intended to kill her. Still, maybe she could simply refuse. "I don't like this, Rhiannon. I have had enough."

"Gillian, I am shocked by yer behavior. One would think ye enjoy being ill. Is that it? Do ye want to lie abed and have people worrying about ye night and day?

"Nay, Rhiannon. I hate being sick."

"Then I will hear no more about the medicine tasting bad. Drink it." Bodie growled again. Gillian felt like growling. She had never heard Rhiannon take that sharp, demanding tone with anyone.

"I'll drink it. But first, would ye send someone for the laird please? Perhaps ye are right about Bodie. He'll go out with Fingal."

"I saw the laird leaving on horseback this morning. He isn't back yet. Ye are stalling, Gillian. Drink yer medicine."

Gillian put the cup to her lips again and spilled more into the pillows. She shuddered again. It wasn't an act. Even the bit of moisture left on her lips as she spilled it was foul enough to make her shudder. But half the mug was gone now.

"Are ye beginning to feel better yet?"

"I feel drowsy," Gillian said honestly. She didn't think she was in danger of losing consciousness but she needed to act the part. She lifted the cup again, spilling still more of its contents into the bed.

"I knew this would work. It will all be over soon, Gillian."

"What do ye mean?" She poured the rest of the tisane down the side of her face and into the bedding. She rubbed her face drowsily, wiping away the moisture so Rhiannon wouldn't suspect she hadn't consumed the tisane. She handed Rhiannon the mug. "If there was something that would help me feel better so quickly, why are ye only just giving it to me now?" She yawned and blinked as if trying to stay awake.

"Oh, dear me. Did I say it would make ye better? It won't exactly do that, Gillian. Ye will be falling asleep very soon and ye will never wake up."

Gillian tried to act surprised. "What do ye mean I will never wake up? Am I dying?"

"Yes, ye are. It has taken ye long enough. I thought ye would be dead weeks ago."

The meaning of her words sank in. "Have ye been poisoning me? With the tisane?"

"Aye, I have. But ye have a much stronger constitution than yer Aunt Meara."

"Aunt Meara too? But why?"

"Has yer mother never told ye the prophecy?

"Prophecy?" Gillian's thoughts really were muddled. Perhaps the few sips she took had been enough. She forced herself to focus.

"Aye, the prophecy about Fallon rising above the rest."

"I don't understand."

"Ye are dying, Gillian, but if ye want a bedtime story while ye slip away, I will be happy to tell ye one. I'm sure ye've heard tell that I'm a seer?"

"Aye," she whispered, forcing her eyes open.

"The Sight isn't what people believe it to be. It is simply wisdom, the ability to read a situation and sometimes to help a prediction come true."

"What do ye mean?" Gillian's voice sounded weak and reedy to her own ears.

"Well, secrets are always a good place to start. Ye know yerself, not much stays completely secret within a clan and I am especially good at ferreting them out. Secrets make an excellent starting place for predictions. I assure ye, Gillian, yer mother has a deep dark secret that she believes no one knows."

Gillian gasped.

"Surprised are ye? Well 'tis true. So, I simply used that knowledge to make the prediction about Fallon 'rising above all others'. It was a truly brilliant prediction."

Gillian's head was swimming. "I don't understand."

"Aye, I'm sure ye don't. Never mind. Another thing to remember is that the best predictions are those that people want realized. They will do everything in their power to fulfill such prophecies and yer mother wanted this prediction to come true. At first she thought she carried a boy who would rise to greatness. Of course my real hope was that the baby would be a girl who could marry my own son and I was overjoyed when the little raven haired beauty was born. I have worked for years to convince Lana to see Fallon betrothed to Coby."

"I thought that was mother's idea."

"Well, she thinks it was. But ye're father wouldn't hear of a betrothal for Fallon before ye, and I had no interest in Coby marrying ye. Lana tried again when Meara was chief but she wouldn't hear to it either."

"Good for Aunt Meara," muttered Gillian.

"Gillian, tsk, tsk. Meara might be alive today if she had agreed to it."

Tears welled in Gillian's eyes.

"As I said, she was much more cooperative than ye in that. But then, before Meara had been adequately mourned the king interfered and named Fingal MacIan as laird. Many in the clan were shocked that Lana didn't encourage ye to enter a convent. She had been so wrapped up in the idea of Fallon's destiny, it seemed the answer. But, Lana would never have allowed Fallon to marry Fingal and when ye married Fingal all of my plans were on the verge of crumbling when ye married Fingal. So she tried again. So far yer husband hasn't agreed to the betrothal either. However, I'm sure the elders will agree when yer grief stricken mother begs them to settle Fallon with my son. Together Coby and Fallon will rule this clan."

Gillian could no longer keep her eyes open. She couldn't stand to look at the evil glee on Rhiannon's face any longer. "But ye would need to kill us both for that to happen." She was so very sleepy. She needed to pretend the potion had had its desired effect anyway, but it wasn't hard.

"Aren't ye the clever lass. Aye, I had to kill ye both. And now I have.

As Gillian drifted off to sleep the last words Rhiannon said penetrated her consciousness. *And now I have.*

Chapter 26

Rhiannon watched Gillian for a few moments. Her breathing became slow and shallow but didn't stop. She had given her much more than enough to kill her. It might have been enough to kill a horse, but Gillian had revealed her tenacity over the last few weeks and this had to work. Rhiannon should really have made sure the ill-fated lass was truly dead but she didn't want to wait. Of course now that Gillian slept, it would be easy enough to put a pillow over her face and smother her. Rhiannon moved closer to the bed. Aye, that is what she would do. She reached across Gillian to grab a pillow. Bodie growled and snapped at her. She jerked away, but his teeth still managed to puncture the back of her hand. She sucked on it to stop the bleeding.

The dog stood over Gillian, his teeth bared, growling. She couldn't do anything with him there. She had to leave or the noise he was making would draw unwanted attention. "It doesn't matter, ye mangy beast. She will be dead soon anyway." She quickly grabbed the mug, rinsing it and dumping the water in the hearth. If anyone had tasted the residue they would know instantly that Gillian had been drugged. Rhiannon couldn't risk that.

Pulling the sleeve of her *léine* over her injured hand, she left the room and made her way to the great hall. "There ye are, Lana. Gillian took the tisane for me."

"Good. Thank ye so much. I am so worried about her. I'll just go up and sit with her for a while. I hate to leave her alone."

"Actually Lana, she is sleeping and I believe she needs the rest. Perhaps we have been pushing her too hard."

"Are ye sure? Ye seemed so very certain about the black bile."

"Aye, and I am still convinced that is the problem. However, since trying to build her blood up hasn't worked, I am going to reconsider a purgative to rid her of the black bile. That will be hard on her, so some rest before I give it is a good thing.

Just don't let Fallon or Ailsa, or any young woman for that matter, near her. We wouldn't want the devil to find his way into them."

"Nay, of course we wouldn't. I will let her rest for a while and keep the others away."

Rhiannon hurried out of the keep. When she reached the gate Tarmon asked, "How fares Lady Gillian today?"

"I fear she is no better. She is resting now. I think a purgative is called for. I am going home to prepare it.

"Mother, ye don't look well," Coby observed.

"Truthfully, son, this whole ordeal has made me sick at heart. I just wish I could do more for the poor child." She put her face in her hands and feigned a sob.

Tarmon patted her on the back. "Rhiannon, ye have done what ye could to ease her suffering."

"But it's just not enough," she sobbed.

"Coby, perhaps ye should help yer mother home. Clearly this is taking a toll on her."

Tarmon called up to one of the men on the wall. "Gavin, send a man down to guard the gate with me. Rhiannon isn't well and Coby needs to take her home."

When they were well away from the village, Coby finally asked. "Is she dead yet?"

"By now she probably is. I couldn't risk waiting for the foxglove to work. Fingal sent for Laird and Lady MacIan. If she is any kind of healer at all, she would recognize foxglove poisoning. I couldn't risk it. I had to get the herbs back. I gave her enough extract of poppy to kill her several times over. She isn't our problem now but the laird is."

"What do ye mean?"

"I knew when he became desperate enough he would grasp at anything. I told him he needed to collect two twigs from a rowan tree that he had never seen before and fashion a St. Andrew's cross from them."

"How would that old legend help rid us of him?"

She clucked. "Coby, when will ye learn to trust me? I sweetened the legend a bit. I told him the charm would be more powerful if he plucked the twigs from a tree growing in adversity. I took him to the cliff and pointed out such a tree growing from a fissure in the rock. After he leaned out to look at it, I gave him a little shove over the edge."

Coby stopped in his tracks and laughed aloud. "Mother,

ye're truly wicked."

"Malcolm's illegitimate get should not be ruling this clan. Even if she couldn't bear him any children, Nuala MacRae didn't deserve what he did to her and I will see the insult repaid."

"Mother, ye do live by an odd set of rules. Ye still intend for me to marry Fallon don't ye?"

"Of course I do. But don't fall in love with that pretty face. As soon as she has produced a few heirs for ye, I will rid the world of her too."

"I almost feel sorry for Fallon."

His mother arched a brow at him.

"I said almost."

"Well, we still have one tiny problem."

"What's that?"

"I'm not entirely sure the laird is dead."

"What? Mother, how could ye be so careless? Surely he noticed ye push him over the cliff. What happened?"

"Don't make more of this than it is. He went over the cliff but was caught in a tree about a third of the way down. I think he's dead. I couldn't tell for sure. At least he was unconscious, one arm was obviously broken and the back of his head was covered in blood. I suspect he cracked it open as he fell. If he is not dead already, he will be soon. Even if he regains consciousness, there is no way he can climb out."

"We can't risk that. I'll go up to the cliff and make sure he is dead. What did ye do with his horse?"

"I left it where he tethered it. It will look more like he had an accident that way."

"*This* accident had better work."

"Well son, ye have fouled up all the other ones."

"So now this is my fault? The problem with making accidents happen, mother, is that they must *look* like accidents. Did ye expect me to stand up on the wall and throw a stone block at him? Someone would have noticed."

"Ye said ye had a perfect shot when ye were searching for those raiders."

"I did. I fell far enough back that no one saw me pull the bow. He turned away at the last minute. I couldn't very well take a second shot. But ye were the one that gave me the drug for the wine the night I set the fire. Christ almighty, I was barely through the passage door when he woke."

"I gave ye more than enough in that to knock them out. I can't help it that he didn't drink it."

"And I can't help it that underbrush kept him from breaking his neck on the hunt. His luck has been uncanny. That is why we must make sure he is dead," Coby said.

~ * ~

Coby left his mother in her cottage and made his way through the forest to the cliff as quickly as possible. He passed Con, still tethered to the bush. The horse nickered and snorted. "Tired of standing there are ye lad? Never ye mind, a search party of worried MacLennans will be through here by dark I warrant, then ye can go home." He made his way to the edge of the cliff and looked over.

"Hell fire and damnation!" He could see the damaged tree a third of the way down, but the bastard was gone.

"Coby, so kind of ye to come looking for me."

Coby spun around to see Fingal come from the other side of a large boulder, sword in hand. His clothes were torn, his hair was caked with blood and his left arm was obviously broken, just as his mother had said. And yet somehow, he had managed to climb back up. *Well, he should be easy enough to finish off.* Coby drew his sword.

In spite of his battered condition, Fingal parried his blows easily. Brute force wasn't going to work; the laird was too skilled. But he looked to have lost a lot of blood. If Coby could spar long enough to tire Fingal, perhaps then he could best him. Maybe goading him to anger wouldn't go astray either.

"Ye are quite a skilled swordsman, Laird. How embarrassing will it be for everyone to learn ye died, tripping off the edge of a cliff?" Their swords clashed but Fingal remained in control.

"I didn't die. That should be fairly obvious. For that matter I didn't trip either. Yer sweet mother gave me a little shove." Fingal was the aggressor this time and Coby had to focus solely on his opponent's movements.

"Do ye wonder why?" He needed to distract Fingal.

"Nay, I know why. When I came to after the fall, I figured it out." Fingal went on the offensive. It was all Coby could do to defend himself. "Ye seem to be having trouble, Coby. I suppose I look like easy prey, but I wasn't hurt that badly. I have a broken arm and a raging headache. And all these years I thought Niall was the one with the hard head. Seems mine's fairly resilient."

Fingal lunged, slicing deeply into Coby's left arm. White hot pain coursed through him as blood blossomed on his sleeve.

"I figure yer mother thought it was all worked out," Fingal continued. "Gillian is sick. If Rhiannon could get rid of me and see ye wed to Fallon, ye will be the next laird." Fingal lunged again; pain shot through Coby's right hip. Fingal stepped back, giving him a moment's break. "Do I have that right?"

Fingal attacked again. Coby stumbled, but recovered and parried. He had to focus. He had to distract Fingal. "Well, there is a bit more to it than that."

"Do tell," Fingal said, forcing him ever closer to the edge of the cliff.

"Gillian isn't sick, she's dead. Mother saw to that this afternoon."

Fingal screamed like a berserker.

Chapter 27

It was with tremendous relief that Eadoin met Niall's party late morning, just several hours ride from Brathanead.

"Laird MacIan, Lady Gillian is dreadfully ill."

"She has gotten worse?" Quinn asked.

"Aye, she has. The laird fears for her life. He expected ye a week ago. This morning he sent me to fetch ye."

"We couldn't come sooner. There was a problem with Rowan's wedding, but that's another story," Niall said.

"What's happening with Lady Gillian?" Katherine asked. "Quinn told us about her having lost the baby. He also said that Agnes passed away, I am so very sorry to hear that. She was a good woman."

"We have another healer, my lady," Eadoin said. "Her name is Rhiannon and she believes it's melancholia."

"That can certainly happen, especially when one has suffered so many losses, but it isn't life-threatening."

"My lady, she is sick all of the time. She can't hold anything down and has no energy. Today the laird couldn't get her out of bed."

Katherine frowned. "Niall, we must hurry. I don't like the sound of this. I don't think it's melancholia."

Niall shook his head. "We can't travel any faster with the wagon."

"Then let me ride ahead. It isn't that far now," Katherine said.

"Ye are not riding ahead without me and I am not leaving the wagon carrying our children and Edna unguarded."

Katherine laughed. "It is hardly unguarded, Niall. Half of yer garrison is with us."

He frowned. "Not half."

"Well nearly. I'm riding ahead. Ye can either send guardsmen with me, or leave them with the wagon."

"Katherine, ye would try the patience of a saint," Niall said, but clearly he had capitulated. "Turcuil, Keavy, and Alan, ride ahead with Lady Katherine. Quinn, ye and Eadoin go too. We won't be long behind ye."

Eadoin understood Niall's desire to protect his wife, but more than anything, he needed to get Katherine to Brathanead as soon as possible. "Thank ye, Laird. I promise ye Lady Katherine will be well guarded until ye reach Brathanead."

Katherin rode up to Niall and leaned over to give him a kiss. He cupped her face in his hand, returning her kiss. "Be careful, love."

"I will be. And Niall?"

"Aye, love?"

"No one will ever confuse ye with a saint."

He laughed heartily as she rode off, surrounded by her guard.

~ * ~

It was early afternoon when Katherine rode through the gates at Brathanead. It had been nearly two years since she had arrived the first time. Then she had been traveling with Niall on their way to the Highlands after their wedding. She had been extremely ill at the time and could barely remember it.

On the ride to Brathanead, Eadoin told her everything that had happened since Quinn left. At Duncurra, Quinn had shared everything he knew about the attempts on Fingal and Gillian's lives, including Fingal's concerns about Gillian's mother. She remembered Duncan's wife, Lana, from her first visit. Lana had been less than warm at the time, but Katherine had been an outsider. She had a hard time believing that any mother would seek her child's death and yet, she knew Eithne would have.

Katherine didn't know what to think, but her first order of business would be to see Gillian. As they entered the keep, Lana came rushing towards her. "Lady Katherine, I am so glad ye are here. My daughter Gillian has been terribly ill."

"That is what I hear. Take me to her and I will see what can be done."

"She is sleeping now, my lady. Our healer, Rhiannon, left just a few minutes ago. She said to let her sleep. She believes a purgative is required and wants her to be rested first. When she comes back, ye can see Gillian with her."

Katherine smiled. "Lana, I understand that Gillian has been extremely ill and only grows worse."

"Aye, she has my lady. That is why she needs to rest."

"Rest is certainly important, but if she is as sick as ye say, I think it best if I see her now."

"But Rhiannon said no one should disturb her."

Katherine was done arguing. "Eadoin, will ye show me to Lady Gillian's chamber please."

Lana's mouth fell open in shock.

"Aye, my lady, come this way."

Katherine followed Eadoin up the stairs with Lana on her heels. Quinn and Turcuil followed them. She tapped on the door but there was no answer.

"I told ye, she is sleeping," Lana said.

Katherine tapped again and opened to door. A large brindle hound stood on the bed beside Gillian's still body and barked. So as not to startle the animal, Katherine crossed to the bed slowly, offering the beast her hand. He sniffed it, then whined and licked his mistress's face. "Ye've guarded her well, lad, let me see to her now. She shook Gillian gently by the shoulders. "Gillian, wake up. My name is Katherine." She didn't wake. Katherine put her hand on Gillian's chest and her ear to Gillian's lips. The dog whined again. "Wheesht, lad, let me listen."

Lana looked on, horror-struck. "She's not...Gillian, wake up," she ordered, her voice strident.

Katherine felt Gillian's forehead, then gently brushed the hair from her face. She felt moisture in her hair and investigated further. "Her pillow is wet. Very wet." She carefully lifted Gillian's head and removed the wet pillow, replacing it with a dry one. "The sheet on this side of her is wet too." She lifted her fingers to her nose to sniff the moisture then tentatively touched her tongue to it. "It's poppy and it's very strong." Turning on Lana she demanded, "dear God, how much did ye give her?"

"I didn't give her any poppy. The only thing I have given her is the herb tisane Rhiannon prescribed."

"What was in it?"

"Mint, comfrey, thyme, and chamomile. Recently she added St. John's wort to ward off the devil."

Katherine rolled her eyes. She knew the value of herbs in treating illnesses but she believed prayer and faith kept the devil at bay, not a bit of dried weeds. "Is that all that's in it?"

"I-I don't know. Those are the main ingredients that I can taste."

"Really? Does this taste like chamomile and mint to ye?" Katherine thrust the pillow at her.

Lana touched the wet spot and lifted her fingers to her lips. "Nay, that is poppy. My lady, I swear there was no poppy in the tisane I sent up. I wouldn't hurt my daughter. Why would ye think that?"

Katherine wanted to believe her. "Lana, she is barely breathing and her heart is beating much too slowly. If ye didn't give her the poppy, who could have?"

"The only person who saw her was Rhiannon and she would never hurt Gillian."

"The healer who told ye to let her rest before she purged her?"

"Aye."

"Where is she?"

"She's gone to her home. It is beyond the village, near the edge of the forest. She said she would be back this evening. Shall I send for her?"

"Nay. I need to speak with Fingal, immediately." As sick as Gillian was, Katherine was frankly surprised he wasn't at her bedside.

"He rode out of the keep this morning, my lady, and hasn't returned."

"What? Where did he go?"

"I don't know, he didn't say."

"How long has he been gone?" demanded Eadoin.

"He left shortly after ye did."

"He has been gone for hours, alone, with his wife lying ill and no one thought that strange?" Quinn asked. "Where is Bran MacBain?"

Eadoin ran his hands through his hair in frustration. "I'm sure he has been on the training field with the men. I'll warrant no one told him the laird left alone. We need to find him. Turcuil, ye and Quinn stay here and guard Lady Katherine and Lady Gillian. Lady Katherine, I will send a maid and Tira MacBain up. Tira may be some help and the maid will fetch ye anything ye need. Ye are not to leave the room until we know what's going on."

Lana shook her head. "Ye needn't take anyone away from other work and Tira is a midwife. I don't see what help she can offer. I'll help Lady Katherine."

"Nay, ye won't, Lana. Ye will stay in yer chamber, under guard."

"Why?"

"Someone has been trying to kill Fingal and Gillian for weeks," Eadoin said. "Now it appears Gillian has been drugged with poppy, again."

"What do ye mean again?"

"She was drugged the night of the fire. We suspect that it was not the accident it appeared to be."

"Surely ye don't suspect me?"

"Lana, I don't want to believe ye could do this, but I will take no chances."

Tears welled in her eyes. "Eadoin, I love her. I would never harm her. I know I have always been closer to Fallon, but I had my reasons. It doesn't mean I love Gillian less. Please, Eadoin, let me stay here with her."

"I'm sorry, Lana."

"Eadoin, wait. Tira and I will both be here, and Turcuil and Quinn will be right outside the door. Lana will not be able to hurt Gillian or anyone else, even if she wanted to."

"My lady, I don't think the laird would approve."

"Why would ye say that, Eadoin?" demanded Lana.

Katherine put up a hand to silence her. "I am aware of his concerns, Eadoin. I promise ye, Gillian will be safe."

"All right. Quinn, Turcuil, one word from Lady Katherine and ye will remove Lana from this room and see that she is guarded until I return." They agreed, taking up their posts outside the door.

When they had left, Katherine turned back to Gillian. She checked her over carefully, but other than her shallow breathing and slow pulse could find nothing. She was too thin, but Eadoin had told her Gillian had been unable to eat for days.

"Is there anything ye can do to help her, my lady?" Lana asked.

"Right now we can only wait for her to wake. I can't imagine a miscarriage leading to all of this. How long had she been pregnant? It couldn't have been very long. They had only been married a little more than eight weeks when it happened."

"I think it was less than that my lady. She had only begun to complain of morning sickness a week earlier and she wasn't sure of the timing of her last courses but she thought it had been a little over a month."

"That wasn't very long. If she wasn't sure she had missed her courses yet, it was the morning sickness that made ye think she was pregnant?"

"Aye, it was most distressing. Rhiannon's tisane was the only thing that helped."

"So she went to Rhiannon because she was sick? Not Agnes or a midwife?"

"Nay, she hadn't gone to any of them. Rhiannon gave her the herbs for the tisane the day after her wedding. She told her to drink a mug every day and it would help her conceive fine strong sons."

Katherine smiled. She knew many people who believed that one potion or another would help them conceive sons but she had yet to find one that actually seemed to work. "Do ye have any of the herbs? I'd like to see what is in this fine blend."

"I had the packet but Rhiannon brought it up when she gave the tisane to Gillian earlier. She thought perhaps a stronger brew was needed. They should be here somewhere." She began looking around the room. Tira MacBain arrived while Lana searched.

"Ye must be Lady MacIan. I am Tira MacBain. How is Lady Gillian?"

"It is lovely to meet ye, Tira. Please call me Katherine. I must be honest, I am worried about her. It appears that someone gave her poppy."

Tira frowned. "Poppy? Are ye sure?"

"Aye, but much of it was poured onto the bedclothes. I don't know how much she consumed."

Tira glanced at Lana, who was now riffling through a chest, and raised a questioning brow.

"She was trying to find the packet of herbs she used to make the tisane Rhiannon prescribed," Katherine explained.

"Here it is. No, wait this is the first packet from weeks ago. I thought it was gone. Well, it should have been much the same anyway, except Rhiannon added St. John's wort as I mentioned."

She gave the packet to Katherine, who spilled some into her palm and looked closely at it. She rubbed some of it between her fingers and sniffed it. Then she put a pinch of it directly on her tongue to taste it. She frowned.

"I told ye there was no poppy in it."

"Aye, and ye were right but there is more than just mint, thyme, comfrey, and chamomile." She handed it to Tira. "What do ye taste?"

Tira too examined it closely before tasting it. Her eyes widened. "Tansy and pennyroyal."

Katherine nodded but Lana shook her head. "Nay, Rhiannon wouldn't put tansy and pennyroyal in something meant to aid conception. They do the opposite, bringing on courses. They can even cause a lass to lose a baby. The brew didn't taste of pennyroyal or tansy."

"But when the herbs are steeped in water, all the flavors blend together. Also, the mint becomes especially strong and masks the other flavors. It is only by sampling the dry herbs that ye can taste each separate one."

"Let me taste." Lana took a pinch of the herbs and placed it on her tongue. A look of horror crossed her face. "Oh dear God, ye're right. If she was drinking this every day it might have been enough to cause her to miscarry."

"Did ye taste anything else?" Katherine asked. Both of the other women shook their heads. "Rub a nice bit of it hard between yer fingers to release the oils, then touch yer finger to yer tongue."

Tira tried it. "Something is a little hot, but I don't recognize it."

Lana's eyes filled with tears and Katherine asked, "Do ye recognize it Lana?"

"Aye," she sobbed. "It is foxglove. Rhiannon has been poisoning my daughter slowly with foxglove."

"I fear she has. It would certainly account for many of her symptoms. It might have been the cause of her nausea in the first place. It certainly would explain why it continued afterwards."

"But the tisane always seemed to help."

"Aye, it would for a while, but as her body absorbed each new dose of poison, it would come back. There isn't much in this. It would be enough to make a young, healthy woman feel sick and perhaps fatigued if she drank it every day, but it would take quite a while to kill her."

"After Gillian kept getting sicker, Rhiannon changed the recipe. Maybe she put more in, but I can't find the newest packet. She had me give it to her three times a day."

Katherine went to the bed to check on Gillian. She was still barely breathing. "Well, she should recover. It may take a while for it all to leave her body but with time, it will." The real question was whether she would ever wake from the poppy sleep.

Chapter 28

Niall found Brathanead in an uproar. He and the remainder of their party arrived less than an hour after his wife and her guard. Alan met him in the courtyard. "Laird, things are bad. Fingal's concerns were not unfounded. Someone drugged Lady Gillian with poppy. Lady Katherine is with her, but fears she may not wake."

"She is in the laird's chamber?"

"Aye, Laird."

"I'll go to her. Ye and Keith find a room for Edna and the children and keep them under guard."

"I will, Laird, but there is something else. Fingal is missing. He left the keep on horseback this morning and hasn't been seen since."

"God's teeth." Niall swore. "Does anyone have a clue as to where he might have gone?"

"Several people remember seeing him ride through the village, but no one paid attention to where he went. We are forming search parties and will head out soon. I assumed ye would want to go along."

"Aye, let me check on Katherine and I'll be back down in a moment."

He took the stairs two at a time. Katherine stepped into the hall when he knocked on the door.

"How is she?"

"She was given poppy this afternoon and is in a deep sleep. But that isn't the worst of it. Do ye know the woman called Rhiannon?"

"Aye. I think she had been a companion to Malcolm's wife at one time. She was married to one of Malcolm's father's guardsman. They have a son. If I remember right, I think her husband was killed at Halidon Hill. She has always been a bit odd. People whispered about her."

"What did they whisper?"

"The usual things one hears about odd women who live apart. Some said she was a seer and held her in high regard. Others thought she dabbled in the old ways and were suspicious. But why are ye asking about Rhiannon?"

"Because I think she is the one who drugged Gillian. What's more, it looks like she's been slowly poisoning her with foxglove."

"Rhiannon? Are ye sure it couldn't be Lana as Fingal suspected? I can't see what motive Rhiannon would have."

"I don't think it's Lana. She seemed genuinely shocked, not to mention heart-broken when I discovered the foxglove in Rhiannon's tisane. She had been brewing it for Gillian and encouraging her to drink it all this time. She is feeling profound guilt. I can't imagine she would take any responsibility if she were behind it."

Niall rubbed his head. "I don't know what to think. I trust yer instincts but please be cautious until we know more. I am going out now with men to search for Fingal. I will make sure Rhiannon is guarded until we can get to the bottom of this."

~ * ~

Fingal knew not to let rage overtake him in battle. *Physical prowess means nothing without cleverness. Lose yer wits and ye will lose the battle every time.* His father had drilled this into him, over and over, and it had served him well.

Today that proved false.

He was more badly injured than he had let on. When he had awakened, caught and hanging upside down in the rowan tree he had been sure he would not survive it. Blood dripped steadily from the back of his head. His left arm was broken as were several ribs, based on how it hurt to breathe. He had no idea how long he had hung there, unconscious. Every move he made hurt but he knew he had to keep going in spite of the pain. He was certain Gillian's life depended on it. His memory was fuzzy and it made no sense to him, but he was sure Rhiannon had pushed him off the cliff. And if she did, was it possible she had been involved in the other attempts on their lives?

So, with the help of the dagger he wore strapped to his leg, and sheer determination, he had worked steadily to extricate himself from the branches of the tree, then climb up the cliff. Inch by painful inch, his progress had been excruciatingly slow. It must have taken the better part of two hours. The top part of the cliff, while a steep incline, was not a sheer drop. His body had probably hit it several times as he tumbled down, accounting for his battered state. However, it also made it possible for him to climb out and perhaps was what gave the rowan tree a place to take root. Below the tree, the cliff face cut sharply back. Had the tree not been there, he would have plummeted to his death.

As he had struggled to climb, his thoughts whirled, trying to make sense of what had happened. It hadn't taken him long to determine, as he originally expected, that this had something to do with Fallon. He was even more inclined to believe that Lana was involved in some way because she had pushed so hard for a betrothal between Fallon and Coby. He still didn't believe that Fallon was remotely involved. This was something Rhiannon and Lana must have conspired over. Although the only way that Fallon and any husband selected for her would take over the leadership of the clan was if both he and Gillian were dead, with Gillian so very ill it would take little effort to kill her. This would be made even easier if the person trying to kill her was the one supposedly working to heal her.

That was it. In spite of the throbbing pain in his head, everything became crystal clear. Rhiannon was causing Gillian's mysterious illness. It had to be the tisane. He remembered how Gillian searched for the herbs the morning after they had first made love, because Rhiannon told her the brew would help her conceive fine, strong sons, the same tisane that he and Lana had practically forced down her at Rhiannon's insistence, believing it would cure her. This single realization is what helped keep him climbing upwards, in spite of all the pain. He had to get to Gillian before whatever was in that tisane did kill her.

When he reached the top of the cliff he heard someone speaking. Not sure who it was, he hid on the other side of the huge boulder. He heard Coby curse. Of course. Rhiannon had sent Coby to make sure he was dead. Coby too was clearly involved. Fingal made a split second decision. Better to go on the offensive, letting his opponent believe he was not seriously injured, than to hide and let him think he had the upper hand.

Fingal pulled on every last reserve of energy. He willfully ignored the pain in his arm and ribs. He focused his mind on a single purpose—defeating his opponent. His father believed mental focus was more important in battle that brute strength and

Fingal prayed it was true, for God knew he had precious little strength left.

And it had worked. Coby may have started the fight over-confident, trying to goad him, but Fingal kept his focus. He did not allow Coby to distract him. Even severely weakened, Fingal had struck flesh several times. Then Coby had said the words that caused Fingal's heart to freeze. *Gillian isn't sick, she's dead. Mother saw to that this afternoon.*

Engulfed by rage, all rational thought fled. Fingal emitted an unearthly scream of rage and pain. He lunged at Coby, intending to bury his sword in the cur's gut.

Taken by surprise, Coby stumbled backwards to avoid the thrust. He fell over the edge of the cliff screaming. Fingal watched in horror as he fell. The rowan tree did not stop Coby's descent. His scream ended when he hit the bottom of the gulch.

Fingal fell to his knees, struggling to breathe. His beautiful, strong, funny, passionate wife was dead. He didn't know if the searing agony he felt was because of his broken ribs, or his broken heart. Part of him wanted to throw himself to his death to end the misery of loss that he knew would shadow him for the rest of his days. The other part—the stronger part—wanted to see the teeny, grizzled old git brought to justice.

Eventually, he rose from his knees, made his way to Con, mounted, and rode towards Brathanead. It would never be home again without Gillian.

Chapter 29

After Coby left for the cliff, Rhiannon gathered up her stores of questionable herbs. She certainly could not risk anyone finding the carefully dried and ground foxglove in her cottage. She placed them in a cloth sack and tied them under her skirts until she could find a place to hide them. She also quickly made a mixture of mint, thyme, comfrey, chamomile and St. John's wort, creating a packet that looked just like the one she recovered from Lana. If anyone asked for it, they would find nothing untoward in it.

She intended to clean and dress the puncture wounds on her hand when she heard someone ride into the yard. Blaze barked madly. Again, she pulled her sleeve down over her hand before going to the door.

"Tarmon, what brings ye here?"

"I've come to fetch Coby back to the keep. The MacIan's have arrived and the laird is missing. No one seems to know what has happened to him. We are sending out search parties and need every able body."

"Oh, dear. He isn't here." Curse it all, she thought she would have more time. She needed an excuse. Glancing around the yard, her eyes landed on their small byre. "My cow strayed. Ye know how they do when they are ready to calf. He went to find her." The cow had wandered off that morning and would wander back that evening as she always did but it made a good excuse. "Ye go on back to the keep. I'll go now and find him."

"Thank ye, Rhiannon."

He remounted and rode back towards Brathanead.

She grabbed her walking stick and started up the path to the cliffs. She hadn't gone far when she heard a horse on the path ahead of her. It couldn't be Fingal. Coby must have decided to retrieve Fingal's mount. She glimpsed the horse through the trees. A bloodied man was slumped in the saddled. She fairly dove off the path, hiding herself in the dense undergrowth. He raised his head, as if he had heard her. She held her breath as he rode past. He hadn't seen her. She had to find Coby. They could not let Fingal reach Brathanead.

As soon as she was sure it was safe, she made her way as fast as she could to the cliff. Surely she would find Coby there, searching for Fingal. Having found no sign of him, dread gripped her heart. Approaching the edge of the cliff, she looked over, covering her mouth to keep from screaming. Her son's crumpled body lay at the bottom. She clenched her teeth as tears streamed down her face. "I will avenge ye, son. I swear. Malcolm's bastards will not win."

She could not return to her home. She had to find a place to hide until she could act. There was only one place where she could hide and still have the access she needed to exact her revenge. She walked westward along the top of the cliff to where the slope wasn't as steep and a path was worn into it, winding downward. Before reaching the bottom she came to an opening from which an underground stream flowed, feeding the burn that wove through the bottom of the gully. It looked like little more than a crack in the rock wall but once she squeezed through, it opened into a wider cave.

She hadn't come prepared with a torch and the light from the cave opening only penetrated a few feet. Still, she knew the way. She placed her right hand on the wall and walked. As long as she kept her hand on the wall, always taking the path to the right, she would come to the door. She knew the walk through the cave from the cliff wall to the door could take upwards of two hours but she was in no hurry. Someone would patch the bastard up but she would see him dead soon enough.

Chapter 30

Fingal emerged from the forest near Rhiannon's cottage to find mounted men spreading out from Brathanead's village. His brother Niall pounded on Rhiannon's door as Blaze barking wildly on the other side.

"By everything that is holy, Fingal, what in the hell happened to ye?" his brother demanded.

"I was desperate, Niall. She was dying. I was willing to try anything." Fingal had to stop for a moment. It hurt so damn bad to breathe.

"Wheesht. Tell me later. We need to get ye back to the keep."

The fear on Niall's face told Fingal that he looked as bad as he felt. He saw stars and feared he would pass out but he had to continue. "I went with Rhiannon to cut twigs from a rowan tree to make a charm. She pushed me over the cliff. I climbed out. Killed Coby." Despair filled him and everything began to go black. "She killed Gillian."

~ * ~

He woke later to an excruciating pain in his arm. Some hellish demon was pulling it while a giant held him down.

"I'm sorry, Fingal, I had hoped ye would stay unconscious for that."

The demon had a sweet, very familiar voice. Nay, not a demon. "Katherine," he whispered.

"Do ye still need me to hold him, my lady?"

Well he had been half right. A giant held him down.

"Nay, Turcuil, I'm finished. Now that the bones are aligned, I just need to splint it."

His foggy brain cleared a bit more. He looked around. It was late. The windows were dusky twilight and candles lit the room. He was in one of the chambers at Brathanead but not the one he shared with Gillian. *Gillian.* Memories came flooding back.

Coby's taunt gutted him. *Gillian isn't sick, she's dead. Mother saw to that this afternoon.* "Rhiannon killed Gillian," he whispered.

Katherine took his good hand in hers. "Nay, she didn't Fingal. Gillian is still alive."

Could it be true? When he thought her dead, all light had left his world. He struggled to sit up. "Alive? I must see her."

"Nay, Fingal. She is sleeping. Let me finish patching ye up first."

"Don't worry about me. Katherine, she is terribly ill. I fear Rhiannon and maybe her mother tried to poison her. Ye can't let either of them near her."

"I know, Fingal. I don't think that Lana was involved, but Rhiannon was definitely trying to poison her. She mixed small amounts of foxglove in the herbs she gave Gillian."

"Her son is dead, but where is she? I will see justice done. She must be held accountable. If Gillian...nay I won't even think it. She must live and Rhiannon must not be allowed anywhere near her. I want the vile woman under lock and key."

"No one gets near Gillian unless Bodie says they do. Rhiannon is missing anyway, but Niall has at least fifty men out searching for her. Fingal, I do think Gillian will live through this. She has a strong spirit and now that we know what was making her ill, I think she can recover fully."

"Are ye sure? Coby said Rhiannon killed her this afternoon. Yer sure there isn't something more?"

"Well, she certainly tried to kill her this afternoon. It appears she drugged Gillian with poppy. I'm not sure how it happened but much of it was spilled on the bedding. She is still in a deep sleep, but her breathing is becoming more regular and I am hopeful that she will wake soon."

"Where is she? Who is with her?"

"Father Stephen is—"

"Father Stephen? Dear God, has she received the last rites?"

"Nay, Fingal, calm down. Father Stephen is just worried about her, as we all are. Edna and Lana are with her too and Quinn is standing guard."

"I don't want Lana near her."

"Fingal, I told ye I don't believe Lana knew anything about the poisoned herbs."

"Ye are too trusting, Katherine."

She harrumphed and rolled her eyes. "Well, there is no doubt ye are Niall's brother. Fingal, I assure ye, she is safe. As soon as I finish splinting yer arm, I will take ye to her. Ye had the good sense to stay unconscious while I stitched yer head and nothing but rest will fix those broken ribs."

When his arm was firmly strapped between two narrow boards, she helped him sit up. His head swam and throbbed and the movement caused waves of pain to shoot through his ribs but it eased after a moment. Then he remembered something. "Katherine, do ye have any red thread?"

She smiled and cocked her head, clearly confused by the question. "Aye. Why?"

"Where is the sheath for my dagger?"

"Here it is." Turcuil handed it to him. Fingal fumbled with it using only his right hand for a moment before sighing and handing it back to Turcuil. "There are two rowan twigs in it. Can ye get them out for me?"

When Turcuil handed them to him, he positioned them into the shape of St. Andrew's cross. "Katherine, can ye help me bind these with the red thread?"

Turcuil nodded, finally understanding, but Katherine, who was not from the Highlands, said, "Aye, but why?"

Turcuil explained, "It is a very ancient practice. The rowan was sacred in the old ways. Some folks still believe the rowan can protect ye from evil if ye pluck two twigs and bind them in the shape of St. Andrew's cross."

"It was why I went with Rhiannon to the cliff in the first place," Fingal said. "I feared Gillian was dying and Rhiannon offered no other hope. She said the protection would be greater if the tree was very strong and the person collecting the twigs had never seen it before."

"Aye, so it's said," agreed Turcuil.

Katherine looked skeptical. "I know it is superstition, but Katherine, the tree these twigs came from saved me. It stopped me from falling to my death. I figure it is a powerful tree and if it protected me, perhaps it will protect her as well." He gave her a sheepish grin. "It can't hurt."

Katherine smiled. "I would have to agree." She bound the twigs and handed him back the small cross they formed.

He stood up and Turcuil grabbed his uninjured elbow.

"I can walk, Turcuil."

"Well, ye didn't walk in here, so while I believe ye, thousands wouldn't."

Fingal took a few steps and suppressed a groan. His body definitely was telling him that he had tumbled down a rock face today but nothing would keep him from Gillian.

When they reached his chamber, Fingal and Katherine entered while Turcuil stayed in the corridor with Quinn.

Fingal went straight to the bed. Gillian was pale and so very still, but the steady rise and fall of her chest told him she lived. Bodie lay beside her. He raised his head and wagged his tail. Fingal caressed her cheek and kissed her forehead before greeting the others in the room.

Edna embraced him gently. "Fingal, thank God ye survived that fall."

"It shouldn't surprise ye. Ye've always said I was hard headed. It's come in handy a few times of late."

"Well, ye'll be right as nails soon. Lady Katherine will see to that. And she'll see to yer beautiful lass too. Mark my words."

Father Stephen also stood to greet him. "Laird, I agree. Surviving that fall was nothing short of a miracle. I continue to pray that the Lord sees ye both through these dark hours."

"Thank ye, Father. Gillian and I both appreciate that. I have a small favor to ask though." He held the rowan cross out to him. "The tree that saved me was a rowan. I know the tradition is left over from the old ways, but this saltire is made of twigs from that tree. I...well...I want to put it near Gillian to protect her. Will ye bless it?"

"Of course I will. May almighty God, St. Andrew, and all the angels and saints guard and protect her." He said a blessing in Latin and after making the sign of the cross handed it back to Fingal.

Lana stood near the hearth. "Laird, I too am glad ye are well."

"I'm not sure I'd jump straight to 'well' but I'll live."

"Please God, Gillian will too." Lana looked pale and drawn, exactly as a distraught mother should.

He couldn't help it. He would not be able to tolerate being in the same room with her or allowing her near Gillian until he knew.

"Lana, what do ye know about all of this?"

"I know what ye know, Laird. Rhiannon tried to poison

Gillian."

"Ye had no role in it?"

Father Stephen was shocked. "Laird, surely ye don't suspect Lana of harming her child."

"Nay, Laird! I would never harm Gillian."

"Would ye not? Not even to see Fallon 'rise above all others'?"

Lana trembled. Tears welled in her eyes. "Laird, perhaps I deserve yer suspicion. I have treated Fallon differently. There were reasons that I don't expect anyone to understand. Still, I would give my own life this instant, if it meant saving Gillian's. I swear to ye, by God's holy bones, I knew nothing about the poison in the herbs Rhiannon gave me. I gave Gillian the tisane, just like ye did, hoping to see her well again."

"If ye and Rhiannon were not working together, why did ye try so hard to get me to arrange a betrothal between Fallon and Coby?"

"I—I have wanted that for years."

"Have ye? Why? What was so special about him that ye nagged yer husband then me to see them wed? He had no great skills, an average warrior at best. He was neither wealthy, nor particularly handsome or charming. In fact, he was ordinary in all things. Surely lovely, warm-hearted Fallon, the child ye believed was destined to 'rise above all others', deserved more than mediocrity?"

"I never looked at it like that. It was just always meant to be."

"It was meant to be. Why would ye think that? Oh, let me guess, Rhiannon *predicted* it."

"Nay, she didn't. Oh, she talked for years about how nice it would be for them to marry but she didn't predict it. I respected Rhiannon, nearly everyone did. I was flattered that she wanted Fallon as a daughter by marriage. She thought it was to be a good match and I agreed. We dreamed about sharing grandchildren. It pleased her so to think of them married."

"I'm sure it did. It would also give her a very good motive for wanting Gillian and I dead. If Rhiannon had succeeded in killing us, and she could manipulate ye into marrying Fallon to Coby, her son would become laird."

"Laird, I love my daughter. All of my daughters." Tears spilled down her cheeks.

Fingal did not know what to think. His head throbbed. He remembered the story about how Lana had wanted Fallon to be recognized as chief over Gillian. That simply didn't make sense. It led him to question her innocence in this now. He sighed. "I want to believe ye, Lana, but at the moment there are too many unanswered questions. Until Rhiannon is found, and I know more, I do not want ye in here."

"Laird, ye can't mean that. Gillian is gravely ill. I need to be with her."

"Katherine, do ye believe Gillian will wake from the poppy?"

"Aye, Fingal, I do. Her breathing is strong and steady now."

"Is there anything I should do when she wakes?"

"If she wakes, send for me," Katherine said. "The best thing for her is to drink lots of fluid to help flush the poisons from her body. Give her some water to drink. If she is able she should have some food too, to help build her strength, but I suspect some broth at first is all she'll be able to manage. If she wakes, I'll see to it. But Fingal, ye have a bad head injury and have lost a good deal of blood yerself."

"Give her water and send for ye. Even in my questionable state, I can handle that." At her frown he added, "but if it would make ye feel better, I will instruct the men standing guard to wake me every hour or so to make sure I'm still among the living."

"I suppose that will have to do."

"Very well, then I will say good night to everyone. Katherine, if Niall returns with any news, please send for me. Otherwise I will see ye all in the morning."

Chapter 31

After they had left, Fingal realized that he still held the rowan saltire in his right hand. He turned toward the bed. Bodie sat up and wagged his tail. Fingal scratched him behind the ears. "Katherine says ye have kept a good watch, Bodie. I need to rest now too, would ye mind making a little room for me lad?" Bodie moved to the bottom of the bed, resting his head on Gillian's feet. Fingal climbed into the bed on her left side. Maneuvering with his rigidly splinted left arm was awkward at best but he managed to slide his right arm under the pillow and around her shoulders. He rested his hand, holding the blessed cross over her heart.

He lay awake for quite a while, praying fervently to every saint whose name he could remember. *Please protect her and make her well.* He did doze after a while but slept lightly. The men standing guard entered the chamber to check on them as he had asked. Most often they needed only to call from the door, "Laird are ye well?" to wake him.

He woke several other times to Bodie standing at the foot of the bed and growling. "That's a good dog, Bodie. Do ye hear the men in the hall? It's all right. They're meant to be there lad." Eventually Bodie laid back down.

Just before dawn he was awakened again. His beautiful wife lay facing him, gently stroking his face. "Fingal, ye're here."

"And praise be to God, so are ye, my sweet, lass." He kissed her and rose from the bed, putting his hand out to steady himself a bit. His head throbbed and spun, reminding him painfully of his own images.

"Fingal, ye are hurt. Rest."

"I will in a moment. I promised Katherine I'd let her know as soon as ye woke." He found Alan on guard in the hall and sent him for Katherine. He also poured a mug of water from the pitcher and brought it to her. "How do ye feel? Katherine said ye should have some water if ye woke."

"I-I feel a little better, I can manage some water." She sat up and took a drink before saying, "did ye say Katherine? Are Niall and Katherine here?"

"Aye, love. Drink a bit more, Katherine says it is the best thing for ye."

She obliged. "Truthfully, I am dreadfully thirsty. But Fingal, ye look awful. What happened to ye?"

"I had a little fall. 'Tis a long story and I don't want ye to worry about me. I'll be fine."

"I'll worry about ye unless ye come back to bed yerself and tell me what happened."

Fingal sighed, but he wouldn't argue with her. He adjusted the pillows so he could sit up propped against them and slid back under the covers. "Ye were so very sick yesterday I was terrified I was losing ye. Nothing we did was helping. I was desperate for anything. I went to see Rhiannon and she told me about an old charm made from rowan twigs."

She smiled. "Aye, I know the one."

"She said the charm would be stronger if I had never before seen the tree and if the tree itself grew out of an inhospitable place. She said she knew of just such a tree growing near the top of the cliffs. I went there with her. She showed me where the tree was and when I was on the cliff's edge she shoved me off."

"Oh, dear God, Fingal. Are ye all right? How did ye survive?"

"Oddly enough, I only fell part of the way before being caught by a *rowan tree*. As ye can see my arm is broken. Katherine stitched up a gash in my head and I have a few broken ribs, but I will heal. Sweetling, I am so sorry to tell ye this, but it appears Rhiannon is responsible for yer illness too. She has been poisoning ye and she tried to kill ye yesterday with poppy."

"I know. After a few swallows of the tisane she brought me, I knew. She said the new ingredient would 'put everything to rights'."

"If ye knew, why did ye drink it?"

"I didn't, certainly not all of it. The first few swallows were incredibly strong. I tried to refuse it. Then I tried to get her to send for ye. She got angry with me. I was too weak to get away from her. I thought it better to let her believe I was drinking it. I assumed she would leave once she was sure I had. I kept pouring little bits of it down the side of my face, into the pillow. Still, I had consumed enough that it was having an effect. When she thought I had drunk it all, she gloated about poisoning the herbs for the tisane. I don't know what it was but apparently she killed Aunt Meara with it too."

Fingal remembered the king's words. *She died suddenly. When that happens one can never be sure it isn't murder.* "Katherine believes she mixed tiny amounts of foxglove in the herbs she gave ye. It is what was making ye so ill but ye will get better now." Taking her right hand in his, he lifted it to his lips. "I am so sorry, Gillian. I never imagined that the person charged with caring for ye would ever intentionally hurt ye."

"Do ye know why she did it?"

"I suspect that Rhiannon intended for Coby to marry Fallon, as your mother wished, making him laird. A few weeks ago Eadoin told me about a prophecy concerning Fallon. It is hard to believe that anyone would do so many horrible things just so it would come true."

"As Rhiannon gloated, she said the 'sight' isn't what people think. She said something about reading situations and helping predictions come true. Perhaps that last part is the most important."

"What else did she say?" Fingal didn't want to tell her he suspected her mother may have played a role in this, but if Rhiannon had told her more, he needed to hear it.

"She talked about secrets being the source of good predictions. I didn't understand it all. She said my mother had a secret. She talked about trying to convince mother to arrange the betrothal between Coby and Fallon. She said she had to kill us both and that she had accomplished that."

"I'm sure she thought I was dead, or close to it. She sent Coby back, I suspect to ensure I had died. I had managed to climb out by then but he drew his sword intending to finish me off. I killed him, Gillian. But as of last night, Rhiannon had vanished."

She moved close to him, resting her head on his right shoulder. "She'll be found. But it's over now. She won't be able to hurt us again."

He put his good arm around her and kissed her head. He wanted to believe her reassurances, but he wouldn't let his guard down until he knew for sure that Lana too wasn't involved. "Aye, she won't hurt us. But, sweetling, I must be sure no one else was involved."

She pushed back from him, a shocked expression on her face. "Ye don't suspect Fallon?"

He pulled her close again. "Nay, of course not." She seemed relieved.

"Fingal?"

"Aye, sweetling?"

"When did ye make this?" She opened her left hand, revealing the rowan cross.

He smiled. "When I awoke, stuck in that rowan tree on the cliff, I decided if that tree could save my life I would give it the chance to save yers as well. I tucked two twigs in my dagger sheath and Katherine helped me bind them together last night. Father Stephen blessed it. Where did ye find it? It was in my hand as I went to sleep."

"When I woke, it was laying on my chest, under yer hand, over my heart. I knew what it meant and I knew ye had made it for me. Thank ye."

Their quiet moment ended with a knock on the door. Katherine arrived with servants, trays of food, and supplies for tending Fingal's wound. She fussed over them both, insisting they stay in bed.

"But I thought that was the worst thing for melancholia and an excess of black bile," Gillian said.

"The only thing ye have had an excess of over the last weeks was foxglove. All of the symptoms ye had, nausea, headaches, the weariness and sadness ye felt, all of it was caused by the foxglove. Ye need to drink a lot, build yer strength back by eating well, and get lots of rest, preferably cuddled up next to yer husband because he needs rest too."

Fingal was happy to comply. Shortly after noon, Ailsa, with Duff at her side, forced her way through the gauntlet of adults who tried to turn her back. She burst into the room and ran into Gillian's arms. "I was so worried. No one would tell me anything. Then they carried the laird in yesterday, and Gillie, if ye think he looks bad now, ye should have seen him then."

"Ailsa, that's rude."

Fingal laughed. "Aye, but it's true. I'm sure I was a sorry sight."

"I told ye, Gillie. What happened to ye both anyway?"

Fingal was unsure how much to tell the lass, but Gillian

stepped in. "Ailsa, sometimes people make very bad decisions because of their own selfish desires."

"Like when Laird Malcolm tried to take Duncurra from the MacIans?"

Gillian nodded. "Precisely. Well, Rhiannon has done something similar. She decided that she wanted her son to marry Fallon and be laird."

Ailsa looked confused. "He couldn't be laird by marrying Fallon. Fingal is the laird. Fallon doesn't even want to marry that old Coby. She likes Quinn MacKenzie."

Gillian smiled. "Aye, I think she does. And ye're right, before anyone else could become laird, Fingal and I would both have to die, so Rhiannon tried to make that happen."

"Are ye saying Rhiannon tried to kill ye? Both? How could she do that? What happened?"

"She has been mixing poison with the tisane she gave me. Instead of making me better, it was causing me to get sicker. And when Fingal wanted to make a rowan charm for me, she led him to the cliffs to find a special tree, then she pushed him off. He didn't fall far, but that's how he got hurt."

Tears filled her eyes. "Are ye going to be all right?"

"Aye, pet, don't worry. Lady Katherine thinks I'll be fine."

"And ye'll be fine too, Laird?"

"Aye, little one, I'm just a bit banged up."

"What's going to happen now?"

"What do ye mean, pet?" Gillian asked.

"What is going to happen to Rhiannon? I don't want her to hurt ye ever again."

"Don't worry about Rhiannon either. My brother is looking for her and we will make sure she can't ever hurt anyone again."

Ailsa nodded. That seemed to be enough information for her because she switched the topic, chattering on about her new best friend, Maeve MacBain.

Before long they were interrupted by a knock at the door.

Eadoin and Quinn entered. "Laird, I've come to tell ye, Laird MacIan has returned. If ye are feeling up to it, can ye join him in the great hall? Quinn will stay here and keep Gillian and Ailsa company."

Ailsa's face was wreathed in smiles but Gillian's brow furrowed. "Don't worry, love. Everything will be fine," Fingal assured her.

Chapter 32

When Fingal reached the great hall, Archie, Owen, Nolan and Daniel had gathered there as had a number of others.

"What in the hell has been going on here?" demanded Nolan. "Gillian is sick and ye were nowhere to be found yesterday."

Owen added, "Not to mention the fact that no sooner do the MacIans arrive in force than they accuse poor old Rhiannon of harming Gillian."

"Calm down and let the laird speak. Surely there is an explanation," Archie said.

"Is she any better at all, laird?" Daniel asked.

Fingal sighed wearily. One glance at Niall told him he didn't have good news either. "Gentlemen, please sit down. There is a good bit of information that ye need to know." Fingal explained everything that had happened the previous day. Shocked silence filled the hall when he was done.

"Ye are certain Rhiannon pushed ye off the cliff? Could ye have just slipped? Ye clearly hit yer head. Maybe it didn't happen quite the way ye seem to remember it?" Nolan asked.

Fingal had expected Nolan to be the most critical of the elders. "Even if ye don't trust my memory, the fact she sent Coby back to make certain I was dead should leave no doubt."

"She might have sent him to save ye and in yer delirious state ye killed him," Owen said.

"I was in pain but not delirious. He drew his sword on me and he said his mother killed Gillian."

"Say ye," accused Nolan. "Coby is dead and there are no other witnesses."

Fingal hadn't considered having to defend himself. "Aye, there are no witnesses. However, Coby had guard duty yesterday. He was assigned to the gate. As I understand, Rhiannon arrived here at midday. Surely if she intended to help me, she would have sent help then. I understand she visited Gillian, then left with Coby, never mentioning my fall. Is that right, Tarmon?"

"Aye, Laird. I even asked her if she had seen ye because I thought ye might have been heading to her cottage when ye left. She said she hadn't seen ye."

Owen harrumphed. "There ye have it. If Rhiannon hadn't seen him, the laird could be making this whole thing up. Maybe she knew nothing about it at all and Coby just happened on ye, the poor man. Ye could be the one who attacked him and shoved him off the cliff. Yer injuries could have been from yer fight. That is easier to believe than the story ye tell about surviving a fall off the cliff. What do ye have against Rhiannon and Coby?"

Fingal gritted his teeth. "I had nothing against them. I trusted Rhiannon with Gillian's life and she repaid that trust by poisoning her."

"Ye're sure Rhiannon poisoned the herbs? Could it have been anyone else?" questioned Nolan.

Fingal sat quietly for a moment before answering, "I am certain it was Rhiannon who tried to kill Gillian yesterday. She admitted it to Gillian herself. Coby said it to me. However, I cannot be completely certain she acted alone."

"What do ye mean?" Daniel asked.

"As I said, it seems she wanted to eliminate me and Gillian, so that Coby could marry Fallon and become laird. Lana tried to get me to agree to this betrothal some time ago and I refused."

Nolan frowned. "She tried to get us to agree to it too, after Duncan died."

"It is hard to believe Lana could be involved, but she did put a lot of faith in that blasted prophecy. She has always favored Fallon," Daniel said.

"She denies any knowledge of Rhiannon's plans," Fingal said. "I don't want to believe she could willingly harm one of her daughters but I will not risk Gillian's life on what I wish to be true. I must know."

"I don't believe Lana played any part in this. I think it is another attempt to shift blame. Ye yerself could have been the one poisoning Gillian. Ye didn't want to marry her any more than she did ye. Perhaps now that ye are laird of this clan ye wanted rid of her," suggested Owen.

"Owen, ye are out of line," Daniel said. "First, ye are

forgetting he was laird by royal decree before he married her. Besides, it's clear he has come to love her. He would not try to kill her."

"Are ye suggesting her mother doesn't love her?" demanded Owen.

"Enough!" shouted Nolan. "There is no denying I was not happy when the king made Fingal MacIan our laird. However, there is also no denying Lady Gillian was given poppy yesterday, enough to kill her if she had consumed the whole mug. By all accounts she was awake and alert until after Rhiannon saw her. Therefore, the laird could not have given it to her before he left the keep in the morning."

Owen backed down. "Fine. I'll accept that the laird didn't give her the poppy."

"And if Rhiannon tried to kill Gillian," Archie said, "it stands to reason that the laird is telling the truth about her attempt on his life and Coby's involvement in that. But I refuse to believe Lana was involved without proof. Rhiannon must be questioned."

"Unfortunately, we can't find her," Niall said. "Tarmon was the last to see her. She told him Coby was out searching for a cow that wandered off. She left her cottage ostensibly to look for him. If ye believe she attempted to kill Fingal, then clearly this was not true. She knew Coby had gone to the cliff and that is where she went. She must have realized her intrigue was discovered when Fingal was not there but Coby lay dead in the gully. She didn't return to her cottage. My men have searched through the night and haven't found her."

Owen started to interrupt him, but Niall cut him off. "Before ye say it, if she was innocent and merely lost, searching for her cow, she would have been found. I can only conclude she is in hiding somewhere."

"Then we must allow Lana to defend herself," Archie said.

"I want to speak with Lady Katherine as well," Nolan said. At Niall's scowl he added, "don't get yer dander up, Niall. I know she is a good woman. The men who were captured after the siege on Duncurra said she was nothing but kind and cared for them well. I just want to hear her thoughts on all this from her own lips."

After a moment Niall agreed, so Fingal sent men for both of them.

Gavin brought Lana to the hall. Her eyes were red and swollen as if from crying and she appeared to have had little sleep.

Eadoin arrived minutes later, looking grim. Not only was Katherine with him, but a pale and drawn looking Gillian was as well with the ever present Bodie at her side. She went to her mother, wrapping her arms around her, causing Lana to burst into sobs. The hurt in Gillian's eyes tore at his heart.

"I'm sorry, Laird. I found Lady Katherine with Lady Gillian," Eadoin explained.

"Gillian, sweetling, ye don't need to be here," Fingal said. "Katherine, I'm surprised ye stood for this."

"I do need to be here, Fingal, and although she tried, Katherine could not stop me. I gather that ye suspect my mother had something to do with all of this?"

"I told ye I intended to make certain no one else was involved," Fingal tried to reassure her. "I don't want to believe she would ever hurt ye, but I must know for sure. Please, love, go back to bed."

"Nay, this concerns me and I will stay."

In spite of her current frail state of health, she stood tall, the picture of strength and dignity. He was reminded of how she looked standing on the wall the night he arrived and as she left the keep on Daniel's arm the next afternoon. "Ye are right. It concerns ye. Come sit with me. If ye get too tired we will take a break." She nodded and joined him at the table.

"Laird, ye can't believe I would harm my ch-child," Lana said, her voice catching with a sob.

"Lana, I don't want to, but I must know. Rhiannon clearly tried to kill both of us yesterday. Someone has been poisoning Gillian for weeks. Rhiannon admitted to Gillian that she intended to see Coby and Fallon wed and thus Coby made laird. Ye yerself have pushed for such a match for ages. Can ye at least understand why we might be concerned?"

"Aye, Laird, I can. I agree I wanted Fallon to wed Coby. I told ye that last night. Rhiannon was my friend. I thought it was a good match. I never intended for Fallon to replace Gillian as Lady MacLennan."

Owen scowled. "That's not true, Lana. After we learned that both Malcolm and Duncan were dead and we were argu—er, discussing—who should become chief, Meara suggested Gillian and ye were firmly against it. Ye said Fallon would be a better choice."

This did not come as a shock to Fingal. Eadoin had told

him as much.

Lana sputtered, "Aye, I did. I always believed it was her destiny."

"Because of Rhiannon's prophecy?" Daniel asked.

"Aye—nay, not just that. Fallon is special. Ye don't understand."

At Gillian's soft gasp, Fingal took her hand in his. More than anything this is why he didn't want her here for this. There was no way to avoid hurting her. "Help us understand, Lana."

"I can't," she spat, some of her old defiance showing. "No one can understand. Rhiannon believed Fallon would be special and she is. That doesn't mean I love Gillian less. Gillian, I would never hurt ye. Surely ye believe that."

Gillian sighed. "Aye Mother, I do."

"We are getting nowhere," Nolan said. "Lana, what was supposed to be in the herb mixture?"

"Mint, thyme, comfrey, and chamomile."

"And Lady Katherine, ye are sure there was more to it than that? Ye are certain Gillian was being poisoned before yesterday?"

"Aye. I tasted foxglove in the herbs."

"I would like to taste them."

"I thought ye might and I brought the packet with me. Do ye know what foxglove tastes like?"

Nolan frowned. "Nay. Now that ye mention it, if it is a poison how do ye know?"

Katherine laughed. "I began learning healing arts from my mother as a little girl, then from an old healer in my clan. Both of them made sure I could identify poisonous plants, especially those which can be confused with others. Young foxglove plants are very similar to comfrey but they taste different. You can tell instantly if ye crush a leaf and just touch it to yer tongue. There is a bitter burn to it." She gave him a pinch of the herb mixture. "Rub it between yer fingers to release the oils in the leaves." He did as she instructed. "Now just touch yer tongue to yer finger. Ye will feel a very slight heat."

"Aye, I feel a bit of something."

"If ye did that with a fresh leaf it would be much stronger. There isn't much foxglove in that blend, but it doesn't take much to make someone sick."

"And the rest is as Lana says? Mint, thyme, comfrey and chamomile?"

"Well, there are some other herbs too."

Katherine had only mentioned foxglove to him. "What else is there?" Fingal demanded.

"There is also pennyroyal and tansy. Neither of them are poisons, but they are known to bring on monthly fluxes."

"Ye mean it could have caused her miscarriage?" Archie asked.

Fingal felt Gillian begin to tremble. He leaned close to her and whispered, "If this is too much, my love, we can stop."

She shook her head, blinking back tears, waiting for Katherine to answer.

"Aye, Archie, it could have caused a miscarriage. But Gillian, it could have been the foxglove that brought on the sickness ye thought was morning sickness."

"Are ye saying I wasn't carrying?"

"I don't know if ye were or not but it's possible that ye weren't."

Fingal wasn't sure it mattered. Either way they felt a terrible loss."

Nolan shook his head. "So we are certain there was foxglove, among other things in the herbs Gillian used for the tisane, but we don't know for certain who put them there."

"I think we do," Gillian said. "Mother, the packet that Katherine has, that isn't the one ye have been using to make the brew recently."

Lana shook her head. "Nay. Rhiannon took that one upstairs yesterday. I couldn't find it in yer chamber last night, but I found this one."

"That proves it," Gillian said. "Nolan, Rhiannon gave me this packet the day after the wedding. I have had it the whole time. Mother never had access to it. She couldn't have put the foxglove in it."

"Is there any chance she made a mistake?" Archie asked. "Lady Katherine, ye said foxglove and comfrey appear similar when they are young. Could it be she made an error? Perhaps all of her store of comfrey has foxglove mixed in?"

Fingal shook his head. "Archie, I don't think Rhiannon's recent actions suggest this could be an accident, but I am happy to check. I can have her herbs brought here for Katherine to review. Do ye mind, Katherine?"

"I would be happy to, but I would learn more by seeing her

stores for myself. However, it may take a while for me to sort through them. Fingal, both ye and Gillian need rest to recover. Perhaps we can address this tomorrow after I have had time to assess things."

"Aye, that's an excellent idea. Gillian and I will retire."

"Not yet, Fingal. Are ye all convinced yet that my mother played no part in this?"

"I'm convinced," Daniel said. "If the first herbs Rhiannon gave ye were tainted and yer mother never had access to them, I don't see how she could have."

Archie and Owen both agreed.

Nolan eyed Lana shrewdly. "I'm not completely convinced." At the surprised looks on the other elders' faces he added, "oh, I believe Lana didn't adulterate the herbs, but I'm not sure she and Rhiannon weren't working together."

"Fingal, what do ye think?" Gillian asked.

The hope in her eyes gave him pause and he considered his answer carefully. "I love ye with my whole heart. I want ye to be safe and happy. Like Nolan, I still worry. However, I also respect ye and yer judgment. What do ye think?" She opened her mouth to answer, but he stopped her. "Gillian, I haven't been married to ye long, but I have learned ye rarely think of yerself first. This time, I am asking ye a question and I only want ye to answer what yer head and yer heart tell ye. I don't want ye to give me the answer that ye think a good daughter or a good clan leader would give. Do ye understand?"

"Aye, I do." She took a deep breath. "My mother has hurt my feelings, perhaps without meaning to, on many occasions. It has always been obvious to me as well as to Ailsa and Fallon that Fallon is special to her in some way. I know she would have been happier if Fallon had been recognized as the leader of this clan."

Fingal glanced at Lana. Gillian's words were honest but they held bitterness. Lana's mouth was set in a tight line and her chin quivered, but she did not interrupt.

Gillian continued. "Still, I have never doubted that my mother loves me and I do not believe she would ever knowingly attempt to kill me. Fingal, she is not involved in this."

Fingal nodded. "Fair enough. Nolan, are ye satisfied with that?"

"I am for now. If other information comes to light, we may all need to reconsider."

Chapter 33

Perhaps it was still the effects of the foxglove, which Katherine had said would linger for several days or it was the after effect of the poppy Gillian had consumed yesterday, but she was exhausted. At Fingal's urging she had a bit of soup and drank as much water as she could stand. Katherine assured her it would help wash the foxglove from her body. When she could not swallow another mouthful, she curled up in bed. Bodie climbed up to lay at her feet as he usually did.

"I know it's still early, Fingal, but ye need rest as much as I do. Come to bed."

"Ye needn't ask me twice. I just want to speak to the guards for a moment first."

He stepped out of the room and when he returned, he removed his plaid and climbed into bed.

"Fingal, if Coby is dead and Rhiannon is missing why are there still guards posted at our door?"

"Mainly because I still don't know if Coby and Rhiannon worked alone."

"Ye said ye believed my mother wasn't involved."

"And I do. But that doesn't mean they didn't have other help and I won't know for sure until Rhiannon is found."

"If she is never found, will ye post a guard in the hall forever?"

"Nay, my love, I won't. But right now, I'm not in prime fighting condition. I'm not able to guard ye adequately. So until I have healed sufficiently, I will ensure ye are guarded by other means."

She sighed and rested her head on his chest. "I love ye."

His good arm encircled her. "I love ye too."

~ * ~

Gillian woke to Bodie's low growls. She wasn't sure how long she had been asleep, but the room was dark. "What's the matter, Bodie?" She glanced around the room. Only the moonlight streaming in the window lent any light at all but still, there was clearly no intruder.

Fingal was awake too. He sat up and reached to scratch Bodie behind the ears. "He did this last night too. I think he hears the guards in the hall. Good dog, Bodie, letting us know when ye hear something."

They settled back into sleep easily, but Bodie woke them three more times during the night.

The sun was well up the next morning when they awoke.

Fingal yawned and stretched before giving Gillian a gentle kiss. "How do ye feel this morning, my love?"

"Considerably better than I have in days, in spite of the interruptions to my sleep," she teased, rubbing Bodie and pulling him into an embrace. "Ye need to heal quickly so we don't need the guards in the hall or Bodie will never let us sleep through the night again."

"Yer wish is my command." He gave her another kiss. "I don't think I have ever slept this long past sunup. I'm sure it was good for both of us."

When they had dressed and left their chamber, they met Quinn standing guard in the hall. "Good morning, my Lady, Laird." His smile seemed strained.

Fingal must have noticed it too because he asked, "Quinn, what's happened."

"Nothing, Laird. It has been a quiet morning."

"But something is troubling ye. Please tell me what it is."

Quinn sighed heavily. "It's Fallon."

Gillian's heart leapt to her throat. "What's wrong with Fallon?"

"Nothing. Well nothing physical. Yesterday evening she heard about what happened in the hall. She knows that Rhiannon did all of this hoping to see her become Lady MacLennan, with Coby at her side. She is distraught and she blames herself."

Gillian huffed. "It is certainly not her fault. Did ye tell her she isn't to blame?"

"Of course I did, my Lady. She won't listen. She insists that she is going to enter a convent."

"I understand why she feels this way. I felt the same way when I learned what Malcolm and Eithne had done supposedly on my behalf. Don't worry. We will talk some sense into her," Fingal assured him. "By the way, I haven't had the chance to ask ye yet. What was yer father's answer to my request for a betrothal?"

Quinn grinned. "As soon as he read it, he flat out refused. He accused ye of using a bonny bride to try to lure me away for good."

Fingal frowned. "And that pleased ye?"

Quinn laughed. "Nay, Laird, not in the least. We argued several times. My mother tried talking him around but he would not hear a word of it. Then all hell broke loose at Rowan's wedding."

"What happened?"

"My lady, it is a long story for another day. Suffice to say, after it was all over, he decided there was some merit in allowing me to choose my bride. He signed the betrothal."

"Perhaps Fallon will reconsider the convent when she hears the news."

Gillian shook her head. "The two of ye are daft. This has been a terrible shock to all of us. Give her time. We will not allow her to make any permanent decision until things are sorted out."

"We?" Fingal asked with a smirk.

"Do ye disagree?"

"Nay, my love, I don't." He kissed her and her irritation melted. "Quinn, ye are officially off duty. I suspect today's discussions will be no less stressful than yesterday's. I'm not sure we have a hope of keeping Fallon away, but I would appreciate anything ye can do to keep Ailsa occupied."

"That shouldn't be a problem. When Katherine returned from Rhiannon's yesterday evening, she brought little Blaze with her. Ailsa has already declared she will care for him until Rhiannon returns."

Gillian smiled at this. "She has always loved that wee beastie. Aye, Blaze and Duff should be able to keep her attention today."

~ * ~

With her illness and everything which had happened over the last few days, Gillian had completely forgotten that today was Pentecost. Second only to Easter in importance, it celebrated the birth of the Church, commemorating the outpouring of the Holy Spirit to Christ's disciples after His Ascension. Such an important feast day couldn't pass without at least a small celebration. They acknowledged the gift of the Holy Spirit at Mass with the sprinkling of red rose petals, symbolizing the tongues of flame. Gillian herself had not been able to plan the traditional huge feast. Still, with Jeanne's help, Fallon and Tira had managed to plan a modest midday feast to mark the occasion. All discussions of Rhiannon and what Katherine discovered at her cottage were put off until afterwards.

Quinn sat with Fallon doing his best to charm the haunted look from her eyes. When the meal was over, he was able to coax her into leaving the keep with Ailsa and the dogs.

"Can I go too, da?" Maeve MacBain pleaded. "I want to play with the dogs."

"Me too, Da," Kieran said. "Tomas, do ye like dogs? Maybe Da will let ye come too." Apparently, Tomas MacIan and Kieran had become great friends over the last few days.

Fingal's wish for Quinn to keep Fallon and Ailsa occupied was quickly turning into something much larger. Gillian leaned close to Fingal's ear. "Quinn may return to his father if ye saddle him with a gaggle of children," she teased.

He winked at her, whispering back, "Not a chance. There are more children at Carraigile." Then he said, "Niall, it is a fine day and we have some things to discuss. Perhaps we can trouble Kira and Edna to join this outing and help mind all the children."

Niall nodded. "Aye, Turcuil and Keavy can go as well. They are just wee lads in big bodies themselves." Everyone at the table laughed.

"And since that's the case, Laird, perhaps I should go too, to keep an eye on the lot," teased Bran MacBain. "Do ye mind?"

"Nay, go right ahead. Take anyone ye need."

The message was clear. The children would have an outing, but only under the watchful eye of a substantial guard.

After they had all left and the tables were cleared, Fingal and the elders were ready to hear the results of Katherine's search of Rhiannon's cottage. Her initial statement came as a surprise to everyone.

"I found nothing but some commonly used safe herbs, no foxglove."

"Ye found nothing suspicious at all?" Gillian was certain that Rhiannon had been responsible for everything. If she didn't have any of the herbs, who else could it have been?

"I wouldn't exactly say that. In my opinion, finding

nothing was suspicious in itself. Pennyroyal and tansy are common enough herbs and when used in the right way, they have benefits. I would have expected her to have some of both of them. Also, we know she gave ye poppy extract. She had none of that either."

"She had none?" Archie asked. "But she gave it to me once when I was having terrible pain from gout. She seemed to have quite a large supply."

"That is why I think it odd. Most healers have some."

"Aye and someone drugged the wine I drank the night of the fire," Gillian observed.

"What?" demanded Nolan. "Someone tried to drug ye before? Why are we just learning of this?"

Gillian realized this hadn't been common knowledge as soon as she had said it. Now she had to explain. "Nolan, there has been more than one attempt on our lives."

Daniel too looked affronted. "More than one? We should have known this before now? Were ye trying to get Gillian killed, Laird?"

Fingal shook his head. "Nay, I wasn't. But I wasn't completely sure it wasn't an accident at the time. Some guardsmen knew, still I wasn't sure who to trust."

"What else has happened?" Archie asked.

"My fall during the boar hunt was not an accident. Hearn found that someone had cut partially cut through the cinch on my saddle. We also suspect the fire was not an accident. Gillian drank from a decanter of wine in our chamber, but I had only a mouthful. It tasted odd, but I couldn't place it at the time. I know now it was poppy I tasted. I suspect whoever put it there did so to keep us from waking as they entered the room to start the fire. I did have trouble waking Gillian when I discovered the blaze. If we had both drunk the wine, we would have died."

"Whoever did that had to have access to yer chamber," observed Owen. "Neither Rhiannon, nor Coby would have been able to do it without being noticed. Rhiannon rarely comes to the keep."

Archie shook his head in disgust. "That brings us squarely back to Lana."

Nolan watched the exchange with his brows furrowed, a pensive expression on his face. "Nay, it doesn't."

"Of course it does. Who else would have a motive to help Rhiannon?" Owen asked.

"No one. But Rhiannon might have known a way to access the room without being seen."

"How is that possible?" Fingal asked.

"Niall, does Duncurra have a bolt hole?" Nolan asked.

"Nay. Built on the crag as it is, it is practically impregnable but there is no secret escape route."

"Well there is one in Brathanead."

"Do ye mean to tell me someone can just enter Brathanead through a secret door? Where the hell is it?" demanded Fingal.

"It is in yer chamber, Laird. One of the pillars of the mantel slides forward, creating a small opening behind it. A narrow set of stairs is built into the wall, winding down to a man-made tunnel below the keep. There is a fortified door that locks from the inside where it connects to a natural tunnel. The natural caves honeycomb the area under the cliffs. If ye don't know the way, ye can become lost. There is but one exit and it is apparently through a narrow fissure, near the bottom of the cliffs."

"Why did no one inform me of it?"

"Frankly, Laird, almost no one knows. The existence of the bolt hole and the route out of the caverns is something which was passed from father to son. Clearly ye wouldn't wish enemies to know it exists, even though the entrance is nearly impossible to find if ye don't know the way. It was intended to remain secret and I thought Malcolm took the secret to his grave."

"But ye know where it is?"

"Aye, I do. But while I know how to open it, I don't know how to traverse the caves to the exit. I would sooner face an enemy than go blindly into those caves."

"If it is such a well-guarded secret, how could Rhiannon know about it?"

"Nuala must have told her," Owen said.

Noland nodded. "Aye, I suspect so. Nuala would have known. Rhiannon was her friend and companion. I suspect Nuala told her."

"That would explain how she gained access to our chamber to drug the wine. I suppose if the entrance is by the hearth, she wouldn't have had to open it far to nudge the log out. That's how I slept through it."

"Laird, it is a very narrow opening to begin with and it opens nearly silently. It would have been unlikely to make enough noise to wake ye even if fully opened."

"Considering the opening to the caves is in the cliff wall, I'll wager Rhiannon is either hiding in the caves or the tunnel." Niall said.

"Show me, now," commanded Fingal. "Gillian, ye stay here. Eadoin, Alan, and Gavin, ye stand guard until we return."

~ * ~

Fingal led Niall, the elders, and a number of men to his chamber. Nolan went to the pillar on the right side of the hearth. "This is the one. Ye just put yer hands on either side, then pull." He demonstrated and the pillar slid silently forward across the width of the mantel. "It was meant to serve as an escape for women and children, so I expect that is why it opens with such ease."

Fingal shook his head in disbelief. "Get torches. We need to search the tunnel for her."

Niall poked his head through the opening. "Fingal, ye have to stay here."

"I have no intention of staying here. I must find her."

"I understand that, but the passage is extremely tight. With yer broken arm, ye'll never be able to maneuver. I'll take several men. If she is in the tunnel we will find her. If she isn't, we'll come back for rope so we don't get lost searching the caves."

Fingal too entered the passage to see for himself and to his irritation, he realized Niall was right. When the men returned with torches, Niall entered with them. Fingal and the elders waited.

A shocked expression suddenly crossed Archie's face. "Dear God, I just realized, ye and Gillian have been sleeping in here the last two nights. She could have entered and killed one or both of ye."

Then Fingal remembered. "I think she may have attempted to. Bodie woke us growling several times over the last few nights. I thought he heard the men in the hall but I expect the grizzled old git did try again."

Sooner than any of them expected, Niall squeezed his huge frame back through the entryway. "We found her in the tunnel, but she's in a bad way. She is burning up with fever and delirious."

Another man backed out of the entrance, holding Rhiannon under the arms, followed by a second man who had her feet.

Rhiannon was clearly not in her right mind. "Ye'll see,

ye'll see, ye can't get through that way. Go the other way. I told ye, left out right in. That beast won't let ye past this way. He'll bite yer arse, mark my words."

Fingal jumped to action. "Let's get her to a room. Niall, please fetch Katherine."

"Rhiannon, ye are safe now. Calm down," Owen said.

"Owen, ye auld bag of wind. No one is safe from that beast."

The men carried her to an empty chamber. Fingal held the door as they passed.

When Rhiannon saw him she shrieked, "Malcolm MacLennan, I thought ye went to hell."

"Should we restrain her before we go, Laird?" one of the men carrying her asked.

Fingal shook his head. "Not unless she causes trouble. She seems weak and confused."

"Ye belong in hell, Malcolm. Ye had to dip yer wick in any lass that wiggled her arse in yer direction didn't ye? How dare ye disgrace my sweet Nuala that way?

Nolan arched an eyebrow at Fingal. "Well ye do look a lot like Malcolm."

Niall, Katherine, Gillian, and Lana entered the room. Katherine carried her bag of healing supplies.

"Och, and there's one now. The laird kept ye for a bit on the side didn't he, Lana? Even after he married ye off to his cousin ye spread yer unworthy legs for him. I know ye did."

Lana went ashen but Gillian asked, "What is she talking about?"

Katherine crossed to the bedside and touched Rhiannon's leathered face. "She's burning up with fever and is delirious, Gillian, pay no mind." Katherine didn't have to look far for the source of the fever. Rhiannon's hand was red and swollen to twice its size. Red streaks went up her arm and pus oozed from puncture wounds on her hand. "She has been bitten by something."

"It was that hellhound Gillian keeps." Rhiannon raised her head to get closer to Katherine and whispered loudly, "she simply would not die. All I was going to do was take a pillow from the bed and help a bit. That crazed beast bit me. But it's all right. She was dying anyway."

Ignoring her, Katherine took a damp cloth and began to clean the wound. "Lana, would ye mind fetching me some hot water." Lana nodded and hurried from the room.

"Lana has a secret. I almost told it to Gillian, but she died."

"What secret is that, Rhiannon," Katherine asked calmly. Everyone in the room remained quiet.

"Ye're very pretty."

"Thank ye. But ye were telling me about a secret."

"Och, which one? I know a few."

"Lana's secret."

Rhiannon snorted.

"Has Lana been helping ye?" Katherine persisted.

"With what?"

"With Fingal and Gillian."

Rhiannon snorted again. "Nay, certainly not. She is much too stupid. Stupid people are so easy to manipulate."

"Then she didn't help ye kill Gillian?"

"Nay. That was all my idea. No one but Coby helped me. After all, he stood to gain the most. She is pretty too, but I warned him not to fall in love."

"Who's pretty? Why should Coby not fall in love?"

Rhiannon's face turned into a mask of rage. "Because Malcolm's bastards must not live. I told Coby to get a child or two off of her then we would rid the world of another one."

Katherine was confused. "Another what, Rhiannon?"

"Are ye stupid too? Another one of Malcolm's bastards." Gillian glanced around and saw her own shock mirrored on the faces of everyone in the room, including her mother who had just returned with a jug of hot water and a mug.

"How do ye know that, Rhiannon?" Katherine asked gently.

"It wasn't hard to guess. Lana had panted after Malcolm for years. She flirted openly with him even after she was married."

"I-I—" Lana started to protest.

"Not now Lana," Fingal ordered in a hushed voice.

Rhiannon continued as if she hadn't heard them. "There were whispers. I thought it possible the babe was his when I made that silly prediction. That's how *the sight* works, ye ken. I make calculated guesses. Nuala was barren. If Malcolm had a bastard son in his own clan, I knew he would recognize him so I predicted the babe would *rise above all others*." She evidently found this amusing. She cackled hysterically.

Katherine worked while Rhiannon babbled. She measured herbs from one of her bags into the mug and filled it with hot water. Then, taking the bowl from the washstand she added different herbs and filled the bowl with hot water. "But yer prediction was wrong. Lana didn't have a son."

"Nay, but a lass can become a leader when there are no sons and *my* son could marry a daughter."

"I suppose he could."

"But the damned king interfered. Fallon and Coby should be leading this clan." She grinned malevolently. "But I fixed it. I killed the bastard and his wife."

"How did ye manage that?" Katherine dipped a towel into the hot solution and wrung it out.

Rhiannon gloated. "I poisoned Gillian with foxglove but she wouldn't die. Meara was much easier to kill. So I gave Gillian enough poppy to kill a horse."

"And the laird?"

Rhiannon cackled again. "I shoved him off the cliff."

Katherine wrapped the hot towel around her hand. Rhiannon screamed, "Hell take ye, lass, what are ye trying to do?"

"I have to draw the poison out, Rhiannon. Ye are healer, surely ye know that."

"Shhhh. That's not where I keep the poison. Don't tell anyone I have it."

"I won't, Rhiannon. Other than Meara, Gillian, and Fingal, have ye killed anyone else?"

"Nay. Not here leastways."

"Did ye intend to kill more people with the fire?"

"I didn't set the fire, Coby did. He didn't want to burn the keep down. After all it was to be his. He just wanted to make a lot of smoke. He wet the rushes ye see, and pulled the burning log out. They were supposed to stay asleep. I had given him poppy to put in the wine. If everything had gone right, the smoke would have strangled them while they slept." She sighed heavily. "I don't know what happened. Coby swears the decanter was empty. They should have slept. That was a mistake."

"I see." Katherine rewet the cloth to rewarm it and wrapped it around her hand again.

Rhiannon didn't react as strongly this time. "Lass, that hurts. I told ye the poison isn't in my hand." She closed her eyes but tossed her head restlessly.

Katherine slipped her arm under the old woman's shoulders, raising her from the bed. She put the mug to her lips. "Ye need to drink this now, Rhiannon. We need to bring yer fever down."

Rhiannon took a mouthful then spit it out. "Don't drink that lass and don't give it to me. The tisane is poisoned."

"Nay Rhiannon, this one isn't the one that was poisoned. Ye must drink it."

Rhiannon narrowed her eyes before slapping the mug in Katherine's hands, spilling most of its contents. "Ye can't poison me. I won't make that mistake."

"Rhiannon, I promise ye it isn't poisoned. I'm trying to help ye." Katherine tried again but Rhiannon pursed her lips, turning her head away as a balky child would.

"I. Won't. Drink. It." She closed her eyes.

"All right, Rhiannon, I won't force ye." Katherine rewarmed the cloth again.

When she wrapped Rhiannon's hand with it, the old woman groaned a little but offered no further complaint. After a moment, she opened her eyes and they were filled with tears. "Coby died."

"I know Rhiannon. I am sorry for your loss."

Tears spilled down her cheeks. "Coby made some mistakes. He missed with the rock and the arrow. But he was my son."

"I know, Rhiannon."

Rhiannon closed her eyes again. Katherine replaced the warm cloth before turning to address those standing in the room. "The wound is very bad. It is poisoning her body. I will keep trying but there is little to do for her."

"Will the tisane help?" Fingal asked. "Maybe we can help get it down her."

"It has willow bark in it. It would ease her pain a little and maybe help break her fever but the wound has gone too long without being tended. I fear it is festered beyond my ability to heal it. Perhaps ye should send for Father Stephen."

"She doesn't deserve God's blessing," Owen said.

Fingal frowned. Part of him agreed with Owen. Rhiannon had done unthinkable things. She killed Meara and very nearly killed Gillian. He didn't even want to think about the tansy and pennyroyal. Still he would not deny a priest to a dying person.

"That isn't for us to decide. God's mercy is His own to give."

"Ye are right. It isn't our decision," agreed Gillian.

Daniel nodded. "I'll find him."

"I'll continue to do what I can for her but I don't think she'll wake again. Fingal, ye and Gillian don't need to stay here. None of ye do. Rhiannon and Coby clearly acted alone in this."

"I will not leave ye here alone with her no matter how ill she is," declared Niall.

"Aye, and while she seems to have revealed everything, I will stay to hear it in case there is more," Nolan said.

"I'll stay too," Archie said. "I am shocked by all of this, but I considered her a friend."

"Very well then. Send for me if ye need me for any reason." Fingal put his arm around Gillian, gently guiding her out of the room.

~ * ~

Gillian was still very weak from the foxglove in her system and the revelations of the day had further drained her. She and Fingal went straight to their chamber. It wasn't long before Lana knocked at their door wanting to speak with Gillian about the things Rhiannon had said. "I need to explain it to her. I need her to understand."

Fingal refused her. "I agree there is explaining to do but there will be time later."

"But I have to tell her. I need to make things clear. I don't want her to think ill of me."

"Lana, listen to yerself. I, I, I. For once, think about what is best for Gillian. She has been ill and needs rest. She also needs time to think about all of this. Your needs will wait. Besides, the person who needs to hear the truth from you is Fallon."

"I don't want to tell Fallon."

"Would ye prefer I tell her? It seems she is my sister."

"Nay, she doesn't have to know, does she?"

"Lana, after all yer years of deception and everything that has happened do ye really believe trying to hide this from her is the best idea?" In a gentler tone he added, "go talk with Fallon. This will be hard but yer daughters all love ye. That won't change."

Fingal closed the door and turned to Gillian. She couldn't keep the tears from welling in her eyes. She remembered the night he arrived, barely three months ago now. One of the first things he had done was insist that Lana allow Gillian time to think without pressure from her mother or the elders. He revealed his instinct to protect her and at the same time respected her opinions from their first moments together.

Seeing her tears, he went to her, pulling her close with his good arm. "Sweetling, I'm so sorry. If ye wish to speak with her, I'll call her back. I just thought ye might need a bit of time first."

"Nay, ye're right. I am not ready to hear any more."

"Then why are ye crying?"

"Because I love ye so very much. How could I have ever tried to hate ye?"

"I have no idea. I am perfectly charming," he teased.

She smiled, wiping the tears from her cheeks. "Aye, ye are."

"Oh, and don't forget, devastatingly handsome."

She looked up at him. Even with scrapes, bruises, and ugly stitches in his head he was the most attractive man she had ever encountered. She smiled. "Aye, devastatingly handsome and so very humble too."

"That too. And very grateful to my king for his interference in my life." He cupped her cheek and kissed her tenderly. She wrapped her arms around him, returning his kiss full measure.

Chapter 34

Katherine was right. Rhiannon never regained consciousness again. She lingered for another day, fighting her own demons in delirium but ultimately died in the wee hours of the morning the next day. When preparing her body for burial, Katherine found the bag containing the foxglove and other questionable herbs tied under Rhiannon's skirts.

Fingal sent men down into the bolt hole to ensure that the door to the natural caves was barred from the inside. He suspected that it hadn't been barred in years, perhaps not since Rhiannon lived at the keep. They discussed this at dinner one evening.

Nolan said, "Ye may as well seal that door. If anyone made their way through the tunnel and into the caves, they would have little hope of making it out without knowing the way."

"It has crossed my mind," agreed Fingal. "I have already taken steps to have the entrance in our room barred from this side. Still, knowing that if the worst happened our wives and children could escape is a comforting thought."

Owen asked, "What was it Rhiannon said as yer men brought her through the opening?"

"I've been thinking about that too Owen," Fingal said. "She told them to go the other way because she was afraid of Bodie. She said, 'I told ye, left out right in.'"

"Aye, that was it. I've heard that said about labyrinths. If ye put yer hand on one wall and keep it there, ye will eventually reach the center."

Fingal nodded. "Aye, but ye could wander for ages in caves like that."

"Perhaps not in this one. Perhaps that is the clue. Turn left and put yer left hand on the wall as ye enter the caves. The reverse would be true if ye entered from the outside. Left to go out, right to come in."

"That could be it. It will be easy enough to check," agreed

Fingal.

The next day he sent men down to test the theory. "Stay to the left. If ye don't reach the exit eventually, turn around and stay to the right. It will bring ye back to the door."

They were gone for hours. Fingal was ready to send men searching for them, when they arrived at the gates of Brathanead. It had worked. The simplicity was brilliant. With the door to the cave secured again and a locking mechanism on the door from their chamber, Fingal no longer worried about anyone secretly gaining access to Brathanead.

~ * ~

Gillian avoided her mother for several days but she could put it off no longer. She and Fallon sat in the solar and listened to their mother's explanations.

"It wasn't that I didn't love yer father Gillian but I had loved Malcolm from the time I was a little girl. I thought he loved me too but his father forced him to marry Nuala MacRea."

"Ye thought he loved ye?" Fallon asked.

"Aye, pet. Ye can tell when a lad loves ye. He can't keep his hands off ye."

Sweet, innocent Fallon snorted. "Mother, I'm not sure that is love."

"What do either of ye know about love?" she snapped back.

"I know that a man who loves me will show me respect. He may desire me but would never compromise or hurt me in any way," Fallon answered.

Lana snorted this time. "Ye're a dreamer Fallon. Men like that don't exist."

Gillian frowned. "Nay she isn't, Mother. Men like that do exist. Fingal is one and Da was too. I believe Da loved ye. He showed ye respect and affection. He would never have hurt ye. Surely ye know that?" Thinking of what her mother had done caused her heart to ache for her da.

Lana sniffed. "I guess he did, in his way. But it was different with Malcolm. We had a great passion."

Fallon rolled her eyes. "It was a great passion because he couldn't keep his hands off ye? Mother, how blind can ye be? He couldn't keep his hands off of Eithne and who knows how many other women either."

Lana looked hurt. Fallon reached out and took her hand. "I'm sorry, Mother. Evidently ye have clung to this idea that Malcolm was the great love of yer life for years now. But it was Da who truly loved ye."

"Malcolm is yer da."

"Nay he isn't. My da is the man who raised me, and loved me. If Malcolm had wanted to be a father, he could have been. Although, it would have broken Da's heart, so I am glad he didn't."

"Someday ye'll see, Fallon. When the laird finally decides to settle ye with some ally of his, ye will see what it's like."

"I have no intention of marrying. Who would have me now? As soon as things here are settled, I intend to enter a convent."

"Ye will do no such thing. Ye are Malcolm MacLennan's daughter and don't forget that."

"Stop it, Mother. I am Malcolm MacLennan's bastard and I'm not proud of that! I was Duncan MacLennan's daughter."

Lana stood. "Ye will not enter a convent. I won't have it." With that she turned and left the room.

Fallon shook her head. "She doesn't understand."

"And she probably never will, Fallon," Gillian agreed. "I don't suppose we can control who we love. For whatever reason, Mother thought she loved Malcolm. It has colored the way she has seen everything else in her life, including ye."

"I know, and I'm sorry."

"It isn't yer fault. But I agree with her about one thing."

"What?"

"Ye don't belong in a convent."

"I have no other choice. As I said, no one will want to marry me now."

Gillian grinned slyly. "Quinn MacKenzie wants to marry ye."

Tears filled Fallon's eyes. "His father would never agree to that, even if Fingal was inclined to ask."

"Not only is Fingal inclined to ask, he already has and Laird MacKenzie agreed."

Fallon looked up, hopefully. "He did? Really? When?"

"Quinn delivered Fingal's letter to him when he went to Rowan's wedding."

Fallon looked crestfallen. "That was before everyone knew

the truth. Everything has changed."

"Nothing has changed. Fingal is the laird of this clan and Malcolm's illegitimate son. Ye are my sister as well as his. The betrothal has been signed." Gillian suppressed a grin at Fallon's hopeful expression. "Of course, if ye feel a profound calling to the religious life, we won't prevent that. It is a valid reason to break a betrothal."

"Nay, I don't. I mean—I-I—"

"I know what ye mean, Fallon. I think Quinn is a better choice for ye too."

~ * ~

Fingal thought it best to allow things to settle before they announced the betrothal between Fallon and Quinn. They planned a huge celebration to coincide with the feast of St. John the Baptist, over a month later. Of course Laird and Lady MacKenzie were in attendance as were the MacIans and the Chisholms. Quinn's sisters Mairead and Annag came with their families. Mairead was married to Tadhg Matheson, a good friend of both Fingal and Quinn's. Annag was married to Laird MacBain, Bran's brother. A group of MacKays traveled from the northern Highlands also. Fingal still hoped Laird MacKay would allow his nephew, Dougal, to begin training as his squire. The celebration was a huge sign to all the Highland clans that the MacLennans were strong once again.

In addition to the betrothal, there was much to celebrate. Gillian had long since recovered from the poisoning. Fingal too was nearly back to normal. Katherine said he could remove the splint, as long as he didn't put too much strain on his arm.

Eadoin was practically bursting with pride because Alana had given birth to a fine healthy son at the end of May.

Tadhg too had glad tidings, announcing that Mairead was expecting their first child in November.

But Turcuil did something that surprised everyone. As planned, when the MacIans returned to Duncurra in May, Turcuil had stayed behind at Brathanead to help train the MacLennan men. However, Edna returned to Duncurra. This was the first time the shy, smitten giant had seen the object of his affection in over a month. At one point in the evening he stood and called for silence. It took a few moments to subdue the crowd of merry-makers, but when the hall was quiet, he took Edna by the hand, walked with her to the middle of the hall, and knelt on one knee in front of her. She looked flustered and confused.

"Edna, I don't know pretty words. I wish I did. I would tell ye how very beautiful ye are. I would say how much I have missed ye this last month. How my heart ached just to see yer smile or hold yer hand. I would tell ye what fine children ye have and what a good mother ye are. I would tell ye that I cannot live another day apart from ye. But I'm not good with words and they would probably come out all wrong. I would offer ye my heart, but it was yers long ago. So I am just going to say, Edna, please be my wife."

"Oh Turcuil, of course I will. Now get up ye big eejit." Tears streamed down her face as he stood, lifted her in his arms, and kissed her soundly to roars of approval from the crowd.

~ * ~

Ailsa's world had turned upside down too many times to count in the last year. Her father died. Then months later her aunt died. Then the king made her sister marry Fingal MacIan. That turned out to be a pretty good thing. "Duff, he gave ye to me in spite of Mother." She rubbed the large black dog's head and he laid it in her lap.

Then terrible things began to happen. Agnes died and Gillie *lost the baby*. Ailsa still wasn't sure exactly what that meant. Then Gillie got sick. The MacBains came to live at Brathanead and that was a very good thing. She loved having Maeve to play with. She didn't even have to share Duff anymore because Blaze needed a home after Rhiannon died.

Rhiannon. That was the worst thing that happened. Rhiannon nearly killed Gillian and Fingal. She died because Bodie bit her. Ailsa knew she should feel sorry for her but she didn't. Before she died, Rhiannon said things that upset Mother and Fallon. Da wasn't Fallon's father after all—but he was still Fallon's da. Ailsa didn't understand that at all.

Of all the good and bad things that had happened, perhaps the one Ailsa liked best was Quinn MacKenzie coming. Ailsa had never met anyone like him. He was funny and nice like Fingal. He was handsome and strong too. Everyone liked him. Ailsa decided that Quinn might be the most perfect person she had ever met. She told Maeve that when she grew up, she wanted to marry Quinn. Now the entire clan was celebrating because Fallon is going to marry Quinn at the end of the summer.

She sat on the floor with her back to the wall, morosely watching the festivities. Maeve was dancing with her father. Maeve said Ailsa could dance with her father too, but she didn't feel like dancing or celebrating. She could tell Fallon was happy and she knew that should make her happy, but she couldn't help but feel a little jealous.

A tall skinny lad with wavy brown hair wandered through the people dancing and stopped in front of her. "Can I pet him?"

Ailsa nodded, "If ye want to."

The boy bent down and scratched Duff behind the ears before stroking the smooth black fur on Duff's back. "Can I sit down?"

"If ye want to."

The boy sat down on the other side of Duff. "I like dogs. Does he have a name?"

"Of course he has a name. It's Duff."

He pulled his knees up under his chin. He sure was skinny. "I'm Dougal MacKay."

"I'm Ailsa."

"Are ye a MacLennan or one of the visitors?"

"I'm a MacLennan. Lady MacLennan is my sister."

"Oh." He rubbed Duff's belly for a few moments. "Is she nice?"

"Of course she's nice."

"What about the laird, is he nice?"

Ailsa was about to tell the lad to go away and leave her alone when she looked at his face for the first time. His grey eyes glistened and he looked suspiciously like he was trying not to cry. "What's the matter?"

He rubbed his eyes quickly and looked away. "Nothing."

"Yeah, nothing is the matter with me either."

He turned his head to look at her. "Are ye sad too?"

Ailsa nodded, suddenly feeling rather close to tears herself.

"What's wrong? Was someone mean to ye? Just tell me who." Although he seemed close to tears a moment ago now he looked poised to do battle.

"Nay, it isn't anything like that. I just had my heart set on marrying someone and now he's marrying someone else."

Dougal relaxed. "Aren't ye a little young to get married? What are ye, eleven?"

"Twelve." How could he possibly think she was eleven?

"Oh. Well, that's still young to get married. Who is it ye wanted to marry, anyway?"

"Quinn MacKenzie," she said as if the world was coming to an end. "He is absolutely perfect and it turns out he's marrying my sister Fallon.

"Oh." He nodded sagely.

Ailsa didn't want to think about her permanently broken heart any more. She asked, "How old are ye?"

"I'm almost fifteen."

"Almost fifteen isn't an age."

"Well, I'll be fifteen soon."

"How soon?"

"October."

"It's June. That's not almost October. I think ye should just say ye are fourteen."

Dougal scowled at her. "Fine. I'm fourteen. That's still better than twelve."

Ailsa nodded her head. "Aye, it is." They both patted Duff for a few moments before Ailsa asked, "So Dougal MacKay, why are ye sad?"

"My da and mum have decided to let me train here as Laird MacLennan's squire."

"Well, that's not so bad. Fingal is nice. He is really good with a sword too. If I were a lad, I would want to learn how to use a sword from him."

"Really?"

"Of course. And there are other really good warriors here too. Ye can learn a lot from them."

"I just—well I..."

"Oh, ye don't want to leave yer home."

He blushed bright red and looked away. "Aye."

"Ye might really like it though."

"Da said I couldn't bring my dog."

"Ye could have. Fingal would have let ye. He likes dogs. My sister's dog saved her life."

"It isn't that. He isn't just mine. I have a younger brother and sister and cousins who live at Naomh-dùn. Da said it wouldn't be right to take him away from them."

Ailsa considered him for a moment. He was awfully skinny. But, he had pretty eyes. They weren't bright blue like

Quinn's but they were still pretty. She couldn't imagine having to leave home and not take Duff with her. "I wouldn't make this offer to just anyone, but ye seem nice. I will share Duff with ye while ye are here."

"Would ye really, Ailsa?"

"Aye. He seems to like ye anyway."

Dougal smiled at her, scratching behind Duff's ears with both hands. "Thank ye. That's really nice of ye. It will be much easier to be away from Naomh-dùn if I can share Duff with ye. Oh, and Ailsa?"

"Aye?"

"If ye don't find someone to marry ye when ye get old enough, I will."

Ailsa beamed.

~ * ~

The celebration continued until nearly sunup. Fingal was finally able to escape with the woman who held his heart. He gathered her in both arms, capturing her lips in a soul stirring kiss. She moaned and melted into him. "I have missed holding ye in my arms."

"I have missed it too." She twirled her fingers in the hair at the base of his neck.

"The feast was wonderful. Everyone seemed to enjoy themselves. I know it took days of work and planning to get ready for it. Thank ye."

"Ye are welcome, husband. I agree, it was wonderful. Fallon is deliriously happy."

Fingal grinned. "Quinn is too."

"And what about Turcuil?" Gillian asked. "For someone who doesn't know *pretty words* he sure managed to wield a few."

"Aye, I guess it took Edna's absence to finally get him to act. Tadhg and Mairead seem very happy too. I was a bit worried at first when they were married. She has always been a sweet little thing, but very shy. I'm glad to hear they are expecting."

Gillian sighed. "I want a baby. I loved the idea of being pregnant even if I might not have been. I want to be a mother."

"I want to be a father too." He kissed her again.

"Well, husband, I only know one way to make ye a father but it is a bit harder to do standing here by the door."

He emitted a low growl of pleasure and lifted her into his

arms, carrying her to the bed.

"Put me down, Fingal. Katherine said not to put too much strain on yer arm yet. I'm too heavy."

"Nay, ye aren't, but if it is the bed ye want, it's the bed ye'll get."

She laughed as he feigned dropping her on it, but then lowered her gently, capturing her lips again, kissing her deeply. He trailed kisses down the long slender column of her neck. She purred and leaned into his touch, closing her eyes. He stroked her body with both hands as he hadn't been able to do for over a month even as she boldly explored his body with her hands. He was sure there was no feeling this side of heaven to rival her touch. They kissed and caressed each other leisurely, giving and taking pleasure in equal parts. Finally, he joined with her. The world disappeared around them. They existed in a place of pure sensation and unending pleasure. He was poised at that moment of anticipation, just before release—sheathed in her, one with her. Her muscles contracted in a shuddering climax and her release became his own.

Afterwards, he held her long, slender body in his arms, simply savoring the feel of her. She was his perfect mate in every way. He looked forward to years of bliss in her arms.

"Fingal?"

"Aye, my love?"

"I'm not sure if that worked or not."

In his drowsy, replete state, he didn't understand what she meant. "I'm sorry, sweetling, ye don't know if what worked?"

"I don't know if I made ye a father."

Fingal chuckled, realizing she was teasing. "I hear it takes a while to know for sure if it worked."

"Aye, so they say. Still, perhaps we should try it again in the morning."

"Ye'll get no complaints from me. We can just keep trying until we know it worked."

"Mmm."

He thought she had dozed off when she asked, "Fingal?"

"Aye, my love."

"We don't need to stop trying, even once we know it works."

"Whatever ye wish, Gillian."

Epilogue

Eighteen year old Ailsa MacLennan sighed as she watched the men on the training field, searching for the one man who made her heart flutter.

"Aunt Ailsa," five year old Ian poked her with his wooden sword, "I want to go play swords with them."

Ailsa bounced eighteen month old Duncan, Gillian and Fingal's other son, on her hip while Duff ambled around at her feet. "Ian, how many times has yer da said, ye can't go near the training field without him?"

"We are near it now. We can see it."

"Aye, we can see it, but we are way up on this hill, we aren't near it."

"Da might think we're near it."

Ailsa suspected he was right, but what Fingal didn't know wouldn't hurt him and he was unlikely to find out. Fingal was with Gillian while she delivered their fourth child. He was the only man she knew who defied the midwives and stayed with his wife during labor and birthing.

"I could go ask him," Ian offered.

"Ian, yer da is busy at the moment. Do ye want to watch the men or not? I can take ye to Aunt Fallon if ye don't. That's where Adaira is."

"I don't want to go to Aunt Fallon's. The lassies are no fun to play with and her lad Evan is just a baby like Duncan. Even ye and Duff are better than them."

Ailsa knew she had wielded the right weapon. Ian would rather do anything else than spend the afternoon with his three year old sister and Fallon's five year old twins, Suisan and Cecilia. "Then wheesht about being too near the training field and watch."

Ian pretended to fight with his wooden sword, imitating

the moves of the men on the field. After a few minutes he asked, "Aunt Ailsa, why do ye like watching the men train? Ye don't even have a sword."

Ailsa blushed in spite of herself. Unlike her young nephew, she didn't climb the hill to watch the men train in order to learn how to use a sword. There was one warrior in particular who she came to see. She thought he was the most handsome man alive. Watching his strong, muscular body move with fluid grace as he sparred with another warrior gave her a strange fluttering feeling in her belly.

Ian poked her again with his wooden sword drawing her from her reverie. She frowned at him. "Stop that." Ailsa tried to imitate Gillian's "mama isn't happy" look, but feared she failed miserably.

"But I asked ye a question. Why do ye like watching the men train if ye don't even have a sword."

"That's a good question, Ian."

Ailsa spun around to see Fingal's nephew, fifteen year old Tomas MacIan walking up behind them. Tomas had become Fingal's squire two years ago after Dougal MacKay had outgrown the role. Evidently he was a good squire but for her it was like having an annoying little brother. "What are ye doing here?" Ailsa demanded.

Tomas' eyes twinkled, "I think ye should answer Ian's question first."

Ailsa blushed. She had no intention of telling them the real reason. Thinking quickly she said, "Well, not that it is any of yer business, but I do have a sword."

"Ye do?" asked Ian. "Where is it?"

"That's my sword," she said pointing to Ian's toy.

"It is not," said Ian. "Tomas gave it to me, didn't ye Tomas?"

"Aye, lad, I did." Tomas grinned.

Ailsa smiled smugly. "And where did Tomas get it?"

Ian frowned. "I don't know."

"Uncle Fingal gave it to me." Tomas said.

That was just the answer Ailsa had expected. Her smile broadened. "And where did yer Uncle Fingal get it?"

"I'll play yer game," Tomas said. "I don't know. Where did Uncle Fingal get it?"

Turning her attention to Ian she said, "Yer da, got it from

yer mama. And yer mama got it from me. But I only loaned it to her which means it's still mine."

Ian frowned, putting the sword behind his back. "What does a lass need with a sword and why did ye have one anyway?"

"The reason I had it was because yer grandda, Duncan, who ye are named after, little man," she said to Duncan, tickling his belly, "really hoped that I would be a lad. He made it for me before I was born." At the look of concern on Ian's face, she said, "But don't worry, Ian, ye can keep the sword. I don't need it and I'm sure yer grandda would be glad ye have it." She smiled at her nephew before turning back to Tomas. "Now that I've answered Ian's question, I believe ye owe me an answer, Tomas. What are ye doing up here?"

It was Tomas' turn for a smug smile. Pointing over his shoulder at Brathanead keep he said, "Ailsa, ye do know this hill can be seen from the laird's bed chamber don't ye? As I understand it, Uncle Fingal's furious with ye. He sent Peggy to find me, to tell ye to come back to the keep with Ian and Duncan."

"I told ye Da wouldn't like it," said Ian.

Tomas laughed. "Smart lad. Come with me Ian," said Tomas. "I'll teach ye how to slay a dragon with that sword." Tomas headed back towards the keep and Ian ran along beside him. Duff started to follow, but stopped and looked back when Ailsa too didn't immediately join them.

Ailsa sighed. She cast a wistful glance over her shoulder before following Tomas and Ian.

~ * ~

This had been the easiest bairn so far. Gillian had given birth to her newest daughter after only a few hours. As had become tradition, Fingal stayed at her side throughout her labor. Tira had teased him, "Laird, this is the fourth baby ye've delivered, why do ye even bother calling me?" As soon as the baby was born and they had Gillian tucked into a freshly made bed, Tira and the other women who had helped left them.

Fingal stood at the window, cradling his new baby daughter in his arms. "My sweet wee lass, yer Aunt Ailsa will be the death of me."

Gillian laughed. "Fingal, Ailsa wouldn't let Ian or Duncan get hurt."

"That's not the point. She knows I don't want them that close. Why does she insist on watching the men train anyway?"

"Fingal, can ye be that much of an eejit? She fancies herself in love."

"Ye need to nip that in the bud."

Gillian snorted. "I need to nip it in the bud? We are talking about my sister Ailsa aren't we? I don't think we need to worry. She falls in and out of love more often than we change the rushes in the great hall."

"Aye but that young man has the reputation of being a rogue." The baby began to squirm and root, becoming fretful when she couldn't find what she sought. Always alert for trouble, Bodie, who lay in his usual spot by the hearth raised his head, his ears perked.

Gillian chuckled. "She's fine Bodie. Bring her to me Fingal, she's hungry. And don't forget, ye had a bit of a roguish reputation at one time too."

"I know I did. That's why I want him to stay away from her." He moved away from the window, "Tomas is bringing them back now anyway." Fingal placed their daughter in Gillian's arms.

Gillian pulled her shift down so the baby could nurse. "I wouldn't worry about it just yet."

Fingal frowned "She's eighteen. We need to arrange a betrothal for her."

"Now ye sound like my mother." His scowl deepened causing her to laugh again. "Perhaps we have put it off too long. Give me a few days to recover and we will talk with Ailsa about it."

"I'll give ye all the time ye need, but I may have to knock a few young men in the head if we wait too long."

Gillian's heart swelled. She loved how protective Fingal was of her family. "Come, sit by me Fingal."

Sitting beside them on the bed, he slid one arm around his wife's shoulder and put the other one under her arms, holding the baby. He kissed the top of Gillian's head. "I love ye Gillian."

"I love ye too Fingal."

He caressed the baby's head while she nursed. Gillian glanced up at his face and smiled. He was lost in adoration. "What shall we name her?" she asked.

"How about, Touch-me-and-my-father-will-kill-you?" he suggested.

Gillian laughed. "I'm sorry, Fingal, I didn't care for that name when Adaira was born and it hasn't grown on me since."

Fingal sighed dramatically, "You may regret yer hasty decision someday. What name do ye suggest?"

Gillian gazed at her beautiful daughter for a moment before saying, "I think we should name her Jean."

Fingal stroked the baby's tiny hand and she tightened her grip around his finger. "Jean. Aye, perhaps that's a better name. Jean it is then."

"Jean," Gillian whispered.

They sat like this in silence and Gillian's mind wandered to those early days of their marriage when she wasn't sure she would ever like Fingal, much less love him. How very wrong she had been. The MacLennans had been on the brink of ruin. Over the last six years he had helped rebuild them to the powerful clan they had once been. That had earned him everyone's respect. And if saving her clan wasn't enough, he had also gently and persistently worked to win her heart from their first moments. He was a strong leader, a loving husband and a devoted father. She could ask for nothing more and she loved him with every fiber of her being.

Jean had stopped nursing and fallen asleep. Gillian pulled her shift back up.

"Shall I put her in the cradle and let ye rest?" Fingal asked?

"Nay, I'll hold her for a while. Perhaps ye should go fetch our other three wee hellions and bring them to meet their new sister.

Fingal kissed her tenderly. "Whatever ye wish, Gillian."

About the Author

Ceci started her career as an oncology nurse at a leading research hospital, and eventually became a successful medical writer. In 1991 she married a young Irish carpenter who she met at a friend's wedding. They raised their family in central New Jersey but now live with their dogs and birds in paradise, also known as southwest Florida. With their youngest off to college, Ceci is breaking away from "primary efficacy endpoints" and writing a few "happily ever after's."

Don't miss The Scrolls of Cridhe, Volume One – Highland Winds, a collection of historical Scottish novellas by The Guardians of Cridhe, six incredibly talents authors of Scottish romance: Suzan Tisdale, Sue-Ellen Welfonder, Katherine Lynn Davis, Lily Baldwin, Kate Robbins and Tarah Scott. The bundle will be available on November 17, 2014.

Follow Ceci on social media:

Website: www.cecigiltenan.com
Facebook: https://www.facebook.com/cgiltenan
Twitter: https://twitter.com/CeciGiltenan
Other Books by Ceci Giltenan:

Highland Solution

Duncurra – Book 1

Laird Niall MacIan needs Lady Katherine Ruthven's dowry to relieve his clan's crushing debt but he has no intention of giving her his heart in the bargain.

Niall MacIan, a Highland laird, desperately needs funds to save his impoverished clan. Lady Katherine Ruthven, a lowland heiress, is rumored to be "unmarriageable" and her uncle hopes to be granted her title and lands when the king sends her to a convent. King David II anxious to strengthen his alliances sees a solution that will give Ruthven the title he wants, and MacIan the money he needs. Laird MacIan will receive Lady Katherine's hand along with her substantial dowry and her uncle will receive her lands and title.

Lady Katherine must forfeit everything in exchange for a husband who does not want to be married and believes all women to be self-centered and deceitful. Can the lovely and gentle Katherine mend his heart and build a life with him or will he allow the treachery of others to destroy them?

Highland Solution is available as a paperback or e-book at Amazon and Barnes & Noble, as an e-book at Kobo and as an audio book at Amazon, Audible and I-tunes.

Highland Courage

Duncurra – Book 2

**Her parents want a betrothal, but Mairead MacKenzie can't
get married without revealing her secret and no man will
wed her once he knows.**

Plain in comparison to her siblings and extremely reserved,
Mairead has been called "MacKenzie's Mouse" since she
was a child. No one knows the reason for her timidity and
she would just as soon keep it that way. When her parents
arrange a betrothal to Laird Tadhg Matheson she is horrified.
She only sees one way to prevent an old secret from
becoming a new scandal.

Tadhg Matheson admires and respects the MacKenzies.
While an alliance with them through marriage to Mairead
would be in his clan's best interest, he knows Laird
MacKenzie seeks a closer alliance with another clan. When
Tadhg learns of her terrible shyness and her youngest
brother's fears about her, Tadhg offers for her anyway.

Secrets always have a way of revealing themselves. With
Tadhg's unconditional love, can Mairead find the strength
and courage she needs to handle the consequences when they
do?

Highland Courage is available as a paperback or e-book at
Amazon and Barnes & Noble, as an e-book at Kobo and as
an audio book at Amazon, Audible and I-tunes.

The Guardians of Cridhe

The Legend:

Long, long ago, in the time before time, seven sisters were called from the far reaches of the realm. Each brought unique talents, but had one common gift; the ability to weave ageless tales of love and courage. An evil witch coveted their gifts and locked them in a tower, silencing their voices upon threat of death. But the Highlands are enchanted, and magic will not countenance seven pure hearts such as theirs to be lost.

With no one else to hear them, they sang their stories to each other. Fate blew a braw Highland wind to their prison, and the sweet, high timbre of the sisters' voices enthralled it. The wind gathered close their silver words as it raced past each day, and carried their love and goodness throughout the world...then across the ages.

Today, their words live on in the Guardians of Cridhe, seven sisters who have sworn to preserve those pure and musical hearts so long as they live. It is said these seven descend from those ancient female bards. Only their words can bear witness to that truth...

The first collection of novellas (~35,000 words each) by the Guardians of Cridhe, Highland Winds will be available on November 17, 2014, as an e-book and in paperback.

The Scrolls of Cridhe
Volume 1 – Highland Winds

Suzan Tisdale - *Stealing Moirra's Heart*
"She didn't believe he was a thief when she rescued him…until he stole her heart"

Sue-Ellen Welfonder - *The Taming of Mairi Mackenzie*
"A forbidden love so powerful it could destroy them both."

Katheryn Lynn Davis - *A Tear of Memory*
"How can a seer paint 'Truth' when she's lived a life of lies. Will she allow a man who has twice deceived her to open her heart to the truth?"

Lily Baldwin - *A Jewel in the Vaults*
"Beneath the ruse is a woman aching to break free."

Ceci Giltenan - *Highland Revenge*
"Does he hate her clan enough to visit his vengeance on her? Or will he listen to her secret and his own heart's yearning?"

Kate Robbins - *Spirit Stones*
"Sheona MacLeod has a gift, Malcolm MacDonald seeks change. Together they can change destiny—if they dare."

Tarah Scott - *Lord Grayson's Bride*
"She can't allow his love for her to destroy him."

Find out more about the Guardians on their website
www.scrollsofcridhe.com.

Highland Revenge

Hatred lives and breathes between medieval clans who often don't remember why feuds began in the shadowed past.

But Eoin MacKay remembers.

He will never forget how he was treated by Bhaltair MacNicol—the acting head of Clan MacNicol. He was lucky to escape alive, and vows to have revenge.

Years later, as laird of Clan MacKay, he gets his chance when he captures Lady Fiona MacNicol. His desire for revenge is strong but he is beguiled by his captive. Can he forget his stubborn hatred long enough to listen to the secret she has kept for so long? And once he knows the truth, can he show her she is not alone and forsaken? In the end, is he strong enough to fight the combined hostilities and age-old grudges that demand he give her up?

An excerpt from Highland Revenge:

Eoin MacKay hadn't gone terribly far when he caught a glimpse of white halfway up a massive oak. She was well hidden. Her plaid was dark green; he wouldn't have noticed her among the leaves if he hadn't been specifically looking for her. He strode closer to the tree, stopping once he could look up through the branches.

There, perched in the crotch of two thick limbs was a woman so perfectly beautiful she might have been part faery. He was left momentarily speechless. Her skin was fair, with a faint pink blush to her cheek. He couldn't see the color of her eyes, but they were ringed with sooty lashes. Something told him that, regardless of their hue, they would sparkle. Her rosy lips were full and soft—lips that were made to be kissed. The late afternoon breeze ruffled the mass of black curls around her shoulders. Her léine was torn, but otherwise she appeared none the worse for wear. She is not a fairy, she is a MacNicol, he reminded himself.

She looked down at him silently with her head cocked to one side, as if she was trying to solve some puzzle. She didn't seem remotely frightened. That would have to change if he was to exact his revenge. "Have ye had a lovely day perched in yer tree, watching us search for ye?"

"I suspect my day was better than yers."

Her impertinent answer irritated him. "Well ye've had yer bit of fun, but it's over. Climb down."

She ignored him. "Who are ye?"

"Yer captor, and I ordered ye to climb down. Do it now."

"Nay, I asked ye a perfectly reasonable question, and ye aren't my captor if ye can't reach me. Until I know who ye are, I think I'd just as soon stay free, even if I am up a tree."

"Free? Nay lass, ye're as good as locked in my dungeon, and I promise ye will regret yer impertinence."

He called to one of his men. "Donald, it fair breaks my heart, but the MacNicol lass doesn't wish to join our company."

"An arrow would bring her down quick enough."

"Aye it would, but ye heard her guardsman. This is Fiona MacNicol, Bhaltair's niece. I wouldn't want to harm a hair on her wee head."

Donald snorted. "Ye have no love for the MacNicols, and neither do I. Have ye forgotten? One of my older brothers rode with ye that night."

"Ye're right, Donald. I have no love for the MacNicols, but the ransom this one will fetch will hurt Bhaltair's greedy, black heart nearly as much as a steel blade thrust into it. Mark my words, we'll have our revenge. We are leaving. Climb up, drag her down and bind her. She managed to evade us once and I won't have it happen again. We have already wasted too much time on her." He didn't spare her another glance but called over his shoulder, "By the way, lass, I am Laird Eoin MacKay, and ye're most assuredly my prisoner."